A MAGIC BLADE

was Bazil Broketail's "Ecator," crafted by Elvish smiths working under the direction of a Great Witch. It cut through armor and sank into the monster's helmet with a great flash of white sparks and a sound like the rending of a giant bell.

The creature stumbled forward a step. Bazil heaved his sword free and waited for the monster to topple. Nothing could live through a stroke like that. And yet the giant warrior did not fall.

The battledragon felt a chill go through him. This foe was not alive, it had no blood. This was like fighting a ghost, a ghost built of steel. . . .

BATTLEDRAGON

Christopher Rowley

A ROC BOOK

ROC
Published by the Penguin Group
Penguin Books USA Inc., 375 Hudson Street,
New York, New York 10014, U.S.A.
Penguin Books Ltd, 27 Wrights Lane,
London W8 5TZ, England
Penguin Books Australia Ltd, Ringwood,
Victoria, Australia
Penguin Books Canada Ltd, 10 Alcorn Avenue,
Toronto, Ontario, Canada M4V 3B2
Penguin Books (N.Z.) Ltd, 182–190 Wairau Road,
Auckland 10, New Zealand

Penguin Books Ltd, Registered Offices:
Harmondsworth, Middlesex, England

First published by Roc, an imprint of Dutton Signet,
a division of Penguin Books USA Inc.

First Printing, October, 1995
10 9 8 7 6 5 4 3 2 1

Cover art by Daniel Horne

 REGISTERED TRADEMARK—MARCA REGISTRADA

Printed in the United States of America

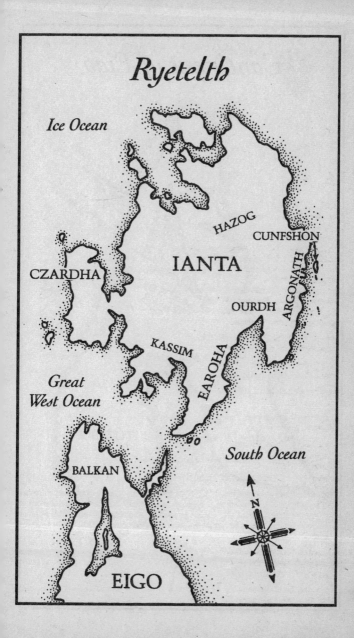

Ryetelth

Ice Ocean

HAZOG

CUNFSHON

IANTA

CZARDHA

OURDH

ARGONATH

KASSIM

EAROHA

Great
West Ocean

South Ocean

BALKAN

N

EIGO

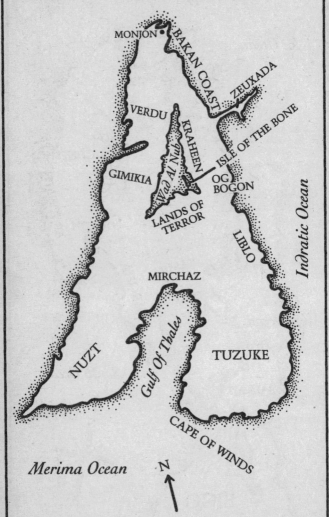

Continent of Eigo

MONJON

BAKAN COAST

ZEUXADA

ISLE OF THE BONE

VERDU

KRAHEEN

Wad Al Nub

GIMIKIA

OG BOGON

Indratic Ocean

LANDS OF TERROR

LIBLO

MIRCHAZ

NUZT

Gulf Of Thales

TUZUKE

CAPE OF WINDS

Merima Ocean

N

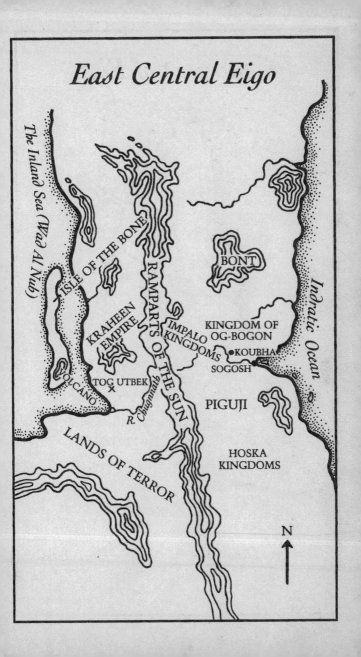

East Central Eigo

The Inland Sea (Wad Al Nub)

ISLE OF THE BONE

RAMPARTS OF THE BONE

BONT

KRAHEEN EMPIRE

IMPALO KINGDOMS

KINGDOM OF OG-BOGON

KOUBHA

SOGOSH

VOLCANO

TOG UTBEK ×

R. Chignaath

RAMPARTS OF THE SUN

PIGUJI

Indratic Ocean

LANDS OF TERROR

HOSKA KINGDOMS

N

CHAPTER ONE

In the land of the Kraheen, in the heart of the dark continent, three grim-faced men stood beside a long, ebony box in the temple of the God of Stone.

Their leader, a burly fellow of six foot or more, nodded to the high priests of the God of Stone, who stood before them clad in feathered headdresses and leather aprons studded with gold.

"Ye have come to see the miracle?" he said in heavily accented Kraht.

"We have come, O great Kreegsbrok, as ye commanded."

"Then ye shall see with thine own eyes and be enlightened. Know this, that the power of the Great One is beyond that of any other in this world, whether man or god or goddess."

The priests bobbed their heads at this, but their dark brown eyes reflected a lack of certainty. These men from beyond had brought many dread things to their land. Their master was indeed a mighty force. But to raise the Prophet from the dead? Surely this was impossible.

"Open the box," said Kreegsbrok.

The high priest snapped his fingers, and men lifted the lid that covered the sacred visage of "He Who Must."

Kreegsbrok looked within and smiled. He saw the body of a lean-fleshed man who had died in his early thirties, struck down by a sudden brain spasm during the height of a raging incantation. The black flesh was neither hard nor soft, the hair still curled in coiled locks about the massive head. The Kraheen had long excelled in the art of preserving the bodies of the dead. The body of the Prophet would be good material for the magic of the Great One.

"May I?" he asked in the same flat voice.

The feathered headdresses bobbed again, the eyes like black pebbles, unreadable.

Kreegsbrok nodded to Gulbuddin and Verniktun, who wore the same black uniform as he. They withdrew flasks of fluid and dust from the small packs they bore and took up a long-necked funnel of semirigid leather. Carefully Verniktun oiled it and made it flexible.

Under the intense gaze of the priests, they opened the mouth of the long-dead Prophet and forced apart the yellowed teeth that had been shut for a thousand years. Into the withered throat they eased the neck of the funnel.

From within his cloak, Kreegsbrok withdrew a small notebook.

They bowed together while he intoned a prayer to their Master. Then they began to chant the harsh syllables prescribed for the spell.

The priests stepped back, ashen-faced at the grating sounds that now came from the mouths of the pale men from beyond. The atmosphere in the tomb of the Prophet became thick and dark. A smoke was rising from the floor. The hair on arm, leg, and neck began to rise along with it. A smell of burning stone filled their nostrils.

Into the funnel Verniktun poured the sparkling black powder invigorated by the Great One. The first flask went down smoothly. Then followed a second.

Now Gulbuddin stepped up with a flask of blue fluid. It had an evil shimmer within its glass.

Kreegsbrok spoke words of power, and the fluid was poured into the funnel. A reddish vapor arose along with a hissing sound as both fluid and sparkling powder sank into the flesh of the long-dead Prophet of the God of Stone, "He Who Must."

After a moment, while the material still hissed within the body cavity, Kreegsbrok put out his hand to Verniktun and received a small silver flask. From this he poured a clear liquid into the funnel.

"Now for the invigorative."

Gulbuddin stepped up and held a black marble the size of a man's fist over the dead Prophet's forehead. He closed his eyes and tightened his lips.

Kreegsbrok called out in a harsh voice to the roof of the tomb. Verniktun struck a flame and touched it to the funnel.

There was a blinding flash. Gulbuddin screamed in agony but held onto the stone in his hand, which now glowed with an intense red light. Carefully he pressed it against the forehead of the corpse in the coffin.

The corpse shook and jerked abruptly within the box. The hips rose and then subsided. The legs kicked. An arm shot up.

Kreegsbrok pulled apart the ancient teeth. Verniktun lifted the leather funnel. Red viscous stuff surged up from the mouth. Gulbuddin's cries were obliterated by a primal bellow suddenly erupting from the long-dead throat, a sacral scream that rattled the bones of every man in that room, a shriek that announced new life in that which should never have moved again.

Gulbuddin barely stood back in time. His mouth working as red stuff oozed from the corners, the Prophet sat up.

The high priests stared with bulging eyeballs. It had come to pass, even as the pale men had claimed. Then with mouths agape they fell on their knees.

"Cry joy for the love of Ajoth Gol Dib!" they sang. "Cry joy for the mercy of the One Who Must!"

The three men from Padmasa exchanged grim smiles. The work was begun.

CHAPTER TWO

It had snowed the day before, and the woodlots at Dashwood were covered in a smooth, ankle-deep layer, virtually unmarked. The dragons' breath came in great steaming clouds as they hewed the young oaks and ash that were grown for firewood. Great axes fashioned from troll battle axes were their weapons of choice. Wood chips sang as they flew from the blows.

Dragonboys danced around the dragons, attaching cables for the mule skinner teams who hauled the trees back to the big, horse-driven saw that cut them to three-foot lengths.

"Watch it Jak, your foot's inside that harness," called Relkin of the 109th Marneri Dragons. Jak shifted his foot and snapped tight the studs on the tree collar he was fitting. When he looked up Relkin had gone, but Jak saw his back for a moment between two trees. Relkin was a dragoneer now and felt an all-consuming responsibility for the unit. Sometimes it riled the rest of them, but Jak knew that Relkin was simply anxious in a way he'd never been before. As dragoneer he was in charge, and any injuries were held against him.

"This dragon is thirsty," said a huge inhuman presence, standing ten yards away beside a felled oak.

Jak whistled to the waiting mule skinner and skipped clear.

"You want kalut?" he asked his dragon, a green freemartin named Alsebra, famous for her skill with dragonsword.

"No, just water." Her big dragon eyes fixed on something in the distance, over Jak's head. He didn't bother to ask what. In this mood she was unlikely to tell him.

Jak hoisted the big water can and set off back to the clearing where the saw was working. The water cart was set up nearby, with others that dealt out hot kalut and fresh bread. There were a hundred men, ten dragons, and forty mules at work in the woodlots that day. It was cold but dry, and the air was still. The work went well, and they had sent more than a hundred cords of wood, cut and split, into camp.

Jak was looking forward to getting back to Marneri. The 109th had almost finished their two-month stint at Dashwood and would soon march back to the city. Their alternates, the 66th Marneri Dragons, would then come up to Dashwood in their turn. In the city Jak had a girl, a girl whom he had been wooing for six months now. Her name was Kati, and she was the sweetest thing in the whole world, especially as she'd let him kiss her several times on the last occasion they'd been together, lurking in the alleyway behind her family's pantry, down near Templeside. Jak sighed. Just a few more days, and they'd be back together. How could he survive the wait?

Dragoneer Relkin paused beside his own dragon, who stood back while another oak gave a creak and slid down to the ground. The dragon, the famous Bazil Broketail, gave a grunt of satisfaction at the clean fall of the tree.

"Ah, boy finished minding everyone's business. Ready to take care of dragon. Where is kalut?"

"Kalut is brewed, and I'm going for some right now."

"Kalut would be here, going down into dragon stomach if boy attended to job."

Relkin nimbly slipped a hauling collar around the trunk of another felled tree, and jumped out of the way as the big mules hauled it back.

"If only it were that simple, Baz."

"You check too much on everyone else. Bring this dragon kalut. And some bread if they got any, with akh."

"There's no akh here. No akh until dinner."

"When is dinner?"

"You know when is dinner. At the end of the day, back in camp."

"That is a long wait for some akh on some bread."

"It'll be all the better for the waiting."

"This is a dubious human concept. Dragon doesn't agree."

Relkin was already on his way to the kalut stall with a big jug over his shoulder.

He passed the saw. Twelve huge mules provided the motive force, heaving around a drive-limber that ran a belt over their heads to the saw itself, which was a circle of steel spinning its way through the tree trunks with a massive whine.

Beyond the saw were the splitter and loader teams, sixty men under the command of Lieutenant Angloss. From their direction came the steady thud of hammers on mauls amid cheerful banter.

Lieutenant Angloss gave him a friendly salute.

"Good day, Dragoneer."

Relkin returned the greeting and went on to the kalut stall. It was a new experience being an officer, and he was still getting used to it. Of course he was just a brevet dragoneer, filling in while they waited for a real one to be sent to them. But in his heart, he still nursed the slight hope that he would be confirmed as full dragoneer for the Marneri 109th. There were, admittedly, several points against him. He was young, not yet nineteen, and though he had four and a half years of service in the legions, he knew they never promoted anyone to command before they reached their twentieth birthday.

Then there was the trial against him. The blood of a civilian, Trader Dook, dead on a riverboat from Relkin's dirk, now stained his record. Relkin had been found innocent of murder after a lengthy trial the preceding summer, but he'd won by virtue of the testimony given by dragons. This had set a major new precedent. Wyvern dragons could speak the tongue of men, and they were known to be intelligent, as far above the rest of the animals as were humans. Still, such a decision rankled with some men. The subject was politically sensitive. As a result, Relkin's chances of promotion were compromised.

For a moment he thought of Dragon Leader Turrent, the stern critic who'd ruled their lives for the last year and a half. Turrent had mellowed, especially from what he'd been like when he first came to them, but he had always been a sharp commanding officer and never really one of them, never truly part of the unit. Relkin, of course, was utterly identified with the 109th. He'd served in it since its inception. Turrent had warned him that the trial would ruin his chances for advancement. And yet when Turrent left, he promoted Relkin to the temporary command.

Things were a little looser now that Turrent was gone, except in the area of practice. Relkin insisted that everyone, dragon and boy, go through combat exercises every day, with a hike in full rig once a week, which always ended with a quick round of the Dashwood obstacle course.

There'd been some grumbling from the usual suspects, like Swane and Mono, who were Relkin's age, but everyone knew in their hearts that he was perfectly right. They hadn't seen action in eighteen months, and it was pretty certain they would be sent up to the Axoxo front sometime in the coming spring or summer. So it was important to keep skills as sharp as their swords.

Relkin wondered how Dragon Leader Turrent was handling his new unit, the 167th Marneri Dragons. He should have reached Fort Dalhousie by now and joined them. One thing was sure, there'd be ten dragonboys in Dalhousie who would be really sick of polishing their kit after Turrent had had them for a while.

He brought back a full can for Baz, took a mug for himself, and spent the rest of the day getting felled trees pulled down to the saw. In between, he tried to keep a visual check on everyone else, although a voice in his head kept telling him to relax. They could take care of themselves. He wasn't there to nursemaid them. He had a dragon of his own to take care of, and that was enough.

At last the cornet blew, ending the day's work, and they formed up, axes over their shoulders, for the two-mile march back to camp.

Dashwood was the alternate quarters for the legion garrison of the city of Marneri. It was a well-worn, comfortable camp of wooden-stockade construction, thoroughly furbished over many decades of use. It was blessed with excellent water from crystal pure springs.

The forest around it was managed by the legion to heat the Marneri garrison and outposts throughout the winter. Great stacks of green wood were set out by the road. On the other side were stacks of seasoned wood. The road from Dashwood to Marneri was paved throughout and very busy at this season with wagon traffic.

Past the wood stacks loomed the big gates, and as they marched in, they caught the heady aromas of fresh bread and simmering buckets of akh, the pungent, spicy concoction beloved by wyvern dragons.

Dragonboys were soon in motion, wheeling carts loaded with buckets of noodles, slathered in akh, down to their dragons in the Dragon House. Others scurried by, weighed down by a dozen loaves of long bread.

Barrels of beer were delivered from the legion brewery and rolled directly to the dragons, who sat in a loose circle in the center of the Dashwood Dragon House and ate and drank their fill.

Leaving a bunch of contented dragons to their favorite recreational activity, the dragonboys got their own meals and were able to choose from steaming cauldrons of polenta, beans, noodles, and a hearty chicken soup. There was more fresh bread, hot out of the ovens, and for flavorings there was butter and lime and salt and even akh for those with strong taste buds.

To wash it down they received their daily allowance of a pint of mild beer, followed by a second pint of real ale.

They sank back into their coats, feeling warm while the fatigue crept up from their bones. They would drink their ale, perhaps sing a round or two of the "Kenor Song" or "La Lillee La Loo," and turn in for the night. And soon, just a few more days, and they'd be heading back to the city.

Swane was trying to hunt up a game of cards among the younger boys. There were five new faces in the unit since the Battle of Sprian's Ridge. Calvene, at seventeen, was the oldest of the new boys followed by Endi of Blue Hills, Roos, Aris, and little Shutz, who at fourteen was now the youngest in the unit.

Endi and Roos were the only boys willing to take Swane's offer, but that was enough for a few hands of Bezok, and the cards came out and were shuffled and dealt.

Swane groaned and moaned. The others winked to each other. They'd seen Swane's repertory of deceptive moves by now. When Swane groaned like this, it meant he thought he had great cards. They all exchanged cards with the deck and bet lightly on the change.

Swane's groaning increased suddenly in volume.

"I bet I can go the full Bezok," said Swane, as expected.

"How much do you bet?" said Endi with a sly smile. Endi was only sixteen, but Relkin knew already that he was better at cards than Swane would ever be.

"Three bits," said Swane, hoping to lure them on.

"Matched," said Endi.

"I'll take it, too," said Roos, a bullet-headed youth from the hardscrabble hills of Seant, who knew to follow Endi's lead in something like this.

"Exchange," said Swane, holding out a single card.

"Taken," said Endi, giving Swane another card from his own hand and accepting Swane's discard.

Swane's groans continued, but now there was a more gen-uine note to them.

"Cut for trumps," he said. Endi did, and they all stared at the two of clubs.

"Clubs it is," said Roos with satisfaction. Swane groaned a little more deeply.

"Lay 'em down," said Roos.

Swane led off with the king of cups. Endi chipped in the three, and Roos dropped the eight. Swane swept them up with a sigh of relief.

"One down, Bezok to go."

Swane played the prince of cups. Endi chipped in the five of cups. Roos gave a wicked smile and produced the four of clubs, trumping Swane's prince.

Swane's groans increased in volume. Endi tried to goad him into increasing the bet, but Swane refused to be drawn.

"Let's have the third card," said Roos with glee, but Swane never got to play it. There was a loud rap at the en-trance to the Dragon House, and a lad from the stables in-formed them that there was a fancy carriage in the camp's main square and someone was asking for the 109th Marneri.

They looked at one another. Most shot Relkin a glance and then looked away. Relkin tried not to think, but they all crowded down to the gate of the dragon quarters and beheld a white, covered carriage, pulled by four horses, rolling up to the gate. The coachman found that his horses were most unhappy. They fidgeted, neighed, and chewed at the bit, ter-rified by the smell of dragon.

The door opened and out came a tall, well-fed young man, clad in an outdated style of dragon leader uniform with knee breeches and high boots and a long coat with tails. An over-sized cap badge was attached to the fellow's antique hat with the numerals 109 inscribed upon it.

Relkin's heart sank.

A soft, feminine voice spoke from inside the coach. The fellow in the uniform turned back to say something, and there was a squeal of giggles.

The eyes of the 109th widened. If old Commander Toup found out about this, there'd be hell to pay. Commander Toup ran a hellishly tight camp at Dashwood.

The plump fellow in the antique uniform turned back to them with a confident swagger. He paused to survey them for a moment, as if waiting for their salute. The 109th were too stunned to remember their manners.

"Good evening all, I am Dragon Leader Wiliger," announced the apparition with an air of jaunty good humor. "I have been assigned to command this squadron.

"I know that we are going to get along very well." He beamed at them. "I'm sure because I know this is a disciplined unit, and by the Hand, I swear I'll maintain discipline!"

They stared at him with blank expressions. Manuel was the first to wake up. He nudged Jak in the ribs and whispered and then whispered louder.

"Salute, you idiots."

Relkin awoke, from nightmare to a reality no better. They saluted raggedly, with more whispering.

Dragon Leader Wiliger smiled and returned the salute. He produced a scroll from under his arm and read out to them his "Orders of Appointment." Thus they learned that he, Dragon Leader Wiliger, had, by the authority vested in the Appointments Board of the Marneri Second Legion, been ordered to take the command of the 109th Marneri Dragons.

"I will make a short inspection now. I want to get to know you all as quickly as I can."

They stared back at him, eyes rounded in amazement.

"And if you don't mind, I will bring in my companions and show them around. I am staying at the house of my good friend the Duchess of Belova, quite close by, and so I thought I would take the opportunity of coming over and assuming command. We've been having a marvelous party, and my friends did so desire to see the dragons."

They struggled for words. Finally Relkin managed, "Uh, yes, sir. Of course."

Dragon Leader Wiliger looked to Relkin. "Introduce yourself, boy," he said.

"Acting Dragoneer Relkin, 109th Marneri, sir."

Wiliger broke into a broad smile. "Wonderful"—he put out a hand—"it's good to meet you, boy, let me shake your hand. You're a legend. One good reason I was so happy to get this command."

Relkin felt his mouth go dry. There were horrible implications in the man's words. Had he bought his commission? Things like that happened from time to time, but never in the Dragon Corps. Casualties were too high in the Dragon Corps for the sons of the wealthy.

"And now I'd like to ask my friends to come inside. They will assist me in my inspection." He laughed, amused by this thought, and they smelled the wine on his breath.

The spell was broken, and the dragonboys scurried away to their individual stalls. They were blessed by the fact that the dragons were still eating. Thus they had room to move quickly around in the stall while they frantically tidied up. Harness, tackle, sewing projects were swung up to the highest lockers. Spare equipment, satchels, even weapons, were scooped off floors and beds and hung on their appointed hooks.

Dragon Leader Wiliger brought in his companions, the ladies Siwili and Jelene Mayro, and the brother of Jelene, Autur. The ladies wore the furs and satins of the aristocracy. They rustled as they walked, and their perfume filled the stalls and brought blushes to the cheeks of some dragonboys and a hardening of expressions in the eyes of others as the boys were caught between bashful youth and adult lust. The ladies giggled at the sight of these "stalls" with the piled-up straw for the dragon and the little high-set bunk for the boy, so odd, so quaintly squalid with all these things hanging on the walls. And they enjoyed Wiliger's performance of going through the boys' kit and demanding that items be better polished. He was playing it up wonderfully. Autur Mayro thought so and continually commented on how witty Delwild Wiliger was. Never would have thought so from his reputation, but he was glad to have met him. Such a funny man.

Gradually a mood of intense dislike solidified among the dragonboys.

Dragon Leader Wiliger called them out to the exercise hall to parade. They formed up. Relkin in front, the rest in a line, and they came to attention crisply. They'd done it a thousand times for old Dragon Leader Turrent, so it was an automatic gesture, but one fit for the parade ground.

"Oooh," squealed Lady Siwili to her cousin, "they look so fierce, cousin, don't you think?" Lady Jelene's whispered response sent Siwili into fits of giggles.

Autur Mayro chuckled. Wiliger beamed at them, belched, and sent the odors of wine and a rich dinner wafting into their faces. Their expressions hardened into masks of stone.

And then there was an interruption. A door crashed open and there came a heavy tread.

"Where is Manuel?" said an all-too-familiar voice, loud, belligerent, and perpetually grouchy. No one said anything.

"Who are these?" it went on to say.

Dragon Leader Wiliger and the well-fed ladies from the party stared up into the scowling visage of the Purple Green of Hook Mountain, whose bulk towered over them. His big jaws opened slightly to reveal rows of teeth.

With a collective intake of air, all four of them fell into dragon-freeze. Instinctive terror of four-ton carnivorous monsters blanked their minds. They were incapable of movement.

Relkin rolled his eyes. Wiliger was stiffer than the rest of them. There could be no doubt now. This was some poltroon from the upper class who had never worked with dragons in his life. There had to be a mistake. They were the fighting 109th, the pride of the Marneri Second Legion. Surely they wouldn't be given over to this idiot.

There was a long, awful moment. The dragonboys stood at attention. Wiliger and his friends stood frozen on the spot. The Purple Green grunted acidly, "Normally dragonboys make more noise than a pack of hyena, but now they are silent as stones. Why is this?"

Relkin set about breaking Wiliger out of dragon-freeze. He snapped his fingers loudly in front of Wiliger's eyes and whistled sharply into his ear.

Swane and Manuel were doing the same for the ladies and Autur Mayro. One by one they came awake, but Wiliger remained locked in a trance.

The Purple Green was already lumbering back the way he had come, while Manuel went to mix some more akh. The dragon's enormous wings were folded around him, his long tail flicked sinuously behind him, and his tread caused the ground to shudder, but at least he was going away. The ladies' breath came back, little sobs escaped their throats. The dragons they'd seen in parades had never seemed so enormously frightening. Autur began to retreat to the outer door.

Another dragon appeared in the doorway. Autur tumbled back from a smaller beast, with bright green skin.

"More akh," said Alsebra.

"Manuel's gone to get it," said Jak.

Wiliger was coming out of dragon-freeze, but the moment he found himself eye to eye with another dragon, a sinuous green one with a look of penetrating intelligence, he gasped for air and his gasp cut off as he went rigid once more.

CHAPTER THREE

The globe spun beneath the emperor's fingers until the great tropical continent Eigo was prominent. He was alone, but for the witch Lessis, who stood by the window.

"This Path of Power you have mentioned, tell me more."

"Your Majesty, it is forbidden to be explicit. You understand that this is a glimpse of other worlds, other places on the great sphere board of destiny, that pearl of possibilities that lies forever in the palm of the Mother."

Her words seemed muffled by the gloom and the luxurious surfaces of the emperor's private study.

"Humor me, Lady, I beg."

The pale light of a stormy day illuminated the slender, careworn face of a woman in late-middle years. Her clothes were simple and grey, her demeanor was entirely undramatic. It was difficult for those who did not know her to understand her place in history.

"Your Majesty, the Path of Power is one possible path for the world to take. If skills and technology are allowed to develop without control, then our world will take that road. Down it lie weapons more terrible than anything we can imagine."

The emperor's brows remained lowered, his dark eyes thunderous. This news was not to his taste. She went on.

"What I can tell you is that there are seven dead worlds in the Mother's palm, worlds covered in ash and a dust that never cools under the poisoned clouds. Those worlds took the road to power. That road begins with the weapons that are being developed now in the heart of Eigo."

The emperor pursed his lips and turned the globe with his fingers as he traced out the route from the Argonath to distant Eigo.

"It seems so far away."

"It is no farther than Czardha." She lofted an eyebrow.

"And this development will put to naught all your great work in Czardha."

His brow furrowed. The Czardhan mission had been a rousing success, and they had signed treaties with the Trucial States. Trade had already swelled. They had combined forces against the great enemy in Padmasa, and for once they had the initiative and were pressing that enemy hard. He had staked his reign on the initiative toward Czardha.

"There really is no alternative?" The Emperor Pascal Iturgio Densen Asturi did not often seem to sulk, but there was a distinct pout to his lips. "This will take a huge fleet. To transport two entire legions, with their dragons and adequate cavalry. I don't know. Can we divert that much shipping?"

"The details are being nailed down right now in our office. It will take sixteen to twenty ships, all of the first rank. The force will be gone for at least two, more probably three years."

"It will make it impossible to take full advantage of the opening we have with the Czardhans. The Trucial States are producing new steels, better than anything we have ourselves. They can teach us so much."

"We understand that, Your Majesty. If there was any other way to go about this, we would try it. The Great Enemy has sent one of their own, their dread leader himself, to attend this project. He nourishes it in the distant heart of Eigo. And with it, he will demolish our power and establish a state of terror that completely girdles the world."

Pascal turned away from the globe. He moved across the room and stood by the other window and looked out across the storm-tossed harbor of Andiquant. Wind-driven rain rattled against the glass. In the harbor rode two white-hulled vessels, frigates. Farther out, invisible in the rain, other, greater ships were riding it out in the Cunfshon estuary.

He had this one great opportunity to place his mark on history and bring the long war with Padmasa to a successful conclusion. Combine with the Czardhans, spawn new tech-nologies from the trade between them, rout the Masters back into their holes, and finally destroy them there.

Any delay might be fatal. Two years previously the Great Enemy had thrust out his hands for their throat. The enemy's invasion of the Argonath had almost succeeded, and would have but for the fanatical defense of Sprian's Ridge by a small force of battledragons, legionaries, and hill tribesmen from an ancient clan. But for them, Padmasa might well have dismantled the cities of the Argonath one by one and thrown the empire back on the Isles, as it had been in the Dark Ages.

Pascal was terribly aware that if he made only one mistake in this war, they would lose and Padmasa would overwhelm them.

To take two entire legions and send them off for two or three years was a great risk. Their defenses were already strained by the great effort they were making to capture the enemy's bastion at Axoxo. To pull two legions out would make it hellishly hard to keep adequate force levels in the forts in Kenor. And if they were lost? Emperor Pascal did not care to think about such a possibility.

"Your Majesty, Heruta himself has gone to Eigo. He is so confident of victory that he has left behind the defenses of Padmasa. What can that mean?"

Pascal heard her. He nodded slowly. The wind beyond the panes was coming in gusts now, throwing the rain hard against the lovely walls of his city. He spoke with a sadness to his voice. How many would die in this great and terrible endeavor? How many would he, the emperor, send to their deaths?

"Then, it must be attempted. I will send Baxander to command. He has all the energy in the world, and he will need it. Steenhur might make a good second in command. Steenhur is much like Baxander, but younger. They will need to be strong. The diseases in Eigo are terrible. We will lose many men just to those tropical plagues."

Lessis was perfectly still and solemn. The witches had plans to deal with the diseases of the tropics.

"We will take losses. It is a great risk, but we must stop them, and quickly. Once this jinni is out of the bottle, we will never put it back."

Emperor Pascal Iturgio Densen Asturi came up with a wry smile. "Indeed, on the face of it this is a task for the Mother's Hand itself. To throw an army halfway around the world and into such remote and forbidding territory, why it invokes a pride fit for the old gods."

Lessis let a trace of a smile show on her own lips, but her words held no comfort.

"If Heruta is given enough time, we will lose everything to him within a century."

"The sea voyage alone will take months."

"With favorable winds a fleet could be there in sixty days."

"Winds in midwinter will not be so favorable."

"Then in ninety days. Once ashore it will take several months to cross the Ramparts of the Sun and get within range of the enemy. We have a plan. Let me show you. He will know we are coming, of course, but he will not be able to do anything to stop us until we are deep within his guard and have our blade close to his heart. If we are in time, then we shall defeat him and end this threat. If not, then we will fail, but we fail if we do nothing, either. This demon we must put back in its bottle."

CHAPTER FOUR

The following day Relkin risked requesting an interview with Commander Toup. The boys of the 109th had learned more in the morning concerning the appearance of Dragon Leader Wiliger. The only good news had been that he wasn't due to actually join them until they returned to the city. In the meantime Relkin continued as brevet dragon leader.

Relkin's point, the only one he felt he could legitimately bring up, was that the, uh, Dragon Leader Wiliger seemed unsuited for service with dragons. He had no experience with dragons, and he went into dragon-freeze very easily. Dragons wouldn't work well with a person who was terrified of them. Had there been some mistake perhaps?

Toup glared at him for a long while, and then banged on the desk with the flat of his hand.

"I don't like this sort of thing, Dragoneer, and I warn you I will not countenance insubordination!" He hesitated for a long moment. "I know full well that you have a damned fine record as a soldier of the empire. That is the only reason I don't have you thrown out of here and placed on a charge."

Relkin waited while Commander Toup's grey eyes bored into him.

"Come see me tomorrow; I'll look into it."

The next day Relkin was called to Commander Toup's office right after lunch. Toup wore an unusually savage expression. The reason soon became plain.

"The man Wiliger is your new dragon leader. It's official, and there is nothing that can be done about it now I'm told. He has powerful influence in the queen's court. His father is one of the most prosperous merchants in Marneri."

Relkin had a desperate ploy. Manuel had done some research.

"I would like to request a review of the appointment, sir, on the grounds that it appears the Dragon Leader Wiliger has not spent any time at all in service in the Dragon Corps. That means he has not been in the legions. Clause thirty-eight states . . ."

"Silence!" Toup banged on the table. "You are impertinent, sir! Dragon Leader Wiliger has transferred from the Marneri Fourth Regiment. Now get back to your command, Dragoneer, and don't let me see you again on this tour of duty."

Relkin stumbled out, stunned. The man had transferred from a crack regiment to a dragon squad! It was unheard of.

Old Toup was clearly very upset about the whole thing. Bought commissions were an evil that the legions fought against but had to accept occasionally. Until now, no one had ever bought their way into the Dragon Corps. In truth, not many had tried since the Dragon Corps consisted of gigantic, uncouth beasts and equally uncouth orphan boys who were conscripted at the age of seven.

The 109th finished out their tour in the woodlots and then formed up and marched away, down the roads to Marneri through the snow-covered winter landscape. The air had warmed in the aftermath of the snowstorm and the snow was melting, but their roads were all well-paved ones and quite clear and dry, so they made good speed, stopping every two hours for a quick boil of stirabout for the dragons and kalut for everyone.

Halfway there they met the 66th Marneri Dragons going the other way. The two units complemented each other on the Marneri tour. While the 109th were in the city, the 66th would be at Dashwood.

The 66th had no news. Everyone in the Marneri garrison was still waiting for word on when they would be sent to Axoxo. That they would finally get their turn on the front this year they accepted as absolute. The only question was whether they would march up to Razac and take a riverboat down the Argo, or take a ship in Marneri and sail to Kadein for the southern route, through the High Pass above Arneis and down the Lis.

They marched into a snowbound Marneri by the tower gate an hour after sunset and, illumined by torchlight, made their way down to the Dragon House where they resumed occupation of their familiar stalls. Cloaks, helmets, and great swords were hung up on the appropriate hooks while shields were stacked against the walls. After a hearty dinner the dragons went up to the plunge pool to join the resident legion champions, lead by mighty Vastrox. These champions helped train all the youngsters that came through the Dragon House, and they were always glad to see their former pupils. They even made welcome for the Purple Green of Hook Mountain, the only dragon in the legions who had not passed through the training in one of the nine Dragon Houses of Argonath.

The dragonboys busied themselves unpacking and reordering their lives. Relkin found a message scroll waiting for him. A letter from Eilsa Ranardaughter of the Clan Wattel, to whom his heart was pledged, and had been for eighteen months, most of them spent in separation.

In her letter Eilsa brought him up to date on her life, the problems of sowing and reaping oats in a year of too much rain, the problems of childbirth among her kin. Old Margian was still dying. A tough old woman in her ninetieth year, she was taking a long time about dying. She'd been dying when Relkin had been introduced to her more than a year before. Eilsa wished, as she ever did, that she could be free of the inheritance of Ranard, her doughty father, and free of the hills of Wattel so that she could come back to Marneri and be with Relkin.

Relkin closed his eyes for a moment as he imagined such a life. Eilsa living somewhere in the city of Marneri. The two being together at some point in every day. Ah, bliss!

These eighteen months of letter writing had done wonders for his skill with a pen, and now he wrote a quick letter in return and told her that he was back in Marneri, safe and sound, as was the dragon, and that his temporary command of the unit was over. He was a plain dragoneer first class now, not a full dragoneer in command of a squadron. He had explained many times to Eilsa why this confusing nomenclature existed and why both ordinary dragonboys and the man who commanded dragon squadrons were called dragoneer. Unless, that was, they had been promoted to dragon leader, the equivalent to being a captain in the infantry. Briefly he mentioned that they had a new dragon leader. As always, he pledged his undying love. He dropped the short scroll off at the Legion Postal Office. Mail was free for all in the legions, a privilege rarely used by orphan dragonboys.

Out on the pavement of Tower Street he paused and considered. The skies were clear now, and the stars twinkled in the cold air. He was tired but too excited to sleep. His anger concerning the new dragon leader was too strong, and any time he received a letter from Eilsa his heart would always pound for hours; he would think about her and wish that she could be with him. He turned about and headed downhill into the city. The sidewalks had been shoveled free of snow and much had melted during the day, but what was left was crusting over as the temperature dropped.

He crossed Foluran Hill, the so-called Quarter of Wealth, with its fine houses of five and six stories and white stucco exteriors. Farther down he crossed Broad Street with its commercial buildings and then plunged down to the dockside.

The lights of the city were echoed by the lights of several dozen vessels at anchor in the harbor. He noticed that one of the really huge white ships of Cunfshon had anchored in the outer harbor. Her lights seemed to stretch across the harbor out there.

His destination lay in a narrow side street, the Blue Bear, a tavern much haunted by sailors and betimes by legionaries. There was nothing Relkin liked better than to sit quietly by the bar and listen to a group of sailors tell stories of the world. Having himself undertaken two long journeys beyond the frontiers of the Empire of the Rose, he understood something of the breadth of the world. He hungered for the rest. He often thought, if he were to lose Bazil, and war was a risky profession, that he would seek a second life at sea, as a sailor aboard one of the white ships.

Inside the Blue Bear, he found the rooms warm from the fire and tight with a good crowd. At the bar he ordered a pint of the slight ale and scanned the throng. He exchanged nods with dragoneers Givens and Weeve, who tended the champions Gerunt and Xaunce. He saw two legionaries, men of the First Regiment from the black borders on their grey outer cloaks, hunched over a dice board in the corner.

Dragoneer Weeve came up to the bar to fetch in a round.

"Evening, Dragoneer Relkin, we was sorry to hear you'd lost your step to full dragoneer."

Relkin did his level best to seem nonchalant. Weeve shook his head. "Dirty shame if you ask me, I don't know what this fool can want, I only hope it ain't a case of a man with a taste for boys in his bed."

"He'll be in for a sad awakening if that's his problem. But something tells me that that's not it."

Weeve's eyebrows rose, but Relkin would say no more.

"Well, you've got your reasons I'm sure. Anyhow, did you hear that the *Barley* came in on the tide."

So that was the big ship out there, the *Barley,* the biggest of all the white ships at three thousand tons, the queen of the oceans.

"I saw her as I came down the hill."

"Word is you're all going out on her. Two days' time, lickety-split."

Relkin expressed surprise. He'd heard nothing, but then again he'd been up at Dashwood and they were a little cut off up there.

Weeve made a joke about the legendary lack of warmth in the Dashwood lavatories, then turned serious.

"I've heard that this won't be what you might think, either."

"What's that?"

"Well, I heard that you're to pack tropical gear, not cold weather."

Relkin's eyebrows shot up. Weeve smiled and put a forefinger to the side of his nose, then took up a couple of mugs of strong ale and went back to his friend Givens.

Relkin sat there rocked with surprise. Tropical kit? Then they wouldn't be going to Axoxo after all.

Unless Weeve was wrong about this. Rumors were always just rumors until you had the orders, one of the earliest lessons of the military life. Relkin was still determined to get those second liners for the freecoats. He could always cache them here in the Dragon House if they weren't needed, but if they were going to Axoxo then he would really want one. That would be a long, cold march from the western bank of the great river to the White Bones Mountains and all the way would be over the flat steppe of the Gan. The winter winds coming down from the north would be bitter.

Relkin found he'd finished his slight ale. He looked at his glass for a moment and fought off the temptation to indulge in a strong one. Instead he had another slight ale. There was still a bit of work to be done on the kit, including sewing by candlelight. One thing he didn't want was to be caught out by the new dragon leader. Relkin had had such a hard time with Dragon Leader Turrent at first. Turrent had really borne down on him hard, from jealousy, or so it had seemed. He didn't want to go through that again.

He sipped the slight ale and settled back on the wooden settle by the bar. The settle was two-sided, and behind him some sailors were loud in conversation. They talked of the marvels each had seen on the faraway coast of Bakan. He heard about floating cities, dreamstones, and a battle between magicians in which pink bubbles contended in the air with blue clouds.

Their talk was wide and general, and quite took him out of himself. A bell rang for the third hour before midnight, and Relkin shook himself free from a reverie in which he and Eilsa Ranardaughter floated away on their own sea schooner.

Outside he found a cold wind blowing down Tower Hill. He pulled over the breast flap on his freecoat and buttoned it down. There were patches of ice here and there on the pavements. To avoid one of these he almost bumped into another swift-moving figure, at the corner of Broad Street, under the Candle Maker's Lantern.

With a cry of recognition, the two embraced and clapped each other on the back.

"By the breath, young Relkin. I didn't know you were back in the city," said Captain Hollein Kesepton.

"We transferred today. Believe you me, we'd been looking forward to it, too. We've had a long wintermonth up at Dashwood. Cut a lot of wood."

"Worked up an appetite, too, I expect. You'll be asked to the Tarchos' tomorrow. There'll be quite a feast."

"I look forward to it, sir. And how is the Lady Lagdalen, and the child?"

"Well, well, absolutely blushingly blooming, and Laminna has several new words. You'll find her changed."

"I expect so, sir."

Hollein walked beside him, and they mounted the hill at a good clip. Any effect from the slight ale was passing quickly. Relkin raised the rumor he'd heard from Weeve. Hollein downplayed the rumor, but Relkin had the thought that Hollein's disregard rang a little false. No one had to tell Relkin something important twice. They don't want the dragonboys talking about this, he thought. And for sure, Captain Kesepton said as much when he finished the subject.

"I have heard that something unusual is happening, but it

is a delicate operation and there is a great deal of secrecy attached. It would be best if this rumor wasn't made too much of in the Dragon House, do you see?"

Relkin nodded. "I see."

Kesepton switched tacks.

"I was sorry to hear that they didn't give you the step to dragoneer. A wretched business if you ask me."

"We'll not make it hard for him sir, sir, I can assure you of that."

"Mmm, well, you'll have to keep a check on some of your fellows, that Swane of Revenant for instance. He's a hothead if ever there was one."

"Oh, we've learned a few tricks for cooling old Swane down."

"A wretched business, and you will have to make the best of it. Of course, if he's absolutely hopeless, then everyone will soon know and there'll be a change ordered. I've heard that he's brave enough. He led a crazy charge that recovered a key position in the battle of Cudburn's Shoals. They said he was braver than a lion that day."

"Oh, I don't doubt his courage." Relkin thought back to Wiliger's appearance at Dashwood. To show up like that, with his lady friends and presume to inspect the 109th Dragons took courage of a sort.

"No, it ain't courage we worry about, sir, it's his judgment. He's never served with dragons in his life."

"By the breath," muttered Kesepton, his face darkening.

They parted outside the Tower of Guard, Hollein to climb to the great apartment of the Tarchos where he lived with Lagdalen and their child, while Relkin went to his right through the Dragon Gate and down the steps to the Dragon House.

As he came in he started to trot; he was late and the last boil had already been dished out. The cooks were already cleaning their equipment and stacking things ready for the next boil. The fires were damped down for the night.

Back at the stall he found Bazil finishing up a bowl of stirabout.

"Ah, damn boy back at last. This porridge no good, not enough akh."

"I'm sorry, I met Captain Kesepton on the street and we chatted too long."

"Bah, you never a good liar. This dragon can smell beer on your breath."

You couldn't fool a wyvern's nose, that was for sure. Relkin attended to the kit. Some studs on the joboquin had begun to strain during the last practice bout and needed attention. The joboquin was the essential heart of the dragon's armoring system. It was a sleeveless jacket of leather strips, each equipped with buckles, studs, and eyeholes that could secure the other pieces of a battledragon's kit, including his armor plate, his scabbard, his cloak, and the pack he wore on a route march.

There was something on the dragon's mind. He set down the bowl, having scraped it clean, licked his spoon, and drained the last of a bucket of ale. But instead of lying down as usual for a nice long sleep, he remained hunched over in a corner, idly scratching his sides and the back of his thick neck.

"What is it?" said Relkin.

Bazil's eyes popped. Why did dragonboys always know when dragons need something. It was uncanny to dragons.

"Look, you can't hide it, I know there's something or else you'd be down and snoring."

"By the fiery breath . . ." he began. "I need to get a particular kind of fish, a large one. I need to have this fish roasted."

"What kind of fish?"

"What we call a sternfish. You know this?"

"Sure, and they have a deadly reputation. The shark that swims behind a ship near shore."

"They will eat anything it is said, but they also make good eating themselves if they are roasted properly."

"It will be expensive."

"We have plenty of silver in our savings account. I do not ask for this thing lightly."

"Yeah, I know."

Relkin understood. It was the ongoing rivalry between Bazil and the Purple Green. Ever since they'd been stationed in Marneri, the Purple Green had been riding Bazil about the so-called tastelessness of fish and other seafoods. In Marneri the dragons ate fish twice a week and shellfish as well in soups and chowders.

"All right, I'll check the fish market tomorrow. See what I can find."

"That would be good." The dragon settled his two and a quarter tons out on the pile of fresh straw that took up two thirds of the stall.

Manuel stuck his head in. Bazil began to snore, his huge belly rising and falling in perfect cadence.

"Dragons are down," said Manuel.

"Thanks for stepping in, I was, uh, talking to Captain Kesepton."

Manuel's face wrinkled in disbelief.

"No, really, I was." The disbelief didn't disappear. "Well, you're right, I was down at the Blue Bear earlier."

"Yeah. Well, there's still no sign of the Dragon Leader Wiliger."

"Thank the gods for that."

"You and your gods. Thank the Mother and be done with it."

"Not after Sprian's Ridge. Old Caymo rolled the dice for us that day."

"That's not what you were saying when we were there."

"Well, in hindsight it seems clear enough."

Even as he said this Relkin knew he didn't believe it.

"She'll despair of you, Relkin, before your time."

"I think she already has."

"I keep hoping that someone will intervene to stop what's happening. Before he gets here."

"I told you what Toup said. 'Nothing to be done about it.' Have to face it, we're stuck with him for a while. Captain Kesepton said that if he were to show himself as being positively harmful, then he'd be relieved."

"I'm more afraid that he'll turn out to be just minimally competent, and we'll be stuck with him until there's an emergency."

"Who knows, he may turn out better than we think. The captain said he was conspicuously brave in a fight at Cudburn's Shoals during the invasion."

With this crumb of consolation they had to be content. Manuel went on to his own stall and a list of small tasks to complete while his dragon, the Purple Green of Hook Mountain, the only wild dragon to ever serve in the legions of Argonath, snored his thunderous snore.

Relkin returned to reinforcing the threading on the affected studs and brooded the while on the new dragon leader. Life under old Dragon Leader Turrent had been hard enough, but this could be ten times worse.

When he'd finished the studs, he slipped out and took a final turn about the Dragon House to be sure that all was well. Everyone was asleep. He doused the big lamp in the center of the hall and took himself to his own bunk.

CHAPTER FIVE

They awoke to a day of sullen gray skies, a cold northerly wind, and a distinct threat of more snow.

The central fire in the Dragon House was blazing when Relkin went down for hot kalut and a bucket of water. A quick check showed no sign of Dragon Leader Wiliger nor any message from him. That meant that Relkin was still in command, and he took the opportunity to urge everyone to make sure their kit was complete and all metal cleaned and polished. They didn't want the new dragon leader thinking they were a slipshod outfit. The responses varied from mildly surly to insolent, but everyone acknowledged the point. Of course, they had already polished every single scrap of brass and steel and checked and rechecked every item on the long list of things that every dragon and dragonboy ought to have, but they accepted that this was a time to make double sure.

The breakfast boil was announced by the bell, and dragonboys moved to fetch immense cauldrons of oatmeal stirred with butter and salt. They returned for loaves of fresh bread and bacon, which was given the dragons every other day while they were in the city of Marneri and which they ate with relish, whole sides at a time, slab roasted on a medium hot fire.

After breakfast Relkin received an invitation to dine that very day with the Tarcho clan. Lagdalen insisted that he come. Relkin had no reason not to, and he deputed Manuel to stand in for him during the evening hour. Bazil would have been invited, too, but the Tower of Guard was not designed to allow ingress by dragons. Their friend Lagdalen of the Tarcho promised to come and visit him very shortly, however.

Relkin worked swiftly through the morning. He checked all the brass fitments and gave them a last-minute buffing.

Then the steel, starting with scabbards and going on to blades and morningstars. He forced the dragon to sit still for half an hour while all his talons were filed once more and burnished to a deep glow. All the dragons were being exhorted not to do anything boisterous for the rest of the day. There were to be no scratches, let alone chips or cracks, in those talons today. At length he finished and let the dragon retire to the plunge pool.

Relkin went out in the forenoon and trod quickly down to the dockside through a chill wind. He noted that the *Barley* had been joined by another white ship, only a little smaller than the *Barley* itself. Scattered flakes of snow were whipping along in the wind. Two white ships could carry a full legion, without horses, and with everyone crammed in tight. Relkin turned over the rumors in his mind. Whatever else was true, there was clearly a voyage of some kind in the offing. They'd have to work hard on the ocean discipline with the wyverns. It would be best if the dragons were kept belowdecks as much as possible on a sea voyage. The smell of the sea brought on ancestral longings, and there was always the danger they would go feral.

At the dockside he turned right and made his way around to Fish Place, a broad stretch of cobbles along the wharves where the city's fishing fleet docked. Facing the boats stood a row of solid three- and four-story buildings, dominated by an even larger one in their midst that had a large front gate with the doors propped open. He dodged through this gaping entrance and was enveloped in the odors of the fish market.

Sweating dockworkers were moving huge slabs of ice on which reposed mounds of fish—cod from the Cunfshon banks, tunny and swordfish from the Bright Sea. A halibut large enough to have swallowed a dragonboy was wheeled past on another ice block.

With a roaring clatter, a train of dollies bearing tubs of salted herring was thrust past by a team of burly lads. Relkin caught sight of their red faces, heard their cheerful banter, including a few insults tossed his way that he ignored completely, and he wondered briefly what it must be like to be one of them. To live here in the city as a civilian, to grow up here with a mother and a father and a firm place in life. It was so unlike his own existence that it actually had a romantic tinge to it.

He inquired at the stalls along the sides of the market, but sternfish were rare these days in the Long Sound. No one much fished for them anyway, and they were rarely brought in for sale.

"No demand for that," he was told on more than one occasion.

"Ol' mansnapper? No, son, we don't carry that. Too strong a flavor. No one likes that."

After trying with a few fishing skippers and finding no chance of a sternfish, he left and returned up the hill to the Dragon House. The snow was thickening steadily now, and the wind seemed even colder.

At lunch he reported his failure to the dragon. There was an ominous lack of response. Relkin realized he had a very sulky dragon on his hands.

The dragons were to exercise after lunch, and this day they were watched over by anxious dragonboys alert to the slightest chip on a nail as they went through their routines with dragonsword and shield, crushing the big dummy trolls and cutting deep into the softened wood butts.

When exercise was done and joboquins, swords, and shields had been retrieved from the dragons, and the great beasts had taken themselves back to the plunge pool with much grumbling, the dragonboys dispersed on their own errands.

Relkin dug into his chest and put on his best blue breeches, his special occasion boots, and his formal dragoneer jacket. On the right jacket breast, he wore three rows of honor ribbons that represented the actual medals themselves. Four white ribbons for his silver Campaign Stars, five scarlet ones for his Battle Stars, plus four special honors including a white-and-green one for the Legion Medal of Honor and a golden square with a black circle for the Legion Star, the highest honor the legion could bestow. The medals themselves reposed in his safe chest, deposited with the quartermaster of the Dragon House.

On his head went his Marneri cap, blue with a red outline thread, and at his waist he wore his best dirk and scabbard, already polished to a frightening degree.

Then he set off for the Tower of Guard. Leaving the ground floor, which was open to the public, he showed his invitation to the guards and was allowed through. He climbed to the Tarcho apartments and was admitted through the wide double doors into the gracious hallway of white plaster walls and red tile floor. He passed the line of ancestor portraits, at least twenty in that one room, and met Lagdalen at the door to the receiving salon.

They embraced as if they were brother and sister, and in a way they were. They had served together in the legendary campaign to Tummuz Orgmeen. At one point they had been alone, lost in the darkness beneath the dread city, all their companions taken or dead and with no company except a dying witch.

Lagdalen patted his chest with her fist.

"You are grown to be a man, Relkin of Quosh."

"And you are the mother of the most beautiful child in all Marneri, Lagdalen Dragonfriend."

"Hush, she will hear you praise her and awake, and we have only just gotten her down. At the age of two and a half our Laminna has become quite imperial in her demands. We are kept busy satisfying her, believe me."

Captain Kesepton came by and waved away Relkin's salute. "Within these walls we can dispense with the salute, my friend. Come, you must meet the company."

Lagdalen introduced him to her father, Tommaso, and her mother, Lacustra. They both inquired after the health and well-being of the broketail dragon.

"Verily do I wish that he could be here," said Tommaso. "I pray that we will be able to entertain him in the summer months and receive him in person at our house in Gatchby."

There was little chance of that, thought Relkin, if they were all to be shipped off somewhere, but he smiled and replied as politely as possible.

"I know that he would be honored to attend. But he would be very hungry. You know what that could mean."

Tommaso laughed. He had served in the tower for more than twenty years, but once he had fought in Kenor with the legions and he knew how hungry a dragon could become.

"You had better listen to him, Mother, I don't think you've ever served dinner to a wyvern. Why just one of them could eat this entire banquet!"

"Tush!" she replied, "we could afford to feed one dragon whatever he wanted." She peered at Relkin for a moment. "And this young man looks famished. I don't think they feed you enough in the legion."

Relkin, Hollein Kesepton, and Tommaso roared at this,

knowing as they did that the legions ate enormous meals, albeit of basic foodstuffs.

Relkin was led in and introduced to a couple of uncles, to Lagdalen's younger brother, Rozerto, a beaming fifteen-year-old with a well-fed look, and to Aunt Solomia and a train of other ladies of mother Lacustra's circle.

There was a long table, and Relkin was seated at the end on the right, beside Tommaso, with Hollein Kesepton beside him, Uncle Iapetor opposite, and young Rozerto beside him. A course of heggeli cheese with wafers and limes was served, and they drank to the emperor's health with glasses of white wine from Kadein. Then came a plate of oysters, and then roast ptarmigan, served with a light red wine from Minuend. Relkin surreptitiously let out his belt a notch. In truth, this was a rare feast for a dragonboy who usually had noodles and vegetables for his dinner.

"Another great ship in the harbor, Uncle?" said Rozerto.

"Aye, nephew, it is *Oat,* and a lovely sight she is. I served on her myself, when she was very new."

Uncle Iapetor had been a sailor all his working life and had retired after six years as captain of the white ship *Hoptree,* a vessel of one thousand tons with a crew of one hundred and fifty.

There was considerable speculation at the table about the mission of *Barley* and *Oat.* The most popular notion was that the ships were to sail for Kadein via the cities of Bea, Pennar, and Ryotwa, and that they would pick up men and dragons in each and deliver a large force, perhaps two legions, at Kadein. This force would then proceed to Axoxo and form the core of a massive assault planned for the summer that would end the long siege.

Relkin noticed that Hollein Kesepton did not contribute to this conversation with much more than a smile and a nod. He found himself thinking about tropical kit. Following the expedition to Ourdh a few years back, the legion commissary had evolved a lightweight suit of clothing to replace the wools normally worn in Kenor. Relkin had had a set of this kit, including a special lightweight cape for the dragon made of a wonderful linen from the Isles of Cunfshon. Somewhere along the line, however, most of it had disappeared. A lot had been lost during the year of the invasion and the battle at Sprian's Ridge. Dragon Leader Turrent had never inspected the tropical kit, and it had not been replaced.

The ptarmigans were followed by the first of the major courses, a great, steaming calf pie, four inches thick and four feet across.

Young Rozerto had grown bolder by degrees as he drank his second cup of wine and water. He began to ply Relkin with questions about the Dragon Corps. He was most interested in warfare, it appeared, which he identified as the most exciting and honorable pursuit for a man. What was it like to fight in battle alongside the wyverns, he wanted to know.

Relkin replied that dragonboys fought from just behind their dragons and that often one's main concern was to keep one's head down when the dragonsword was flying. The usual death for a dragonboy was, in fact, being crushed by the dragon or decapitated by the dragonsword.

The boy was awed. He kept glancing furtively at the three rows of ribbons on Relkin's jacket.

"How did you win so many honors?" he said at last, unable to restrain himself.

Relkin looked up, his mouth full of the calf pie.

Rozerto's question, while somewhat impolite, had drawn the interest of Uncle Iapetor, even while Tommaso frowned at his youngest for asking such a question of an honored guest.

Relkin swallowed the calf pie, took a sip of the fine Spriani wine. Iapetor and his neighbors on his left were looking at him expectantly. Some sort of response was called for.

"I've served in the legion for four years. It just so happened that there was a lot of work for us to do."

"Work? You mean campaigns," said Rozerto. "All those silver ribbons are for campaigns. I know that much. And the red ones are for battles." Rozerto turned to his father, "Papa, it is too exciting. I want to join the legions and go to war."

Relkin saw the glow in the boy's eyes. The naiveté of it sent a chill through him. He spoke sharply in a cold voice.

"You might not enjoy the excitement, though. War isn't about glory. It's about killing and being killed. It's not something you ever enjoy."

He sounded more severe perhaps than he meant to be. It was just that he had lost so many young friends in battles both large and small. Youths not much older than Rozerto.

Rozerto's face had fallen.

"But school is so boring. I want to run away to sea or else become a dragonboy."

Relkin actually had wistful feelings when he thought of the concept of "school." He'd only had a couple of years in the village school of Quosh, and he'd always regretted his lack of education.

Everyone else was laughing, however. Poor Rozerto flushed.

" 'Tis only orphan boys that are accepted in the Dragon Corps, young Rozerto," said Uncle Iapetor, attempting to be kind.

Kesepton corrected him.

"Actually other boys can join, but they have to go through the training at the academy. The classes have been expanded lately; there is a greater need than ever for dragonboys."

Tommaso smiled, but his eyes were uneasy. After the troubles he'd endured with his daughter, Lagdalen, he worried about his son.

"We will talk of this another time, Rozerto. You have a place reserved for you in the Officer Training School. We expect you to try for the First Regiment, to follow in my footsteps."

Rozerto looked downcast. "I know, Papa."

The talk shifted away for a moment to a discussion of the remarkable red wine they were drinking.

"It's a Spriani from the year of the great battle," said Tommaso.

"From a lucky vineyard, so many were destroyed that day."

"They had dragons treading in the grapes," said Iapetor.

"They had trolls and ogres, too. The painting of the battle in the auction house is most explicit," said one of the men to Relkin's left.

"You were at Sprian's Ridge, I believe, Dragoneer."

Relkin acknowledged the truth of this.

"You will allow us to drink to your health, then." They stood and raised their glasses.

Relkin kept a fixed smile on his face, although he was self-conscious, even embarrassed by this attention. He tried not to remember that day, which he thought could only be glorious to those who hadn't been there. It'd been a slaughterhouse with the dead stacked chest-deep. He would never forget the smell of blood, nor the dark red eyes of the enormous ogres.

He was rescued by mother Lacustra's demand that he come and sit beside her and Lagdalen for the next course or so. He was the guest of the entire family and not just a pack of men sitting at one end of the table.

Relkin moved to a place that was opened up for him in time for a great slice of gamecock pie served with roasted leeks. He was beginning to feel full, but he knew there were several further courses to come.

Now, surrounded by the matrons of the family, he endured another inquisition, this time chiefly concerning his marital status and what he intended to do about it. He explained carefully that he was affianced to Eilsa Ranardaughter of the Clan Wattel and that he had another five and a half years to serve in the legion before he could wed.

This occasioned a round of condemnation of the legion for making young men serve such a long time without marriage. At the same time, there were many whispered asides among the ladies. The name of Wattel was little known in the lands of the coastal cities.

There were many other inquiries about himself and his dragon, and he was kept busy so that it took a while to finish the gamecock pie. At once a great serving of roast venison was put before him, garnished with roasted turnips and caramelized onions.

The venison, he was told again and again, had been slain by Uncle Iapetor himself, a fine buck taken with staghounds and spear in the forest of Rogollo. Iapetor rose and toasted the stag and sang the hunter's song. He had a fine, clear tenor, and the table broke into determined applause when he'd finished and sat down.

Relkin struggled manfully with the venison, although by now he felt quite gorged. Nor was it possible to let out his belt, not with all these eyes upon him.

He ate on while Lagdalen tried to correct an aged aunt's impression that Lagdalen had been a dragonboy herself at some point in her life. Relkin chewed and swallowed. The venison seemed endless. Lagdalen's efforts, however, brought the threat of giggles to his lips.

At length he finished; not a scrap of venison or even leek remained. His plate was instantly snatched up.

No sooner was it behind him than the first of the desserts

was brought in, a glistening cake five feet high, capped with a green dragon fashioned in marzipan.

Somehow he managed to devour it; in truth, it was remarkably light and tasty. Lagdalen shot him a look of sympathy.

"I'm stuffed," she whispered. "I bet you are, too."

He fended off more inquiries about his fiancée from some of the more nosy ladies of the tower, and then was allowed to make his excuses and return to Tommaso's end of the table in time for the second dessert, a heavy, jellified trifle.

With a ghastly smile, he contemplated a large plate of this confection. A glass of sweet wine was set at his elbow.

The talk now switched into the dangerous channel of the state of the legions and bought commissions. This last, despite Hollein Kesepton's efforts to head it off.

Relkin labored through the trifle. Really, he could not manage another mouthful, and felt as if he might burst.

Uncle Iapetor thought bought commissions were all right, but that the prices should be raised considerably. Tommaso thought the whole thing was damnable.

Relkin was finally asked his opinion. He chewed, swallowed, looked around desperately for a moment.

"Well, the thing that we don't understand, is why it's allowed in the first place. You take units that are highly trained and motivated, and you give them to the command of men who have no training and perhaps no understanding of the training."

"Exactly," said Tommaso, slapping the table.

Iapetor spread his hands. "But the revenues, remember the revenues. Marneri keeps two legions and a dozen frigates for the defense of shipping. The cost is enormous. We need revenue from wherever we can get it."

"The damn Aubinans are manipulating the grain markets again," said one of the men to the left.

"The exchequer is in a lamentable state," said another.

"We need to sell more commissions, not stop the practice. A good way to raise revenues."

This all seemed suddenly too ignoble a conversation, and Tommaso changed the subject and asked Relkin to describe his visit to the hidden stair of the kings of Veronath. Relkin was glad to do so, pushing his chair back, feeling his belly stretched taut. The trifle was finished, at last.

Lagdalen came and forced Rozerto to let her share his

seat, for she had had no time alone with Relkin, who was her friend first and foremost, before any of the company.

Relkin had described the lesser stair and then the mustering of Clan Wattel and the opening of the cliff to the secret main stair when there was an interruption.

The major domo came close and whispered in Tommaso's ear. Lacustra signaled him to tell her, too. Tommaso's face had gone grey. The major domo moved toward the other end of the table.

"What is it, brother?" said Iapetor.

"We have a visitor, an unbidden one."

Lacustra suddenly gave up a wail. "No, not again, my heart won't bear it."

Relkin looked up to the door and saw a small figure in a simple robe of grey come in. He stared, amazed. It was the Lady Lessis.

"Greetings to you all," she said with a simple bow. Artfully she cast a spell of attraction over them with a fluid gesture of her arm. They responded very well; frowns and gawps were replaced by smiles for the most part.

"I see some faces here that I know well, and I see other faces that think they know me too well." She laughed sadly. "Thus are we divided in our struggle with the Great Enemy. Good Master Tommaso and Mistress Lacustra, I offer you a thousand apologies for this interruption. It is absolutely unkind, I know, but it is vital business of the empire. I am afraid I must speak with Lagdalen alone. The need is very urgent."

Tommaso had risen to his feet, his face a war of emotions. For a moment he could not speak, then he mastered himself.

"Lady, we did not know you were even in our city."

"No, I came only very recently."

And Lagdalen knew at once from Lessis's tone that she had, indeed, only just stepped through the Black Mirror, after a flight through unimaginable danger in the ether of chaos.

Lagdalen rose and went with the Grey Lady, and when she was out of the room, Lacustra wept aloud and could not be comforted. It was too much to be borne. These witches came as they pleased and stole one's children out from under one. There was nothing a mother could do. The poor child had already served enough, more than enough, enough for several lifetimes. Why couldn't they leave her alone? Why couldn't they leave the family alone?

Relkin's eyes met those of Hollein Kesepton and read there a hidden knowledge. Something was happening, but even though Lagdalen was his wife, Hollein would not break his silence, especially not at a dinner like this.

A foreboding began to build in Relkin's heart. He resolved to immediately investigate the matter of a tropical kit.

Lacustra was lead away by some of her ladies, and the dinner ended on a quiet note with the conversation much reduced. The last course was a marvelous pudding of rose water, flour, suet, and currants. It was extremely filling. Relkin struggled to finish it and left the Tower of Guard feeling as stuffed as one of the suits of armor that stood on the landings of the higher floors. Going downstairs was uncomfortable at first, and he had to pause for a moment at the second landing.

Outside in the cold air and winter light of evening, he took several deep breaths and felt somewhat better. The tropical kit surfaced on the uneasy brew of his mind. Lessis the Grey was in Marneri. Something unusual was in the works.

He made his way back to the Dragon House and found the rest of the 109th lined up in the midst of a full kit inspection, with everything spread out before them and Dragon Leader Wiliger standing there glaring at him with icy rage.

"You are derelict, Dragoneer. Where have you been?"

Relkin explained that he had been away to dinner with friends, special friends who had invited him to their home. He mentioned that while he had been away, he had deputized Manuel to stand in for him.

He made the mistake of saying further that he had heard nothing from the dragon leader since they had first met at Dashwood and that he had no idea that he would be joining them that day.

Wiliger's fury intensified, but he visibly checked himself.

"I hardly consider that good enough. However, you have an alibi. I will investigate. Should it prove false, then you will be up on a charge. Now, fall in with your own personal kit for inspection."

CHAPTER SIX

The obstacle course for dragons was built on heathland well beyond the walls of Marneri. Here, in a group of sandy drumlins, the legion had constructed a series of climbs, slides, crawls, and wallows, connected by a path roughed with dozens of rocks and felled trees.

Over this course went the 109th, each dragon carrying on his back four hundred pounds weight of sword, shield, and equipment. This in addition to helmet, chain mail, and the joboquin with breastplate and arm protectors.

Through the muddy wallows they splashed, throwing up a bow wave as they went. At their head were the younger dragons, such as Roquil, a leatherback from Blue Hills. They pushed themselves hard, even the big brasshides like Oxard and Finwey. Behind them came the older dragons: Alsebra, the green freemartin, generally in front; then the leatherbacks, Vlok and Bazil Broketail; and then the heavyweights, big Chektor, an oversize brasshide, and the huge Purple Green of Hook Mountain, the only wild, winged dragon that had ever joined the legions. He'd been forced into it when the minions of the Blunt Doom of Tummuz Orgmeen clipped his wings and robbed him of the power of flight.

As they went on around the course, a pattern began to repeat itself. The youngsters started well, but by the halfway mark they began to lose stamina. They tired quickly on the twenty-foot climbs. The older leatherbacks and Alsebra caught up and passed them in a while. Now these three plodded on, increasing the lead, down on all fours for most of the time, with sweat pouring from the glands down their backs and along their tails, despite the chill wind from the north and the snow under their feet.

By the end they were a minute or more ahead of the younger dragons and a full three minutes ahead of Chektor and the Purple Green.

As always, the Purple Green disparaged the course and the thinking behind it. The others drank the water brought by dragonboys and ignored him. He always complained about everything. They knew that the course was a physical challenge and that they had met it and well. Even the Purple Green had completed it within the twenty-six minutes alotted. They knew they were lean and fit for anything. The month at Dashwood had hardened and tightened their massive muscles.

After the water they sipped kalut and endured inspection by dragonboys anxious about every talon and every fragment of equipment. Then they formed up and marched for Marneri, keeping up a brisk four-miles-an-hour stride that brought them within the walls by the evening hour and well in time for dinner.

In the Dragon House they stood still while dragonboys undid armor straps and stays. Joboquins came off and were immediately inspected for the slightest rip or tear. Dragons cooled down from the march in the plunge pool. Then they headed into the refectory and sat in a circle around the central fire.

Dragonboys wheeled in cauldrons of cornmeal stirabout. Pots of akh were handed out. Dragonboys returned with kegs of beer, which were eagerly seized up by the dragons as they were broached.

The cornmeal vanished in minutes. Already the boys were back, however, wheeling in an enormous "gift" course, this one from a subscription among the fishermen of the city taken up to honor the "fighting 109th" of Marneri. It was a pie of "three fishes," easily twelve feet long, eight feet wide, and two feet deep. The pan it rested in had been especially cast for the occasion. Within were cods by the half ton, pequerel by the half ton, and runido in the same measure. This had been simmered with onions and garlic and then covered with a pastry shell and baked to a turn.

Two hogsheads of the finest ale from the Barbican brewery were brought in on a donkey cart and drawn into tall steel pails. The dragons sang happily after the first toast.

The pie was cut and shoveled into great platters that the dragons ate off with the same oversize spoons they used for everything else.

The wyverns much appreciated the pie. Their breed had originally been coastal predators, wild sea-dragons of the north, and they always enjoyed the flavors of the ocean. The Purple Green from Hook Mountain, however, disparaged the flesh of fishes.

"Pallid, insipid stuff," he proclaimed after cleaning two platters clean.

"Hardly worth the effort of devouring," he said as he accepted a third.

There were cries of disagreement. "Not so," said several of the wyvern dragons. "This is excellent pie. The cod is bland enough, but it supports the flavors of the runido and the pequerel."

"You just have a fixation on eating flesh, it comes with the wings," said Bazil Broketail.

The Purple Green scoffed. "You remember that horse we roasted? Now wasn't that incomparably better than this?"

"They're not really comparable at all," said Alsebra, who was taken by all of them to be uncomfortably quick-witted and intelligent. None of them liked to get into an argument with her. She always seemed to get the better of them.

"Fish is disgusting stuff, and these shellfish you talk about have no flavor at all!"

They listened for a while to the Purple Green's raving, but finally Bazil exploded. "I know of a fish that even you will have to admit is a great thing to eat. I will get one."

The Purple Green allowed that it would be something he would love to taste. Bazil swore by the fire of old Glabadza that he would and in a day or so, too.

Only later did he really put himself to imagining how to go about it. The boy had already tried to buy one without success. To go and try and get one on his own would have been an obvious solution, except that it went against the great prohibition.

It was forbidden for wyvern dragons to swim in the ocean. All the dragons in service to the legions were absolutely banned from the waters of the sea. Men feared that the ocean would reawaken the dragons' true identity, and they would cast off their alliance and reassume the wild way of life. "Turning feral" it was called with dread by all dragonboys.

Bazil fell silent as he contemplated the fix he'd gotten himself into.

While the dragons ate, the dragonboys checked and cleaned

equipment. An ungodly amount of mud had attached itself to everything.

They worked, mostly quietly, around the hot-water tub in the scullery, but dissension broke out when an orderly brought a message. Dragon Leader Wiliger invited Manuel, Relkin, and Mono to dine with him at the Wolf & Pheasant, an expensive restaurant on Foluran Hill.

"What's all this about, then?" said Swane, who was clearly miffed at not being included.

Relkin was still trying to work it out himself. The last he'd seen of Wiliger had been an unpleasant little interview in which he was castigated for being a troublemaker. Wiliger had told him in no uncertain terms that he would have anyone given ten lashes and field punishment if he thought they were playing the fool or trying to rag their dragon leader.

Now, just hours later, there was an invitation to a dinner more handsome than most.

"He's invited the three oldest of us," said Manuel.

"I don't understand," said Mono. "He was so hellfire runkly this morning. Told me I had to rework old Chek's shield handle by tomorrow."

"I guess we'll find out," said Relkin as he finished cleaning Bazil's breastplate and arm protectors.

An hour later the three of them left the Dragon House. They wore their very best blue coats with red trousers in Marneri twill and knee-high boots that gleamed with the polishing. Their best caps were aligned in perfect horizontal fashion with the brass squad badge aglow on the front. They marched down to Foluran Hill and stood outside the Wolf & Pheasant, admiring its polished-brass fittings and the green awnings that curved above its three windows on the street.

Without hesitation they elected Manuel to go first. Relkin and Mono were orphans, Manuel was not, a real rarity in the Dragon Corps. Manuel had had an education. He belonged in some way to the world that included the Wolf & Pheasant. They did not.

Manuel found the headwaiter, and the name "Wiliger" was enough to secure them instant attention. They were shown to a fine circular table set in the far corner of the main room, near the immense fireplace in which a whole pig was roasting.

A few moments later Dragon Leader Wiliger himself joined them. His self-invented uniform had been toned down somewhat. He still wore the long blue coat with tails, but he'd switched from breeches to pantaloons, and they were of the correct red for dress uniform. He had turned to a wide-brimmed hat, like a cavalry trooper, which was all wrong of course, but worse still he wore the oversize cap badge with those sacred numerals, 109, in what looked suspiciously like gold.

They did their best not to fixate on this vulgar, incorrect item. Having spent so much of their lives considering such details under the stern eye of Dragon Leader Turrent, they were intensely aware of how wrong it was.

Wiliger was oblivious to their concerns. He settled in at the table, ordered ale for all of them, and plunged into a determined attempt to be friendly while pumping them for information about the unit. He seemed utterly unconcerned about the incongruity of this. In the morning he was the roaring taskmaster, demanding this and that, poking about their kit and complaining that things weren't polished enough, including items that were never polished at all and never exhibited on parade. Now he was attempting to be their friend and intimate.

It was difficult in the extreme. But as one ale was followed by a second, and their attention was drawn to sizzling chops and slices of roast pork, it became a little easier. Manuel did most of the talking. Mono was the quiet sort anyway, and Relkin didn't trust himself to speak. He was still too astonished by this turn of events.

Wiliger wanted to know about the great fight at Sprian's Ridge, and he listened intently to Manuel's descriptions, venturing little in reply except an occasional "my word!" or "by the Hand."

When he'd heard it all, he congratulated them quite handsomely and then told them of his own fight, at Cudburn's Shoals. He seemed quite unself-conscious as he spoke.

"The enemy had thrown a large body of imps across the shoals, and my regiment was in danger of being cut off. There was this group of rocks by the river's edge. It was absolutely crucial, but we'd been driven off them. I took up the fallen standard and rallied some of the men, and we retook those rocks and threw the imps into the river. Saved the day, I think."

"Of course it was nothing compared to what you fellows did at Sprian's Ridge, but it was hot enough that day." They listened and exchanged puzzled glances. This was a transparent effort to win them over. They were supposed to accept that Wiliger was a real soldier and not some overfed fop with a wealthy father when all the evidence was to the contrary.

Wiliger next asked them, one at a time, to recount briefly their life stories.

"Where were you born, for instance, Relkin?"

"Village of Quosh, sir, in the Blue Stone country."

"Ah, the Blue Stone. Such pretty country, I've always enjoyed it. My uncle has an estate there, he holds it in fief from the Baron of Borgan."

Relkin's eyes widened for a moment. He and Bazil had once worked for the Baron of Borgan, a disastrous period for them both.

"So, where were you schooled?" said Wiliger.

A course of pigeons stuffed with foie gras arrived. Relkin admitted to having been to the village school in Quosh for a couple of years.

Wiliger frowned. "You mean that you have only had two years schooling in your life?"

"Yes, sir."

Wiliger muttered something under his breath.

"And you, Mono, where did you attend school?"

Mono looked down. "I never did no school, sir. Farmer Gool's wife learned me the skill of reading, but I never did too well at the writing. I can count, though, she learned me the counting and the multiplying."

Wiliger's eyes popped. " 'Tis extraordinary, and yet they allow you to serve in the legion."

He turned to Manuel.

Manuel had been to school from the age of seven and had attended the academy in Dragon Lore and learned much concerning the physiology and behavior of the dragons.

Wiliger at once asked Manuel his opinion on the great Chesler Renkandimo, renowned author of *Knowing the Dragon* and the great *Care of the Wyvern Dragon*.

Manuel hesitated. "Renkandimo is not much favored at the academy. He lacks a grounding in the principles of the biologic. His prescriptions are whimsical in some cases."

"Whimsical? Dear me, surely not. The great Chesler whimsical, it can't be." Wiliger seemed most upset by this news.

The incredibly filling stuffed pigeons were at length picked clean. More ale was brought, and all three dragon-boys were feeling the effects by this time. Manfully they drank it down and prepared to tackle the desserts as they arrived, beginning with the wondrous house apple pie.

For the second day in a row, Relkin was feeling over-stuffed to the point of bursting. Worse, this time his head was feeling wobbly from three pints of the best ale. He normally never drank more than two. Now came a fourth and a huge wedge of black currant pie.

Having exhausted his interest in the lives of the dragonboys, Wiliger turned back to Relkin.

"I have ordered new cap badges for the unit. Like my own, with larger numbers, a great idea don't you think? This is a proud unit, a legendary one. We want people to see our number and give us the respect we deserve."

He'd taken off his hat and was pointing to the horrid great flashy thing.

Relkin choked for a moment. When he got his breath back, he struggled to find words. Something impelled his tongue to truth, perhaps all that ale sloshing around inside him.

"Sorry, sir, they're irregulationary. Can't be used."

"What?"

"Cap badges will be one inch long, seven-sixteenths of an inch high, three-sixteenths thick, made of Cunfshon brass and polished to a high shine." Despite being drunk, Relkin rolled the oft heard syllables off his tongue like some religious chant. Manuel and Mono nodded in time.

Wiliger's face darkened.

"What do you mean?"

"It's Legion Regulation 243, sir," said Manuel quickly. "Cap Badges Will Be." He saw Wiliger's confusion. "Our former dragon leader used to recite the dress regulations to us at every parade, sir. I think we know all of them by heart. Cap badges are strictly prescribed for in size and material."

There was a long, pregnant silence while Wiliger went scarlet. They all kept their eyes on their plates. The rest of the meal was an agony of embarrassment, and they were all glad to escape at last and scurry back to the Dragon House.

CHAPTER SEVEN

The land of the Kraheen bore a well-earned reputation for cruelty and the rule of savage kings. Their neighbors avoided them, in part because of the legends concerning cannibalism and their dark terrible ways, but also because their land was isolated beyond the Ramparts of the Sun, in close proximity to the ancient forests known as the "Lands of Terror."

Wealthy Kraheen women poured fortunes in fat down the throats of tame pythons and fed them on slave children. High Priests carved totems from especially fattened, living men and women. Hung on hooks from the chins of the gods of Stone and Fire, these living emblems howled out their propitiation of the deities. Sometimes they lived for weeks this way. At every rising of the full moon, the priests bled human sacrifices and then bathed themselves in the juices.

The Master Heruta Skash Gzug had sent Kreegsbrok to end this world and replace it with another. He had been given five hundred men, the pick of the armies of Padmasa, with fifty troll and five thousand heavy imp. This force had been enough to shatter the army of the Kraheen nobility and scatter it to the winds. Kreegsbrok had taken the royal family prisoner. Through them, he had become the ruler of the land of the Kraheen. He promulgated enormous reforms, especially to the use of the land that was to be distributed among the peasants.

This was an enormously popular step. At once the people rallied behind the new regime. The orders went out for the arrest of all the old nobility.

When Kreegsbrok and his men had finished with the old nobility of the Kraheen, there was a mound of skulls ten feet high standing at the gates of the new fortress that was rising on the Island of the Bone.

The last holy men of the old gods had been made to swim

for their lives with the bones of their high priests still smoldering in their mouths. The old ways were no longer needed, for the Prophet had come to life.

"He Who Must" strode the world once more, a legend from a previous millennium. From his fingertips danced blue fire that could heal the sick. From his eyes emanated a strange force that brought calm to the souls of the mad. He spoke with a voice of honey and brought balm to the back of the ancient people. The Prophet had the power in him and demonstrated it before the people every day.

And so they came to him, in vast throngs, pouring into the capital city from the hinterland. They returned speaking of the marvels they had seen, bearing among them the lame who could now walk and the blind who could now see.

And thus did Heruta Skash Gzug fashion a hand to carry his other great weapon, the were-sword, the destroyer of worlds, cast of metal in great forges built on the Island of the Bone.

Kreegsbrok had been summoned one night and flown on the back of a massive batrukh across the waters of the Inland Sea to the Island of the Bone. There within the new fortress he was received by the Great One himself. The Master, great Heruta, commended his servant. Kreegsbrok had done well and had repaid the faith shown in him by his Master.

He was given a new task in life. He was to manage the Prophet, to control the strange thing that Heruta had created from the long-dead flesh of "He Who Must."

"He lives, but he knows in his heart that he is dead," said the Master in that eery rasping voice. "This makes him vulnerable to the suicidal impulse. Death is generally sweeter than life for such as he."

"Yes, Master," said Kreegsbrok.

"You must keep him alive, good Kreegsbrok. With him alive, we shall have an army of a hundred thousand Kraheen who will willingly fight to the death. Such a host will be necessary for the next steps in our mission."

Kreegsbrok said nothing, his eyes fixed on the ground, unwilling to gaze too long on the whorls of sparkling horn that covered the Great One. Heruta floated a few inches from the floor in utterly inhuman form. He understood the effect his appearance had on his servants, and he relished the fear it grew in their hearts.

"Kreegsbrok, good Kreegsbrok, you are a creature of war.

You have served our power faithfully for many years. You understand something of the great struggle we are engaged in."

"Yes, Master."

"Since the disaster of two years ago, we have been on the defensive. It is imperative that we regain the initiative and gain enough time to rebuild our strength. That is our mission here. We must succeed!"

Kreegsbrok clenched his fists. "We shall win!" he said in a tight voice. The Great One smiled for a moment.

"Of course we can expect our enemies to take some action. Our presence here is now known. It was inevitable that they would find out somehow, they always do. Still, it will take them years to mount a response, and even then I doubt they will be able to take effective action. We are too far from the coasts they dominate with their filthy fleets. But I expect the hags of the Witch Isle to try their best. They will come in various guises. You will need to be very alert. They will try to subvert our work upon the old Prophet. You will notify me at once if you detect the slightest sign of witch magic!"

"Yes, Master."

And thus Kreegsbrok had become the keeper of the Prophet. A strange business, watching over a man who was not a man, alive but not alive.

At times Kreegsbrok detected a definite personality within the husk, a glimmer of the ancient man who had been consumed by his ascension to "He Who Must." It came alive when he spoke to the crowds. He was a captivating speaker, imbued with an energy that moved people to ecstasies. Afterward there would be a light in his eyes, and he would speak to Kreegsbrok in broken Verio, which ancient tongue he had known something of in bygone times. Kreegsbrok was conversant in Verio, along with several other languages learned during the campaigns of his youth. The Prophet would question him about the world as he knew it. The answers always excited the Prophet, and at times he would rage off in Kraht, completely unintelligible for a while. At other times he would simply laugh and ask more questions.

And then the eyes would go out and the body would stiffen. Though it moved and even spoke, it seemed to have no life within it.

When it slept, it was as if it were truly dead. To waken it,

Kreegsbrok forced black drink into its mouth. The black drink had a powerful effect on the thing. It always wanted more and Kreegsbrok had to be careful to keep it from intoxicating itself.

"You don't understand man-who-still-lives," said the Prophet one time. "You don't understand a thirst built over a thousand years."

But the Prophet lived enough to speak to the people, and that was all that was required of him. Every day the heralds went forth from the new temple to summon the crowds.

And they rose up and came to see him, in their tens of thousands. They came with the thunder of drums and the ululation of the multitude. They came with fierce joy in their hearts and a flame lit in their eyes. They came to worship the Prophet and to relish his message.

Darkness fell, huge fires were lit on the water and out of the night He came and stood before them, bathed in light from two orbs that were lit upon the base of the pinnacle. He wore the cloth of gold and strode a white carpet. He raised his hands and silence fell.

In the distance there was a great flash of light from the Bone. A few seconds later a dull boom shattered the night and echoed off the cliffs of the Place of the Pinnacle.

From the great crowd there came an ecstatic sigh.

The Prophet came to them and in him was the power. He preached it to them and the power went out into them; and they felt the joy in their hearts grow louder.

When he paused, their ululations rose to the heavens. A harsh birthing cry of the legend of the Prophet. Ajoth Gol Dib, the One Who Must, who came to the Kraheen alone, promising an end to their misery, an end to disunity and slavery.

Cry joy for the love of Ajoth Gol Dib! The Great One Who Must!

Across the white carpet he came, tall, beautiful, with the fires of destiny blazing in his great dark eyes. The masses swooned at the sight of his beauty. They drank up his words like sweet wine.

The message was a seductive one. Accursed by all other peoples, the Kraheen would rise up at the last and assume the rule of the world. For too long had others cheated the Kraheen. For too long had the coastal peoples kept the Kraheen from the riches they deserved.

In the name of Lugad, the God of the ancient Kraheen, they would go forth and spread the message of the Prophet. Fall down and worship Lugad, all else is forbidden on pain of death. For Lugad had given the world to his faithful Kraheen, and it was now time for them to take it.

And he told them to throw down all other rulers and to know no other gods but the One God, Lugad. And he promised them that if they did this, then Lugad would look upon them with great love in his heart and would raise them up and make them the mightiest people of the world.

And they brought to him cripples and the mad and he held them and the power went out from him into them and they were cured and they stood up and they spoke like sane men and the crowd went wild and the drums thundered and the ululations cracked against the skies.

And they brought to him the condemned and they wept and wailed and they were bowed down with chains. And they were hung up on poles beside the Prophet, who preached against their crimes. He damned their treachery, their apostasy, and their heresy in denying Him, "He Who Must." Then he raised his hands and once more they were silent.

And the condemned began to howl as their bodies distorted. Their cries rose into shrieks of agony as their ribs rose and muscles stretched taut. Then the distended chests finally burst in a shower of blood, with the sound of meat under the ax, and their hearts were given up to the Prophet's hands.

The crowd went mad with excitement, the drums rose to a thunderous pitch. The Prophet waited until they were exhausted, and then he raised his arms and hushed them. He blessed them and departed, disappearing behind a dark screen that cut off the brilliant glow of the orbs at the base of the pinnacle.

Far away on the Bone there came another enormous flash of light and shortly thereafter a final heavy thud that reverberated in the warm, wet air.

CHAPTER EIGHT

The bell atop the temple rang for the second hour of morning. Apart from a few lights showing around the fish market and in the taverns hard by it, the city was asleep.

At the gate to the Dragon House, the sentries were nodding on their spears. Light snow was falling, and the skies were dark with hurrying clouds.

Suddenly there came a loud crash from the direction of the rubbish yard, next to the stables across the way from the Dragon House.

The sentries woke up, blinked in irritation, and peered across the cobbled passage to the dark mouth of the rubbish yard, a small court in which the garbage from the Tower of Guard and the Dragon House was mixed with other refuse from other official buildings before being mulched and transported.

They looked at each other and shrugged.

Suddenly there came another crash.

They looked at each other again.

"Come on, Gerse, we better take a look."

"You go. I should stay here."

"Both go, just in case. Might be a lunatic."

They peered through the snow.

"Come on."

Cautiously they made their way across the passage to the entrance to the rubbish yard. Gerse had brought a torch, which he thrust in ahead of himself. The other, Irodle, came behind him with his spear leveled.

The torchlight revealed mounds of debris, all carefully graded and tidied away. Two enormous cats glared at them from the dark, then sidled swiftly away behind the bone bins.

"Just them cats," said Gerse.

"I dunno," said Irodle, "it was pretty loud for cats."

But the piles of discarded clothing, dirty hay, vegetable compost, and builders' scrap stood there mutely in rebuttal.

"No lunatic," said Gerse with relief.

"Damn cats."

But it was not the cats who were solely intent on the rats drawn to the place. Nor was it a lunatic.

Neither Gerse nor Irodle glimpsed the tall, massive form that had slipped out of the Dragon House while they were in the rubbish yard.

It moved through the snow with a light, anxious tread, and turned out onto the wide space of Tower Parade, which led down the hill on the south side of the height on which stood the Tower of Guard.

Here Bazil Broketail paused for a moment. He was out of sight of the guards. Their job was primarily to keep people out of the Dragon House rather than dragons in, since wyverns only rarely entered the city, apart from the fortress set about the Tower of Guard. Still, he didn't want anyone to know about this mission, because he was about to break a most fundamental rule for the Dragon Corps.

From here on questions would certainly be raised about his conduct. But his determination remained. The damned old Purple Green was going to eat a fish and enjoy it. He'd been listening to the wild dragon go on about how distasteful fish was for months, and he was tired of it. So were all the others. It was up to Bazil to do something about it.

He set off southward, down Water Street, a steep lane that wound down through the Lamontan Graveyards to Sawmill Lane and then to Old East Street, where it changed pace. Now it dogged southeast and went straight down a smooth, gentle slope toward the East Bay. Here stood the homes of prosperous merchants, sea captains, and the like, in a fine row of white-fronted houses, each with a square portico held up by plastered pillars.

In the day a thousand eyes scrutinized this street, but at this hour there was no one to observe the progress of a two-ton wyvern dragon, partly concealed beneath his great cloak, as he hurried down the center of the street.

At the dockside he paused. On this side of Chandler's Point lay the East Bay. Here the water was shallow and just offshore the current was swift. There were shoals in the bay so it was not favored for shipping, which congregated on the west side of the point, inside True Bay.

Bazil crossed the promenade of the Southside and passed through the ornamental gardens to the ramps that led down to the sandy flats that fringed the water. Among the wealthier families, a ride on the exposed sands was one of the pleasures of the day.

The tide was low, and so he would have to cross a hundred yards or more of tidal flats. This wouldn't have been a problem except that across the bay he saw a fire on the beach, near the East Gate, where someone, perhaps drovers waiting for the morning's market, were staying warm and passing around a bottle of whiskey.

He removed his cloak, folded it roughly, and stuffed it beneath a bench. Then he dropped to all fours and slithered down across the cold wet sand to the water of the Long Sound.

He reached the meridian between two worlds and breathed deeply of the scent of the ocean. He pressed on, his feet slipping through the foam, feeling the delightful coolness of it as it splashed above his ankles.

This was seawater, and thus it was forbidden. Men feared that wyverns could not withstand the lure of the sea and that, once affected, they would leave and never return. Bazil had swum in the sea as a youngster, however, breaking the prohibition many times, and although he knew the pull of the sea he did not desire it above all things. And in his service in the legions, he had swum both lakes and rivers. Of course, freshwater was not the same; it had no echo in the heart for wyvern dragons, who were natural predators of the shore and the shallows.

The water came up to his belly, and then he was off his feet and swimming. It was cold, which he enjoyed. As a wyvern dragon, he burned at a higher temperature than men. He slid into it gratefully and inhaled the scent of ocean.

All at once a great orchestra struck a chord in the back of his mind, and he felt as he had never felt before. He swam in the natural way for wyverns, breathing several times quickly to fill his lungs and then keeping his head below the surface as his great tail thrust him along, with steering provided by his legs and torso.

Memories awoke from his youngest days in Blue Stone. Days when he had chased tuna over the offshore banks. Deep feelings moved inside him like whales working in the depths, inchoate things, never voiced before.

This was how to live, wild and free, swimming in the sea, the way the wild one had been when his wings were strong and he roamed the northern skies, pouncing on whatever he saw that he desired to eat. This was where a wyvern dragon belonged, where he ruled the shallow waters and the beach lands.

He surfaced to breathe, sucking down long deep breaths and expelling them loudly, supercharging his lungs. Then he lowered his head into the water, enjoying the feel of it, tasting ocean and her silky vastness, her distant shores and enormous reaches. He swam, sampling the water, seeking the trace odors of potential prey.

He noticed at once that there was a considerable stench coming from the True Bay on the other side of the headland. Marneri treated most of its sewage, but from the ships that docked and occasional spills from storm sewers, enough pollution reached the small, tight True Bay to make it stink to a nose as sensitive as his. He turned away from it and swam eastward, against the current, into clean water, keeping about half a mile from the land.

He sensed a school of mackerel ahead of him that took fright and fled out of the bay into deeper water. The sardines that the mackerel had been pursuing escaped down the coast inshore of him, and he chuckled to himself and wished the small fish well.

He crossed the Sequile shoals and detected a big eight-arms, intent on a crab until the wyvern was quite close. The octopus sensed him when he was right overhead and fled in a jet of black ink. Bazil lifted his head from the water and laughed from the sheer pleasure of it. This was the life, ruling the margin of the sea.

Why should he ever go back?

The question rose suddenly into his mind. Why return at all? Let them forget Bazil Broketail, he would become what he was meant to be, a great predator of the coasts, hunting for seals and bears on land and for whatever he could catch in the water. He would swim the surf from one end of the continent to the other and feast on the fish and the animals. No man would rule him, no one would make him wear man's things, the clothing and equipment that marked one as being the property of the legions. It was a dangerous life being a battledragon, why should he die for man?

Men, destiny, flashing thoughts struck through him, visions of the legions and their organized life.

He refused the call of these visions. Instead he would go free. He would taste the life of a wild wyvern.

He recalled with shame the disastrous attempt he had made some years before to desert and go wild with the Purple Green and the boy, hunting in the forests of Tunina. They had discovered that in a world of speedy elk and deer, two great multiton predators were simply too slow to survive. But here, in the ocean, the wyvern came into his own.

A savage exultance filled him, intoxicating him with its euphoria. He drove himself forward through the waters, thrilling to the sensation of pressing aside the sea, the mighty sea. He rose to the surface and sucked·in a giant breath of air and rolled over onto his back and continued to power along, but on the surface, looking up into the silvery night-born clouds. Snow was falling lightly, being whipped away over the water by an offshore wind.

Suddenly, with painful clarity he visualized Relkin's face. He thought of the pain the boy would feel on learning of his desertion. He thought of the others, the dragons in the 109th, his close friends.

They would forget him, said the new part of his mind. His destiny was to live wild and swim the sea.

He would not forget them, said the older part of him, and he would live with shame that would grow and grow and consume his heart in the end.

After all they'd been through, he couldn't abandon Relkin. And then he thought of their dream, to retire after their ten-year stint and take up the free land in Kenor. They'd have savings to buy a few draft animals and plenty of tools, and they'd clear good land and build a prosperous farm. In time he would fertilize the eggs and beget more wyverns for the villages of the Argonath. He would live a productive life and a comfortable one.

The new part of him shouted its rejection of this human scheme. It demanded that he turn away from the land forever. Forget the men and their wars, none of it meant anything to a wyvern dragon hunting free along the shore.

Except that there was a good reason the dragons served the legions, and for a moment a dark cloud obscured his thought; from the cloud projected the fangs and hateful malice of the great enemy. And then it was gone, for the new part of him refused to accept it. He would turn away from all of that.

He swam on, thoughts quite blank, sometimes lying on his back and other times on his belly with his head down and his nose questing for the scent of prey. Slowly an unease spread through his euphoria, clouding it as effectively as the eight-arms' cloud of ink in the sea. All around him in the sea he felt this change, a wave of concern; creatures everywhere were dispersing away.

And then he caught another odor, darker, heavier than that of most fish, a stench filled with terror. Instantly it brought back memories of a night when he was young and played truant from the village and swam in Blue Stone Bay.

A great stern fish swam nearby, not the common kind that grew to ten feet and five hundred pounds, but the very rare, terrifying giants known as white death, which could reach fifty feet and thirty tons.

The unease he had felt had hardened into something considerably less pleasant.

On that occasion in his youth, he had been saved only by his good fortune in reaching the Bareback rocks a few seconds ahead of the monster that had pursued him. He had stood there shivering as the huge dorsal fin curved past the rocks and then sank into deeper water and vanished.

It was a rare moment that a wyvern dragon felt fear of another animal. Bazil recalled the feeling of awe and rage when he'd stared into the face of an ogre at the Battle of Sprian's Ridge. The ogre stood fifteen feet high and weighed as much as Bazil or more, but there'd been no fear, no genuine terror, for in his hands Bazil had held the great sword Ecator, nine feet of shining steel and fit to cut down any living thing. There had never been a sword to match Ecator, and he loved the weapon more than any other brute thing in the world. Only now he had no great sword in his hand, but merely a tail sword, with its short blade and sharp point, perfectly sufficient for dispatching a sternfish, but not what he would have chosen for this situation. Nor was he standing on firm ground, sword ready, connected to all his training and experience in war. Instead he floated in the watery universe and had to depend on his instincts.

He submerged and tried to locate the great fish. Nothing could be seen. The stench was stronger, and he sensed that the monster was near and that it knew he was there. It was contemplating him. He was larger than most sea animals, and though it ate anything it came up with, including sick whales, it had the caution of its kind when there was no blood in the water. The presence of large quantities of blood drove all squalae into a frenzy, even leviathan, but in this situation it would carefully inspect a potential prey of Bazil's size.

Bazil swam slowly toward the shore, turning his head backward frequently. It was closer, but still circling him. He felt it moving just fifty feet away, nosing past, curious but not yet moved to attack.

By Glabadza's ancient fiery breath, it was huge! He floated head down in the water, gripping the stubby hilt of the tail sword and keeping as still as possible.

The fish was gone. Even the stench receded. The moments ticked away with a dreadful slowness. Then he sensed a pressure coming toward him from the land. Closer and closer it came. It could no more see him than he could see it, though he could sense a deeper blackness pushing toward him, but it knew precisely where he was.

Then it was upon him. A darker mass coursing through the black water, a great mouth opened, teeth six inches on a side gleaming faintly through the murk.

Bazil ducked down, drove himself deep with two intense thrusts of his tail and curved up again.

The monster's jaws slammed shut a foot behind him with a clash like the end of the world, and he rose up alongside the vast body as it went past.

He swung, the short sword struck and stayed fast, lodged in the monster's tail.

It gave a tremendous heave, Bazil felt himself lifted up and broke the surface for a moment, still clinging to the sword hilt. He sucked in a great sobbing breath of air before the next thrash of the tail drove him back under the surface and dislodged the sword. He was hurled away, tumbling.

The giant was already turning back on its own length, and again its jaws clashed shut barely inches from dragonhide. This time his evasive twist brought him into violent contact with the shark's belly.

It was like bouncing off a gravel road; rough skin rubbed him raw and he shot away quite helpless to strike a blow.

Again the monster turned. There was some of its own blood in the water now. This produced an abrupt effect on the giant shark. It charged, jaws snapping repeatedly, a sound with a concentrated crack in it that hurt the ears.

There was no time to dodge; he survived because the monster had entered a frenzied state and bit at the bloodied water as much as anything solid. The huge bulk slammed him aside and for a moment he felt the giant's dinner-plate size eye under his talons, but he was spinning and could do no harm. The shark bucked under the stimulation of the blood. For a fraction of a second he was suspended over its side. He stabbed home with the blade and felt it sink to its hilt. The wall of flesh reacted angrily. He clung with all his might and felt the blade cut itself free, delivering a terrible wound; then he was driven deeper by a solid slap from the great tail.

Foul-smelling blood clouded the water. The giant hurtled away, turned, and then flung itself back.

Bazil was several feet below the blood cloud when the shark passed through and this time he stabbed upward and the tail sword sank into the great fishwhite belly and stuck. In a moment it was torn from his hand.

Bazil arched backward and drove himself down deeper, spiraling away from the scene. With no weapon he could do no more harm to the shark, and if it detected him now, he would die in those terrible jaws.

He heard them snap shut twice more in quick succession as the monster curved back into the blood cloud. Then it was gone again, leaping away into the darkness.

He drove himself deeper still, and sensed another, smaller shark, attracted to the blood. They passed unseeing, the shark barely noticing the dragon so intent was it on the blood ahead. A moment later Bazil touched bottom and clung to seaweed to hold himself there.

The smaller shark, a mere eight-footer, attacked the blood and a moment later was cut in half with one monstrous slam of enormous jaws.

Bazil clung to the bay kelp and held his breath. Another small shark went past, very close, traveling at top speed.

Up above, the monster returned, took the remains of the smaller shark and flashed away. The blood from both its own belly and the smaller shark was widely distributed now, and more sharks were gathering every second. The waters just off a port city were good grounds for some kinds of sharks, and there were dozens in motion now.

Bazil recognized that this was becoming a very dangerous neighborhood. A five-foot-long blue shark drove itself at him until he stunned it with a punch on the snout that left it to float away, feebly twitching. Moments later he felt it crumple under the assault of several of its fellows.

Bazil drove himself across the seabed, crouched low, heading in what he prayed was the direction of the shore.

Behind and above him he heard the terrifying sounds of a feeding frenzy underway. Dozens of powerful fish were hurling themselves in and out of the blood cloud while snapping at everything in their path. At regular intervals this background roar of teeth was overlaid with the clashing of the giant's jaws as leviathan cut through the crowd of smaller terrors, destroying them as he went.

The water shallowed beneath his feet, a sandy bottom. He caught the sour stench of human pollution from the lower bay. He had to breathe, which meant risking a rise to the surface. But he could go no farther without air. He kicked himself upward, broke the surface, and sucked in several deep breaths before he dove and powered himself down to the seabed again. The frenzy continued as sharks hurtled through the water above him.

The sandbank climbed to a bar, and he found himself wading across tidal flats in waist-deep water. Ahead lay a channel of deeper water yet and then the flats again, now bared at low tide.

There was a fire going on the beach. Probably the same drovers he'd seen before. He envied them their cheerful drunken sing-along, completely oblivious to the terrors of the cold water of the Long Sound.

He crept up the beach as far from the fire as he could and slipped back across the promenade. He had been gone less than an hour and the streets were still empty as he padded up the hill and reached the Dragon House.

The guards had resumed their customary slack pose. Bazil looked around for something to divert them with and observed a hay wagon, parked up the slope by the wall of the Novitiate. He pulled the wagon free of the wall, kicked away the brake block, and let it roll slowly down the cobbles, heading toward the top of Water Street. As it went, it picked up speed and began to rumble.

The guards woke up and gave a cry. Since they were the only folk awake at that hour in that part of the city, no one responded, and in a moment they were both pursuing the wagon down the street, trying to turn it and head it into the stone wall of the Dragon House where it could do no harm.

Neither of them observed the great wet dragon that slipped into the entrance behind them.

CHAPTER NINE

In the morning Relkin awoke with foul breath and a muzzy head. It was enough to make him instantly regret the strong ale of the night before. For a moment he wished he could stay just where he was, tucked up snug in his cot, eyes closed like armor against the world, but then the sounds of morning in the Dragon House intruded and with them came the remorseless demands of routine.

He stretched, ducked himself in cold water to chase away the cobwebs, and went down to the kitchens for hot kalut and a cauldron of stirabout for the dragon.

Carefully balancing kalut and pushing the cauldron on a dolly, he came back bristling with gossip. The cooks were full of the news that they were to pack their kit that very day. Something was definitely in the wind.

He found his dragon still sound asleep and proceeded to wake him with a lively whistle in the ears. The big eyes snapped open.

"Why does boy feel compelled to wake this dragon?"

"We've got a busy day ahead, that's why. I think we'll be moving today, likely to go on board one of the ships in the harbor. You're usually awake by now anyway, so what's the problem?"

"Shrill, snappish boy, that's what." Bazil accepted the cauldron and fumbled off the lid.

"No akh?" he said in a deeply injured tone.

"How the hell you manage to eat that stuff at this time of the morning I don't know."

"Eat it because it is good."

Relkin drained a cup of kalut, his second, which seemed to revive him a bit, and threaded his way back to the kitchens in pursuit of akh, the pungent, mouth-burning condiment favored by wyverns on all food.

The delicious smell of fresh bread greeted him. He took a

deep breath and then felt a playful punch on the arm. Swane wanted to know all about the dinner with Wiliger.

Up to that point Relkin had managed to obliterate all memory of that embarrassing horror, but now it came crashing back, including that awful moment when they'd informed the new dragon leader he couldn't have his own design of cap badge for the 109th fighting dragons.

"You had too much ale, I can tell."

Relkin merely groaned. Swane chortled. Up to this point he had felt seriously left out.

"What did Wiliger want?"

Relkin groaned again.

Manuel had come in unheard behind them. His sudden voice made Relkin jump.

"We are twitchy today."

"Yes," agreed Relkin, "we are."

Manuel shouldered past Swane and tore himself a piece of bread.

"In answer to Swane's question, Dragon Leader Wiliger was trying to be friendly," he said. "Trouble is he's inept. Told us about some fight he was in up in Kenor. He doesn't want us to think he's had no combat. Made me think he's an idiot."

"He's probably crazy," muttered Relkin, gathering up a pot of akh and a half dozen fresh-baked long loaves.

"What's that the Quoshite said?" said Swane.

"Wiliger's barking mad, that's what," replied Manuel between swallows of fresh army bread, straight out of the oven.

"Well, I already knew that, academy boy," growled Swane.

Relkin spoke again. "The cooks say they've been told to dismantle the kitchens and prepare to embark today."

"By the breath, why didn't you say so?"

"You didn't give me time to."

Swane grabbed up an armful of loaves and set off for the stall he shared with Vlok, a stolid, perhaps even unintelligent, leatherback dragon who had become the third longest serving dragon in the 109th by dint of luck and hardiness.

Relkin took bread and a pot of akh back to his own stall and fed the dragon, drank more kalut and ate some bread himself. His head felt better by degrees, and he soon noticed that his dragon had some fresh abrasions, with crusted blood, along his side, on his tail and his forearms.

"What are all these cuts?" he said indignantly. One slaved over the great beasts, keeping them in perfect health and what did they do? They horsed around in the plunge pool and broke their limbs, or rolled in sharp grit and cut their skins to shreds, which was what it seemed Bazil had been up to.

The dragon ate but said nothing.

Relkin sensed something was wrong.

"Come on, tell me, you've been rubbed raw in places here. What the hell did you do?"

Bazil stuffed another loaf of bread into his mouth and chewed thoughtfully.

Relkin tried different tacks, to no avail. The dragon would make no response. Relkin gave up with an elaborate sigh. Finishing up his breakfast, he made a quick inventory of things he wanted from the commissary and headed out.

"Will boy go to fish market again and try for sternfish?"

He looked back. "They won't have any."

"They might today."

Relkin eyed him suspiciously. What did that mean? But the dragon gave every sign of refusing to answer any more questions. Pushing a sulky dragon was not the way to get anywhere. Relkin went on his way, thoughtfully chewing his lower lip.

At the commissary he ordered new hooks and studs for the joboquin, plus a new set of nail clippers, his old ones having grown dull. Dragon talon was doughty stuff and soon blunted steel. Then he turned to his requests for various items of tropical kit.

The clerks checked and found that some of his requests had come in, but were not yet unpacked. He was told to come back later in the day.

Outside, with some time free, he enjoyed the feeling of sunshine beating down from a sky clear of clouds for the first time in days. The air was cold and fresh, and the colors of the city were bright and sharp. He decided to stay outside in the sun, and for something to do he wandered down the hill to the dockside. He would just stick his head in at the fish market. The dragon's hide had already scabbed over; later he would examine the cuts and perhaps use some Old Sugustus. Then, maybe, he would get the truth.

Down Tower Street he went, passing through the crowds that thronged it every day. At Foluran Hill he saw a party of sailors, very visible in their white pantaloons and bright blue coats and hats. They were hauling handcarts laden with trunks and other items of personal luggage. As they passed, they sang a shanty, a tune unfamiliar to Relkin that ended each line with a rousing "away- a- way- oh!"

The city of Marneri, of course, was utterly used to sailors, and nobody turned a hair, except for a few ex-mariners who joined in on a few choruses. Relkin watched them go before crossing the street, and he felt an odd exaltation in his heart. He had fond memories of two previous sea voyages, the longer of which had brought him back from Ourdh, all the way around the Southern Cape. Great weather, no dragon leader, weeks of fine sailing on steady seas with little to do except relax and fish for bonito in the evenings. Of course, it was now midwinter, but still he found himself looking forward to the sea. It was an advantage, of course, that he had never felt a moment's seasickness, where some of the others had been prostrated.

He took a deep breath. His hangover from the night before had miraculously faded. He went on down the pavement whistling the "Kenor Song."

At the dockside he observed more sailors passing crates and bags onto the dock to be ferried out to the great white ships sitting in the deeper anchorage of the bay.

After gazing at the ships where they glittered in the cold winter sunlight, he turned and went on up the dockside to the fish market. Inside, enveloped in that peculiarly powerful odor, he came to a stop and felt his jaw drop.

A gang of men with a crane was raising the head and jaws of the largest shark ever seen in Marneri. Chains had been passed through the jaws and out through the neck. With a mighty heave-ho on the block and tackle, they ran the rope back and the great head rose from the floor and wobbled ten feet into the air.

It swung around and for a moment Relkin stared into jaws so huge they would have swallowed him whole like a bonbon.

A crowd had gathered.

"Eight foot across those jaws are," said a grizzled old fish cutter in a leather apron who was wiping a long knife on a towel.

"Eat a man like a rasher of bacon," said someone else.

"Ha," said another, "eat a whole boatload of men like a rasher of bacon."

"Who caught it?" said Relkin.

"Caught it?" said the fish cutter. "Oh, it wasn't caught. They found the head and the tail beached in East Bay this morning. The rest was eaten. Found some other dead sharks today, too, washed up on the point."

"What is it?" said Relkin, staring at that huge head with awe.

"They call him the white death, lad," said the fish cutter.

"Doesn't seem white to me."

"The head is darker, 'tis true, the white is on the belly, none of which was recovered."

Relkin whistled to himself at the great jaws, bristling with six-inch teeth.

"I wouldn't wonder if we ain't looking at what happened to Jonas Faller and his boat *Peaspod,* said another man with the square-cornered hat of a fisherman and a yellow water-proof.

Several other fishermen rumbled in response.

"A plague on all sharks," said one at Relkin's elbow. The fish cutter had gone to stand directly beneath the swinging head of white death.

"Fortunately the damned things are very rare, else the oceans'd be empty." He reached up and knocked loose a tooth with his knife. He caught it as it fell and handed it to Relkin.

"There you are, young sir; show that to your young uns. That's the tooth of white death."

"And pray to the Mother that they never see him again!" said the nearest fisherman.

The tooth was triangular and bigger than Relkin's hand in area. He ran his thumb along the edge; it was sharp enough for an edged weapon.

"Jonas Faller, Mother care for his soul, he was a careful man, but it doesn't matter how careful you are if one of those monsters finds you. They can sink a fishing boat all right."

"Boat?" said another bitterly, "remember the brig *Lally*?"

They fell to reminiscing about the mysterious loss of this brig, which had its bottom torn open in waters with no shoals and no rocks.

Relkin found a couple of smaller sharks displayed on a slab of ice. Both had been bitten about the head but were otherwise intact.

He bent down and sniffed the larger of them.

"That's perfectly fresh today, sir," said a fishmonger. "It was brought in still bleeding. I wouldn't sell it otherwise."

Relkin bought it. His dragon had been right. The shark was seven feet long and weighed three hundred pounds gutted and cleaned. Yet for its size it was cheap enough, and he obtained the whole thing for no more than two pieces of silver. Then he threw in a groat for the porter to have it shipped up the hill to the Dragon House.

"No call for 'em, sir, most folk won't eat a sternfish."

That afternoon it was roasted over an open fire under the anxious direction of a certain leatherback dragon. Then the great fish, cut into foot-wide steaks, was served up to the dragons of the 109th, gathered in a private conclave around the open fire.

The platters were cleaned. Wyverns looked up expectantly at the Purple Green. The wild one avoided their eyes.

"Well?" said Bazil after a while.

The Purple Green had finished his shark steak. He was eyeing the remains of the shark; there was still plenty there.

"Ah, I wonder if this dragon could have another piece?"

Bazil exchanged a look of triumph with the others. Another huge piece was passed to the wild dragon, who fell to eating it immediately.

"So, did you like the sternfish?" said Alsebra, laying a green hand on the massive purple-black forearm of the wild dragon.

"Oh, yes, it was good."

"You're sure now?"

The Purple Green's platter was empty again. With an odd look he scanned the shark's remains.

"All gone?" he said plaintively.

Bazil clacked his jaws. "Not quite. I have one more piece."

"Oh?" Caution warred with greed in the Purple Green's eyes.

"But I'm only giving it to a dragon who admits that this is one fish he really enjoyed eating."

There was a long moment. The Purple Green looked at the

other wyverns. They were all staring at him with unmistakably smug expressions.

By the ancient gods of Dragon Home, though, that sternfish had been damned good. Unlike anything he knew from land-bound game. And wild dragons are absolute slaves to their stomachs. He simply could not resist the lure.

"Oh, all right! Yes, I did like it. Now give me the last piece."

The wyverns exploded into loud dragonish mirth, a sound quite terrifying to all other forms of life. Happily they broached a couple of kegs of ale and drained them and sang together while they ate every last scrap of the shark, along with cauldrons of noodles covered in akh, fresh bread, and wheels of cheese.

The beer was almost gone, and they were at the height of the singing when a messenger poked his head in and announced to Manuel and Mono that General Steenhur had ordered that they be issued with tropical kit very shortly. There would be a full inspection, section by section, immediately afterward, and then they would go aboard the *Barley*.

The orders were not unexpected, except for the tropical kit. It was clear they were not going to Axoxo. This was generally welcomed since Axoxo meant marching hundreds of miles across the windswept Gan and then a siege campaign amid snow and ice in high mountainous country.

Tropical kit sounded far more promising, at least to dragonboys.

Evening arrived and with it came the new kit. Lightweight jackets and pantaloons, cotton shirts and mosquito netting, a wide-brimmed hat for protection against the sun. There were any number of new medicines both for boys and dragons. Anti-vermicides, fungicides, and fresh supplies of Old Sugustus's disinfectant and liniment, bales of bandage, poultice covers, sterilized thread, even new needles.

Relkin had already acquired several choice items that were rare, including a lightweight belt with compartments to take many small items. Then there were a pair of well-fitted, legion sandals. These were hard to get. Swane was already cursing the ones he'd been issued.

Back in his stall, he packed everything away in his knapsack and roll, and went over all his equipment for one final check. Everything was present.

He heard Dragon Leader Wiliger's voice in the next stall, the inspection had begun. Relkin waited confidently.

Wiliger appeared a moment later, still clad in his odd, self-assembled antique uniform. However, he wore no cap badge, the flashy oversize thing was gone.

Wiliger nodded curtly to him, all friendliness forgotten.

"At ease," he said, and then began to call out each item on the long list of equipment.

Relkin produced them or pointed to them one by one until they came to "Tail Sword, double-cross karket style."

There was no tail sword, it was missing from its scabbard. Relkin looked to the dragon, but found no answer there.

"Tail sword, Dragoneer Relkin?"

"It seems to be missing, Dragon Leader."

"Dragoneer Relkin," said Wiliger in a bored and disgusted tone, "it cannot *seem* to be missing. Either you have a tail sword or you do not."

"Do not, sir."

"Why not, Dragoneer?"

"Don't know, sir."

Wiliger peered intently at him.

"Dragoneer, if you try and play games with me, I will break you, I swear it. Am I understood?"

"Yes, sir, but I truly do not know. I only just this moment discovered that the sword is missing. I checked yesterday. Everything was correct."

"Well, it's not good enough. Jump down to the armory and get another, and hurry, because we're leaving very soon."

Relkin jumped, his mind whirling over the possibilities. It was hard to imagine that anyone would steal a tail sword. Bazil used an unusual style, with two big raised crosses on the hilt, it went better for his unusual, "broken" tail.

The armorer was displeased. He broke anew into his peevish lecture about the expense of replacing these weapons. Then he reported that there were no tail swords in inventory.

Relkin begged him to check the depot. After a long wrangle an assistant was sent. Relkin waited, anxiously biding his time.

At last, with the cornet blowing for assembly, the assistant came back with a worn, but serviceable tail sword. It was a karket, but with a single knob for the gripping tail. The dragon would be sure to complain about it.

In which case he could explain what had happened to the old one. Relkin ran back to the stall, pulled on his pack, tucked the tail sword into Bazil's kit, and marched out beside his dragon with the drum thumping and Dragon Leader Wiliger calling out the step.

Down the hill they went, past curious groups of men standing outside the taverns and clubs.

At the dockside they embarked on lighters that bore them across the bay to the side of the *Barley*. There they clambered up the ship's side on specially designed rope ladders made of number-ten cable that could bear the weight of dragons.

By the third hour before midnight they were all aboard, along with a thousand legionaries. The galleys produced an evening meal of the usual legion fare and ale to wash it down.

On the tide, the ship pulled up her anchors and stood out into the sound and began the run down to the open waters of the Bright Sea.

CHAPTER TEN

The white ships of Cunfshon were the ultimate expression of the power and resourcefulness of the Empire of the Rose. The largest, swiftest vessels in the world, they had carried trade and diplomacy to every harbor and every nation. In extremis they had ferried legions to Ourdh and more recently from Cunfshon to the Argonath during the frantic days of the invasion.

Now they carried a small but powerful army halfway across the world on a desperate bid to snuff out the greatest danger the world Ryetelth had ever known.

Day after day, through a brisk northwest gale the great ships plowed south, keeping the land well sunk to the west. At this time of the year the captains were keenly aware that the gale could swiftly swing about to the northeast and thus turn that western wall of land into a dreaded lee shore upon which any ship might be driven if the gales grew too furious.

As it was they were being driven many leagues to the east, well out of their course, which was south, south and west, directly to Cape Hazard at the southern tip of the continent.

The seas were sharp, short but high, a common and unpleasant aspect of winter sailing in the Bright Sea. Even the *Barley,* at three thousand tons, was behaving wickedly, shoving her nose deep into the troughs and jerking upward on the short swells with a distinctly nervous energy, like that of a startled horse.

The results were predictable. In her holds and all through the lower decks the ship was filled with seasick men.

On her decks were her crew, constantly at work trimming the few sails that they could set, and those were largely furled up themselves. But the wind was variable, always fierce, but prone to sudden changes, and therefore the sails could not be left alone for a moment. Captain Olinas and her first and second mates had been on the quarterdeck all night and all day with three crewmen hauling on the wheel as they ordered shifts in sails. The captain was a weather-beaten woman, at sea since she was eight years old and a full captain in the empire's service for nigh on twenty years. Her face was drawn, but steady, and her eyes flicked constantly to the barometer, checking its steady fall.

Down in the holds with all the seasick men of the Marneri and Kadein legions were thirty dragons without the least hint of sickness. Dragons were amphibious beasts, bred for the ocean, but that was not what protected them, for they were no more evolved to ride in this jerky, leaping fashion across the waves than were men. Instead, it was simply their oddly evolved organs of hearing that employed pads of a stiff jelly. Since men's sense of balance is governed by fluid in the inner ear, the rhythmic shifts of the sea produced the nausea of seasickness. By contrast, dragons balance themselves by the action of stiff hairs growing on the inside of a sinusoidal process at the base of their large brains. They possess no fluid to slosh about and disorient their systems. Thus they remained cheerful and vigorous of appetite no matter what the motions of the ship.

This made life for dragonboys harder than ever. Stifling nausea while fetching cauldrons of hot steaming food was a grim task.

For the fortunate few who were immune to seasickness, there was a lot of extra work. Some of the boys could not drag themselves to their feet. Little Jak was absolutely prostrated, along with Roos, Aris, and Shutz. Relkin, Swane, and Manuel, helped by Mono when he could manage it, brought the food for Alsebra and Oxard, Aulay and Stengo.

The gales lasted almost a week before finally ameliorating and leaving in their wake days of bright sunshine, with steady cold northerly winds that helped drive the fleet south. The motion of the ship became more regular, less impassioned.

They passed the guano islands, beneath great clouds of seabirds, puffins, auks, guillemots, even pelicans, that swarmed about them as they crossed the cold upwelling waters of the Cunfshon current.

The guano islands themselves were visible only as distant blurs of grey on the horizon, soon lost behind. The seabirds disappeared by the end of the day, about the same time that the hardier souls among the sick recovered enough to take a turn on the foredeck, which was allowed to the passengers, when conditions were favorable.

On the tenth day out Relkin came on deck in the forenoon, to draw some of the good, clean, but cold, air into his lungs. The atmosphere below was growing strong. Thousands of men and dozens of dragons confined in packed quarters were producing a fetid stench despite rigorous, daily cleanings and scrubbings. Having so many men and dragons had forced the ship's carpenters to cut many new heads, but during the gales many men had been unable to face the heads, located along the bows of the ship, below the forecastle. Consequently the bilges had grown foul and had had to be pumped clean with fresh seawater every day. Captain Olinas ordered up a wind sail every so often to direct a freshening blast belowdecks, but nonetheless it was growing close down below.

Relkin gripped the rail and breathed deep. Ahead, a half mile away, could be seen the mighty *Oat,* two thousand tons, under a pyramid of gleaming white sail. On the starboard beam rode the *Barley*'s sister ship *Sugar*. Behind came the old, slow *Potato,* smaller than the *Oat* class and normally kept for the grain trade between the Isles and the Argonath. Beside her rode the *Malt,* another older ship. Neither of these vessels had enjoyed the recent blow, losing spars and sails, while the troops aboard had been forced to man the pumps when their aged timbers began to work and let in water.

They were too massive to be really threatened, however, and now they held their position, as did the rest of the fleet, both ahead and astern. Despite the rough weather, the components of the fleet had come together smoothly off Cape Balder, eight ships from the Argonath and eight ships from the Isles of Cunfshon. Those from the Argonath bore an expeditionary legion made up of units from Marneri, Kadein, Bea, Talion, and Pennar. Taken from units that had been available in the cities or reservists hastily called to active duty. The ships from Cunfshon carried the famous Legion of the White Rose. Now sixteen great ships, hurriedly, and secretly pulled away from their normal trading schedules, bore away into the south, heading for the Indramatic Ocean.

Swane and Manuel were also on the foredeck, taking a breather before the bells went for lunch.

"Wiliger's up on his feet," said Swane. "Manuel saw him in the galley." Dragon Leader Wiliger had been stricken since the first day at sea. Indeed, he had sickened directly following his fierce and public dressing down by Commander Voolward. This had been brought about by the debacle of Wiliger's luggage. This had originally consisted of twelve huge trunks, including one that carried nothing but sweetmeats and potted foods, another of expensive wine. Wiliger had forty shirts and sixty pairs of stockings packed in yet another. Voolward told him he was allowed a single trunk, and that only half the size of any of those he had brought aboard the *Barley*.

When Wiliger's trunks had been transshipped to a lighter in the Long Sound the next morning, Wiliger had disappeared to the sick bay and had hardly been seen since.

"I can't say as I've missed him," said Relkin.

"Nor me, either," grunted Swane. "Manuel said he was a bit green in the face."

Relkin shared in Swane's amusement. This pleased Swane enormously.

"Pity they never packed him off home with all those trunks of his," said Swane.

Manuel was intent on the other ships, craning his head around the rigging to get a view of the *Potato*.

"There's a frigate coming up," he said. "She's moving very fast."

The others crowded to the side, leaning out until they earned a sharp rebuke from a sailor in the waist.

"You silly buggers fall in and ye'll not survive, not in winter sea. Nor will any of us'n jump in to rescue ye."

"There's a frigate coming," shouted Relkin.

"Aye," said the sailor, calmly. "That be the *Lyre* all right, Captain Renard. My cousin Shephuel is third mate. She's a flyer, is that *Lyre*."

Clearly the sailors had all been aware of the frigate for a long time.

Now the smaller ship, under a tremendous press of canvas, came racing up to starboard and then pulled up just a cable's length away. A cutter was set down to the sea and bore across the gap under the powerful strokes of six men. The captain of the frigate, Captain Renard, came aboard the *Barley* and brought with him two small figures clad in hooded robes of a soft grey.

Relkin saw them climb onto the sacred quarterdeck, and he knew at once who it was. On the quarterdeck the small grey figures were greeted with considerable ceremony by the captain herself, who introduced her mates, and then they were conducted down the steps to the rear cabins and were lost from sight. Down those steps, Relkin knew, lay the staterooms and grand salons where the admiral of the fleet had his quarters. The admiral's long golden pennant flew from the mainmast. The admiral had come aboard from a frigate that had brought him from Andiquant, slightly ahead of the rest of the Cunfshon fleet.

"Who was that, do you think?" said Endi, who had joined them from below.

Swane looked to Relkin and held his tongue. Swane knew who they were but couldn't tell, even though he longed to. It was up to Relkin.

Manuel did not feel the same compulsions. "Witches," he muttered. Like most citizens of the realm, he found it difficult to accept the women of the magic arts. There they were, these people who could control anyone with a spell or two. They moved secretively through the society of the empire, and no one could control what they did. Manuel, as an educated person, tended to distrust such small but powerful groups. The other dragonboys, largely bereft of education, had less distrust, but even more awe, a sense verging on that of the religious.

Endi looked sharply at Relkin for confirmation.

Relkin nodded, noticing Endi's look of apprehensive awe.

"What do you think they want?" said Endi.

"I expect they're talking to Admiral Cranx. The witches like to control everything at the top level." Manuel voiced his suspicion bluntly.

Endi again looked anxiously to Relkin. Relkin shrugged.

"Don't ask me, your guess is as good as mine, but I expect it's something to do with our mission, whatever that may be."

"I'd love to know," said Endi.

"So would the rest of us," growled Swane. "Packed off to sea with virtually no warning. Up and down like galley slaves for days in weather that's not fit for fish and still no idea of what we're in for."

The door on the quarterdeck opened again and one of the figures in grey emerged. Captain Zudith Olinas conversed with the witch for a few minutes, gesturing to the rigging now and again, clearly showing off her ship, of which she was justly proud. Then the hooded figure came forward, stepped lightly down from the quarterdeck into the waist and made its way along the gangways and up onto the foredeck.

"Relkin, I hoped I'd find you here," said Lagdalen of the Tarcho.

"I'm glad you did." They embraced. Then Relkin introduced Endi, whom Lagdalen had never met before, and then she shook hands with Swane and Manuel.

Endi was awed into silence at the sight of this beautiful young woman, clad in the grey of the sisterhood, obviously a personage of great importance and yet consorting with dragonboys!

"Are you with us for long?" said Relkin.

"I don't think so. We will go back to the *Lyre* and then go on, the Lady hopes to reach Bogon well before the rest of the fleet."

"Bogon?" said Swane. "Where in the name of the Mother is that?"

"For shame, Swane, to take the Mother's name in vain," said Lagdalen.

"Sorry, lady, I was just, surprised."

"You should say contrition." Lagdalen saw Relkin's eyes on her. Her sad half smile admitted the truth of his unspoken accusation. Who was she to be giving contrition? She had grown very high and mighty since they'd first met, when she was a failed novice in the temple service and he was a young provincial scruff trying to get into the legions illegally. Both those young people were gone, transformed into more serious minds. It seemed a very long time ago.

"And to answer your question, Swane, Bogon is on the east coast of Eigo. It is a tropical land, with great forests and enormous rivers."

"And why would we be going there?" said Manuel.

"This is the first we've heard about anything to do with this mission. It's just been 'very important' and 'top secret' since we first heard about it," said Swane.

Lagdalen was clearly wondering how much she could tell them. "All I can say is that we're not going to Bogon itself. We're to leave the ships there and move inland."

"But why?" said Manuel.

"I'm sorry, I cannot say." She smoothed down the front of

her robe, exchanged a smile with Relkin. "How did the dragons do during the storm?"

"They quite enjoyed it, I think. They would come up here to get splashed by cold seawater. They were really hungry the whole time."

"They are the strangest, most wonderful creatures. To think of wanting to eat during all that heaving and shuddering. Everyone was sick, except the crew of course. Even the Lady was sick!"

Relkin smiled. "Were you sick, Lagdalen?"

"A little, not as much as the others, though."

"So we're going to Bogon, way across the ocean. All jungles and monsters and things like that," said Swane, wonderingly.

"We're going to Bogon," said Manuel, "and then we're going to go on, into the interior of Eigo, the dark continent."

CHAPTER ELEVEN

"The very heart of the dark continent, does anyone know what lies there?"

"Myths, legends, and most recently direct, terrifying intelligence."

Admiral Cranx nodded, then sipped his cup of kalut. "I can remember only too well your address to the Imperial Council in which you outlined that intelligence."

The woman he spoke to was uncannily ordinary in appearance. Indeed, if anything, she looked undernourished. Her garb was plain, a grey woolen robe over a white cotton blouse and trousers. Her thin, pale grey hair was pulled back loosely behind her head. She wore no jewelry, no cosmetics, no accentuations whatsoever.

Cranx was aware, however, that this woman was hundreds of years old, that she was one of the greatest sorcerers of her time, and that she was anything but the plain person she appeared to be.

She fixed him with pale grey eyes that were peculiarly intense.

"This menace is well known to those who Serve the Light," she said softly. "It is the first step to the road of absolute material power. At the end of this road, men will take control of the very stuff of matter and make weapons with it. Weapons that can destroy an entire world in a matter of moments."

"So the wise inform us." Cranx smiled sadly. "Myself, I am a man of tide and sail, and I leave these things to others with greater wisdom, though I will admit that we have developed many weapons ourselves. We have these great ships that can outsail any enemy, and when we cannot avoid a battle, we have our weapons, terrible weapons indeed."

"Yes, Admiral, fire arrows and catapults are fearsome things for causing destruction, but believe me when I tell you that they are toys compared with the dark fruit of the road to power."

Cranx put down his cup. "Then we must see to it that we destroy the seeds of this terrible fruit."

"Indeed, sir, and if your fleet can deliver this force to the shores of Bogon intact within three months, then I think we may succeed in doing so."

"As to the duration of the passage, all that can be said is that much depends on our catching the tail of the winter winds in the Gulf of Ourdh. Once we round Cape Hazard, we should pick up those winds, and they will carry us half-way to Bogon with steady sailing, if they are still blowing."

He pointed to a chart of the Indramatic Ocean on the wall. "However, once we have ridden the winter winds to their end, we shall be in the Mother's Hands. The airs in the tropics at this season are notoriously vague and fickle. We might sit there for months."

"Let us pray not, there is not a moment to lose."

Cranx gestured to the pot of kalut on the table. "Would you care for another cup?"

"Yes, thank you. It is a most excellent, invigorating draft." For a moment they sat there, contemplating the chart and the immensity of the ocean that lay ahead of them. Six thousand miles sailing, from the cold waters of the Bright Sea to the tropical doldrums of the western Indramatic, it inspired awe, even in such an experienced mariner as Admiral Cranx. Then he turned away from it to pose a question that had been on his mind for days.

"I wonder, Lady, if you have any news of the situation at Axoxo? Since we left Andiquant harbor I have heard nothing."

Her eyebrows rose a fraction.

"I am afraid I have had no communications regarding the siege. I expect that it will continue. We will take Axoxo eventually."

"I ask because my grandson, Ericht, is serving there in the Talion Light Cavalry. I think of him often."

"I am sure he will have much to do."

"He was in a cavalry action two months ago. We received a letter with very dramatic descriptions of the fighting. It appeared that our forces had held their own against the enemy's tribal forces."

"There is a possibility that Axoxo might fall before next winter."

"It would be a famous victory."

"But if we fail in our present mission, it will not happen. The enemy will overthrow all opposition to his rule."

They finished the kalut, and Lessis made her good-byes, most especially to Captain Zudith Olinas. Then she noticed that Lagdalen was absent from the quarterdeck.

"Your assistant went forward," said Olinas. "She seems to be on great terms with the dragonboys."

"Dragonboys? What units are you carrying aboard?"

Captain Olinas pursed her lips. "We have three dragon squadrons, ninety tons of the great beasts, can you imagine?"

"Carry them safely, Captain, they are priceless."

"Their appetites are what's priceless." Olinas signaled to her second mate, a lean, hollow-looking man with an eye patch.

"Eents, what are the unit numbers for the dragons?"

"Thirty-fourth Bea, 66th Marneri, and 109th Marneri."

"Ah, the 109th," said Lessis rolling her eyes, "I should have known. I must join her."

Lessis moved quietly past the sailors in the waist, leaving behind a somewhat puzzled Captain Olinas, who wondered why a personage like the Grey Lady would wish to talk to a bunch of scruffy dragonboys.

On the foredeck the conversation came to a sudden stop at the appearance of Lessis. She stopped in front of Relkin.

"Just as I expected, Relkin of Quosh." Lessis embraced Relkin. "How good it is to see you, young man."

Relkin was unaccountably nervous. He recalled the last time they'd spoken; she was then a small bird with terribly bright eyes, and they'd floated on an underground river.

Lessis laughed, a light sound.

"I can tell you this much, my friend, it is much easier to see you and talk to you than it was at our last meeting!"

The others were staring at him agog.

"Well, Relkin, once again I find you caught up in great events. I am more than ever convinced that the Mother has selected you for some great and peculiar destiny."

"Destiny?" That word again! "Oh, no, not again. My last experience with destiny was enough."

Lessis laughed again. "Yet you survived. You always survive, young man. Perhaps old Caymo is rolling the dice for you after all."

Relkin's eyes widened to hear a Witch of the Great Mother so casually speak the name of one of the old gods.

She looked up. "And these are members of the 109th fighting Marneri dragons, too, I take it."

"Yes, Lady. May I present dragoneers Swane, Manuel, and Endi."

They stiffened to attention and saluted.

"I am honored to meet you," said Lessis, taking their hands one at a time. "But, alas, time is pressing, and I am afraid we shall have to depart."

Lessis turned to Lagdalen, and shortly afterward the two small figures in grey went down the ship's side to the cutter along with Captain Renard. Shortly afterward the *Lyre* clapped on more canvas and slipped ahead of the *Barley* and forged into the open sea.

CHAPTER TWELVE

The fleet made the passage of Cape Hazard in the space of two days on fortunate winds. Almost immediately they picked up the winter winds out of the Gulf of Ourdh and enjoyed three solid weeks of fine sailing, making one hundred and fifty miles a day and advancing across the Indramatic Ocean in a long gentle slant, west and south.

During this period, life aboard the white ships settled into a steady routine. Men and dragons exercised in shifts on the foredeck. Kit and drill was inspected at noon. Enormous meals were served out three times a day, and in the evenings there was a ration of whiskey for the men and ale for the dragons. This usually started everyone singing, which would go on until sleep claimed the hardiest.

While the men and dragons were thus occupied, the crews of the ships concentrated on their work, which was not onerous in these conditions. The crews were of mixed sex, in the Cunfshon way, women and men working together in absolute equality. Of course, such women as these were strong enough to pull their own weight, able to climb the rigging and swing out on the yards to set and reef sails as well as the men, not to mention hauling on lines and heaving on the capstans.

In the normal course of their lives at sea, even over long voyages, the crews of the white ships of Cunfshon adjusted to their situation. The rule was that romantic interludes between crew members were forbidden and that if they occurred then the parties would be set down at the end of the voyage and written out of the ship's company, in effect retired from service. For the most part, this had served the Cunfshoni navy well, and the tradition continued in the fleets of the Argonath. Indeed, the kind of woman who generally took to the seafaring life was not the marrying kind and often enough had little or no interest in men.

The great white ships primarily carried cargoes of grain, lumber, livestock, and the like. There were passengers, of course, but never more than a hundred or so, and these were berthed in the stern and were rarely seen anywhere except on the quarterdeck. Passengers were taken care of by a special team of servants, and there was almost no contact between passengers and crew. Thus the normal sailing life was one of calm attention to routine, with occasional periods of storm and trial and other, more pleasant interruptions in foreign ports and exotic locales.

Using the great ships as troop ships, packing them with thousands of young men in the prime of their youth, put the institutions of the Cunfshon naval service to their sternest test.

Even the most hard-bitten old sailor gal, with sunbleached hair, craggy face, and arms thick with muscles, became the focus of ardent intentions. Some were amused, at first, others outraged from the beginning. After weeks of it, they were all hot and bothered. One or two were even guilty of enjoying little flings with carefully chosen legionaries. Such cracks in the wall between crew and passengers inevitably sparked wild rumors and caused problems.

Aboard the *Barley* there was friction between a couple of young female sailors and some men from the Talion Light Horse. These particular women had no interest in men, and they very much resented the attentions of the horsemen. There was some verbal back and forth. One of the horsemen grew rancorous and attempted to clamber into the rigging to chastise one of the young women. This put him at a disadvantage, and in the ensuing clash he was cut on the arm and unceremoniously dumped off the yard to land ignominiously in the side netting where some older hands, men, had to help him out and pat him down before his fellows could take him to the sick bay to have his wound attended to.

This reverse put the men of the Light Horse on their mettle, and some were muttering about getting their swords out when Captain Septeen of the Talion brigade came on deck and quelled things for the time being.

But the mere presence of hundreds of young men starved for the affectionate company of women served to keep the temperature high. All of the female sailors felt the constant pressure of hungry male eyes directed at them.

The crew berthed in the forecastle, well away from the legionaries crammed in the holds and the orlop, but after one drunken corporal was found trying to break into a sailor's cabin, the crew demanded a guard be set. Commander Voolward issued a stern order forbidding any interference with the crew and threatening flogging if he was disobeyed.

For a week this kept the peace, then a fool from the Pennar Third Regiment attacked one of the youngest sailorwomen and tried to rape her. She beat him off and escaped, but he was seen and captured at once.

Captain Olinas summoned Commander Voolward to the quarterdeck and demanded punishments as laid down by the Great Weals of Cunfshon.

Voolward blanched, then refused. "You know well enough that we do not castrate in the Argonath legions."

Their voices rose and on a ship, even one as large as the *Barley,* loud voices could be heard all over the ship. Captain Olinas took her case to Admiral Cranx.

In the end Voolward promised to mete out field punishment for the man if he was found guilty by a drumhead tribunal. He agreed that in this situation it was impossible to wait until they returned to safe harbor where a full courtmartial could be held.

Commanders from four regiments gathered to hear the case. The evidence was overwhelming, in addition to the accuser, there were three eyewitnesses to the latter stages of the attack.

With the drum tolling, the man was seized up to a grating and given fifty lashes. This put a damper on things for quite a while. None of the crew, male or female, would speak to the soldiers and vice versa.

The only groups not included in the hostilities were the dragon squadrons. The crew tended to venerate the dragons and to accept that the dragonboys were different from the mass of soldiers belowdecks. They were only youths and boys, after all. When two dragons exercised on the foredeck, the crew would watch with awed expressions. The dragonboys found themselves in the role of unwilling intermediaries between crew and soldiers. It was surprising how much trade went on, in such commodities as batshooba, tobacco, betel, sugar candies, even religious tracts and books.

It was from his enthusiastic participation in such trading that Swane found himself with a terrible problem in the person of one Birjit Oolson. Birjit was a she-hulk of great size and strength. She served in the mainmast section and was a powerful hand with rope and line. Swane acted as go-between for a set of scrimshaw chessmen, exchanged for tobacco, which Birjit liked to chew and which had long ago stained her teeth a dark brown.

Swane discovered his predicament one evening when Birjit lured him to her cabin in the forecastle with the offer of some rum. Swane was at an age when he would often get himself into trouble quite thoughtlessly. Here he failed to notice the signals of approaching difficulties. The heavy breathing, the weird smiles that contorted Birjit's angular, leathery visage, the strange simpering expression that came over her when she watched him during the morning hosing down on the foredeck.

In the cabin Swane drank some of her rum and then had to fight off the burly Birjit when she put her arms around him and tried to kiss him. It was quite a struggle, for while Swane was the biggest and strongest dragonboy, he was still not yet full grown, and Birjit had strength to spare. Swane's only advantage was that he knew how to fight, even in confined spaces. This kept the match interesting. However, he found that hitting Birjit was not unlike hitting a big sack of grain. She didn't seem to feel it much, and things were getting desperate when by chance he bounced against the cabin door and it burst open and he escaped.

Swane told nobody about his not-so-secret admirer. He hoped the blows he'd struck would convince her to leave him alone.

He was wrong. Birjit Oolson had a head as hard as the good oak decking of the *Barley*. A few love taps from the boy of her dreams could hardly restrain her.

She hovered nearby whenever he was on deck, and when she was off duty and awake, she lurked around the 109th berths in the forward hold on the chance that she might see Swane.

The other boys found it all highly amusing. Poor Swane would be found hiding in someone else's stall or in the heads, or up on the deck in poor weather, while a tipsy Birjit would be wandering around the hold with a fierce brown-toothed smile. Swane and Birjit jokes proliferated.

One day the fleet found itself in the midst of a meeting of herds of whales. A great herd of sperm whales was heading east while smaller pods of fin whales were passing through the sperms to the west.

Everyone, man and dragon, was drawn to the foredeck during this passage to take a look, The sea was filled to the horizon with spouts and the sounds of whales.

That evening after dining on bread, fish pies, and a soup made with generous helpings of akh, some of the dragons of the 109th sat together on the foredeck to take the air before bedding down for the night. They passed a keg of ale around.

Below them they heard the usual discordant uproar of dozens of different singing groups, some restricted to the old favorites like "La Lillee La Loo" and the "Kenor Song" and others with far more sophisticated repertoires that they performed with wildly varying results. Whales were still passing, smaller herds of sperm whales, following in the wake of the great herd they had seen in the daylight. Every so often a whale would come to the surface so close to the ship that they would hear the spout clearly, even glimpse it in the moonlight.

The Purple Green gazed out over the softly heaving sea.

"I wonder what they taste like. Has any of you ever eaten one?"

This produced a strong response.

"You try to eat one of those, and they eat you!" said Vlok merrily. "Even wild dragon be nothing but a meal to those kind of whales, they got teeth!"

"No one eats whales," said Bazil Broketail. "It is like the horses, men do not eat them and dragons do not eat whale."

"I have heard that some men eat whale."

"Men will eat anything," said Vlok.

"Not horses," said Bazil.

They paused a moment, while the keg went around.

"I wonder what it is like to swim with whales," said Bazil.

"Ha! Listen to him," rumbled the Purple Green. "Vlok tells us that whales would eat dragons, and so Broketail wants to give them the chance."

"At least he can swim," said Alsebra.

"I, too, can swim. I have learned from you!"

"Ho ho, the wild one thinks he can swim!"

"You swim like a giant frog," said Vlok, chortling.

"So I do not swim as well as you, but then none of you have ever flown a flap."

"That is true, and you have learned how to wield a sword and take your place in the line of battle," said Bazil generously, knowing how touchy the great wild dragon could be. For all his strength and power, he was often defensive and prickly.

Another leviathan broached near the ship's side. They heard the stentorian whoosh of its spout.

"There is a beauty in them," said Alsebra. "I think they are the true rulers of the seas. Their life is not like ours, but I can sense that it is a grand life. They taste many oceans, live within great horizons, and are perfectly free."

"We could be free ourselves if we swam with them."

The others fell silent. Bazil had broached the forbidden subject. Even the Purple Green kept quiet, knowing how difficult this area was for any wyvern. Immediately, Bazil regretted saying it. Unfortunately Vlok, as always, had to have it all explained to him in detail.

"Broketail dragon forgets something, all dragon forbidden to swim in seawater."

Bazil took a swig from the keg and set it aside.

"Vlok is right. This dragon stays right here, but when I see the whales I wonder sometimes."

"If you swim in salt water you will experience the wild reaction, you will go wild yourself. That would mean you would starve to death since you are not adapted to deep-sea living like whales. Wyvern dragons are meant for the shoreline. We rule the surf." Alsebra, as usual, knew more than the rest of them.

"Why can we swim in streams and lakes?" said Vlok.

"That water is fresh, it does not have the smell of ocean. If once the smell of ocean entered your nostrils that way, you would be changed. Can you not feel it just floating over it in the ship? I can. We are all restless. It will be better once we reach the land again."

"So that is why it is one of the great rules of the men. Dragons must stay out of the sea," said Chektor, who rarely spoke. "I never understood it before."

"The men are wise in this," said Alsebra. "If wyverns swim in the ocean, they rediscover their true selves and cannot fight in the legions ever again."

"Then why don't you all go overboard and enjoy your wild lives?" said the Purple Green.

"Because we know that it would be dangerous and hard

and hungry. We eat better in the legions, and we not have to work hard," said Vlok, who, though not bright, knew a good thing when it was carefully explained to him.

Later, when Bazil was lying on his pallet, feeling the ship move slowly from wave crest to wave crest as it plowed southwest, he raised the topic again, with the dragonboy this time.

"Boy, tell this dragon, what would happen to a dragon if he dove into sea and swam with whales?"

Relkin looked up sharply. "He'd be left behind, and he'd starve to death in the sea."

"What if he swam back to the ship? Not be left behind."

"Then I suppose he'd be put on trial and given the ultimate punishment. To tell the truth I don't know exactly what would happen, but it would be the end of that dragon and his dragonboy. You aren't thinking of doing this are you?"

"I watched the whales today, they are so very beautiful."

"They are, I watched them, too, but they belong in the sea. Dragons don't, or at least, not dragons that must serve in the legion."

"Serve in the legion, yes, that is it. That is why I did not do it, why I could not do it. But it was hard at times to stop myself."

Relkin knew that the dragons were all skittish from being transported across the ocean. Seawater was their natural home, and it was well known that for a dragon to taste salt water was to turn him feral.

"To swim in salt water is forbidden, Bazil. It is one of the prime rules."

"I know, not to strike a man, not to strike a woman, not to strike a child, not to taste salt water, not to hunt the beast of the field and the fish of the stream."

Baz paused. "But this rule we have broken, for we have often hunted for fish in the stream."

Relkin had to agree. "But you know that that rule is not so important. And we needed to fish to survive."

"Break one rule, break another," muttered the dragon, upset as dragons often were, by human deceits and contradictions.

Relkin suddenly had a great flash of insight.

"Hunting of fish," he said.

Bazil looked up, and there was an unmistakable guilt in his eyes.

"You did!"

Bazil said nothing, unable to respond. Despite their reputation in human myths, dragons were very poor at lying, especially to dragonboys who knew them all too well.

"You did, you went out and killed that monster they had in the fish market. How?" Relkin broke off, stunned, appalled, and amazed all at once.

"I don't know what to say," he said after a moment.

Bazil said nothing, but felt a certain low misery brought on by his guilt. In a way he had betrayed the basic compact between himself and Relkin.

"And you risked your life. I don't know how you killed it, that shark was as big as one of these whales."

Bazil's pride ignited. "I cut him open with tail sword. Other sharks came, and they killed each other."

Relkin's eyes went wide. "All that for a piece of fish?"

Bazil looked as sheepish as a dragon possibly could. "I had to show the wild one that some fish taste good."

Relkin stared at him, speechless, then shook his head.

"I'll never understand you. Sometimes I think I might have an inkling of what goes on in that big head, but then things like this happen, and I realize I don't know a thing."

The dinner bell rang, and Relkin went down to the galley to fetch up cauldrons of stirabout and pots of akh.

Relkin found it hard to banter with the others and even the latest Swane joke couldn't raise a smile, which disappointed young Roos, who had thought it up. All the new dragonboys regarded Relkin as something of a hero. They knew he had received the Legion Star and had served in more campaigns than any other serving dragonboy. To make him laugh was an achievement. To receive a kind word from him made them glow with pride.

When the dragon had a sufficiency, Relkin went up on deck and watched the sea. The whales had been left behind now. He was suffering from a quiet desperation. The dragon had broken the prime rule. Relkin knew that Baz had swum in the sea as a sprat, but that had been long ago. He had obeyed the rule through adulthood. Now he'd gone and broken it. He could turn feral at any moment and that would be the end of their partnership. What would he do then? Start a new dragon? Raise up one from the egg? He groaned at the thought of such a task.

A sailor pointed out a dark volcanic isle away to the south, faintly illumined by the moon.

"You see that glinting down there?"

Relkin admitted he did.

"That be the Isle of the Sorcerer, an evil place that we avoid, though it be useful for the navigation. We turn here to be sure of striking the Watering Isle in the doldrums."

"What sorcerer is that?"

"Don't know that he has a name. Some say he's been dead for a long time, leastwise he hasn't been seen or heard of. But then I never met anyone who'd been to his island and escaped. To be shipwrecked off that black isle is a terrible doom."

In a grim desperate mood Relkin stared at the volcano, a distant dark mass. What dreadful secrets did it contain?

Sometimes the world seemed a terrible place, or at best a place where the good and the light struggled against the tides of darkness to keep a small area within its grasp. Relkin had seen much of the world already, and he had seen much of the dark.

Slowly the distant isle slid past on the fleet's lee side. When it had sunk below the horizon, Relkin went below.

By then the dragon had finished his dinner, and the empty pots were set out ready to be collected and taken down to the galley. Relkin completed the last of the day's chores and bedded down. The dragon was already snoring.

He closed his eyes. Normally he was blessed with the soldier's ability to sleep instantaneously, once he was lying in his cot. This night he found it hard. The thought that Bazil would have risked everything by going out to hunt for a sternfish himself was very difficult to accept. The dragon had always been so steady.

He checked himself, because there had been the mad kidnapping episode a few years back. Perhaps the dragon was not so steady after all. Then he remembered that once again it had been the Purple Green's fault. It was the Purple Green's natural chafing at the constraints placed on dragons who lived around humans. The Purple Green voiced the inner dragon, and Bazil listened. Most of the time it just washed over him and he ignored it. Once in a while something struck a chord in the big wyvern brain, and they got into fearsome trouble as a result.

For instance, much of the year previous had been spent in

trials. Relkin had been tried for the murder of Trader Bartemius Dook, slain by Relkin aboard a trading ship. In his favor had been dragon testimony that described the final tense moments in which Dook had threatened the life of one of Bazil's offspring. Dook's behavior had necessitated his killing. Against Relkin was the word of Dook's crew-members and the emotional accusations provided by Dook's surviving kin.

The trial had been moved from Kenor to Marneri to ensure that dragon testimony could be presented. Still, some jurors could not countenance the testimony of dragons, even if they spoke perfect Verio and appeared rational and intelligent. Such folk could not accept equality with any other kind of beings. The first trial had produced a hung jury. The second trial produced a mixed verdict. Relkin was found not guilty of murder but guilty of killing a man in a minor degree of self-defense. Relkin was punished with a mark of censure on his record that would make it hard for him to receive promotion. It would make it impossible for him to be employed by the city of Marneri once he left the legion. Since this was a frequent way for injured dragonboys to earn a living once they were mustered out, this had serious consequences. Relkin's legal advisers appealed this verdict, which prolonged the proceedings into the winter.

The High Appeals Court of Marneri heard the case and removed the mark of censure after lengthy proceedings. But these trials were but half of it, for in addition there were a series of tribunals and inquiries for both himself and for the dragons, Bazil and the Purple Green, who had abducted him and gone absent without leave for a month in the year of the invasion. By Fundament Day, Relkin had been deathly tired of the legal process.

At last it had ended, and he escaped even a mark of censure. And somehow, through it all, it had seemed that the bond between himself and the dragon had grown stronger, despite the adversity.

Indeed, the whole unit had grown stronger. There was a very good feeling in the 109th Marneri Dragons, at least until Dragon Leader Wiliger had appeared.

But now he wondered to himself if he hadn't simply invented these feelings, and that, in fact, something had happened to Bazil, possibly through the words of the Purple Green. Perhaps Bazil had become deceitful, perhaps he would turn feral and either be destroyed or turned out upon the northern shores of Dragon Home. Either prospect brought amazing hurt to his heart.

A scream echoed from the maintops. More screaming followed. There was the sound of feet thudding on the deck above, shouts. Relkin leapt to his feet, found his sword, and looked out the door.

Dozens of other tense figures also bearing swords were standing in the passageway.

The screaming cut off, and there was a storm of other noise and then the voice of Captain Olinas bellowing, "Belay there, nobody fire, it has Meloy."

"By the Mother's mercy, the monster has Meloy!" said someone in a hushed voice.

Soon the dread explanation arrived. A gigantic flying thing had flapped low over the ship, circled, and disappeared into the clouds. Then it had returned suddenly and seized the lookout from the maintops crosstrees.

By this time everyone was awake and asking questions. The answers were so disquieting that the ship did not settle back to sleep that night.

Captain Olinas ordered a better watch kept and asked for good bowmen to be placed in the maintops to protect the lookout. Commander Voolward asked for volunteers and was gratified to receive a powerful response; dozens stepped forward.

A service was said in the memory of poor Fidel Meloy, now lost to the unknown terror of the night. From then on, men and dragonboys were ready at the crosstrees of all three masts. Others waited on the foredeck and forecastle with bows at the ready.

CHAPTER THIRTEEN

The next day the winds died to a whisper, and the fleet was becalmed. The volcano of the sorcerer's isle was still visible, a tiny jut upon the far northeastern horizon.

All day they drifted southwest on erratic airs, and Captain Olinas became concerned that they had lost the winter wind early. This would dramatically increase the length of the voyage.

There was nothing to do, except hope for better winds. That evening they ate quickly, and there was an excited competition to stand guard at the onset of night. Would the flying brute return and if it did, would they be able to kill it?

As the moon rose, a few clouds gathered in the east and slowly filled the sky. Bored and disconsolate, the early watch returned to their bunks and were replaced. Another hour passed and nothing was seen. The intensity of the watch slackened, as the men in the crosstrees talked among themselves.

Then, with a shocking rapidity, a giant form plummeted out of the clouds and plucked loose a man in the maintops of the *Potato*.

His screams rang out across the water with a heartrending intensity. A few arrows sped in his wake, but they were late and missed the batrukh.

Once more the watch was renewed with vigilance. Many an anxious eye was cast up toward the clouds from whence these huge fliers could so abruptly drop.

So intent were they upon the clouds that they did not see the swooping shapes that flew in low, just above the wave tops and then rose at the last minute to pass close over the decks.

Aboard the *Barley* there were a dozen crewmembers standing in the waist, the wind was freshening and they ex-

pected Captain Olinas to shift sails again shortly. At the last
moment they sensed the thing coming and dove to the decking. It flew over the rail, folded its wings with perfect timing
to pass between the masts and snagged a sailor by the name
of Peggs. Peggs's shrieks of woe faded away, even as the arrows from the maintops splashed short in the water.

Now the lookouts were rattled. The things came from on
high or they swept in low, and they came so fast it was difficult to get a shot at them.

Voolward sent more men aloft and lined the rails with others. Grim-faced, they remained alert the rest of the night, but
the batrukhs did not return.

Admiral Cranx was very disturbed. Men had been
snatched from six ships, a total of nine were now missing.
Cranx was not sure whether they were being devoured by
these aerial monsters or taken captives to the sorcerer's isle,
which lay just below the horizon to the northeast.

Worse, the wind that had stirred the clouds during the
night had faded away with the dawn and left the fleet becalmed once more, hull down from the isle but still well
within the range of the enormous batrukhs.

The boats were set down, and they towed all day, but to
little effect since a strong current began that pulled the entire
body of water on which the fleet floated back to the north
and east. Whatever forward progress the boats made was negated by this rearward drift of the water around them.

The Witch of Standing, Endysia, was rowed across from
the *Oat*. She was closeted with Admiral Cranx, who then
summoned Captain Olinas and Commander Voolward. The
witch had confirmed Cranx's worst fears. The sorcerer in the
isle had detected them and sent the batrukhs to snatch away
more men once the first man, poor Meloy, had been taken.
The sorcerer might have decided to try and take more, many
more. Suitably entranced, men could make good slaves. The
witch was sure that great magic had been made, probably
with poor Meloy's life to cement and give it force, and it
was this that had stifled the winter wind and left them becalmed close to the isle. The witch would prepare a spell to
try and break the sorcerer's grip on the wind. However, she
cautioned that she might not have the power to accomplish
that much.

During the day the men worked on defensive procedures.

They ate another hasty meal at dusk, and the first watch took up their posts.

Once again a gentle night fell. The air was warm but still, and the stars were clear and sharp until the moon rose. The men and dragonboys scanned the skies. Where were the things?

Once again nothing happened at first. The bell tolled to end the first watch and the changeover began.

Relkin climbed into the foretops and sat on the little platform where the topmast was fixed to the mast. In his hands rested his Cunfshon bow, a lightly built but still powerful short-range crossbow. On his hip rested his quiver with three dozen points to hand. Let the batrukhs come. He had killed one before, a lucky shot of course, but still it left him with the confidence that these things were mortal, vulnerable to the steel of an arrow head.

However, to be killed they had to be seen.

After a while, staring into the night made his eyes hurt. He had to relax, but found that his body was so tense it was cramping. He sucked in several deep breaths and released them very slowly. It helped a little.

And then he caught a flash of movement, low down, approaching the fleet from the west.

"There!" he pointed, his voice sounding oddly high and shrill.

Other voices arose, on other ships. A dozen of the great flying beasts were making a concerted attack. No one had expected so many.

However, most were detected before they reached the ships, and these ran into a hailstorm of arrows, slingshot, and even spears.

The first batrukh to attack the *Barley* veered away at once, but a second came in from bow on and this one swooped up at the men in the foremast crosstrees. Relkin watched it come with one part of his brain while the rest of him fired, reloaded, and fired again with that remarkable Cunfshon spring, which could be wound up and paid off in sections. He had two shafts in the thing, but it kept coming. A sailor dropped from the mast on a line, distracting the monster. Relkin put his third shaft deep into its head, and it flew straight into the topmast, which broke under the impact. Mast, batrukh, and a great tangle of cordage and block and tackle came crashing to the deck and over the side. The *Barley* shook as the monster landed on the foredeck.

Relkin was all that was left, still perched on the foremast crosstrees, amazed to have survived. The topmast was gone and so were the men who had been above him. The batrukh still thrashed on the deck, and men struggled to put an end to it and free their companions from the wreck. Relkin let out a long breath, and then without thinking, rewound his bow and checked his points.

There was a shout, his head came up and the first batrukh was back, stooping on the men in the mainmast crosstrees.

Relkin brought his bow up and fired in the next moment. His shaft sank home as the batrukh was snatching at a soldier, spoiling the creature's aim. The soldier sank his spear into the brute's wing as it went past. Relkin's second and third shots missed and it swept away, huge wing beats powering it forward.

But it had taken many shafts in that brief moment, both from dragonboys and soldiers armed with the longbow. One of these longbow arrows had driven steel deep into its flesh and cut a vital blood vessel. Within a quarter mile it weakened and then plunged into the sea with a great splash. It began to thrash there and soon attracted the sharks.

Around the fleet the tale was similar. A dying batrukh had clung to the mainsail of the *Oat* and torn it loose as it fell to its death on the deck. Men had been taken, but one had been recovered after the wounded batrukh fell to the sea close by. Other batrukhs had been seen to fall, and all of them had been struck by at least one arrow.

The crews were at work through the night cutting away wreckage and replacing sails, and in the case of the *Barley,* the fore-topmast. No more batrukhs were seen that night.

In the dawn, the Witch of Standing performed great magic on the quarterdeck of the *Oat.* For hours she murmured phrases and built up the volumes of a great spell. At length, she sank exhausted to the deck and had to be helped below. Her spell had an immediate effect, however. The erratic wisps of wind that had come up in the night swelled into a steady breeze from the north.

The winter wind was back! A cheer went up through the fleet, and the sails tightened and then billowed and the ships got underway once more and began to surge south and west.

After an hour, however, the winds began to die again. At the same time the counter current rose once more.

The witch was roused and returned to the deck where she built up another great spell involving the recitation of a thousand lines from the Birrak, plus declensions and a half dozen intractable volumates. This exhausted her strength, but it also produced a change.

The counter current was cut off, and the wind strengthened again. Once more the ships surged forward. The Isle of the Sorcerer receded behind them. Their spirits began to soar. Men broke out into verses of the "Kenor Song," and whole ships rang with the chorus.

Another hour, and a third, and now the ships had a white bow wave, and the mood of elation was confirmed. Captain Olinas was seen to give a little jump for joy when she came back on deck after some sleep.

And then with sickening suddenness, the wind died away and the counter current began again. In a matter of a few minutes, the ships had lost way. Then they began to be pulled back toward the dread Isle of the Sorcerer. An appalling sense of futility and doom settled over the fleet.

Once again the Witch of Standing began her great magic, but she was unable to complete the spell. Her concentration was broken each time by a malicious little voice that would speak inside her head, mocking her, laughing at her store of precious knowledge.

The fleet was hauled back, although the boats were soon over the side and pulling. The entire mass of water in which they floated was flowing north and east, taking them helplessly back toward the Isle of the Sorcerer.

Night fell when they were within sight of the isle once more.

They manned their positions and waited. The moon rose, clouds welled up from the southwest and slowly passed overhead, tinged with silvery light.

The midnight bell rang through the fleet and the watch changed. Still there was no attack.

In the hour before dawn, however, there was seen a vapor rising from the surface of the sea. A ghostly faint vapor, not like a proper fog or mist at all. It rose and moved over the ships. Some men complained at once of a strange feeling, a giddiness almost in their hearts.

The mist faded soon after.

The Witch of Standing attempted a divination spell and was foiled. Nothing she could do could shift the presence she felt in her thoughts.

It began on the *Potato*. Three soldiers on the forecastle began laughing uncontrollably. They tore off their garments, dropped their weapons, and threw themselves into the sea. They began to swim strongly toward the Isle of the Sorcerer.

It spread quickly. Wherever men had breathed deeply of the pernicious mist, the manic laughter began. All of the men thus affected removed their clothes and sought to hurl themselves into the sea. A few were intercepted in time and restrained, but they had to be taken below and chained up to keep them aboard, and the laughter turned to a manic howling that set everyone's teeth on edge.

In the meantime dozens of men were lost, swimming for the isle. The sun rose fully, and by the morning light they were visible for a long time before they were lost in the distance.

The Witch of Standing was rowed across to the *Barley* and closeted with Admiral Cranx once more. The nuisance posed by the sorcerer had now grown into a deadly peril.

The sorcerer had not interfered with shipping for many years and indeed had been quite quiescent for a long time. Nobody had visited his isle, of course; his reputation was not only grim but well established. As the years lengthened, however, shipping had grown more casual about approaching his isle, and since it was placed at a significant point of navigation, ships used it as a landfall on the long haul from Cape Hazard to the Straits of Kassim.

Now, all of a sudden, the sorcerer had reached out to snare their fleet. The witch feared that the sorcerer, an ancient, independent figure, had thrown in his lot with the great enemy in Padmasa. Whatever the case, it was plain that his powers were beyond those of a Witch of Standing. Without the aid of a Great Witch like Lessis, they could not break free. Lessis, alas, was far ahead of them aboard the frigate *Lyre*, speeding for the coast of Bogon.

Cranx met with his senior officers and released a statement to the fleet that reflected his own bafflement. They would stand fast and mount an intensive watch during the night to defend against the depredations of the flying brutes. He made no mention of the mist that drove men mad.

In the forward hold aboard the *Barley*, the dragonboys of the 109th Marneri were gathered around a butt of shafts from which they fashioned fresh arrows. They feathered and fitted steel points. These were then honed on the stone wheel awhile to make them razor sharp.

"It seems like we're done for," said Swane with a vast shrug. "This here sorcerer has got us on a tether, and we can't cut the rope. Our witch just doesn't have enough power."

"And he'll send that mist out and drag us all into shore," said Jak.

"What the hell does he want with us?" said Endi.

"Slaves, of course."

"I guess you'll probably find out soon enough," said Manuel. "We all will."

"No, we won't," said Relkin.

"Listen to that Quoshite. Always the optimist."

"The dragons won't go. They're immune to magic like that. Remember in Dzu, Swane? In the Pit when we faced the Mesomaster. The dragons took no notice of his spells."

"Right, so the dragons will have to sail the ships back home to get more men and dragonboys. We'll all be on that island slaving for the sorcerer."

But Relkin was gripped by a sudden thought.

"The dragons!" he exclaimed.

Endi saw it, too. "Of course. The dragons can do it," he shouted.

They took the idea to Dragon Leader Wiliger in his cabin. He heard them out, then snorted disdainfully.

"It seems fanciful. Would we not be asking too much of the noble lizards? Can they remember so much?"

"They can remember as well as a man."

"And we will be with them."

"What if you are incapacitated? The sorcerer will not react passively to your plan. What will happen if the wyverns have to do this on their own?"

Three dragonboys glared back at Wiliger.

"They will complete the mission," said Relkin solemnly.

Wiliger remained unconvinced.

"But how will they reach the land? You know perfectly well that they cannot be allowed to swim to the strand."

"Sir, we believe that in this instance they could be allowed to do so. We also believe that the rule may be in error, sir."

Wiliger looked up sharply. "And what does that mean?"

Relkin compressed his lips. Any words here were dangerous.

"Well?"

"Nothing, sir, but that we know the dragons, sir. They can do it, and nobody else can. We have to get free of the sorcerer, and the only ones who aren't affected by his wicked spells are the dragons. Magic doesn't affect them much at all."

Wiliger nodded thoughtfully.

"Well, I will take this idea to Commander Voolward and see what he thinks. You are dismissed."

Ten minutes later Wiliger took a written version of the plan to Commander Voolward's office.

Voolward read it and then sat back in his chair with a thoughtful look on his face.

"The dragons, eh?" He pursed his lips. "But they can't be allowed to swim in. Have to go in on boats. Can we do that?"

"I don't know, sir. We will have to ask the captain."

Voolward was a generous sort. He had been unhappy with Wiliger at the beginning of the voyage. Perhaps he had been too hard on him. Now he did his best to befriend the dragon leader.

"Dragon Leader, this is your idea, I leave it to you. Go to the captain and then take it to the admiral, see what he has to say. I will give you a scroll explaining my position, which is one of cautious agreement with your plan."

When approached, Captain Olinas calculated briefly, then conferred with Ship's Master Jiano. Shortly she gave her judgment.

"It appears that we can ferry a dragon in the largest ship's boat, the pinnace. We have twelve such boats in the fleet."

Wiliger applied to see Admiral Cranx. He did not show Cranx the scroll from Voolward. Instead he told Cranx that Voolward was afraid of using the dragons this way and had discouraged him. Wiliger told the admiral that he had risked a reprimand because he felt that this was the best option they had.

Cranx plucked at this straw.

"Dragons are impervious to magic, they tell me."

"So I have heard, sir."

Cranx wished that he had either General Steenhur or General Baxander to pass this burdensome decision onto. If he was wrong and they lost dragons, they might compromise the entire mission. On the other hand, if they stayed here the damned sorcerer would find a way to abduct them all and they would end their lives as slaves in his dark mines.

Cranx ordered the selection of twelve dragons at once. Wiliger scented a great chance for glory and volunteered the services of the 109th Marneri.

"Well, Dragon Leader," said Cranx after a moment's consideration, "since you dreamed up this mad scheme, I think it only fair to allow you to carry it out."

CHAPTER FOURTEEN

The ten members of the 109th were augmented by a pair of volunteers, old Shomble from the Kadein 92nd and Der Stanker from the Marneri 66th, who, though young, was already famous for his sword-fighting skill. Indeed, there were those who said he was the match of the famous Broketail himself.

As soon as darkness had grown thick enough to cloak their activities, and before the moon's rise, twelve large cutters were set down on the calm sea and rowed to the side of the *Barley.*

It was fortunate that the sea was so gentle, for easing the huge dragons down the side into fragile boats that were barely big enough to accept them without swamping proved to be a most arduous task.

Eventually it was completed, without major mishap, although Vlok fell the last few feet and broke davits and lockers in the pinnace from *Oat.* Fortunately the hull held. The Purple Green was carried in the largest pinnace of all, from *Barley,* and even that was driven deep into the water.

With muffled oars they were rowed through the darkness to the glittering strand where small waves broke upon a wide sandy beach.

The moon was just beginning to rise when the dragons crossed the sand and hid beneath the jungle growth that fringed the beach. With the dragons were their dragonboys, Dragon Leader Wiliger, and Dragoneer Feens of the 66th Marneri, who was acting second in command. In addition, there were six bowmen from the Alpha Flight of the Kadein First Legion. They carried heavy compound bows of horn, wood, and steel, and wide quivers loaded with dozens of points. They were risking much, since unlike the dragons they were susceptible to sorcery, but there were strong advantages in having archers, in addition to the dragonboys who had to come anyway.

They waited at the edge of the jungle for a moment while Wiliger and Corporal Fermin of the Kadein bowmen scouted for a path. Dragoneer Feens moved up and down the line checking with each dragonboy for problems.

Behind them the boats were rowing out toward the distant ships, visible now in the moonlight as ghostly pyramids of sails about a mile distant. The small party under the eaves of the jungle were on their own.

Dragoneer Feens was a tall young man of twenty-five who had been a dragonboy for ten years and lost his dragon to the disease called Blue Liver. He had been given the command of the 66th Marneri after the unit was rebuilt in the aftermath of the campaign for Arneis. His own dragons had been disappointed at not being chosen themselves for this mission. Though there were hardly any survivors of the old unit that had fought beside the 109th in Arneis, the 66th still prided themselves on belonging to a crack unit that had fought in Ourdh, in Kohon, and in Arneis. If the 109th were to be sent, then the 66th felt that they should be sent as well.

However, there were only twelve boats, and it was decided to send only twelve dragons. They would be a formidable force, and if they were lost to some unguessable sorcery, then the loss would be limited to only twelve precious dragons. Thus the 66th had to be content with sending only their dragoneer and one dragon chosen by lot. This was the already famous Der Stanker, a young green from Aubinas.

Corporal Fermin came back and signaled to them to follow. Now they hiked inland, moving through the moonlit scrub vegetation toward the volcanic cone. After a couple of miles the scrub thinned out, and they stepped out onto a weird blasted landscape of tufs and lavas. The cone of the volcano started up a quarter mile ahead, forming an enormous mass that loomed above.

Here and there about its circumference the cone bore outlier juts and pinnacles. On one of these, to the south and east of their position, stood the eldritch castle of the sorcerer, a fantastic collection of towers and struts, from which a few amber lights could be seen even at this great distance.

There was no cover, but there was a kind of zigzag trail broken into the flaked tuf that formed the slope. To either side of the crumbly tuf were flows of a black, harsh lava with horrendously rough surfaces. The tuf at the bottom was deep and hard to get good footing on for beasts of two tons or more. Dragonboys hopped around their dragons with considerable anxiety as the monsters struggled up the slope, for dragon feet were tender and no boy wanted his charge to suffer damage.

The trail began to bend to either side, zigzagging up the steepening slope. They rose higher so they could see the castle of the sorcerer more clearly, just a few miles away, with lights burning in some of the towers.

They were all well aware that just as the castle was visible to them, they must be visible to the castle. Dragons were not inconspicuous beasts, except when moving through forest cover when their natural predatory natures made them amazingly quiet. Here, they were set out under the bright moonlight with no cover at all. And still there was no reaction from the castle. The sorcerer appeared unaware of their presence.

After an ascent of more than a hundred feet the zigzag path brought them to a broad road that had been cut into the side of the mountain and paved with massive stone blocks.

This road had been broken up by the most recent flow of lava, and a new road was in the process of being hacked through. There were tools and timbers stacked inside a cut made into the lava.

In the other direction, the road ran straight along the side of the cone to the castle.

They rested briefly. The dragons were hot and thirsty after that climb, but there was only enough water in the dragonboys' flasks to wet everyone's throat once.

Wiliger studied the castle and the way ahead with his spyglass. He conferred with Dragoneer Feens and Corporal Fermin. It seemed that the sorcerer had not seen them yet. They would go on, straight for the castle, and hope to reach it before being detected. The plan remained the same.

Dragonboys checked their charges' feet, which were simultaneously massive and tender and liable to blister. Relkin found that Bazil had come through fairly well. There was a nick on the left ankle from a sharp piece of lava but the soles of the leatherback's feet had held up. Relkin thanked all those hours he'd spent in the last year bathing the dragon's feet in Old Sugustus Skin Toughener. Other dragonboys worked feverishly with blister sherbet and disinfectant.

"I wonder what's up," muttered Swane to Relkin. "Why do you think there's been no defense?"

"Maybe it's a trap," said Manuel, who was passing close by.

"Or maybe the wizard's too busy gloating over the fleet to notice us," said Relkin quietly.

"It could be anything," said Mono, passing the other way, "but keep it down 'cause Wiliger's coming back."

They hunched over their work. The dragons were silent, intent on getting their breath back and cooling down.

Wiliger spoke quietly with Feens for a moment, then they separated.

"All right, everyone, we go on," said Wiliger. "There's no sign of opposition, no sign that they've even seen us. Old Caymo must be rolling his dice for us."

Relkin's eyebrows rose. Wiliger was a follower of Old Caymo, too? One didn't hear his name thrown out like that very often; it was regarded as disrespectful to the Great Mother.

With a few grunts of displeasure here and there, they succeeded in getting the dragons on their feet and then they moved on down the well-paved road toward the castle.

To their right, over the low retaining wall, they could see the lower part of the island and out in the bay the fleet, marooned in a tight flotilla, white sides gleaming in the moonlight.

Maybe Relkin had it right, the damned sorcerer was too busy savoring his triumph to imagine that the fleet might strike back at him like this.

The castle grew close enough for individual windows to be discerned. There were lights in many of the towers. More lights, presumably torches, moved on the battlements.

A shadow fell across them.

"What?" said Wiliger looking up.

"Up there," said Swane in a harsh whisper.

"Batrukh," said several voices apprehensively.

Over the cone of the volcano came the great flying beast, it swooped low over them and rose again with a monstrous shriek of hate that chilled the blood in men's veins.

"That's done it," said Swane.

The batrukh flew to the castle and vanished into the dark open maw of a gate that hung over a precipice.

Not long afterward more lights could be seen on the castle battlements. Then a very bright light was lit within some interior courtyard so that it shone up among the sides of the towers around it. At the same time they heard a dreadful howling begin.

"Sounds like they're readying a reception for us," said Endi.

The howls were increasing in volume. Some of the boys looked worried.

"Anything that howls must breathe," said Relkin with a grim smile. "And if it breathes then it lives, and if it lives then it can be killed." He glanced meaningfully at the dragons, each with his great sword riding in the scabbard on his shoulders.

"Look!" shrieked little Jak. "The batrukhs are coming." It was true. One by one the batrukhs of the sorcerer were appearing from the mouth of the cliff gate. In a matter of moments they were stooping at the dragons from the dark sky.

The bows of the Kadein archers snapped loudly and drove their shafts home. Two, then three, batrukhs broke away from the attack; one fell heavily on the lower slopes of the volcano and tumbled in ruin to the jungle.

The others attempted to grapple with the dragons.

They met twelve shining blades of sharp steel, huge blades that whirred in the soft tropic air and slaughtered batrukhs as if they were no more than turkeys.

Such conflict could not last for more than seconds. The batrukhs dove among the dragons. The swords flashed and batrukhs fell dead in the roadway. Only one escaped, the Purple Green having missed with a stroke that would have cut it in half, and it flew back to the castle with a sobbing, mournful cry.

The dragonboys yelled insults in its wake.

"Silence," snapped Wiliger.

They quietened and then they heard the howling again. It was much closer now and possessed an insane high tonic that set their teeth on edge.

"What the hell kind of hounds are those?" said Swane.

"They aren't hounds," said Manuel. "No hound can wail like that."

"Then what in the name of hell are they?"

"Look, they are men," said Endi.

And around the corner came a mass of men, howling as they came, under the light of great torches that blazed above. They carried round shields and waved swords and battle axes and in their eyes was a deadness that betrayed their loss of will.

Among them were some of the men taken from the fleet.

"Prepare to receive the enemy!" said Dragon Leader Wiliger in a tight voice.

"But they're men from the fleet," said Roos.

"That won't help us any if they get to grips. The sorcerer's done something to their minds."

The dragons pulled free their swords. There wasn't room for more than two dragons to stand and fight in the road, so Alsebra and Der Stanker took up position at the front. Behind were the rest, with Bazil and the Purple Green slotted in second place.

Bowmen deployed in front and kept up a good fire until the advancing horde was within a hundred feet. Then the bowmen withdrew. The howling men came on and threw themselves at the dragons.

Great dragonswords glittered as they rose and fell and brought death's merciful release to men trapped like moths by the sorcerer's flame. Their faces never changed expression even at the moment of death. It was awful work, and both dragons and dragonboys hated it.

Despite the slaughter of their fellows, the mob never stopped their march toward the dragonswords. One or two eventually got past Alsebra and Der Stanker; dragonboys took them down with their little bows. The rest died in front of the two green dragons, whose swords swung back and forth almost mechanically, sundering shields and bodies alike.

The dragons were most unhappy with this work, and Alsebra's dragon speech curses were loud and frequent. The dragonboys were not pleased, either. Slaughtering men who had no control over themselves was unseemly, but there was no choice.

Relkin had seen it before, and it still disgusted him. Men and imps simply could not attack battledragons unless they could rush them from all sides, or they had the support of trolls and other larger scale creatures.

Half the men were dead. Abruptly the howling ceased, cut

off in mid-scream as if by a giant knife. The men stumbled
backward until they were out of bow shot. Their faces were
slack, eyes staring, their minds destroyed by the evil power
of the sorcerer. There was no recognition of either the dragons or their comrades from the fleet in their eyes. They were
lost souls.

A mound of corpses lay in the road.

"Forward," said Wiliger, who alone in the group seemed
satisfied. Alsebra and Der Stanker were ordered to the rear
and the dragons marched, Bazil and the Purple Green at the
front, shields lowered and great swords at the ready.

Without even bows and arrows the sorcerer's pack of demented men could do nothing. They gave ground. The dragons
pressed on and soon had the men trotting ahead of them back
toward the great castle gate on the edge of the pinnacle.

Here a causeway traveled out over a sheer drop of a hundred feet or more and reached the castle wall beneath frown-
ing turrets forty feet above.

As they approached, they saw the gates pulled closed by
teams of dwarves that were chained to the insides of the
gates. The doors slammed shut in the faces of the demented
men, leaving them on the causeway, facing the dragons.

Bazil paused, not liking this situation.

Relkin, too, felt suddenly very cautious.

Wiliger ordered the dragons to thrust forward to the gate
and to push the sorcerer's men aside. If they did not fight,
they would simply be passed back across the causeway and
left behind the dragons.

Relkin shook his head, this was not the time to step out on
that causeway.

"Sir," he said, "this is a trap of some kind."

Wiliger shot him a furious look.

Bazil stepped forward to the edge of the causeway and
poked the men aside with Ecator. They did not hesitate but
moved meekly to the sides of the causeway and began to fil-
ter back across, outside the two rows of dragons.

"Sir," said Relkin, deadly afraid now.

"What is it, boy?" snapped Wiliger.

"I don't know, sir, I just know that it's a trap."

Wiliger looked at the stones.

"It seems solid enough to me," he said. He looked up at
the battlements; there was a gleam of metal up there. Men

were at work with some large device. Quickly he called to Bazil to step back.

"Dragoneer Relkin, I think your instinct may have been right. There's something going on up there."

Then with a groan of metal and the creak of chains, they saw great iron pitchers of boiling oil being raised above the battlements.

Wiliger groaned. Their mission had failed. The sorcerer could sit inside his castle, safe from them, and wreak evil on the trapped fleet.

Manuel caught Relkin's sleeve.

"Up above, up there, what do you see?" he said, pointing up the slope of the volcano.

Relkin saw at once what he meant. Pinnacles of earlier lava had formed, broken out from the main slope by a later lava flow that had among other things created the crag on which the castle sat. These slender pinnacles of old black lava were cracked and fissured and stood above them on the higher slope of a fissure cut in the cone's side.

Relkin turned to Wiliger, and indicated the pinnacles above.

"There, sir, that's all we need."

Wiliger stared at them uncomprehending for a moment. Then he realized what the boys were suggesting.

"Are they capable of it?"

"The dragons? Oh, yes, sir."

The first pinnacle fell within the hour, heaved over by the combined strength of twelve dragons. The lava column fractured as it fell, and great blocks of stone, ten feet to a side, went bouncing down the slope, over the edge of the fault line and then barreled across the causeway to smash into the gate.

The first great rock broke the gate's timbers. The second stove them in, and the third bounced high and smashed the right-hand gate off its hinges and hurled it within.

The silence that followed was broken only by the thin cheering of the dragonboys.

The second pinnacle shook at the first heave by the dragons. It overlooked another, much larger, mass that stood out right on the edge of the fault line, poised a hundred feet above the causeway to the castle.

The dragons gathered themselves and gave it another great push.

The rock column shuddered.

There was a trumpet blast from below.

"Someone's coming," said Jak, who was on lookout.

They all watched with bows drawn as two figures on horseback rode out of the gate under a white flag and then picked their way up the slope toward them.

"A flag of truce. The question is do we accept it?" said Wiliger.

"Can you trust this sorcerer in any way at all?" said Dragoneer Feens.

"Probably not."

And yet they waited, signaling to the dragons to hold off from the pinnacle.

A man holding a white cloth tied to his spear approached. He was a squat, ill-favored fellow with sallow skin and black eyes in which there was a gleam of something akin to madness.

He greeted them with a flourish and a flow of fine words in a courtly style of Verio that sounded very much as if it had been learned from a book.

He explained that he came from the presence of the Honored Master, lord of this isle and its surroundings. He went on to say that the Honored Master was much aggrieved by their presence and wanted to ask them why they proffered such violence to his manse and his creatures. What ailed these great dragon beasts? Why did they make such violent affray and trouble in his kingdom? Why did this fleet pass so insolently close to his isle and not stay to pay proper tribute? Where was the respect that was most naturally owed to him, the Honored Master?

The Honored Master felt that he had legitimate grounds for complaint, and he begged the great dragons and their owners to refrain from committing any more violence.

They were invited to enter in and partake of a banquet with the Honored Master. Once they had broached a cask together and sung the good old songs, then they would find common grounds for friendship.

Yes, it was an unheard-of privilege, but the Honored Master offered them his friendship!

"Is that the Honored Master?" said Wiliger, pointing.

The spokesman waved his hands hurriedly. "Do not point like that, it is terribly disrespectful."

"All right, but tell me, who is that man?"

With eyes downcast, the spokesman admitted that it was indeed the Honored Master.

"Why doesn't he come closer and speak for himself?"

"Why are you so suspicious, man from the north? Why did your fleet not stop and pay its respects?"

"I'm not the admiral in command of the fleet. Why did your master send his flying monsters to attack our ships?"

" 'Attack'? You are wrong. They came to investigate, not to attack."

"We were there. It was an attack."

The spokesman grew flustered. He glanced back helplessly to the other figure, still sitting on his horse fifty yards away. For a moment the tension rose. Then some decision was made. The figure moved forward, slowly, walking his horse up to them.

As he came, he completed a web of sorcery that he cast over the men and dragons like a net. Across the minds of men it fell like a shadow obscuring the light, and their thought became hazy and unfocused. Many stared witlessly at the moon, others giggled and scratched themselves. Dragon Leader Wiliger felt his wits go astray. He could not remember who these men on horseback were, or why he was standing there with them on this hillside beneath the moon. He tried to speak and found himself unable to say more than two words in order.

The sorcerer ignored him and rode up to the dragons and halted about fifteen yards away. His horse would not go any nearer without intensive coercion, and he wanted to have his whole mind free to contemplate these dragons. He had never encountered these famous monsters from the Argonath before.

His spell had had very little effect on the dragons. One or two of the younger wyverns shifted uneasily from foot to foot at seeing their dragonboys silenced like this. These young dragons eyed the sorcerer with some apprehension. They had not seen real battle yet and had never dreamed of fighting wizards.

"What wrong with everyone?" said Vlok, who was perhaps the least affected of all.

"Human magic, this one here in front of us must be the sorcerer," said Alsebra sharply.

"Ah. This is the cause of our trouble, then." The Purple Green stood up and drew his sword. It was a standard regulation blade, eight feet long and massively proportioned. He set it down point first and rested his huge forearms on it and gazed at the wizard.

The sound of steel being pulled from scabbards came from all around him as the other dragons did the same.

Wiliger was struggling to think clearly.

"Hold," he said. "Where you going?"

"Be quiet, man," said the sorcerer's spokesman, "trouble not the Honored Master with your impertinence."

"Stop," said Wiliger, clutching his head. His thoughts were congealing like cold tar. He spun on the spot and fell down in a swoon.

The older veterans of the 109th Marneri had seen magic before, and they remained unconcerned. Magic had little effect on them.

The figure pulled back its hood and revealed a normal human face with thick lips and a very thin nose, although the skin glowed grey under the moonlight. He was hairless; his eyes were set close together.

The sorcerer forced his unwilling mount to go closer until he locked his gaze with that of the nearest dragon, which happened to be the broketail.

Bazil glared back. The man's eyes seemed to pinwheel a little. It was a foolish effect that merely annoyed the wyvern. His glare in return was that of a giant predator, two huge eyes facing forward on potential prey.

The sorcerer found his own focus blurred by his discomfort at being stared at in this way. These monsters were indeed highly intimidating. He concentrated all his strength and pressed his gaze upon that of the dragon, willing himself not to flinch, not to pay any attention to the force and purpose of the giant's own stare.

Now he pressed down with his great willpower and sought to break the dragon's gaze. First make it look down, and then take control of its will.

Nothing happened, except that the dragon shrugged as if to dispel a tickle or a cold draft.

"Stop what you do, man." Bazil took up Ecator. The steel gleamed in the moonlight.

The sorcerer quailed and moved back. His horse became almost uncontrollable.

"I merely wish to welcome you, great honored monsters of the north."

"Funny idea of welcome to attack with stupid bats."

"A tragedy, a complete misunderstanding, I assure you. Now, welcome to my humble island."

There was such a weight of sweetness in his words that they were like some foul honey, an exudate collected from spiders perhaps. One or two of the younger wyverns were even ready to accept this reading of events.

"Wizard, you let fleet go if you want to live," said Bazil. "And first you release dragonboys from your spell."

"Ah, spells, now there's a story to be told." The sorcerer had turned his gaze on Alsebra, but he had no more luck than he'd had with Bazil. Quickly he spun to the Purple Green. This was a mistake. No living thing stared back at the Purple Green, not when the Purple Green was concentrating all his four tons in a glare of hyperbolic venom. The wild dragon roused up and stepped closer to the man and his horse.

The horse reared, and to avoid being tossed by the panicked animal, the sorcerer let it retreat another fifteen yards. There he regained control and brought the panting animal to a halt, looking back to the dragons.

It was an astonishing thing, a complete reversal. Never had he, great Gadjung of Batooj, suffered such a defeat. He was the only living master of the great magical system of the Red Aeon. He knew of the work of the Five who dwelled far to the north in the uttermost Hazog. Their power had grown great, indeed, but they knew nothing of the arts of the Red Aeon, which were the greatest of all on the world Ryetelth. He did not fear them nor any other living man or woman.

These dragons were clearly unreachable. They must be possessed of minds so incredibly dim and recalcitrant that they simply could not be touched by the delicate power of his magic. Well, if he could not master them then he would have to destroy them. He raised his hand, and his servant blew the bugle.

"Behold! We will watch these over-haughty monsters cut down to size."

CHAPTER FIFTEEN

There was a sudden stir among the dragons. Something had appeared in the ruined gateway, something huge that glittered strangely.

There came a harsh metallic shriek, and now the light of the new moon was reflected from brass surfaces and silvery details. With more enormous squeaks and groans the thing came on, rolling on huge gears starved of oil.

It stepped across the causeway and now they saw it clearly, a man-shaped thing almost twenty feet tall. A giant clad in heavy armor, wearing a helm that enclosed the head and carrying a huge round shield.

The sorcerer retreated downslope and finally paused, when well out of bow shot from the Argonathi soldiers. He watched the coming of the great cataphract with satisfaction. He had never had cause to use it before, not since that day when he had rescued it from the pit in which it had lain for aeons and cleaned it of the slime and filth. These haughty reptiles would get a lesson now. He chuckled to himself, a dry leathery sound.

The giant armored man began to move upslope, each stride accompanied by another shriek of dry, rusty metal. He came slowly, weighed down by enormous mass.

"By the fiery breath," muttered the Purple Green.

"That would be a useful thing to have right now," replied Alsebra as she moved away from the others and deployed her beautiful dragonsword "Undaunt."

Bazil stood forward and drew "Ecator." "I have never met a foe that could withstand dragonsword," he said. Ecator fairly glowed in the moonlight, a long ribbon of white steel.

"There can always be a first time, Broketail."

All the dragons were ready now, swords in hand, shields held loosely. There was no need for tail sword, by the look of the armor plates on their opponent. This was going to be heavy-duty work; they could forget finesse.

It came up the slope toward them at the same steady pace, each huge metal foot crunching into the volcano's side as it came down, sinking deep into the surface while plates of tortured steel squawked most horribly.

Perhaps it was the overpowering sound, perhaps the general tension, but the dragonboys started to wake from the sorcerer's spell. His grip was broken. One by one they snapped awake and looked up at the giant towering over them.

"Where the hell did that come from?" yelled Swane, frantically looking for his bow and quiver.

"Mother preserve us," said someone else.

"By the breath!"

They scrambled for their weapons, then looked for their dragons.

There was a sudden shriek of fright as Dragon Leader Wiliger woke and found himself almost beneath the feet of the oncoming thing. No one had seen fit to pull him clear.

For a moment he gaped up at the helmet towering above him. Above the cheek guards there were empty spaces.

Wiliger backed away, mouth working.

"Impossible!" He turned and ran and slammed into Bazil's right leg and almost fell over.

The dragon steadied him with the flat of the dragonsword. The touch of that steel sent a shock through his system. His scream of terror cut off. He ducked sideways then scrambled clear, keeping his head down, while Bazil limbered up, which sent his tail cracking back and forward just over human heads.

Wiliger fought down the terror he felt. The thing had holes for eyes but there were no eyes within them. He gasped for air, fighting the rising panic. Something made him look up, and he saw Relkin examining him from his place behind the dragon, where he waited with bow and arrow.

Wiliger pulled himself together with an effort. He was dragon leader! He would command his unit as he was supposed to! He peered along the slope of the volcano, trying to work out where everybody was.

As far as he could see, they'd made a natural semicircle in which to receive the giant. Closest were Alsebra and

Bazil Broketail, all were armed and ready. They had organized this on their own, without any need of a dragon leader.

Well, he would start earning his keep now. Just as Chesler Renkandimo said in his book on the subject, "Dragons are smarter than horses, they're not quite as smart as people."

From here on he would guide them to victory. He turned back to look at the approaching iron man. The din of its approach was terrifying enough. It wielded a great sword, broader than a dragonsword but not quite as long.

Then Wiliger's view was obscured as Alsebra swung in front of the monster. It halted in mid-screeching stride to engage. Great swords swung together, and Alsebra put her two tons fully behind the blow.

There was a great clangor of steel, as loud as any heard on any battlefield, and Alsebra was forced back a step. The metal giant turned on massive, slow-flexing knees and swung the backhand. It was slow to set up the blow, but it delivered it smartly enough and Alsebra stepped back just in time, her counterstroke already in motion. Undaunt came around and struck the giant's arm above the elbow. Sparks blazed from the site but the blade was repulsed and left no visible mark.

Then the giant's forehand stroke broke upon Alsebra's shield like thunder, and the shield was riven on one side. Alsebra staggered backward. The green freemartin was too lightly built to stand against this thing, and her sword could not cut the outer layer of the cataphragm.

Bazil Broketail swung in to engage, his sword swinging on a forehand cut. The giant surprised him by raising a huge foot and lashing out with it. Bazil deflected the giant's sword, but the huge foot struck his shield and bowled him over. He went down in a tangle of limbs, sprained his tail, and rolled down the hillside for a hundred feet.

There was a roar of anger from the rest of the dragons.

"Let me take him," cried young Aulay, who hurled himself at the metal monster with his sword flailing. Unfortunately, Aulay's charge sent his tail lashing sideways and caught Dragon Leader Wiliger on the back of the head and knocked him cold.

Swords rang off each other once, twice, and then Aulay was driven back on his heels by the third and fell over, quite overmatched. The thing stood over him and raised its sword for the deathblow. Before it could fall, however, the Purple

Green engaged, bringing his sword down in a terrific overhead chop that rang off the giant's helmet in a shower of sparks.

At last the cataphract showed some reaction to a blow. It staggered and took two steps backward, reaching back for balance with its shield.

Roos helped Aulay to his feet and pulled him away, his sword arm completely numb and shivering. Dragoneer Feens had dragged Wiliger to safety.

The Purple Green engaged it again, and there was an exchange of sword blows. The thing was slow to shift position, but its sword arm moved very rapidly to compensate. The combination made the iron man hard to read and difficult to compensate for.

Still, the Purple Green exchanged five great ringing strokes with the cataphract and then his legion-issued dragonsword broke asunder and left him with only a shield. He scrambled backward, almost trampling Manuel in the rush.

The metal-clad giant came after him with a shriek of dry steel in tension.

Chektor moved in to block its path with a swinging two-handed stroke that bounced off the thing's shield and left old Chek off balance. The cataphract's return stroke knocked Chektor right off his feet, and he sprawled there helpless. It would have gone badly for Chektor then, but Bazil Broketail had regained his feet and clambered up the slope to come at the Cataphract from behind. Seeing Chektor's peril, Bazil brought Ecator down on the back of the cataphract's head.

Ecator was a fell blade, made by elvish smiths working under the direction of a Great Witch. Now it cut through the otherwise impervious armor of the cataphragm and sank into the monster's helmet with a great flash of white sparks and a sound like the rending of a giant bell.

The Cataphract stumbled forward a step. Bazil heaved his sword free and waited for the monster to topple. Nothing could live through a stroke like that. And yet the giant warrior did not topple; instead it recovered and slashed back at Baz with a backhand stroke that he barely deflected, so strong was it.

The leatherback stepped backward, downslope. Old Chektor had rolled clear and was getting back to his feet. The

Purple Green was upslope, looking for a weapon. Now Oxard and Stengo had come to the front to engage the thing.

Clearly visible though was the bite in the cataphract's helmet from Ecator. Bazil saw it and felt a chill go through him. This foe was not alive; it had no blood. This was like fighting a ghost, except that this ghost was built of steel.

With a terrific crunch, it broke Stengo's shield and knocked the leatherback dragon sideways. Then it battered Oxard to his knees with two tremendous overhead blows that came so quickly the big brasshide could not move out of the way in time. Its gears shrieked horribly as it moved on the fallen Oxard.

Bazil circled to come at it again from behind and ran up and brought Ecator down with all his strength right into the angle between the head and neck.

Ecator sang its unholy verse of death and bit deep in another shower of white-hot sparks. There was a moment's stillness, then the monster turned, slowly but unstoppably on squealing steel gimbles, and Bazil was pulled off his feet as he struggled to pull the sword free again.

How could it do this? It seemed impossible after a blow like that. Then the cataphract slammed him across the body with its shield, and he almost lost his grip on the sword. His feet came back on the ground, and he stumbled and fell against the thing and almost knocked himself cold. He felt the sword move a little. Then the iron man shoved him away, and he reeled backward as Ecator came free at last.

The cataphract's sword whistled over his head as he tripped and fell. He landed with a stunning crash and slid down the ash, ripping his joboquin from its fasteners.

Steel crunched down on the cataphract again as Vlok attacked with a wild overhand. Vlok's sword "Katzbalger" rang on the cataphragm in a coruscation of sparks, but did no apparent damage.

Their predicament now dawned on all the dragons. Their foe was almost invulnerable to their weapons, and even when cut deeply it took no notice.

Bazil hauled himself back to his feet with a groan. What could they do? His jaws ached.

A voice shrilled behind him, and he stood still for a moment. Relkin had worked his way downslope, and now he vaulted from the dragon's knee to his shoulder.

"Are you hurt?" he shouted.

A tooth fell from Bazil's jaw. He spat blood and reached up to his mouth. There was a large tender area.

"Jaw not broken," he said a moment later.

"Thanks to the old gods for that."

Pieces of equipment fell from the tattered joboquin.

"That whole damned thing is made of metal."

"But hollow, Baz. When you struck him, it rang like a drum. That armor is just a kind of hull."

"It is strong, I have never felt a stronger arm."

There was a shriek of metal, the sound of a heavy blow, and Oxard was sent sprawling. The Purple Green picked up Oxard's sword and resumed the battle.

Endi came over and crouched beside Relkin. "There's nothing inside that thing; it's not alive."

Relkin shivered. The arms could move so quickly through certain prescribed motions.

"How can we kill something that is not even alive?" said Bazil in an appalled voice.

"We're doomed," said Endi.

A sudden realization struck Relkin with an almost physical force.

"The sorcerer must give it its strength. He must drive the thing with his magic."

They squinted carefully down the slope to where the sorcerer sat his horse, a hunched figure of dreadful power. He had retreated well out of bow shot when the cataphract first appeared on the scene. His equerry was beside him.

"If you going to do anything, you better hurry," said Bazil as another young dragon was bounced aside by the giant. The 109th was getting something of a beating by this point. Oxard had been wounded, deep cuts on the forearms, a slash on one side of the rib cage, some broken bones. Roquil also was nursing a wounded side. Everyone else had abrasions and cuts, and their armor and gear were a terrible mess. "If this goes on, it will kill all of us."

Wiliger was out cold. Dragoneer Feens was on the far side of the cataphract. Relkin decided to act. He moved, sliding to his right, low along the ground in a crouch, then dropping into a gulley that snaked downslope toward where the sorcerer sat on his horse.

Relkin checked his bow, and pulled an arrow from his quiver. He darted around a corner, avoiding small boulders, and then a heavy body dropped on his from above. He was driven into the gulley wall.

"What the hell?"

It was Swane.

"I should've known," groaned Relkin.

"Listen, Quoshite, I know you, you'll be trying to hog all the glory again. This time Swane's gonna be in on the action."

There was nothing to be done about it. Once Swane got a notion. . . .

"Well, just don't let him see you, all right?"

They went on down the gulley, which deepened quickly and allowed them better cover the closer they got. The only problem was that they were also getting farther below the sorcerer's position. To get in a good shot, they would have to climb the far side of the gulley, within perhaps thirty yards of the sorcerer, which was a killing range for Relkin and his Cunfshon bow but which would be in plain view of those deadly eyes.

There was nothing else to do, however, so they slipped across a broken mass of lava that had slid down into the gulley and went on through the boulder-strewn ash until they reached a point where the gulley curved to the right sharply. To get in a shot they had to climb here, up onto the right-hand side slope until they could see the sorcerer up above the left-hand slope.

There were a few large pieces of lava perched on the slope, which could give a minimal cover.

"Up there, then," said Relkin.

"Right," said Swane, who immediately set off up the steep, irregular slope. He got ten feet up, and his boot slipped on crumbly ash and he lost his balance completely and tumbled back into the gulley with a wail.

"Shut up!" Relkin threw himself flat on the ash slope and took aim at the edge of the gulley.

Swane's cry had been heard. The sorcerer had nudged his horse closer to the gulley and now peered over the edge into the depths. At first he saw nothing, the dragonboys were hidden in deep shadow, but then he noticed Swane and instantly reached out with his terrible strength.

Swane gave a gasp as he lost consciousness. Relkin released and saw his arrow suddenly sprout from the sorcerer's right shoulder. The figure in black gave a shriek and fell off his horse out of sight. More cries followed. Great Gadjung, high sorcerer of Batooj, was not accustomed to such discomforts. His servant dismounted and ran to his aid.

Relkin climbed down and then up on the left side of the gulley. He knew his shot had not been a kill. But if the sorcerer was down, then maybe Relkin could finish him off.

Panting, heaving for breath, he reached the top and crouched among pieces of raw lava. Not twenty paces away, the sorcerer was being helped into his saddle by his slave.

The sound of the battle had stopped for a moment. Relkin glanced back and saw that the cataphract had slowed; in fact, it was barely moving. Encouraged, the dragons threw themselves at it and their swords now raised a hellish din.

Relkin felt a glow for having guessed correctly how the iron man was powered. He took aim and released. His bowstring snapped, and his arrow bounced off a nearby rock and went straight up in the air for ten feet and fell to the side.

He felt the breath freeze in his throat, and then he was pulling loose the broken string and fishing in his pouch for a new one.

The sorcerer, fortunately, too preoccupied to notice Relkin, struggled to get a leg into his stirrup and failed and slid to the ground with another shriek of pain from the agony in his shoulder.

Relkin's fingers slid the bowstring through the notches, tightened knots, and pulled it taut.

Once again the sorcerer got a foot in the stirrup. There was a terrific clangor from up the slope where the dragons had pitched the cataphract over onto its back.

The sorcerer rose in the saddle, with another cry of pain. He steadied himself, took a deep breath, and then happened to look directly in Relkin's direction, where he crouched among rocks at the edge of the gulley.

Relkin took aim, but then the numbness struck his brain as the sorcerer pounced. His nerveless fingers released as the black cloud came down on his mind and he toppled backward.

When he came to, a few minutes later, he found himself in the bottom of the gulley. Swane was pinching his cheeks and slapping him lightly on the face.

"Enough." Relkin put a hand up to the side of his head and felt blood. His head rang from the blow it had taken. He remembered releasing that arrow. Had he hit his target?

"Damned Quoshite, what are you doing?"

"I don't know, trying to get up, I guess. Everything blanked out there for a moment."

"Everything's gonna blank out for good if that sorcerer gets another look at us."

Swane pulled him to his feet.

"How long was I out?"

"Seemed like forever. Better hurry now."

"Then I must have hit him; he must be wounded badly or he would have finished us off already."

"Come on, let's get back to the others."

They scrambled back up the gulley toward the sounds of dragonswords ringing off the cataphragm.

The dragons had laid the thing over and were pounding it with their great blades. But only Ecator could cut the magical integument of the cataphragm, and not even Ecator could slice off whole limbs.

Relkin looked downslope and saw the sorcerer was back in the saddle, but hunched over and obviously worse for wear. But now the sorcerer straightened himself by sheer willpower. His head came up, and once more the cataphract was instilled with his power. It rolled over and started to get back onto its feet.

Relkin staggered up to Dragoneer Feens.

"Drop that pile of rocks on it, that'll stop it." The Purple Green looked up and noticed the pinnacle again.

"You are right." He started for the pinnacle. Several other dragons joined him, leaving Baz and Alsebra to hew at the cataphract as it struggled back to its feet.

Ecator sank in again, cutting a foot deep into the hip plate of the cataphragm. The metal monster continued to move, although a shudder ran through it as Bazil put a foot up on it to heave the blade free.

The Purple Green gave a great roar as he pressed against the base of the pinnacle. The other dragons fitted themselves in around him; soon there were twenty tons of muscle and sinew at work against the base of the pile of rock. The pinnacle shuddered, and then it gave a heave and began to move.

Bazil and Alsebra were alerted by a shrieking from the dragonboys, and they dodged sideways, feet digging in the ash for purchase.

Too late, the cataphract saw its doom and began to step

backward. The dragons were clear, the sorcerer gave a scream of hate, and the pinnacle toppled and fell directly upon the cataphract.

The great rocks crushed the cataphragm, flattening the helmet, knocking the giant's sword from its hand, and driving it downslope. The boulders bounded on, one tumbling over and over just above the sorcerer himself. Indeed, his servant was plucked from his horse and destroyed utterly by another smaller boulder.

The great rocks from the top of the pinnacle bounced down the volcano's side and then soared off the edge of the upper fissure and rained down to smash into the castle below.

There was a tremendous thud, and a tower collapsed in ruin. Sections of a high wall slid down in clouds of dust. Screams of fear rose up from the ruins.

The sorcerer fled from them, riding hunched over down into the cloud of smoke and dust that billowed up from the ruined gates.

There was a third pinnacle nearby that could be toppled onto the castle. It was larger than the first two, and taller, and correspondingly heavier. They studied it for a moment, and Dragoneer Feens and Manuel hit on the solution at the same time. There was a wide gap between two segments near the bottom. If they could find a wedge-shaped rock, they might lever the whole thing over.

By good fortune there was a sarsen of roughly the right shape not fifty yards away, lying where it had fallen from the volcano's mouth.

The Purple Green, Chektor, and the young brasshide Finwey picked it up and lugged it across. In shape, it was like a wedge of pie. With the aid of the others, they fitted it into the gap near the bottom of the great stack of lava blocks.

Then all the dragons put their weight on the rock and heaved it down.

The pinnacle shook all the way to the top. And then the wedge broke at the narrow end.

The dragons sprawled out on the ash with loud curses.

After a moment they got back to their feet, picked up what was left of the rock wedge, and shoved it back into place. In fact, it was improved by losing the first couple of feet. What was left was thicker and stronger.

Once again they heaved on it, and the pinnacle shook. They pulled down with every ounce in their huge bodies and slowly the pinnacle began to move. Creeping up by inches on one side. Dust and powder began to fly from the downslope side. Finally, there came a sharp cracking report, and then the pinnacle teetered for a moment, a slab slid off the top, and then the rest fell. Huge blocks of rock bounced down the slope, bounded out into the air, and slammed down into the castle.

A cloud of smoke arose from the ruins. The castle was practically leveled.

The men that had been enslaved by the sorcerer cried out in joy at being released. They ran up and prostrated themselves before the dragons and dragonboys. A few were survivors abducted from the fleet.

"Saved. We're saved, shipmates . . ."

Another building collapsed in the castle with a roar of sliding stones and timbers. The smoke was getting thicker. And then a batrukh flew from the outermost tower, where the gate to the rookery of those fell creatures made a dark mouth. On the batrukh's shoulders flew a hunched-over figure. The batrukh gave a last cry of hatred and malice and flew into the north.

Wiliger awoke on the beach while they waited for the boats to come in and collect them. Alsebra was carrying him strapped across her shoulders. His sudden choking alerted her, so she released him and he sagged to the ground with a thud.

Wiliger remembered only the beginning of the fight. The approaching metal monster, then everything blanked out.

"What happened?"

Jak told him the whole story. "You were hit by a tail, sir, been out cold ever since. We was worried about you."

Wiliger was mortified. He'd missed the glory. Getting slapped down by a tail was the dumbest thing a dragonboy could do. Wiliger knew this now, just as he knew how to avoid dragon-freeze. He'd missed the battle, and they'd defeated the sorcerer without him.

Wiliger felt despair warring in his heart with a strange hatred for his own dragonboys.

CHAPTER SIXTEEN

After escaping the grip of the sorcerer, the fleet had run down to the tropics on the northerly winds. At length, though, they had slowed as they reached the doldrums. Weeks went by.

The tropic waters stretched still and vaporous around the becalmed fleet. Sails flapped uselessly against the masts. The heat beat down like a living thing determined to oppress all beneath it, the dragons were morose, the freshwater had become fetid, and despair was once again on the rise.

On all sides warm mists arose from green sea. The other ships of the fleet appeared like ghosts occasionally glimpsed through the murk. In such humidity men sweated simply standing still, but the water had to be strictly rationed; there'd been no real rain for weeks, and they were dependent on the supplies brought from home, which had grown sour and full of bugs after so long in casks.

The heat had laid Dragon Leader Wiliger low. He was in the surgeon's section, receiving treatment for severe depression.

For this the dragonboys of the 109th were extremely grateful. Since his less-than-noble showing in the fight on the sorcerer's isle, Wiliger had been a shrewish, waspy, demanding presence, making their lives hell. Inspections had become even more frequent, and endless hours of punishment details had to be worked off as a result of the slightest infraction.

Having Wiliger off their backs was about the only merciful thing in life, however. They'd been in the doldrums for weeks, endless days of heat and humidity with little in the way of a breeze and hardly any forward way on the ships. Sometimes the fleet sat in the same spot for days on end, until the foulness in the waters caused by thousands of men drove the captains to let down boats and order the ships towed to cleaner water.

The dragons were snappish and difficult to work with. Some still had wounds from the fighting on the isle, and their dressings had to be changed every few hours and fresh disinfectant applied. They did not enjoy this process and complained bitterly. Dragonboys knew better than to reply to any of it, however. Dragonboys knew that this was a time for them to keep low profiles and to share their own feelings only with each other.

On board the *Barley* conditions were tense. Another soldier was flogged for attempted rape. This time it was worse in that the evidence was unclear and the only witness was a good friend of the purported victim. The accused claimed innocence right up to and through his lashes. After this there was outright hatred between some of the soldiers and some of the crew.

Meanwhile everyone was aware of a growing level of anxiety among the generals and admirals. There were almost daily meetings in Admiral Cranx's fine stateroom.

The doldrums were particularly tricky at this time of year, deep winter in the northern part of the world. They had hardly moved in weeks, and the water situation was getting bad. The witch Endysia had tried several weather spells. Her drum could be heard sounding every morning as she tried to summon clouds. Clouds came, to be sure, but they brought no rain, only an oppressive greyness that added to the heat and humidity, and made the conditions perfectly hellish.

The day wore on, much the same as those before it, and as far as anyone could tell all those to come. The heat and oppressiveness seemed limitless.

In the afternoon Relkin finished fetching water for the dragon and took a rest on the foredeck, sitting with little Jak and Manuel. Their conversation centered around the mysteries of the continent of Eigo, to which they were bound. Eigo was a fabulous place, little known in the Argonath beyond legends of people with black skins and enormous monsters that lived in the ancient jungles of the deep interior.

Manuel knew a little more than most, having studied at the academy before passing exams to become a dragoneer.

"I think it will be strange to see nothing but people burned black by the heat of the sun," said little Jak.

"You'll get used to it." Relkin had seen plenty of dark-skinned folk in Ourdh and had grown accustomed to it easily enough.

Jak giggled. "I wonder what the women will be like."

Relkin punched him on the shoulder. "That kind of thinking will definitely get you in trouble, boy!"

"Do you think we'll be just as strange to them, all pale except where the sun's been at us? Maybe they will be afraid of us. Maybe they will want to catch us and put us in cages to look at."

"Maybe they will," said Manuel, "which would be a good reason for dragonboys to stick close to camp."

"But what if they really like us? What if we're like, sort of fabulous and wonderful to them, since they've never seen anything like us? Now, if that's the case, then their women will definitely be interested in us!"

"Wiliger will really come down on you if he finds you out of camp without a pass."

"Oh, Manuel, you always want to do everything just by the book."

"You know something, Jak, you're gonna find that the local traditions can sometimes get in the way of hell-raising."

"Relkin's right, Jak," said Manuel. "The folk of Eigo are fierce, and the men are legendary for their jealousy."

"All right, all right, I'll do nothing but march and fight and eat and sleep, but you have to promise me you'll do the same."

Relkin was usually touchy about his reputation as the great lover in the regiment, what with the Princess of Ourdh and his famous romance with Eilsa Ranardaughter of Clan Wattel. On this occasion he simply grinned knowingly at the younger boy.

Manuel knew better, of course.

"You won't have time for chasing local women, anyway. I heard that soon as we land, we reembark on riverboats and head upstream. No time to be wasted, every moment is precious and so on."

Jak grimaced. "I'm tired of boats. Real tired of this boat."

"Our duty is to serve, doesn't matter where they send us."

That sent Jak onto his other favorite line of thinking.

"I heard that we're going right to the deep interior. There's a sea inside the continent."

Manuel nodded. "We're going to the waters of the Nub as

it's called. The great Nub. I think it means 'water' in the Kraheen language."

"There are sea monsters there."

"So the legends say."

"I was wondering if they could be related to wyverns. Wyverns are sort of sea monsters if you see what I mean."

Manuel was nodding agreement. "Some teachers believe that sea monsters are the ancestors of the wyvern dragons."

The talk of wyverns as sea monsters made Relkin nervous. His trust in his own dragon had been shaken by the strange affair of the sternfish. What had Bazil been thinking of? Or had he just not thought of the consequences if he'd been caught? He gazed off into the murk toward the lumpy mass of *Potato* in the mists.

He sucked in a breath. The haze was twisting around *Potato,* and quite suddenly he noticed that her topmost sails were filling.

Then the first hint of the breeze reached them, and the enormous sails of *Barley* suddenly twitched and rattled.

"A wind!" breathed Jak.

"I think so," said Relkin, who saw the mists clearing rapidly in the direction of *Potato.*

"Well," said Manuel, "maybe we really will get to Eigo after all."

The slight breeze blossomed for a few minutes and then faded somewhat for a while, but then it strengthened again and grew steadily stronger. The mists evaporated, and the flat sea rippled and then broke into waves. Within an hour a strange chop had developed that sent shudders through the big ships. The breeze had become a wind, rising steadily and coming directly out of the east.

Larger waves now appeared, rolling in from the east as well and lifting the sterns of the white ships as they came.

The crew muttered together while Captain Olinas spent much of the time up in the mizzenmast crosstrees with spy-glass in hand investigating the eastern horizon.

The wind shifted slightly, until it was coming from the southeast and now it became gustier, shrieking through the rigging for a few minutes and then dying back to a gentler breeze.

The waves continued to roll in, real ocean combers now, with whitecaps breaking away into the distance. The feel of the sea had changed almost incredibly; now there was something large and ominous about its movements.

By nightfall, the wind had grown to a steady roar, and the ships were racing westward under a few scraps of canvas amid whitecapped combers that came rolling in, lifting the ships by the stern and then buoying them up atop a thirty- or forty-foot cliff of seawater before leaving them behind in the trough, enclosed on all sides by water.

Seasickness soon returned to the weaker members of the legions. Dragon Leader Wiliger did not appear, and dragon-boys, who were mostly resistant to seasickness now, spent as much time as possible on the foredeck watching the wild seas rising and falling.

The moon arose, visible through bands of clouds that were moving very rapidly north, a distinctly different direction from the sea-level wind, which still came out of the east.

However, this soon changed, and the captain ordered a re-setting of sail as the wind veered steadily to come almost directly out of the south. It strengthened again, and sea froth and spray flew over the decks.

Captain Olinas conferred with Admiral Cranx briefly. Then messages were sent by lamplight to *Potato* and *Oat*, which were now the only ships in sight. They then passed on the messages to the ships now over the horizon. Olinas expected that they might be on the outer fringes of a hurricane during the night. She believed that the hurricane was not going to pass over them but was trending northward and would soon turn and head northeast, away from them and off toward Cape Hazard and the Gulf of Ourdh.

Her reasons for this belief concerned the motions of clouds, winds, and waves, and basically centered on her long and extensive experience of the world's oceans.

All ships were to maintain a westerly course. If any were blown off course during the coming onslaught, they were to head for the Watering Isle, which lay about three hundred miles west of their position. The fleet would rendezvous there as soon as possible.

As the night watches wore on, the seas grew mountainous and the winds intensified until vicious squalls broke out in the early morning that caused the white ships to heel over in the water as they struggled with shifting wind directions and cross-cutting waves.

Barley rose and fell with a sickening, jagged motion during these periods that disturbed even such sound sleepers as dragonboys, who found their hammocks tossed violently around. Only dragons slept through it all undisturbed.

Relkin came on deck shortly after dawn and found that the ship was dancing up and down the flanks of enormous waves, while huge packets of spray flew right across the ship's deck at head height. The clouds were gone, however, and the sun shone brightly. When he looked aft, he saw in the distance a mountain of cloud, a vast swirling wall that stretched across the edge of the eastern horizon.

A mile astern rode old *Potato* and beyond her could be seen the sails of *Oat*. To the south Relkin saw *Sugar* and a smaller vessel that he could not identify. He asked a sailor with whom he had good relations and was informed that the smaller ship was the frigate *Flute* and that the fleet was all accounted for, just somewhat spread out across the ocean. Furthermore, since the hurricane had shifted north and east, they had merely been clipped by the outside edge of the storm and were now moving away from it rapidly. The captain had gone to bed long since, and was sleeping soundly.

All that day they continued to sail westward under strong winds from the east that very gradually abated through the afternoon.

The final hour of daylight had begun when a shout from the maintops informed Captain Olinas that *Flute* was in sight to the northwest and had reported sighting land.

In moments *Barley* was trimming sails and shifting her course to the north and east.

CHAPTER SEVENTEEN

The Watering Isle was another mid-ocean volcanic peak, this time with twin cones, both heavily eroded, since their inner fires had long since burned out. A wide coral reef ringed the island, which supported a lush forest and a small population of fisherfolk.

The fleet formed a line after *Flute* had entered the lagoon and pronounced it safe, and led by *Barley*, the white ships sailed carefully through the broad S-shaped channel that led into the inner lagoon.

Once inside they cast their anchors while boats were sent ashore to convey greetings and presents to the native chiefs. Double-hulled canoes came out in great numbers to surround the white ships and proffer them fruit and drink. The natives were a people of large stature, with comely limbs and an attractive easygoing nature. Between them and the white ships, there had always been perfect amity. The mariners of Cunfshon had always paid for their water, and they had always behaved well toward the islanders. Nonetheless, legion commanders spoke to the legionaries before any set foot on the shore and warned them to adopt their best behavior. In particular, they were to leave the native women alone, and they were not to accept drinks of *pulji,* a seductive narcotic that was popular throughout the Southern Hemisphere of Ryetelth. The natives were used to this dream-inducing drink, but it could send those unused to it into wild, terrified seizures in which they thought they were being chewed by insects or pursued by men with worm-ridden faces. Any legionaries who transgressed these rules would face the lash.

Again and again the point was made that this was to be a brief and businesslike visit. They would ship water and greenstuffs, and then they would be gone. They had lost precious time in the doldrums, and Admiral Cranx was determined to try and make it up now that they were on the final leg of the voyage.

At the same time, it was realized by the commanders that all the men deserved a break ashore and a chance to relax on the warm coral sand that made up the inner beach. Parties of one hundred at a time were sent ashore, under the strict eye of sergeants and lieutenants, who were to arrest anyone who got out of line.

Eventually even dragonboys got to stretch their legs ashore when they went with their dragons to draw water.

The spring flowed into a pool of freshwater that was a place of wild floral beauty. Massive gum trees were carpeted with white and pink orchids while enormous magenta blossoms of the scarlet creeper gave off an exotic, overripe scent. Tall graceful palms waved in the breeze, and the pool itself lay over a bed of pure white coral sand.

The dragons sang as they marched up the little stream and happily plunged into the freshwater pool when they reached it. A stream ran from the pool down into a lagoon, from which a flotilla of boats and cutters were bringing the ships' empty water barrels up the stream. They could not enter the pool itself because of a bar of rock and sand at the entrance.

The dragons' job was to push the empty barrels across the pool and position them beneath the flowing spring to fill them. Then they were to heave the full barrels back to the cutters and help load them.

The dragons enjoyed the cold freshwater after the heat and humidity of the tropics. They happily sloshed back and forth, gathering in fours to heave the big ones back into the ship's cutters.

A pair of dragons could do the work of ten or twenty men, and they soon drew a crowd of awed and excited natives. The islanders had never seen Argonathi wyverns before, although they had heard many tales and legends.

A constant line of people stayed around the pool just to watch the wyverns at work. The dragons were used to it. Humans liked to gawk and stand around doing as little as possible. Meanwhile there was plenty to be done. Each of the big ships carried hundreds of tons of drinking water, and refilling all those barrels took time. The process would take several days to complete.

They worked in two-hour shifts in the pool, followed by big meals of stirabout and akh. Dragonboys peeled pineap-

ples for the big wyverns, who ate them by the handful like
grapes. At night they camped onshore, as did a few hundred
trusted legionaries. Mindful of the great prohibition against
swimming in the ocean, the dragons camped near the pool
under the flowing spring so as to be near freshwater and
well away from the temptations of the lagoon.

Dragonboys spent the day gathering brush and firewood
and purchasing meal and fresh fish from the islanders. Having worked hard all day, the dragons ate like titans and
drank kegs of the native "beer," which was fermented from
the *poolki,* a fruit with furry skin and pale green flesh.
Though it didn't suit the dragons as much as Argonathi ale,
they drank it happily enough before they burst into song.

The native folk were stunned by this nighttime uproar.
There were a dozen great campfires blazing on the strand
and upward of a hundred great monsters drinking *poolki* and
roaring together. The sound could be heard right across the
island, and people came out of their homes and stared up
into the night as they heard the great voices in and out of
harmony.

After a while the dragons finished and laid themselves
contentedly out on the sand beneath the stars. They were
quite unaware of the sensation they had caused.

A group of natives approached Dragon Leader Wiliger
where he sat by a small fire. The squadron's pennant flew
from a pole beside his tent, so the natives had deduced that
he was the commander of this particular stretch.

They spoke a crude Verio, but by dint of repetitions and
the use of hand signals conveyed their meaning clearly.

"What you want for one of these dragons? We like to buy
one, or maybe more if they cheap enough."

Wiliger was stunned at first, then he broke into a laugh.

"No, no, my friends, dragons are not for sale."

The native men stared at one another and then back at
Wiliger.

"Maybe you make gift of dragon, then, for friendship with
us island people."

Again Wiliger was forced to disappoint the native men,
who stood around, talking among themselves, and examining the sleeping dragons for quite some time.

Wiliger found this all very amusing and passed it on to the
dragonboys, who did not. With more elaborate sign language, Wiliger tried to explain to the natives that the drag-

ons were soldiers for the Empire of the Rose, as much people in their way as the men and boys, and that when they were aroused they were a terrifying foe.

It was unclear how much of all this was absorbed by the islanders, who were slow to disperse.

The dragonboys did not pass on this insulting story to their charges, who remained sound asleep throughout. The old saying that "a sleeping dragon is best left undisturbed" never seemed more appropriate. However, a watch was posted thereafter.

Relkin drew the first watch, and shinned up one of the palm trees to the thick mass of fronds at the top. The fronds were sharp-edged, but by spreading a piece of matting from the barrel boats, he was able to sit there quite comfortably and enjoy a view of the lagoon with the lights of the great ships at anchor.

The dragons lay spread out in a row of great, snoring shadows on the white sand. All was perfectly still, but for the breeze that came down from the volcanoes bearing a scent of the forest: dank, fruity, and mysterious.

He began to think wistfully of Eilsa Ranardaughter. How much better it would be if she was there with him! Then this exotic and wonderful scene would be complete.

He watched the ships, moored in a long line out in the grand lagoon. Each one of those great white shapes, so ghostly and pale under the moonlight, was a floating world of its own, complete with characters of every type and class. For months now *Barley* had been his entire world, with *Potato* and *Sugar* as nearby, other worlds that might be seen with a telescope but never spoken to. How far away the ships seemed, and so small. He mused on the perception of things for a while. Aboard the *Barley,* the tyranny of Dragon Leader Wiliger became an oppressive center of the universe. From up on the palm tree, it all seemed far away and unimportant.

He would put up with Wiliger and survive him. They had withstood Dragon Leader Turrent and ultimately won him over. It had taken a while but Turrent had mellowed, and the 109th dragonboys had grown much better about such things as cap badges. They would not break down under Wiliger's tyranny.

Relkin knew that Wiliger was under some great stress. His mood swung wildly, and his behavior was unpredictable.

With the dragonboys, Wiliger was under the misapprehension that reading to them from his favorite tomes was going to foster a sense of warmth and appreciation for him.

Alas, Chesler Renkandimo's treatise on *Care of the Wyvern Dragon* was all nonsense as far as dragonboys were concerned. Renkandimo was much concerned with the dragon's soul and believed it to be associated with ocean and rock and the eternal conflict between them. Human souls were linked to air and fire. Dragons could not ascend to the heavens reserved for humans but were instead taken to the red star Zebulpator. Dragons therefore were best treated with red substances; oil of rosewood, turmeric, saffron, and carrot balm were recommended for skin wounds and abrasions.

Dragonboys dismissed all this as airy-fairy absurdity. What worked on wounds and cuts was Old Sugustus's disinfectant.

Even worse were those times that Wiliger read from the expensive little leather volume he carried of Bundt, Bunge, and Bunsome on *Military Practice*. These worthies were insufferable and extremely boring. They exalted spirit and élan above all else, and exhorted their readers to sacrifice life itself, for the slightest aspect of any campaign.

Such sessions with their leader were difficult, and confined aboard the ship, they had been much harder to avoid than would have been the case even in a fort, much less a campaign up-country.

Their distaste for these empty exercises communicated itself to Wiliger on some level, and he was always ill-tempered after them. However, he continued to give these readings, as if he just had to bang enough Chesler Renkandimo into their brains and they would come around and love him and become the perfect dragonboys he hoped they would be.

Relkin sighed. They all sensed that Wiliger was not inherently malicious, simply unstable. He might be as brave as a lion one moment and completely terrified the next. Under the stress of combat, Wiliger had performed modestly enough. However, it had to be remembered that in the crisis, he had been willing to listen to mere dragonboys and to take heed from their warnings. This gave Relkin hope. As far as Relkin understood, a good fighting commander had to have the iron in the soul that all combat veterans possessed. It gave them a phlegmatic dourness in battle. No matter what horror passed before their eyes, they continued to fight and to execute their commands.

Relkin hoped that as Wiliger hardened, he would relax his grip and grow into the role of a real dragon leader.

In the meantime they would just have to endure.

He sighed again. If only Eilsa were with them, somehow. The way it had been in the campaign in Arneis. To know that she was with them would have made it easy to put up with any amount of grief and stupidity from Wiliger.

Alas, there were years to go before he could retire. If he lived through the upcoming campaign. If he made it through the next battle. There were always too many ifs.

Then he contemplated his retirement plans, and for a moment felt a familiar warm glow. He had constructed a pleasant future for himself.

He and the dragon would retire together, take their allotted free land, one hundred acres on the bottomlands of the River Kalens in eastern Kenor. Eilsa's Clan Wattel would lie just to the south.

He and Baz had marched all over that land, and they'd seen some places with good soil that were still completely wild. The area had poor riverine communications because of the rapids on the Bur River. However, the rapids downstream from the Kalens could eventually be overcome by the construction of a system of imperial chutes, like that he had seen in action on the Keshon breaks. In the meantime, they would sell their grain to the Wattels, who grew oats and rye on their upland fells but often had short supplies in deep winter.

Once they'd cleared some land, he and Baz would grow wheat and barley and root vegetables. They'd plant orchards and vineyards, too, and sell all their surplus to the Wattels.

To help them clear the land, they would buy a string of horses in Kohon and bring them over the plateau and down the Bur to the Kalens country.

Relkin and Eilsa would be wed, and they would raise a family. Bazil would win the right to fertilize eggs. That would mean they would have to make a pilgrimage back to the village of Quosh in the Blue Stone country. That would be some day when the famous broketail dragon came home to the village of his birth. There would be such competition for the chance to raise one of the young scions that Bazil would father.

By then Relkin would be a father. What would that be
like? He shrugged inwardly. Was he really ready for that?
Ready to be responsible for children of his own? He wasn't
sure. Not just yet. He'd seen what it had done to his friend
Lagdalen of the Tarcho. She had become such a serious person. It felt as if she had aged a decade or two, even though
she was still just a little older than he was.

Relkin felt uncomfortable at the thought of settling down
for a moment. He loved this roving life. He wanted to see
the world. He didn't want to be cooped up on some farm in
the backwoods.

He giggled. He was getting ahead of himself here. He was
going to see a lot more of the world before he had any
chance at all for settling down.

He prayed that Eilsa would not change her mind; five
years seemed incredibly long when he thought about it. It
made him recall with a start that five years before he'd been
an unknown dragonboy in the village of Quosh, still struggling with his lessons. Five years could be a long time; there
would be many changes in that span of time.

Eilsa Ranardaughter would be under a lot of pressure to
forget the dragonboy and marry someone of importance
within the Clan Wattel. Could she possibly hold out against
that pressure?

Relkin agonized and then dismissed such thinking. Whatever would come would come, and if old Caymo, and the
Great Mother, wished it, then he would be wed to Eilsa and
they would live together as he envisaged it.

His watch ended with nothing to report, and he climbed
out of the tree, slipped into his blanket, and slept like a stone
until awoken by the reveille one hour after the dawn.

The dragons rose, stretched, and watered themselves.
Then they ate enormous breakfasts and resumed their work.
They were reaching the end of the job, and it was announced
that they could rest for the remainder of the day. The fleet
would sail on the evening tide.

The last casks were filled before noon, and they broke for
lunch. Afterward some dragons slept happily in the sun or
swam lazily in the pool.

The dragonboys on the other hand spread out and explored the island. What trouble could they possibly get into
in one afternoon?

CHAPTER EIGHTEEN

Under the inspiration of the reborn Prophet, the Kraheen people arose like a cloud of dense smoke above a forest fire. Kraheen armies, reorganized by General Kreegsbrok, were dispatched to the north and east. The impact was swift. The Kraheen had abandoned the historic style of combat, in which they threw javelins from a distance and achieved victory solely by outnumbering an opponent. Instead, they now closed for a decision and fought with stabbing spears. This proved devastating to all the neighboring tribes, and soon there were legions of captives marching into slavery in the Kraheen lands.

Under Kreegsbrok's guidance, the entire basis of the Kraheen economy shifted to war. The Kraheen, as foretold by the Prophet, became a caste of warriors. Captive slaves worked their fields and took care of all mundane tasks. The Kraheen, long a downtrodden folk, accepted the new order with enthusiasm. Their armies became a terror to the rest of the continent of Eigo.

In the north, they menaced the advanced states of the Bakan. In the east, they threatened the Impalo kingdoms and even the empire of Og Bogon. Other forces were sent to the western shores to spread the message of the Prophet to the Kraheen sister peoples that dwelled there. Mass conversions became the norm. The ancient worship of the gods of Fire and Stone was replaced with the creed of "He Who Must."

An avalanche had been let loose among the unsophisticated peoples of the inland basin of Eigo, and with the creed of the Prophet on their tongues, new armies were on the march in every direction, bringing devastation and ferment in their wake.

The Great One was well pleased at first. His servants were making progress on the Isle of the Bone. All around the inland sea, the work of the Prophet was building armies. In the meantime, as expected, the enemy had discovered what he was up to and had launched an expedition to Eigo. The hags had responded with a swiftness that was both gratifying and unsettling. Heruta Skash Gzug knew that the hags understood how dire was the threat. They took him seriously. They had been forced to give him respect. This made him smile. On the other hand the thought that two full legions backed by thousands of other troops from the advanced parts of the world were on their way to snuff out his experiment raised a frisson of concern in his mind.

Heruta Skash Gzug had learned the hard way that it was unwise to underestimate the forces of that eastern empire. It was those accursed dragons! But for them, the Masters would long ago have achieved dominion over Ryetelth.

Still, there were ways to slow the enemy. Heruta Skash Gzug had sent emissaries to the ancient Sorcerer of the Black Isle, Gadjung, who had promised his aid.

In addition, a massive Kraheen army had been dispatched over the Ramparts of the Sun to take war against the Bogoni, who were the natural allies in eastern Eigo of the Empire of the Rose.

And yet Heruta Skash Gzug felt uneasy. He called on his servants to accelerate their efforts. On the Isle of the Bone, they worked feverishly to master the art of casting iron and forging steel. It was difficult work, dependent on the fiery furnace in the heart of a volcano. Currently the volcano was semi-quiescent. The heat was barely enough for making steel. Progress had slowed.

The Master consoled himself with the success of his other weapon, the Prophet. He summoned Kreegsbrok for regular reports. Kreegsbrok sensed the Master's mood and doctored his reports accordingly. There were disturbing aspects of the Prophet's eerie new life, but Kreegsbrok knew that the Master did not want to hear about these things. He wanted to hear good news. He wanted this very badly. Kreegsbrok had learned that it was unwise to personally bring bad news to the Great Ones.

Still, when Kreegsbrok was deposited back on the battlement of the palace of the Prophet and the batrukh flew away, he was left with the dilemma of how to deal with the increasingly strange and terrible thing they called "He Who Must."

The problem was the Prophet's thirst for killing, as powerful as a young man's lust for women. If denied too long, the Prophet would become dangerous, capable of attacking anyone around it, quite suddenly, without warning.

The first time it had slain Kreegsbrok's servant, Golse, whipping Kreegsbrok's own dirk from his sheath and sinking it into poor old Golse's back.

Kreegsbrok had been forced to bring it slaves for slaughter. Nothing else would do. It could no longer be satisfied with the prisoners that it executed for the crowds. Worse, the more it killed, the more it wished to. It would go on for hours, one after the other. A knife thrust into the throat of a helpless man, bound at wrist and ankle, the deep gouge for the voice box, the fountain of blood. The thing gave out hot gasps of pleasure as the blood smeared its body. Quivering with the pleasure of death, it would rip out the still-beating heart, to squeeze the blood into its upturned mouth as if it were some obscene fruit. Then the energy would fade, the excitement would cool. There would come a shiver, a shake of the head sending bloody drops spattering. The knife would come up again, and it would advance on the next victim.

Kreegsbrok had done his utmost to keep it a secret. It would not do for the Kraheen to learn of this. Their faith in their Prophet must remain unsullied and pure. The knowledge that "He Who Must" was, in fact, "He Who Must Kill" would dampen their ardor for the cause.

Accordingly he had four specially trained guards who disposed of the bodies. This had become a difficult proposition. At first they'd dumped them in the sea, but, of course, pieces floated to shore. Burial was difficult. The Kraheen traditionally burned their dead and buried only ashes. To sequester a large enough piece of land for burial and to keep inquisitive souls away was possible, but it would stir rumors and eventually the truth would leak out.

Then Gulbuddin, his second in command, told Kreegsbrok of the dungeon below the palace of the Prophet. Kreegsbrok investigated and discovered large rooms once used to torture apostates of the cult of the God of Stone. Into these rooms the guards stuffed bodies.

They quickly filled. A stench began to rise from the dead. Kreegsbrok was forced to act again. He commissioned some of the barges used in ferrying goods to the Isle of the Bone

and late at night used a team of slaves to haul the corpses
from the vault and pack them into the barges. Then the
barges made the journey to the Isle of the Bone. The bodies
were moved on carts up the slopes of the volcano and
thrown into the main crater. When the noisome task was
done, Kreegsbrok and the four guards slew the slaves and
threw them after their horrid cargo.

When the barges docked at the palace later that night,
Kreegsbrok found Gulbuddin waiting.

"So you have brought back my barges. I wonder what
you've been up to with them."

"You don't want to know," said Kreegsbrok, who had labored all night and was sick to death of the business.

"Well, I have a cargo that must be shipped to the Bone today. We've dug up every stable in this stinking country. All
the dirt where horses have pissed for years. I've got twenty
cartloads ready."

Kreegsbrok's forehead furrowed.

"The Great One moves in mysterious ways," he said.

"That He does. But you tell me what you think He wants
twenty cartloads of piss stinking dirt for."

"Maybe he is raising a new monster that eats it. You remember the ogres?"

Gulbuddin shuddered. "Damned things ran amok. One of
them ate my friend Kinradrik. Bit his head off just as you
please."

Kreegsbrok laughed. "I saw one once grab someone's
horse and eat that! Alive, too."

"That's disgusting."

Kreegsbrok laughed some more, but agreed.

"How goes it with the Prophet?" said Gulbuddin.

"To be truthful, I am worried. It has grown a little strange,
shall we say. Mostly it sleeps, but when it awakes, aiee."
Kreegsbrok spat eloquently.

"It was strange from the beginning. A dead thing imbued
with a mockery of life."

"Yet it serves our Master well."

Gulbuddin nodded. "Of course, of course."

"It says food has no interest for it."

"Yet it must eat if it lives, surely?"

"Aye, it must eat, but it does not want to live."

Kreegsbrok handed over the barges and went to look in on
the prophet. "He Who Must" was asleep, lying prone on its

back with its mouth open. It would stay that way until he awoke it. Which was a blessing. Once awake it would soon turn to its obsession and demand slaves to kill.

Kreegsbrok tiptoed away nonetheless and repaired to his own chamber. He left two guards on while the others slept. They had had a long night of it. As he composed himself for sleep, he wondered briefly what the Master would want with twenty cartloads of stable dirt.

CHAPTER NINETEEN

Bazil lay quietly in the sun with his legs and tail immersed in the cold, clear water. The difference in temperatures between the top and bottom half of his body was most pleasurable. Equally so was the mere fact of relaxation in the sun. There had been days of work with the barrels, hustling to and fro, and now they could rest.

The only thing he missed was a keg of good Argonath ale. After a hot morning's work a spot of ale, preferably two or three gallons' worth, would have gone down very well.

He turned over and rearranged himself. He'd lost some weight, and he could feel how taut and well toned his upper body had become. These days of simpleminded physical labor had been good for him. Even with regular exercise routines, the confinement of shipboard life inevitably reduced a dragon's fitness. Bazil fervently hoped the voyage would soon be over. He was tired of the crowding and the lack of room. He was also tired of the temptation of all that ocean water lapping around them. It would be better to be well removed from the smell of the ocean. It upset them all, except the Purple Green, of course, and Bazil knew better than most of them just why. At times he had to struggle against a great urge to leap overboard and return to the bosom of the ocean. When they were back on land again, that urge would disappear. They would exist within the military machine of men, and in that routine there was a mindless kind of comfort. They would march and drill and practice and eat. Eventually they would fight. Wyvern dragons enjoyed all of these things, especially food and fighting.

Furthermore, like the rest of the dragons, Bazil was intrigued by the rumors that they might meet with their very own legendary ancestors.

Eigo was the dark continent, a vast tropical landmass, in shape rather like a capital A with the top of the letter in the northern tropics and the equator bisecting the continent. Legends spoke of a vast inland sea in the heart of Eigo. This sea was called the Nub, (N-uh-b) of Eigo and was marked by very deep waters and active volcanoes.

In those strange waters, so the stories went, dwelled creatures long since lost in the rest of the world. Among these were animals like dragons, except that they lived their lives almost exclusively in the waters.

As the fleet drew closer to the coast of Eigo, so they heard more and more of these stories from both sailors and legionaries. Dragonboys had passed on many tidbits.

All of this had sparked a lot of discussion. In fact, it was what the 109th were talking about at that very moment.

Vlok had heard that the sea dragons of the Nub of Eigo had enormously extended necks and four flippers rather than limbs.

"How can these be the ancestors?" Vlok wanted to know.

"I don't think they are," said Alsebra. "I was told long ago that we came from a short-necked kind that lived in northern oceans."

"Can wyvern dragon interbreed with these long necks of the inland sea?" Roquil, the young leatherback, wanted to know.

"Ah, Roquil thinks of fertilizing the eggs of the ancestors," said Vlok with a chuckle.

"We all know that Vlok would rather eat their eggs," snorted the Purple Green in a crushing tone.

"In answer to the leatherback's question," said Alsebra, "probably not."

"But our kind can interbreed with the wild dragons; there are living examples."

Everyone knew that Roquil was talking about Bazil and the wild green dragoness known as High Wings. The young ones, Braner and Grener, had been winged and much like their mother. They now lived in the uttermost north where they haunted the migration trails of caribou and mammoths.

"True, but wild dragon and wyvern dragon share common ancestors. We are two kinds but of one blood."

"Yes, yes, of course.." There was a lot of nodding and several dragons shifted position around the pool.

"We are too different, then?"

"Yes."

A pity, but there it was: there'd be no point in fertilizing the eggs of these monsters of the sea.

Bazil listened with one part of his mind while with the other he thought fondly of his "family." They would be swooping down on polar bears no doubt. Wild dragons were immeasurably fierce.

Possibly too fierce, he mused. His own little ones had evinced very little affection for their male parent. Indeed, they had berated him for lacking wings. He chuckled, indulgently. They were wild and beautiful, just like their mother, but they were also his. Someday he would like to lie with the green dragoness again.

He felt a prod in the shoulder.

He rolled over. An alarmed man in the dress of the islanders, simple white tunic and scarlet headband, jumped back. Behind him were two others and a cart loaded with small barrels.

"Beg pardon, great and noble dragon, but we wish to honor you with this barrel of *pulji*. We have several more for your fellows."

"What is *pulji*?"

They rolled the little barrel toward him, broached it, poured out a cup, and held it up to him.

Bazil sniffed it cautiously. He was aware of other interested eyes.

"You try it," said Bazil. Vlok spilled it with his sniff. Another taste was poured for Alsebra.

"Some kind of beer?" said Vlok with hope in his heart.

"Yes, it is made in a similar way," said the men in the white tunics.

"That is good, very kind of you islander men." Vlok picked up a barrel and crushed one end to open it. He took long pulls at it while the others watched.

"Yes, very good," he said.

"Vlok has never been much of a judge of beer, if you ask this dragon," carped the Purple Green.

"What does a wild dragon know about beer? You drink polar bear blood instead."

Alsebra grunted with amusement.

All the dragons communed for a moment with small guilty voices of conscience, which they quickly overcame.

There were no dragonboys to say no. Dragon Leader

Wiliger was away visiting a native village. Soon they were all drinking the *pulji*.

It was peculiar stuff, not really beer at all and more like wine. It was sweet, and there was a smell both fruity and slightly rotten to it. Still it was wet and cool, and they made the best of it.

They lay back on the coral sands or splashed in the pool. An hour passed, and all of them were lost in dreams. The effect was subtle, but it mounted, and in time they all fell silent and just stared about themselves in an extremely self-absorbed and reflective mood.

The native men in white tunics had returned. Bazil found a pair standing beside him.

"Great monster, we have an offer for you." The Verio was accented but comprehensible.

Bazil blinked.

"We think you should stay on our island. We will feed you and give you much *pulji* and you will live here in the pool by the lagoon."

It sounded kind of nice.

"Yes, you will be good monsters, and we will keep you and send away the other men, and you will tell them that they cannot keep you against your will. You will be ours instead."

"We will be good masters," said another.

Masters? Bazil blinked again. He worked for no "masters" and that very name reeked of the Great Enemy that he fought as did all wyvern dragons.

"No," he said firmly. "I work for no masters, ever." He pulled himself to his feet.

"Oh, but you will, great dragon. Because we will give you *pulji* and you will want *pulji*."

Bazil blinked again. He did not actually care for the effects of *pulji*. It was hard to think clearly. It would be impossible to sing.

"Dragons could be very useful in building things for us," murmured one of the men.

The men were smiling. Bazil did not like their smiles.

"No. I am a fighting dragon, legion dragon. Too busy. Good day to you." He stepped away from them and headed for a stand of palm trees that marked a nearby farm midden. That farmer was getting a heroic addition to his manure pile from the presence of so many dragons. He trod down the muddy

track still muttering to himself about the men who wanted to be
"masters." He recalled the face of the Mesomaster by the Pit
beneath the dread city of Dzu. That was the way this dragon
would deal with any men who wished to be masters of dragons.
Dragons were volunteers in the legions.

He was on his way back to the pool, thoughts returned to
a fond anticipation of dinner, and was negotiating a place
where the path widened and crossed a little hidden stream
making the surface boggy, when he felt something brush his
head and then a net fell across his upper body. A rope was
pulled up from the mud across the front of his legs and he
was struck hard in the middle of the back.

With a startled cry, Bazil toppled forward and fell heavily.
An excited screaming went up, and he looked up to see a
dozen or more of the native men in their white tunics gathered around him. Several of them threw more nets over his
head, others had ropes and poles in their hands.

Bazil saw red. He lost control of his temper quite completely.
Perhaps the effects of the *pulji* even magnified the rage.

With an awesome roar, he surged up from the mud. The
men gave a collective shriek but held on to their ropes. He
fairly howled as he tore at the netting and ripped it to shreds.
Ropes snapped as he kicked his huge legs, and men, still
clinging to their ends, were tossed headlong into the undergrowth. Bazil seized hold of the long pole that had been
used to topple him. When two men tried to pull it back, he
lifted them bodily and flipped them into a tree.

Some fool jumped on his back and struck him with a club on
the back of the head. He reached around, seized the man by the
scruff of his neck, and tossed him into the center of the bog.

Now he swept the pole around him like a club and battered trees, men, rocks, and a small shepherd's hut, which
succumbed entirely.

The remaining men broke and ran with an enraged wyvern
dragon in hot pursuit, still flailing with that long pole. So
much for a leisurely afternoon by the pool!

Yet the dragons were not the only members of the 109th
fighting Marneri who were in desperate trouble.

Relkin had gone for a walk, scaling the slopes of the smaller
and older volcano called Rudwa until he reached a spectacular
viewing spot. From there he could see the fleet laid out in a
line on the lagoon and the offshore reef beaten by the surf.
There was a wonderful tropical quality to the light that fasci-

nated him for a while. Then he'd gone on down into the saddle between the volcanoes to the fertile heart of the island. He wandered past farmland where corn and pineapples grew, and ambled through groves of fruit trees.

The air was warm and soft, redolent with spicy aromas. He felt relaxed and quite at peace for once with only an occasional pang of wishing for Eilsa.

Crossing a little stone bridge over a stream, he found to his great surprise, Swane squatting by a far pool of water. Swane ducked his head into the pool and shook the water off with a gasp.

Swane looked up. Relkin saw that his upper lip was thickened and bloodied. There was a bump on his forehead and a scratch on his cheek that was still bleeding.

"Relkin, you gave me a start. Where'd you come from?"

"What happened?"

"We're in trouble, me and Jak."

"Yeah?"

"Especially me."

"What happened?"

Swane stood up and set off through a grove of trees. Relkin followed him to a glade and found little Jak sitting beside the prone form of Birjit, Swane's hefty admirer from the *Barley*. A pool of blood had stained the ground beneath her.

Jak was green in the face.

Relkin groaned softly, understanding at once what must have happened.

"She followed you?"

Jak nodded in numb agreement.

"Never saw her," said Swane. "Never thought to look really."

"And?"

"She attacked me when I went for a swim."

"What?"

"She told me I had to make love to her or she was gonna cut me. She had a big knife out, too."

Relkin cursed and spat on the ground.

"She wouldn't stop, Relkin, even when I got my own knife out."

Relkin had dropped beside the sailor. Poor woman with her crazy fixation on Swane, why couldn't she have left him alone? Why did it have to end like this?

She didn't seem to be breathing. He felt for her pulse.

Nothing. He cursed bitterly, they were really in for it now. Then he felt it, still coming, but weak.

"She's alive, you dolts! What are you standing there for? We've got to stop the bleeding."

Awakened from their shock, Swane and Jak helped Relkin to turn Birjit over. Swane's blade had gone deep, below the ribs, above the liver.

"I didn't want to do it, I kept telling her to stop."

"That's true, I was there," said Jak.

Relkin worked quickly and methodically to clean the wound with freshwater and to staunch the bleeding with a bandage made by tearing up Swane's shirt.

"You stabbed her, you lose your shirt," said Relkin with no attempt at humor.

"What are you acting so high and mighty for, Quoshite?"

"She's alive, so you two are probably not going to hang, but you think Wiliger will let you go without thirty lashes apiece? I don't."

"By the Hand, I don't think I could take that," whined Jak.

"I don't see that you've got much choice. They might hang you anyway. I'm sure the ship captains will ask for it."

"I didn't do anything," said Jak, appalled.

"I couldn't help it, Relkin," Swane chimed in. "It ain't fair to blame me. *She* attacked *me*."

"Help lift her, get this bandage around her chest and tie it tight. We have to stop the bleeding right now and carry her back. Jak, we need a couple of long pieces of wood as poles, and we need something to string between the wood to act as a stretcher. You understand me?"

Jak headed into the grove and shortly returned, accompanied by a native with a donkey and a small cart. The man had poor Verio, but Jak had managed to convince him to come by the simple expedient of giving him a silver coin and showing him another one and then walking in the direction he wished to go.

The dragonboys pointed to the wounded sailor and then pointed in the direction leading to the lagoon. The farmer understood soon enough, and they carefully lifted Birjit into the cart and walked beside it as it rumbled down the dusty road toward the sea. They trudged in silence, each wrapped up in gloomy thoughts of the near future.

CHAPTER TWENTY

Aboard the *Barley* the catastrophe proceeded to unfold in just as dreadful a fashion as Relkin's worst imaginings.

Dragon Leader Wiliger took one look at them, daubed with blood, Swane puffed and cut, and immediately decided that they were lying and had conspired to attack Birjit. He ordered all three dragonboys arrested and conveyed to the brig in chains. When he reported to Commander Voolward, he demanded field punishment of the third grade. That meant fifty lashes apiece, followed by castration and life imprisonment.

Voolward was stunned. Not only by the crime committed, but by Wiliger's passion over the matter and his determination to see the three youths destroyed.

Voolward decided to interview the dragonboys. The accused were entitled to some kind of trial, after all. And there was something not quite right in the dragon leader's voice, something that hinted of malice and even hysteria.

The dragonboys told another story altogether. It sounded preposterous. The sailor jumping on a dragonboy and demanding sexual favors? Women just didn't do such things. Yet there was something open and honest in these young men and their vehemence when they insisted that they had not tried to rape the woman.

The surgeon's report gave their story a shade of corroboration. Only one boy had evidence of a fight. The others merely had the sailor's blood on them. There was no evidence of a sexual attack on the sailor.

They'd brought her back themselves and admitted to having stabbed her. Wiliger hadn't mentioned this, and the omission chilled Commander Voolward. Surely if these boys had tried to rape her, they would have killed her and tried to blame the islanders. Voolward was deeply troubled. Dragons that lost their dragonboys would be difficult to work with, and in the coming campaign the dragons would have a vital role.

Meanwhile Birjit was unconscious while the surgeons and the Witch of Standing Endysia worked to save her life. They had issued a cautiously optimistic initial report. Relkin's bandage had been excellently dressed and had served well. The knife appeared to have missed the vital organs. The surgeon had sewn up the wound after it had been cleansed and treated with herbs and honey.

From other quarters there came unrelenting pressure. The captains of the fleet were insistent on immediate trial and punishment. The crews were aroused and angry; the situation could become disastrous at any moment if there was another clash. An all-out battle between crew and legionaries was possible. Unless they saw these oversexed dragonboys swinging from the yardarm, they would not rest.

Voolward issued an order for a court-martial. He also issued a statement declaring that until Birjit was able to testify, the court-martial would not take place. Evidence would be gathered in the meantime.

Then came another urgent message. Voolward hurried to Admiral Cranx's cabin; there he discovered that an ugly situation had developed onshore. A native village had been half destroyed by intoxicated dragons. The villagers were hopping mad, and demanding punishment for the dragons and restitution of the village.

Cranx reminded Voolward that relations with the islanders were of great importance to the Empire of the Rose and were particularly important to their own mission in Eigo. Relief ships and supply convoys would all pass this way and require freshwater. To turn the island hostile would be a terrible mistake.

The latest word was that the dragons were still in an uproar, armed with trees they'd torn down to use as clubs and standing in the ruins of the village defying the villagers to return.

The dragons had also announced that they would only communicate with their dragonboys.

"Which dragons are these?" said Voolward with a sinking heart.

"Dragonboys Swane, Relkin, and Jak of the 109th Marneri are mentioned in particular. Along with Manuel and Roos."

"How many dragons altogether?"

"As far as we can tell, the only dragons involved are from the 109th."

"It seems hard to believe. These are veteran wyverns. They've fought in so many campaigns for the empire."

"The Broketail has been in trouble before, you must admit. And the wild dragon is a problem and always has been, since it was first taken in."

Voolward sighed. The admiral had been fed some pretty old gossip. These notions were stale now.

"The wild dragon fought heroically at the Battle of Sprian's Ridge. There are songs about him, how he threw down ogres and killed them with his feet. Can you imagine?" Voolward grew quite passionate.

"As for the Broketail, what needs to be said? That dragon is a legend in his own lifetime. He single-handedly brought down the Doom of Tummuz Orgmeen."

Cranx remained unmoved. "I understand your concern for the dragons, but we really have to punish them for this. The islanders will not be satisfied with anything else."

"How are we to punish them? Are we to set other dragons against them?"

"The islanders suggest that we help them disable the beasts and then leave them here, to be beasts of burden for the natives."

Voolward turned ashen-faced with anger. In a tight voice he replied. "I will not agree to that, Admiral. It is against the basic code of contract between our kind and that of the wyverns. If they are to be punished, then they will receive the exact same treatment as any legionary. They will be arrested and confined until they can be brought before a court-martial."

Cranx pursed his lips for a moment.

"Well, some method of punishment must be chosen, and it must satisfy the islanders."

"You understand, Admiral, that those dragonboys are the very ones that the fleet is determined to see hanged for attempted rape of the sailor Birjit."

Cranx took a deep breath.

"I was aware of that, and I can allow no change in their status. As soon as they have persuaded their dragons to return to the fleet, they must be rearrested. The sailors will be satisfied with nothing less."

Left unspoken were other possibilities, including those of

a rebellion among dragon troops, the worst nightmare for any legion commander.

Voolward took a pinnace and five dragonboys from the 109th, and was rowed around to the beach in front of the village that had suffered dragon assault.

It was dark, but a large fire burned in the middle of the village, around which gathered wyverns clutching tree trunks and drinking from a looted barrel of real beer.

The monstrous great reptiles merely turned their heads to watch as the boat grounded and the commander, with two legionaries and the dragonboys, clambered out.

Voolward half wished that the damned trio of boys would abscond with their dragons and remove the problem from his jurisdiction in one swoop. They could be left to a subsequent fleet. It would weaken the force under his command, but it would save him from a terrible set of problems.

They approached the wyverns, Voolward and his men hanging back a little. In truth, these dragons did look a little wild. And they had done terrible damage to what had been a very solidly built village.

The native houses had been solid affairs of wood beams and wattle and daub walls. There were fireplaces of stone and brick floors. Assaulted by club-wielding dragons, many houses had taken on a shattered appearance with walls broken in and doors smashed to flinders.

The dragons had piled up flammable materials from the broken houses and ignited it from the coals in one of the native kitchens. In just an hour or two, they had done a century's worth of damage.

The dragonboys went up to their dragons. The wyverns were cool, they hardly spoke. Dragonboys murmured affectionate greetings and began the routine of checking their giant charges for damage. The dragons were so used to this that it calmed them immediately. The familiar bonds were reforged. Soon they were able to talk rationally once again.

Voolward waited. After a short while the dragonboys approached. Their reports only made things more complicated.

The dragons had a powerful complaint of their own. The incident had begun with the appearance of native men who gave the dragons small barrels of a beer called *pulji* that had a weird effect on them. Then groups of the islanders had tried to entice them to desert and stay on the island as pampered pets. When that had failed, they had thrown nets and ropes about the wyverns and tried to abduct them.

The dragons had fought off their attackers, but crazed by the *pulji,* they had gone a little too far with their retribution. They admitted as much, but they pleaded extreme provocation.

Now the fat was absolutely in the fire. The entire dragon force of the Argonath would be affected if these dragons were unjustly punished.

Voolward looked up at the sentry's cry and saw a delegation of the villagers approaching from the direction of the palm groves.

They were a well-fed lot, dressed in red linen and thick-soled sandals. They spoke poor Verio, except for one rotund member who had spent time in Kadein in his youth. They had many demands, but the prime one was that the dragons had forfeited their freedoms and should be left behind, in chains, to become the slaves of the islanders.

Voolward gave them the dragons' side of the story. The village elders were outraged and dismissed the charges with derisive insults. The dragons were mere animals and were not to be listened to in such things. It was a blasphemy against the old gods to even think such a thing.

The islanders would not listen to Voolward any further. Voolward signaled to the *Barley.* Another pinnace, this time bearing Admiral Cranx and six armed sailors, arrived.

Cranx and Voolward strolled some distance from the village elders to converse. The admiral felt that first consideration must be given to keeping the natives of the Watering Isle friendly. In vain, Voolward pointed out the need for keeping dragon morale high.

A disaster was shaping up when there came a sudden interruption. A high piping whistle sounded from the palm trees. The villagers turned expectantly. A column of native men wearing armor of coconut matting and shell filed out carrying spears and shields.

The villagers beamed and looked meaningfully at Cranx and Voolward.

Then more men marched out of the palms; these were bound at the wrist and neck, however, by stout cords and driven on by others in the coconut armor. The faces of the villagers dropped. Several began to edge away from the scene.

At the head of the procession came a magnificent speci-men, over six and a half feet tall, wearing red-lacquered ar-mor. He roared commands at both the villagers and his men. Those who had been edging away froze. The armored troops fanned out to surround the villagers.

Voolward and Cranx exchanged amazed glances; the drag-ons and dragonboys tensed. If the armored men tried to at-tack the dragons, there would be a slaughter. The dragons still held onto their crude clubs.

The bound men were brought up and made to lie face-down on the ground while the giant in red explained in ter-rible Verio that they were the guilty parties. They had been apprehended fleeing the scene and taken and questioned. Under careful questioning, their lies had been pierced through and they had confessed. The dragons' tale was con-firmed in virtually all aspects.

Voolward gave a huge sigh of relief. The dragons were ab-solved of blame. The very village that had conspired to drug them had been the one to take the brunt of their rage when they exploded.

With groans of woe, the village elders were rounded up by the men in armor. The leader in red announced that they would be whipped and then made to repair their village.

Further signals were sent to the fleet, and more boats came ashore to ferry dragons to the *Barley.* Once they were aboard, however, the three accused dragonboys were taken below and clapped in irons in the brig.

Admiral Cranx called a meeting of the captains of the fleet, and asked Voolward to attend. The captains demanded an immediate trial for attempted rape.

Voolward requested a delay, at least until Birjit should awake. As yet there had been no actual complaint from Birjit. The charge of rape had not even been made by the victim. After the meeting ended, inconclusively, the witch Endysia entered to confer with Admiral Cranx.

Later Cranx announced his solution. There would be im-mediate first-grade field punishment of twenty strokes apiece, to satisfy the fleet. Voolward protested, and Cranx accepted that the protest would be marked in the log, but the punishments would stand. Cranx admitted that it might even be an injustice, but still it must be done. Nothing else would satisfy the fleet.

CHAPTER TWENTY-ONE

The floggings were set for the forenoon of the next day.
Relkin, Swane, and Jak were chained up in a morose group
in the brig.

That evening Commander Voolward tried to get Dragon
Leader Wiliger to admit that he had jumped to conclusions
and made a hasty and perhaps unfair charge. Voolward felt
a growing sense of desperation as the hour of injustice approached. Wiliger would not budge, and Voolward came
close to losing his temper with the man. However, in such a
situation, Wiliger's opinion counted for a great deal, and
Voolward could not simply overturn it on his own.

When Wiliger was dismissed, Voolward considered carefully and then sent for the witch Endysia. At his request she
visited the dragonboys. She was reluctant, admitting to
Voolward that her sympathies lay with the female sailors for
what they had endured during the long voyage.

Voolward wrote an urgent message for General Steenhur
and dispatched it by boat at once.

Endysia approached her interview very cautiously. She
was aware that all three young men were veterans, allied to
experienced dragons, and one was a much decorated hero.
She was determined not to let such things sway her judgment, for she was in the middle of a very difficult political
situation. The fleet was aboil with rage, fed by weeks of
chafing confinement with all these young legionaries. There
was widespread resentment among the men against unfair
punishments being handed out without even the benefit of a
proper trial. Endysia was charged with expediting the voyage to Eigo. She felt the weight of the responsibility and
looked forward to being free of it. Sometimes she rued the
day that Lessis had walked into her chamber. The Grey Lady
was always a dangerous visitor, they said. Endysia came
from Cunfshon and perhaps erred in siding with the sailors.

in sympathy with her sex. To all Cunfshoni, rape and assault on women were crimes of a peculiar horror. The Isles were prosperously ruled by a matriarchal cult, after all. And their society was regarded as a model of the well-ruled state, with justice and equality for all beneath the small and elastic technocratic hierarchy of the Empire of the Rose. The Common Weal of Cunfshon was certainly the most sophisticated political culture in the world. Endysia was proud of her native isles, and she had a slight degree of suspicion for all outsiders, even for the folk of the Argonath, who were an organic outgrowth of Cunfshon. This led her to build a wall between herself and the hearts of the fighting men. Sexual assault was the worst crime in the world, for it tore at the very basis of the great Commonwealth of Cunfshon. These boys had to be taught a lesson, and if it was summary punishment, then so be it. A trial could be held later, and maybe after that they would be hanged.

Her mind was set on a cool elevation therefore, and her visit was short and changed nothing. She asked only a few questions and did her best not to even make eye contact with Relkin of Quosh. Afterward she suffered a degree of self-reproach and then recalled poor Birjit's pale face. She hardened her heart against these boys. The fleet must come first. Endysia returned to the sick bay and sat beside Birjit, mulling over what to do next. The one remaining hope was that Birjit would awaken and reveal what had really happened. How that might be achieved was a question beyond the competence of a Witch of Standing. If only Irene had been there, or Lessis herself.

Endysia fidgeted. There had to be something she could try. A vague thought stirred her. She rose, went to her book chest, and rummaged for a certain scroll of Cunfshoni spellsay.

Relkin, Swane, and Jak were left to their own bitter thoughts in the dark closeness of the brig aboard the *Barley*. They had fallen afoul of a situation that didn't seem to allow for justice to be done.

Swane gave a harsh chuckle.

"So we gonna get whipped for doin' something we never did." They shared a grim smile.

"No, really, I mean I've done a lot of things that I ought to have got a whipping for, we all know that." Swane's idiot grin lit up the dark. "But they never caught me so I didn't, you know what I mean, Quoshite?"

There was a new vulnerability there.

"I can imagine."

Oh, yes, the younger Swane must have been a jolly roger among dragonboys, hands in everything, a light-fingered rascal, no doubt. But now he was going to get marked for something he'd not done and get marked for life.

"It ain't fair. It ain't right," said Jak in a peculiarly desperate tone. Jak was the most afraid of the three of them. Jak had seen field punishment and had fainted while having to watch a man suffer fifty lashes for desertion. Jak didn't know if he could take twenty lashes himself without screaming and shaming himself forever.

The code concerning this among the men of the legion was strict. You were not supposed to make a sound, especially not with the whole fleet watching. The pride of the legion rested on you. But Jak was sure he would blub and scream.

"You know, Jak," said Relkin in a calm, reasonable voice. "You're right, but it's still going to happen, and we just have to deal with that ourselves. Unless, well, unless Birjit will tell the truth."

"I hear she's still unconscious," said Swane dismally. "The surgeon doesn't think she'll come around."

"What if she don't tell the truth?" said Jak, voicing another fear.

Relkin looked to Swane.

"How likely is that, Swane?"

"How would I know? I just been fighting off the daft woman ever since we got on this ship. It's her that should be getting twenty lashes, not us."

Relkin was almost ready to agree with Swane about that. Twenty strokes! That was not going to be a day to remember.

"What's it goin' be like?" said Jak with undisguised anxiety.

"Gonna strip the meat right off your bones, Jak lad" was Swane's uncomforting reply.

"Not so bad, Swane," said Relkin in angry reproof. "The blood will run, but the scars will heal; Jak's young enough."

Swane snorted and hung his head in the darkness. Both of them knew this was unlikely. The scars left by the cat of nine tails, each a stiff, waxed cord with three knots in the end, would be with them all for the rest of their days.

Swane had caught the tone in Relkin's voice, though, and fell silent, aware that little Jak was taking this all pretty badly and that he ought to make it as easy as he could. The problem for Swane was keeping up his own spirits. It was a short leap for him from ebullience to despondency, and he was starting to run out of bravado.

Meanwhile Relkin's thoughts had drifted away again. He wondered how far Wiliger would let his malevolence take him. This was all Wiliger's fault. He had made the charges, no one else; after all, Birjit was unconscious. Then he'd refused to retract the charges, and as their commanding officer, he could not be made to retract them. Commander Voolward couldn't do it without permission from above, and with the delicate situation with the sailors, General Steenhur would not step in. Wiliger was why they would get those scars in the forenoon.

The important point to Relkin now was whether this would satisfy Wiliger's wounded pride or whether he would go on hating them. Relkin understood now that the dragon leader had suffered a terrible blow to his sense of self-esteem by his ignominious performance during the battle with the sorcerer's armored warrior. Being knocked cold at the onset of the real fight had left him feeling foolish, and for Wiliger this was the worst thing in the world.

Would he be satisfied with scars on their backs? Or would he have to have everyone in the squadron destroyed as well?

And destroyed it would be, because those scars would be there for life. Every time he took off his shirt, every time his beloved put her arms around him, those scars would be there.

How was he going to explain this to Eilsa! How would he tell his children of their father's shame? He saw the image starkly in his mind; the cat cutting his skin and the blood running down his back.

Was there really no way out? What if Birjit awoke? Would she tell the truth? He found himself grasping at straws again.

The only thing that could save them from this would be for Birjit to awaken and confess her own shameful secret, which was that she had attacked Swane. But even if they were saved now, something else would come along sooner or later and Wiliger would try and destroy them again.

Relkin was left wondering what it might take to appease
the dragon leader. They couldn't get rid of him it seemed,
not even Commander Voolward would do that unless
Wiliger showed cowardice on the field of battle. They also
knew that Wiliger had influence back in Marneri because of
his powerful family. That was enough to make commanders
and generals cautious when dealing with him. So they were
stuck with him and his unpredictable ways.

Swane had suggested that they just kill him. A sword in
the back during the next fight they got in. Relkin had dismissed the idea, but still it lingered uneasily in his thoughts.

Relkin shivered. He had done many things, and like
Swane he'd escaped just and proper punishment for a lot of
them, but he'd never murdered anyone, not even Trader
Dook. Yes, he had slain Dook, he had thrown the knife that
ended Dook's life, but he had been forced to do it to protect
the life of a young dragon. The court had acquitted him, and
in his own mind Relkin felt himself innocent of the charge.
But if they killed Wiliger, it would be murder and Relkin
didn't know if he had it in him to murder anyone, even
someone as useless and dangerous as Wiliger.

While Relkin wrestled with his own torments and Jak
tried not to imagine the nine knotted cords slashing his back
and Swane whistled tunelessly while he thought angry
thoughts about sailors and dragon leaders, the witch Endysia
studied Birjit very carefully by candlelight in a small room
connected to the surgeon's rooms.

Her doubts about the case had grown to an obsession, and
she had decided at length to try a very great spell designed
to wake anyone who was still this side of death. It would
stretch Endysia to the very limits of her strength. She was a
Witch of Standing, but not a Great Witch like Lessis or
Ribela. Thousands of lines of the Birrak, along with
Cunfshon spellsay, had to be spoken correctly. Her own
spirit had to grow out of her and seize hold of the very fabric of time and space.

Nonetheless, she knew she could never face the Grey
Lady if she did not make the attempt.

Thus Endysia drove herself through the night, sweating
and straining through the recitations and the voluminates,
and in the hour before dawn, she burned a bundle of yew
leaves and sprinkled them with the dried blood of a
Cunfshon steerbat. Inhaling the smoke, she used it to express

the final volume. Her spell was complete. Now to see if it had been made correctly.

The air in the sick bay had thickened until it was difficult to breathe. Over the prone form of Birjit there hovered an aura, at the edge of visibility.

Endysia breathed a sigh. This had been the most difficult spellsay work she had ever undertaken. Already she felt that it could not have worked. Her clothes felt clammy, clinging to her body. She was simply not good enough for this level. A shudder went through her, and she felt suddenly very cold. There was a long, awful moment of suspense.

There came a little snort from the cot. Birjit stirred and half turned her head.

Success! Endysia let out a little whoop, her heart plucked from the depths and sent soaring into the heavens.

Birjit shortly opened her eyes and stared wanly around the sick bay.

Endysias waited for a few minutes in silence, to allow the wounded sailor time to realize where she was, that she was safe and that she was going to be all right.

The minutes lengthened. Still Birjit made no sound.

"Birjit," said Endysia.

Birjit's eyes flicked up to meet hers.

"You will live, Birjit; I the witch tell thee this truth. You will live. There are things you must tell me. It is urgent."

Birjit stared at the witch with dulled eyes.

"I will not."

She said it clearly and carefully, and then lapsed into a sullen silence.

Endysia was horrified. Had the poor dear been raped indeed? Or traumatized so badly by those boys that she could not face life again?

With tact and great care Endysia sought to question Birjit, but received no response. Endysia withdrew, puzzled and somewhat disheartened.

The surgeons examined the sailor and expressed amazement that she had reemerged from a coma that had seemed likely to last until death. Endysia was happy to receive their awed praise for her efforts. Indeed, she herself felt a little awe at what she had achieved. She was, however, exhausted, and in desperate need of an hour or so of rest.

"Let her be taken up on deck. Perhaps some fresh air,

along with some food, might help her to recover. She has suffered most grievously."

Birjit was carried up to the quarterdeck and installed near the rail on the leeward side. Captain Olinas took great pains to congratulate Birjit, and to promise that the perpetrators of the dreadful deed would be punished. They would have the skin off their backs that very day.

Meanwhile the news spread like wildfire through the ship; legionaries stirring at the first light of day were met with the word. Birjit was awake but she refused to talk.

Because Relkin was in the brig, Bazil didn't hear this story at first, nor did Vlok or Alsebra. The Purple Green, however, was informed by Manuel, and the wild dragon lurched across the hold to tell Bazil and Vlok.

"The woman they are accused of attacking is awake."

"Good. What did she say?"

"She refuses to speak."

"She afraid to speak, I think," said the Purple Green.

"Our boys are going to be beaten unless she speaks. We know the truth of this. She has been down here, seeking fertilization of her eggs for months! Boys have nothing to do with her."

"True, Swane boy say he rather fertilize a horse. I know Swane boy is difficult to understand at first, but . . ." Vlok's analysis of his dragonboy trailed off.

The broketail dragon was gone, hunching over Manuel at the entrance to the Purple Green's stall.

A few moments later Manuel dashed out and darted up the ramps and stairs to the quarterdeck.

He bore a message from the dragon, Bazil of Quosh, requesting that the said dragon be allowed to question Birjit, the wounded sailor.

When he returned a few minutes later, one look at him told Bazil the answer. The captain had refused.

Bazil was in motion a second later treading purposefully to the massive ramps that led up to the foredeck. No one tried to get in his way.

He emerged into the light of day, took a deep breath of the clean ocean air, and looked across the ship to the quarterdeck where Birjit lay. They were separated by the waist, the gangways, and the ship's boats, lashed in place to either side of the mainmast.

It would be a very serious step. He would be risking

much. Dragon mutiny was a terrifying thought to the men of
the legions. But he could not allow them to lash the boy for
no good reason!

Bazil stepped forward, lurched down the steps, squeezed
through a passage designed for men, not dragons, and
headed down the gangway.

Sailors leapt aloft with cries of alarm. On the quarterdeck
more alarms were raised. He passed the mainmast, squeezed
by the longboats, ducked under rigging and a new spar that
was being prepared to replace one that was starting to crack,
and moved on, directly toward the quarterdeck, the sacred,
inviolable place of the captain of the ship.

An irresistible force was coming up against an unbreakable shell of tradition. Irresistible force won. Bazil mounted
to the quarterdeck, although the steps groaned beneath his
weight and he had to squeeze through the narrow access.

Dragon Leader Wiliger ran in front of him. Other men
were there, men with bows drawn, arrows ready. Others had
spears.

"Dragon Bazil, you must stop now!" bellowed Wiliger.

"The woman must talk to me! That is all I ask, all any
good dragon would ask. Let me question her. Then do what
you want."

Wiliger danced back as two and a half tons of leatherback
dragon surged forward.

"Don't shoot!" he screamed. Admiral Cranx was standing
there, his mouth open in an appalled "O." Commander
Voolward came bounding up the steps. Captain Olinas, face
filled with fury, had her hand on her sword.

"Hold your fire!" Voolward shouted. The men obeyed. Arrows came up.

Cranx looked at him with ire in his eyes. "You are above
yourself, sir, giving orders on the quarterdeck."

Captain Olinas threw herself between the dragon and the
cot by the rail.

"You have no right on this deck!" she said, and raised her
sword.

The dragon looked at her. Instinctive, primal terror seized
her mind, and she fell into dragon-freeze. Bazil eased past
her and loomed over the cot. Birjit could not look away from
him.

"I know you not have fear of dragon. I see you many,
many times in our quarters."

Birjit stared at him and blinked. She didn't go into dragon-freeze.

"My dragonboy is wicked, but not that wicked. He stupid, too, but not that stupid. I know my dragonboy never want to fertilize your eggs."

Birjit felt those eyes bore into her.

"My boy will be lashed because he tried to help you. I know what happened. You know what happened, too. You must tell them."

Birjit quailed. The dragon seemed to look into her very soul. Her dishonesty was laid bare before the bright sun of another's knowledge of her shame. Her hands came up to her face, and she broke down into urgent sobbing.

"I don't want to hurt anyone, I just, I didn't know. I feel so ashamed."

"Swane boy, he stab you in self-defense this dragon is sure. He not stab you because he want to fertilize your eggs."

With a wrenching sob, Birjit acknowledged the truth, then looked away over the rail. The dragon swung his big head and gazed back at the assembled officers.

"You heard this. Boys innocent completely. This dragon will go back to quarters now."

And as they stared at him, partly in awe, partly in rage, he stepped gingerly down groaning steps to the gangway, and returned to the foredeck and the entrance to the forward hold.

CHAPTER TWENTY-TWO

"So there it is, Jak," said Relkin, leaning over the lee rail, gazing off to the land, no longer distant at all. "The end to our voyage."

"I can't wait to get back on dry land. We've been cooped up on this ship for so long."

A line of yellow cliffs topped with brilliant green marched southward, the direction they were sailing. White surf boomed on the reef offshore and a million seabirds were in flight around them. Flocks of gannets and boobies went one way, squadrons of pelicans and gulls another.

"The dark continent, we made it, eh?" said Swane coming over to join them.

"We made it." Relkin's tone carried with it the conviction that they had only just made it, and no thanks to Swane.

Manuel came climbing down from the rigging. Of late Manuel had taken up an interest in sailing and now spent quite a lot of time in the rigging learning whatever he could from the sailors aloft.

"We can see Sogosh and the entrance to the channel through the reef."

"How far?"

"Just a few miles now, we'll be there by noon if this wind keeps up."

They all looked up at the billowing white sails. The wind was light and chancey and had died several times in the past few days as they grew closer to the coast of Eigo, a maddening business for sailor and soldier alike, all eager for an end to the months at sea.

"Let's hope old Caymo is rolling his dice for us," said Manuel, who had taken to jibing Relkin for his belief in the old god's helping hand.

"Let's" was all Relkin had to say. Relkin had come away from the great battle on Sprian's Ridge with a firm belief in the intervention of Caymo in his affairs. The Great Mother might rule the heavens but somewhere, somehow, Caymo survived.

"Anyone seen Wiliger?" said Manuel.

"Not since breakfast. He went to visit the admiral, I heard," said Swane.

"Any chance Wiliger will transfer to the fleet?"

They laughed at the thought of the seasick-prone Wiliger becoming a sailor.

"That admiral, he must love Wiliger; they been meeting every day now," said Swane.

"He can smell a fortune. Everyone knows the Wiligers are stinking rich."

"More's the pity."

"Sssh," hissed Jak. "Wili's here."

It was true. The dragon leader had suddenly appeared on the foredeck and was bearing down on them.

"What now?" groaned Swane quietly.

Relkin wondered, too. Since the Watering Isle debacle, Wiliger had grown into a sour tyrant. Gone were the efforts to befriend them. Gone, indeed, was much of the obsessive inspection and exercise regime. Wiliger had spent most of the time locked away in his cabin or else in the spacious suite of the admiral, who had apparently befriended him.

All the time, though, Relkin knew that Wiliger was just waiting for them to make a mistake. The humiliation on the Isle of the Sorcerer had been terrible for Wiliger, but the overthrowing of his sentences on Relkin, Swane, and Jak after the Birjit affair had seemed to unhinge him.

"Stand easy, boys," said Wiliger, acknowledging their crisp salute with his own, much less crisp.

He stood there in front of them, looking over their heads at the yellow cliffs and the exuberant tropical vegetation. His tropical uniform was correct but unpressed, his buttons barely polished. He wore no hat in the heat, so they didn't know yet whether he'd finally abandoned the irregulationary cap badge.

"I expect you boys are all excited by the thought of getting off the ship and stretching your legs on dry land again."

They favored him with a watchful silence.

"You there, young Jak, I bet you can't wait to get your feet on the ground, eh?"

Jak mumbled something. Wiliger's eye gleamed.

"Had enough of the mariner's life, have we, Jak?"

"Something like that, sir."

"And how about Dragoneer Relkin? Looking forward to getting ashore?"

"Yes, sir," said Relkin quickly, in an automatic voice.

Wiliger's mouth worked for a moment, and he looked away again, off to the yellow cliffs of Bogon.

"Well, boys, I don't have to remind you that I will expect only your best behavior during our stay in the town of Sogosh."

Swane stifled his natural chortle of contempt. After months at sea, Wiliger expected Swane not to go hunting for a girl? Any girl?

"Needless to say if I catch any of you absent from your station without my express permission, I will order field punishment of the first class. You know what that means!"

Twenty lashes with the cat.

That put a damper on things. Swane deflated. Relkin stiffened and felt the hairs rise on his neck. Wiliger wouldn't rest until he'd put stripes on all their backs. He would never forgive them.

"Furthermore, boys, we will be joining forces with an army of Czardhan knights that has been waiting for a month. There are also forces from the Bakan states and a regiment of Kassimi cavalry called the 'Desert Panthers.'" Wiliger was clearly amused by such pretensions, but his lips barely twisted in a smile. "General Baxander and General Steenhur have given orders that we are to avoid conflicts with our allies at all costs. The Czardhans in particular are very important to us. Under no circumstances will we do harm to a Czardhan knight."

They stared back at him sullenly. No Czardhans would ever get hurt by them as long as they kept civil tongues in their heads and were reverent of the Mother.

"Is that understood!" he barked. His eyes grew dangerous and wild.

"Yes, sir," they chorused obediently.

Wiliger smiled, looked down, and fidgeted on the spot for a moment. Then he turned and vanished down the gangway.

The dragonboys returned to gazing at the cliffs.

"Phew! What a pain he is," groused Swane.

"Never met a Czardhan," said Jak.

"Horse cavalry, heavy armor, ride really huge horses. Supposed to be unstoppable on a battlefield," said Manuel.

"Ha! You've seen cavalry against dragons, that don't work," said Relkin.

"We've seen light cavalry, and they couldn't get around us because we were in forest. If we'd been out in the open, it would've been different. We'd never have touched them, and we'd be picking arrows out of the dragons all day, every day."

"So, what's that to these knights?"

"So, we haven't seen the dragons receive a heavy cavalry charge."

"But we ain't fighting the Czardhans, are we?" said Jak in mock confusion.

Swane laughed.

"No we aren't," admitted Manuel.

"We don't know what the hell we'll be fighting," said Relkin. "Nobody knows anything solid; it's all just rumor."

"Well, we'll have this heavy cavalry on our side anyway."

"Yeah, and we'll have some Kassimi horsemen, too," said Swane. "Call themselves Panthers. Ho ho."

"I seen Kassimi; there was some Kassimi sailors in Marneri once. They do a lot of trade with Kadein."

"Kassim is an ancient realm with a glorious tradition of chivalry," said Manuel, as if he was reciting a book, which he was in a way.

"Stuff the Kassimi, what about the Bogoni? They're all black."

Relkin shrugged. "So what? They'll be no different from people anywhere. Besides, there were black people in Ourdh."

"How do you know? Since when was the Quoshite there? Nobody's been there, 'cept the witches I 'spect."

"Traders come all the time, Swane."

"I guess it's on my mind because it's just going to be really different from home," Swane demurred.

"Home?" said Relkin. "Where's that? Fort Dalhousie?"

Before Swane could grapple with the problem of having no real "home," unless it was the entire Argonath, Jak piped up.

"Uh-oh, our pirate friends look like they're finally getting serious."

A cornet blew from the maintops.

Jak was pointing to seaward. They all turned to see a flotilla of fast, rakish outrigger vessels bearing down on them from windward. These were the same small piratical praus that had dogged the white fleet's progress since the previous day. More cornets could be heard throughout the fleet.

"Guess they decided it's now or never," said Swane.

Relkin nodded in agreement as a thunder of feet from below sent the *Barley*'s crew into action.

The viperish pirate praus were lightly built but crammed with men. Their technique was to get close and board their prey.

The sailors had raised heavy catapults into position and removed tarpaulins that protected them from the elements. While their winches were turned by chanting groups, the weaponeers loaded the ten-foot-long arrows into the waiting slots. Each arrow carried a massive steel-tipped warhead more than a foot long.

Meanwhile heavy slings had been hauled aloft. These would be used to hurl pots filled with flaming oil into the sails and rigging of the pirates. The slings were ingeniously routed between the masts, aligned vertically, which allowed for a tremendous pull on them and therefore a long range.

Along the rail of the nearest pirate ship, they could see a mass of dark-skinned faces, white teeth gleamed alongside bright cutlasses.

Cornets were blowing throughout the fleet.

"Look!" cried Jak. The old *Potato* was under attack.

With a sound like the cracking of a pair of giant whips, two of *Potato*'s catapults let fly. The arrows struck the pirate hulls with terrific force. Such fragile shells could not withstand such projectiles. Both were holed.

More catapults released and soon the leading prau was checked, holed at the waterline and sinking fast.

The second prau luffed up and after swinging by to pick up the struggling men in the water, turned and rode the wind south, leaving the white fleet behind.

Another prau had approached within firing range of *Barley*.

Captain Olinas gave the order, and ranging shots were fired with whining cracks that hurt the ears if you stood too close. The first shot went right over the prau. The second stuck fast in her mainmast. The third splashed in the water uselessly in front of the prau. A jeer went up from the packed men on the prau, and it veered in closer.

There came another command from Captain Olinas, and this time a volley of great arrows thudded home along the pirate's waterline.

The situation changed at once. The prau slowed in the water and became sluggish. More arrows struck home, holing her again and again. Soon there was just a struggling mass of men and a few elements of wreckage floating in place of the prau.

Barley sailed on unmoved.

The boys saw the fleet's frigates, *Flute* and *Viol* turning to deal with the remaining pirate vessels. The frigates bristled with catapults as they bore down menacingly on the pirates. The black praus withdrew and were soon hull down on the horizon away in the south.

By then the white fleet was already beginning the passage of the gate to Sogosh, a mile-wide channel between the two arms of the great reef.

Ahead lay the whitewashed sprawl of Sogosh.

CHAPTER TWENTY-THREE

The white fleet arrived just after noon, the great anchors splashing down in the deeper water of the outer bay while the cornets shrilled. The town of Sogosh was quite asleep, for in the burning heat this was the only escape. Only the poor, blinded *punkahs* were at work, keeping their masters fanned as they slept.

Sogosh was an old place, a cosmopolitan city at the mouth of the river Awal that controlled the entrepôt trade with the interior. Sogosh had sprawled along the margin of the sea and the river, and overflowed its walls three times over. Three and four-story white-stuccoed buildings hugged the harbor. Graceful villas of limestone and pink tile occupied the higher ground inland. There were many towers, and those that stood above the various temples were topped with brightly colored onion domes.

In the modern era, Sogosh belonged to the Og Bogon, a feudal empire of the Chumar peoples. The ruler was the Suzerain of Koubha. This was the capital of the Chumar and lay several days inland above the great scarp.

The current suzerain was Choulaput, who was young and vigorous and had already fathered one hundred and sixty children. He was known widely as the "lion heart," the "Kwa Hulo" and was much respected in Sogosh where he was wise enough to let trade alone and to keep tax collections light.

The cornets of the fleet made a wild, thrilling sound as they screamed out their salute to the town. For a few moments the echoes played off the distant shore, and then there came a sudden blaring of welcoming horns and the rumble of heavy drums.

Boats were set down at once, and envoys were rowed ashore with gifts and messages for the representative of the suzerain in Sogosh, Lord Tagut.

Slowly Sogosh staggered to wakefulness. The presence of the huge fleet of white ships seemed to overawe the town for a while. Then the more commercially minded folk took to their boats, and a swarm of small craft poured out of the inner harbor to surround the white ships, offering fruit and pigs and a thousand other things with a seller's piercing cry.

The dragonboys stared in open amazement, and some admiration, at the muscular black men and women manning the boats and canoes that swarmed about the *Barley*. They exchanged Marneri silver for bunches of bananas, pineapples, guavas, and pupaws. Figs, honey, and raisins were proffered by others. And now there were sellers of hot spicy cooked meats, jerks, and *pugfluddi,* a pungent sausage of fish and meat.

The fruit sellers' teeth gleamed whitely against their chocolate skins; their eyes flashed; they seemed intensely alive. Relkin was dazzled. This was a moment he would savor, his first arrival on another continent after a voyage of eight thousand miles.

Now came larger canoes carrying teams of drummers who beat out a massive welcoming thunder.

Semi-naked women performed a sinuous, writhing dance in the prows of these larger canoes.

Dragonboys exchanged looks. It looked like this was going to be an interesting place, after all, no matter what the strictures from the dragon leader.

Oh, to set foot on the alien strand! They were filled with a terrible longing for the shore.

The afternoon hours wore by with terrible slowness thereafter as they waited for the envoys to return, and then for more boats to go ashore with officers and forward units, like the engineers, to get things ready for disembarkation.

While they waited, they fed the dragons and fed themselves and tried some of the tropical fruit they'd purchased.

The word came down that there would be no pause, no interruption in the disembarkation, which would go on through the night. Evening boil-up would take place on both ship and shore. They would begin marching out of Sogosh at first light.

Of course, that provoked the question of where they were going. To this there was no answer as yet. Rumor had it they were marching directly upriver. That they wouldn't even get to spend a day in Sogosh.

Where were they going?

Upriver. Into the interior. Into the heart of Eigo, the dark continent.

Large, flat-bottomed barges emerged from the harbor. Some of these were propelled by doubled banks of oars driven by sweating oarsmen. Naturally, these soon outstripped the rest and reached the ships.

Cornets were shrilling and commands rang out as the disembarkation began in earnest.

From here on it was steady work as almost twelve thousand men, a thousand horses, and eighty dragons were moved from ship to shore. With them went supplies of everything an army needs in the field, from canvas to wheat, from kalut beans to iron and charcoal.

The first ashore were infantry, then the cavalry, and finally the dragons. This meant that the dragons spent the night on the ships and did not begin to move until late the next morning. By then their impatience had grown dangerous. This time it was the Purple Green who nearly fell while clambering down *Barley*'s side to the barge. If he'd fallen into the barge, he would have gone right through the fragile timbers.

Before they disembarked, Wiliger insisted on one last inspection. Everyone had a complete kit, and every item was in gleaming shape if it was able to be polished.

Bazil, Vlok, and the Purple Green rode in one barge. They crouched amidships, in a line, and did their best not to step too much in any direction since their weight tended to unbalance the barge.

The sun beat down mercilessly from an empty sky. The dragonboys threw pails of water over their dragons to cool them a little. Green-striped domes rose above the walls of a waterside palace.

Other watercraft piled past them, and the dragons received astonished glances, shrieks of fear, and wild avoidance of the barge. Collisions grew more frequent as they progressed into the inner harbor, which was crowded with small craft.

As they drew closer, they saw squads of legionaries forming up and marching away past a row of warehouses. Then they were tying up alongside, and an especially heavy-duty gangway was thrust across the barge's side. Moving cautiously, the dragons stepped onto the dock and then to the land.

Relkin stepped ashore with a little prayer to the old gods for luck. The unknown continent accepted him and brought with it a whiff of spice, something exotic, something corrupt!

There was a whirl of activity around them. Hundreds of black faces, porters with white pantaloons and red hats, fruit sellers, and the merely curious who gaped while dragonboys pulled together their gear, loaded up the dragons, and then took up their own heavy packs and fell in, ready to march. Cornets wailed up and down the docks as various units assembled themselves.

A steady stream of wagons laden with stores and equipment rolled past. Riding on each were two legionaries to make sure that nothing was stolen. All this equipment was precious, irreplaceable material carried eight thousand miles across the world. General Baxander had ordered that maximum care be given to all legion equipment. They were on their own here, even farther away than old Paxion had been during the siege of Ourdh.

Wiliger put in an appearance, and soon the orders came down for them to march and away they went, falling behind a company of legionaries from the Bea legion. They marched down the dockside, past cheerful, brightly colored crowds to an open square with a monument in its center. Everyone seemed to wear white trousers, skirts, or pantaloons. Most men wore conical red hats.

The monument turned out to be a pillar with a larger-than-life stone head atop it. This, they were told, was the Kwa Hulo, the Lionhearted King of Og Bogon, the Suzerain of Sogosh, Choulaput the Great.

Relkin observed a well-formed face, stern of expression, with a prominent chin and a wide fleshy nose. There was something in the set of that chin and the incipient frown of the eyebrows that was intimidating.

They turned and marched through the city, up a long slow incline, past solidly constructed buildings of two and three stories, all covered in stucco of varying shades of freshness and whiteness.

Farther up the slope there were large houses with trees and gardens. Here the crowds thinned considerably. Small knots of men with spears and long shields stood guard at the gates of some of these larger places. A few riders were abroad wearing colorful silks, white pantaloons, and tall, round hats, usually red. Women wore loose-fitting, white tunics and robes.

In these suburbs the trees became so thick that it was virtually like marching through a palm forest, with occasional patches of enormous ginkgo trees that thrust up far above all others.

To the dismay of all the dragonboys, who'd been hoping for a night on the town, they left behind even the suburbs of Sogosh. Outside, they passed neat fields, where men labored with donkey and ox. Small villages of one-story adobe brick houses with orange-tile roofs dotted the way.

Atop a ridgeline with a view of Sogosh and the harbor spread out below, they halted for a quick meal of bread, onions, akh, and sausage purchased in Sogosh, then they resumed the march. Shortly before dusk, they reached the site of General Baxander's armed camp.

Going by the book, Baxander had determined to build himself a fort as soon as he was able. The site was a fallow field that had been purchased in advance by agents of the Empire of the Rose. Permission had been granted by the Lord Tagut of Sogosh, who was under orders from the king to do nothing to impede the Argonathi.

The place was already well on its way to being a fortress. A ditch had been dug around it and staked against cavalry. Above stood a three-foot berm into which six-foot logs were being set to form a complete stockade. Engineers had completed the layout of the interior with rows of tents for both men and dragons, latrines, cookhouses, and woodpiles. The front gate would eventually have sixteen-foot towers and a drawbridge all fashioned from local wood with the addition of timbers and parts brought from the Argonath. Men, horses, and dragons were still working in a blaze of activity.

They were allocated a couple of large, square tents, partitioned into stalls, and the 109th took a moment to rest their feet. Then, summoned by the cookshack bell, dragonboys returned with basins of noodles slathered in akh while a wagon brought beer for the dragons.

The dragons ate and drank heartily, and were refreshed. When asked to put in time on the construction, they rose willingly enough and went down to help set up the timber stockade.

Dragon Leader Wiliger had settled himself in a small one-man tent nearby rather than taking a space in the big dragon tents. To help him settle in, he had little Shutz and Endi move things around for him. Relkin took the opportunity to slip away to explore the camp before he could be roped into anything. Bazil was working in a gang, deepening the ditch; he couldn't need anything until his stint was done.

Relkin found the smith's bellows going and the forge already hot. Baxander was having spare swords beaten out and sharpened. There was an unmistakable sense of urgency throughout the camp. Wagons rumbled past in a continuous stream before parking in long rows down the center of the camp. Smoke rose above the cauldrons and griddles of a row of large cookshacks. Here he noticed a line of tall, well-formed men, with long blond hair flowing free. They wore chain mail, woolen leggings thonged and strapped with red leather, and boots cut just above the ankle. At their hips they carried short swords and knives.

Relkin realized that these were Czardhans, clearly in a good mood. They'd been drinking beer, and they were chaffering each other in Demmener, one of the most common Czardhan languages. It sounded curiously hard and guttural to Relkin's ears, used to the more silken tones of Verio. Could these coarse, though genial, fellows be knights? Relkin wasn't entirely sure.

Then a party of men on enormous horses came by. Relkin sucked in a breath, for these were undoubtedly knights, encased in gleaming steel and white silk tunics with a medley of colorful signs and images on the breast.

Their helmets were massive and squared off at the top. Most of them had their helms up, and what he could see of their faces suggested large-boned men with blue eyes and hair the color of straw.

So these were the knights, the others were foot soldiers. Relkin pursed his lips, wondering how well they fought together. Relkin knew that most cavalry performed wretchedly against dragons in close-quarter action. Horses could hardly be made to approach dragons in the first place. Riders were placed conveniently for a smooth stroke of the dragonsword. The result was usually butchery.

But without dragon support, it would be a different matter. Legion infantry had many tactics for dealing with cavalry, of course. Archery was usually effective, and staking a position was often enough to keep cavalry at a safe distance.

Still Relkin preferred that these impressive steel-clad knights were on his side in the coming campaign.

The knights rode on into an encampment of their own, within the legion camp. The orderly succession of white, rectangular legion tents suddenly gave way to a jumble of large striped tents, colorful awnings, and marquees. Strings of horses were tethered outside, and to Relkin's stunned eyes, there were women among the camp workers.

As Relkin drew closer, he noticed a sour smell in the air. The place stank due to inadequate sanitation practices. A huge pile of manure was being shoved into place by some Eigoan workers hired for the task. The Czardhans, it seemed, declined to dig proper latrines or to take care of the consequences of stabling their mounts outside their tents.

A pair of buxom young Eigoan women, dark-skinned beauties wearing bright yellow saris strode past, throwing a haughty look in his direction.

Relkin smiled; a year or so ago he would have blushed. Now he simply admired their muscular, firm figures.

He was bumped from behind, and turned to find a group of Czardhan foot soldiers pushing past.

"Watch where you're going," he complained.

One of the footmen turned on him. "And who are you?" said a blond giant in strongly accented Verio.

"Dragoneer Relkin, 109th Marneri."

"Ah, a lizard keeper!" The man turned to his fellows and yelled something in his own rough tongue.

They gathered around Relkin, and there was a lot of jesting at his expense, but since he couldn't understand a word of it Relkin took no offense. He thought the Czardhans were pretty amusing, too, but he was heavily outnumbered here.

"I hope we can fight together well," he said carefully to the one that had addressed him in Verio.

"Don't worry," said the big man. "We are here to protect you and your old lizards. You'll be safe with us around."

Relkin laughed happily.

"I'll be sure to tell them so. They'll be relieved."

But the blue eyes didn't seem to get the joke.

"You dragonboys had better go home. There will be real fighting here, and we will be too busy protecting your damned lizards to save you, too."

"Oh-ho! So this is going to be an easy war for a change. We'll get to sit back while you fellows take care of the enemy. Sounds wonderful. Wait till I tell everybody."

The Czardhan translated some of this to the others, and they all roared and stamped their feet. Then they tramped off to their tents.

Relkin made his way back to his own tent with images of Eigoan beauties and Czardhan oafs jumbled up in his mind.

CHAPTER TWENTY-FOUR

While Relkin lay down to sleep beside a dragon uttering thunderous snores, the senior commanders of the expeditionary force were holding a somewhat anxious conference in General Baxander's tent not far away.

Baxander was a bold, aggressive campaigner, as he had proved in several fights with the Teetol. However, he had never commanded such a large army, and the worry of it all was telling on him. The sheer logistical effort of keeping twelve thousand men, their horses, and the dragons fed and in motion was almost overwhelming. His staff had struggled throughout the first day, in part because of inexperience. That the legions had landed smoothly and gotten their gear ashore without any major mishaps was a relief, but ahead loomed a hundred obstacles and months of campaigning on alien ground. The prospect had the young general nervous.

General Steenhur was even younger than Baxander. He had served well in Kenor during the enemy invasion two years before. Now he too was confronting the many pitfalls of such service and the all-consuming anxiety that it could provoke.

He sipped some kalut while he reeled off the latest rumors to reach him.

"First, there is said to be a plague in the bush up-country. Men are dying by the thousands of black boils that erupt all over their bodies. Second, there is a huge enemy force, equipped with magical weapons that enable them to fight at night. Third, the people of Sogosh are about to rise in rebellion against Choulaput, throw in their lot with the enemy, and cut off our rear. And those are all just within the past hour and half! The rumors are beyond reason, it's madness."

The witch Endysia and Admiral Cranx were the other participants. They sympathized with the young generals' anxiety, but they had their own agendas.

"It's natural enough with ten thousand men standing on a foreign land," said Endysia in her most mother-henlike manner.

"Things will settle down once we get on our way," Cranx chimed in. "My experience in these matters, limited of course when it comes to missions on land, has always followed a similar pattern. At first it seems impossible, and the path ahead appears choked with dangerous possibilities. Still you must go on, and as you do, gradually the fear subsides."

Baxander and Steenhur looked at the old admiral. Such platitudes were all very well for him, he was leaving the scene, to sit off the coast in a frigate and direct the white fleet as it continued with the various aspects of its mission.

"These things will seem less troublesome in a few days as we get into the habits of the campaign," said Endysia. "I hope we can begin to move tomorrow." Baxander looked to Steenhur. This was not to their way of thinking. He coughed and cleared his throat.

"While I, too, wish to begin our march inland, I must insist on the completion and proper fortification of our fort here. We must have a strong anchor to fall back on."

Endysia arched her eyebrows. In fact, she had heard exactly to the contrary from Lessis. It was imperative to march the column straight inland to Koubha.

She remembered Lessis's words quite clearly.

"Keep them moving, Endysia. Don't let them stop and dig in. We're going halfway across this continent eventually; we can't build forts all that way."

Endysia kept her gaze steady. "We must get to Koubha as soon as possible."

"Ah, yes," said Steenhur. "Koubha. Koubha, as you know, is a hundred miles inland. We must gather a lot of provisions before we can attempt such a march."

Endysia suppressed a critical response. They would be traveling more than a thousand miles into the interior, mostly on the great river. They would live off the land. It was time for Steenhur to get used to that idea. Still, these men were grappling with the tremendous burden of responsibilities that came with command of the expedition, and Endysia knew she must make allowances for that. They would come around soon enough, they had been carefully chosen.

"I know that Lessis would beg you to accelerate your plans. Any delay could be fatal to King Choulaput."

"Ah, the Lady Lessis," said Baxander. "I have been asking myself where she might be. I was told that she would be here with intelligence concerning the situation inland. Instead, I find myself with virtually no intelligence except that brought me by my own scouts."

"The Lord Tagut is certain that there are no enemy forces directly in front of us. Nothing until we reach the Great Scarp in all likelihood."

"Can we really trust this Tagut?" said Steenhur.

"I can see no reason not to."

"But where is Lessis; when will we see her?"

"As to that, General, I cannot say. I believe she is in the Impalo country. She intended to go even farther, to the Ramparts themselves."

"The Ramparts of the Sun?" said Steenhur uncertainly.

"And beyond them, to the unknown forests and the inland sea."

"I've heard that it is haunted by demons, a place of terror, so they say."

"So they say," responded Endysia, "but we are going there, General, to bring an end to this new terror."

"Well, I just wish we had some solid information about what we're facing."

There came a short call on a cornet outside the tent. An aide put his head in.

"The Count of Felk-Habren is here to see you, sir."

"Ah, the count. Show him in." Baxander grinned internally. Now the witch could see for herself what he had to contend with.

A large man wearing chain mail under a pale blue silken blouse marched in and crashed to a halt with a clenched fist salute and a guttural cry in Demmener.

The front of his blue blouse bore the heraldic rampant lion and three blackbirds of the house of Felk-Habren. On his right hand he wore the massive amethyst known as the lion stone; on his left hand he wore three massive gold rings with black pearls.

Count Trego Felk-Habren was the titular leader of the Czardhan forces in Bogon. However, his was far from a solidified command. The knights were grouped in "battles" from the many small Czardhan states. There were many enmities between the states. The men of Hentilden could scarcely be made to cooperate with those of the Trucial States for instance. Indeed, the Trucial States were generally unpopular, but they were wealthy, and Felk-Habren, despite its small size, was one of the wealthiest of all, and thus the count was titular commander of the force.

Count Trego was a fairly typical representative of his breed. Tall, good-looking, with a long straight nose and full red lips. His eyes were a washed-out blue, and his hair was so pale it was almost silver. On his right cheek he wore the scars of sabre dueling, a passion among the young men of the Czardhan aristocracy. He was prickly, arrogant, and incredibly ignorant of just about everything beyond the minutiae of the aristocratic hierarchy of Czardha. Thus he knew to within a fraction of a degree who was of higher rank within the knights by virtue of family longevity or size of landholdings, but he knew nothing of Og Bogon or Eigo. He had agreed to come on the great mission because of the urging of his liege lord, King Federio of Lankessan. It would be an opportunity to win much glory and even to gain a fief, perhaps in Gazin. For honor and a fresh fief, he had come and he had become impatient with the long delays. He knew little about the Empire of the Rose except that it was reputed to be run by women, a concept that all Czardhans found inherently amazing.

Still, Count Trego had found it possible to work with General Baxander. Trego spoke good Verio, the tongue of the Argonath and Cunfshon. Because of its great literature and its use as the language of science and engineering, Verio was a popular tongue among the elites of court in the Trucial States. Baxander had spent quite some time in conversation with Count Trego. In the weeks before the main fleet arrived, the two of them had worked out a method of operations that suited the count and the rest of the Czardhans.

In effect, Baxander ignored the Czardhans and made no calls on them for anything. Baxander and his thousand engineers and support staff had an enormous amount to do and only a few months in which to do it. Setting up the logistics in Bogon for the feeding of eleven to twelve thousand men, plus a thousand horses and eighty behemothic eating machines called battledragons was a colossal task. Just getting the thousands of carts built and the oxen to haul them had been a major undertaking. General Baxander now knew to a nicety the prices of oxen in every major market in Bogon.

The Czardhans, endlessly prickly about honor and precedent, were of little use in such matters. Their own supply problems were immense, in part because of their tendency to be late in paying for deliveries of food and hay. So bad was their situation that Baxander had factored in a huge store of emergency food supplies since he visualized having to feed them, anyway, when the time came.

Count Trego had never understood that Baxander had simply left him alone. Trego believed that he had merely been afforded the respect due him. Baxander had no title and thus must be considered a commoner and therefore not of the same social standing as the Count of Felk-Habren. Baxander's small force were busy providing services, that had been enough for Count Trego.

The situation had changed, however, and dramatically. Since the white fleet had landed and disgorged eleven thousand men, horses, and dragons, the Czardhan leaders felt under a severe psychological pressure. They were now the junior partners in the alliance and this brought massive uncertainties regarding the proper respect and deference to hierarchical norms. Such uncertainties were highly disturbing to the Czardhan mind.

These doubts were the source of the reserved tone and pensive expression on the count's face.

"Count Trego, may I present General Steenhur, my second in command." Steenhur saluted. The count repeated his clenched fist and a few words of his native tongue.

"Admiral Cranx, commander of the white fleet"—again the clenched fist.

"And the witch Endysia."

The count stared. Was this some kind of low joke? An incredibly plain and unattractive woman was being presented to him.

There was a long silence as he struggled to understand and failing in that he colored.

"What insult is this?" he stammered in Demmener.

The woman was dressed like a peasant, in plain white woolen robe and a grey shirt or smock. She wore sandals, and her feet were bare and exposed! The count swallowed heavily. Never in all his life had such a creature been presented to him. Did they mock him? His face purpled.

Endysia bowed and smiled at him. Then spoke in Demmener.

"I am honored to meet you, Count. Felk-Habren is spoken of in my order as a place of great honor, home to men of courage."

It was like being struck over the head with a mallet. Count Trego was taken utterly aback. He groped, and his face lost the purple tone. He realized he was being completely graceless.

"Ah, I, uh, thank you, uh, witch, for your words. You speak our tongue well."

"I have studied it for several years now. I enjoyed reading the *Lays of Medon*. They are beautifully written."

Count Trego swallowed. He himself had never read all the *Lays of Medon,* only the most popular parts. His sense of astonishment was now complete.

On the principle of striking when the foe is confused, Baxander broke in.

"Count, we are considering how soon to begin the march inland. What are your views?"

Count Trego was caught between purple fury and his desire to speak his piece. After an inarticulate moment his desire to speak won.

"Armph, harrumph!" he began. "Truly your ways are different from those of the High States. Allowances must be made, I suppose. As to your question, I can assure you that we are all most anxious to move immediately to get to grips with the enemy. The sooner the better. We have been in this pestilential land for far too long already."

Endysia spoke quickly. "It is wonderful to hear that the warriors of Czardha are ready, for we must indeed prepare to leave as soon as possible."

Count Trego stared at the woman again. The woman had spoken of military affairs, in front of these men, and they did not rebuke her!

"I find it surprising that a woman speaks to us in such a way." His eyes snapped blue fire.

Endysia did not flinch.

"Many women serve the Empire of the Rose in all its actions. We have not disgraced our sex by doing so."

The count blinked.

"Among us the women are not involved in such matters as the movements of armies. The women remain in the home and take care of the children and are subordinate in every way to our men."

Endysia smiled politely. "In the Empire of the Rose, men and women are equal in every area of life except service in the front lines of the legions."

"That is quite preposterous. Women cannot think about such matters as war!"

"On the contrary, Count, let me assure you that women can and do think about such things."

The count was about to explode, when there was a loud call on the cornet. An aide put his head inside to whisper to Baxander, whose jaw dropped.

"By the breath, show her in."

He looked up, and his eyes met those of Endysia.

The tent flap opened and Lessis of Valmes walked in, accompanied by Lagdalen of the Tarcho.

The count was stunned. Here were more women, in even humbler garb. The older one, a completely drab, poverty-stricken figure whose lined face and lank hair spoke of semi-starvation and lack of sleep, wore grey cloth that might almost have been rags. The younger one, now that was another matter, for she was a pretty-looking little thing, and in a decent gown with some jewels about her, then he, Trego of Felk-Habren would have been pleased to have made her acquaintance.

"Count," said Baxander. "May I present the witch Lessis." This was the older one.

Count Trego sucked in a breath, unsure whether they made sport of him, and if not, then how could he take these people seriously ever again? Old women in rags invited to Councils of War? Preposterous! His face began to color once more. Lessis raised her hands for a moment, and he felt a sudden relaxation. As if a masseuse had worked on just the right spot in his often tormented back and released taut muscles.

The woman had the strangest eyes; they seemed to bore right through one.

"I," he began, but something ebbed away from his mind, and he did not complete the thought.

"Count," she began, with a smile that revealed even white teeth, "I am so honored to meet you. The emperor asked me to express his personal thanks to you for your support of our mission."

"You," he gasped. "You are one who speaks with your emperor?"

"I have that honor."

Count Trego swallowed. Incredible! Then that was the way it was, just as he'd been warned. These men allowed themselves to be ruled by women! How in the world had they become such a feared and respected power? It didn't make sense to a man like Trego of Felk-Habren. Still, he controlled himself; at all odds he must be polite.

"I thank your emperor for his benevolence."

Lessis moved on; as always with her, time was short.

"Gentlemen, Endysia, I have just come from Koubha. We left only hours ago."

The count spluttered.

"If I may say so, it is not possible that you have come here from Koubha in only a few hours."

The witch smiled at him. "Nonetheless, we were in Koubha, with King Choulaput this very day. And as you can see, we are here now."

Count Trego would have scoffed, but something about this woman told him not to. She would not claim such a thing if it were not true.

"Then, I must say, I wish I had a way of getting myself there with our army this very night. The sooner we get to grips with the enemy, the better for us."

Lessis laughed with the count.

"I wish that were possible, Count. Unfortunately, we have only a single batrukh, and it could never carry a horse."

Only Endysia was moved to mirth by this sally.

Steenhur had seen batrukhs. His eyes bulged. "Did I hear you correctly, Lady, a batrukh?"

"Yes, and a fine fellow he is. I call him Ridge-eyes because there is a pronounced ridge of bone above each of his eyes."

Steenhur turned his astonished gaze to Baxander, who merely shrugged. This was a Great Witch; they were capable of anything.

Count Trego, however, thought Lessis was joking and he laughed heartily.

Lessis brought the laughter to a halt by informing them that it was imperative that they indeed start the army marching for Koubha that very night. There was no time to waste whatsoever if they were to save Koubha and King Choula-put.

"What has happened to require such a drastic response?" said Baxander.

"The Kraheen invaded Og Bogon a month ago. They defeated the king's own army two weeks past at the crossings of the great river. Choulaput is heavily outnumbered and is now besieged in the capital. The Bogoni have been at peace for too long, I am afraid. Their spears have grown rusty. The walls of the city are not in good repair. The Kraheen are a disciplined foe, inspired by their Prophet, and they have sent a considerable force, perhaps thirty thousand in all. They must have bought off the tribes because we knew nothing of their approach before the invasion began."

Baxander hesitated, pressing his palms together as he considered.

"Our fort will not be finished," he began.

"General, I doubt that we will see this fort again for a year or more. We have a great journey to make."

Baxander swallowed. So, the worst had come true: They were actually going to have to march the entire force into the interior. He had prayed that this would not come to pass, even as he and his engineers had worked to make it possible.

"I see." His mouth set in a line. "By the breath, this is a gamble, Lady. Two entire legions."

"We will also have the Czardhans, and the Kassimi army that is marching south from Bakan to join us at Koubha. Plus several small forces from the Bakan states themselves."

"Then, we shall do the best that we can with what we have," said Baxander with a wan grin.

Lessis smiled back.

"Now, I must tell you what we have seen in the interior. Lagdalen, do you have that map?"

The girl came forward and unrolled a map they had brought from Koubha. It was beautifully made, drawn in black, green, and blue, on a piece of antelope skin.

"Here lies the coast, this is Sogosh, this is Koubha." The map unrolled. A great river snaked across the continent. A rampart of mountains cut it in half.

"These are the Ramparts of the Sun, for that is what the Kraheen call them. Here," she indicated a large blue triangle, "lies the great inland ocean they call the Nub."

Floating in the blue was a femur-shaped island.

"And this is the Bone in the Nub."

"He who drinks from the Water of the Bone will never come home, 'tis said," muttered Admiral Cranx.

"Aye, Admiral, it is a bitter draught, and if we are not quick, it will be forced on the entire world."

Shortly, the conference ended, and they filed out of the tent led by Count Trego.

Outside, Lessis found the Czardhan standing transfixed, staring at the huge shape crouched on the ground beside the tent. The batrukh was oblivious to the presence of the men all around it. It was waiting for Lessis, and when she appeared, it gave a low crooning cry and bent its huge neck toward her.

Then, to Count Trego's astonishment, Lessis and the young girl climbed onto the back of the thing, and with a few enormous flaps of its vast wings, it took to the air and disappeared into the night.

CHAPTER TWENTY-FIVE

They marched through a shimmering landscape besieged by heat. Dust arose in great clouds from the marching feet of men, oxen, horses, and dragons. Behind the columns flew a great gathering of vultures, eagerly awaiting the bones and scraps left behind by twenty thousand hungry men every day.

Despite the dustiness of the road, this remained the lush coastal plain, and they were surrounded by mixed forest of gums and palms wherever the land had not been cleared for farming. At times when the road dipped down to cross another small river, they passed through swampland with enormous trees hung with moss and vines. In the higher elevations, there were farms and villages with round-roofed houses and long sheds for the cattle and goats. This was prosperous land, long settled and at peace. As the strange army of pale-skinned foreigners marched through these little places, the people hid themselves. Such things as the knights of Czardha were terrifying enough, but then there were the battledragons. These monsters, with their enormous swords across their backs, were too much for the people to take. In some places the folk broke from concealment and ran screaming when they saw the dragons marching in.

On the third day, the army began climbing a long, gentle slope through mixed forest until at last they emerged from the trees on the higher ground. Around them stretched high golden grasses, with clumps of trees every quarter mile or so.

The Royal Road soon deteriorated into little more than a wide rutted track, dry and dusty at this time, though on other occasions it could obviously be a sea of mud. General Baxander had seen it as both, and he knew how fortunate they were to be marching during a dry spell. He refused to complain about the dust.

In this he was alone. The dust was incredibly pervasive. It dulled their metal, coated their throats, played havoc with the sensitive membranes around dragon eyes, and formed a persistent grit in all their food.

Almost as worthy of complaint were the biting insects, which despite daily spells from every witch in the column, proved a continual torment.

Baxander had learned from the terrible experience of the first night that they could not camp close to water, especially swamp water, of which there was a great deal in the wetlands near Sogosh. At night, vast clouds of gnats and mosquitoes arose from such places. They camped well away from the low spots thereafter, which meant arduous water details for men and dragonboys. Woodcutting and collecting was equally important, since all water for drinking had to be boiled first by order of the witches.

The heat and humidity also corroded leather. Relkin's store of resistant ramgut was more precious than ever, and he refused to part with any except for the most vital purpose.

The dragonboys were forced to make new thongs every day. This was an arduous process in which they took fresh hide, soaked it overnight in salted water, then cut it into strings and dried them on racks placed across their wagons.

The results were crude and lacked the strength of good Cunfshon cordage. The thonging stretched easily and soon rotted and gave way under the strain of holding a dragon's gear together.

Fortunately for everyone the dragons' feet had held up very well. This had been something of a surprise. For the first two days they'd worked feverishly with blister sherbet and Old Sugustus as dragon feet, grown a little soft at sea, blistered and bled. Then on the third and fourth days, the great reptilian feet healed and hardened. Eventually even the Purple Green was marching without much pain.

Everyone felt it was a minor miracle, though some put it down to the conditioning exercises they had gone through for the last year in training, plus the effects of Old Sugustus skin toughener.

Moreover, they had covered considerable ground on each day with the dragons marching the whole way. Baxander's engineers had set up posts along the way and stocked them with oil-soaked torches. These allowed the ox trains to keep moving well into the night. By extending the line of march and keeping the wagon trains in almost constant motion, the legions were able to move as quickly as men and dragons could march in an eight-hour day. Since there was no mud, they had marched every day from dawn until the onset of the worst heat, and then again for the evening into the first hour of darkness. The end result was something close to twenty miles a day. By the end of the week they were close to Koubha.

Now that they were seeing larger villages, a sure sign of proximity to a big place, the rumors were flying again.

The most dangerous one was why the witches insisted on every man taking quinine every day. The powder was dissolved in warm water and gulped down with expressions of disgust at the bitter taste. It was supposed to prevent disease, they were told, but the real reason, they believed, was to suppress their sex urges. This was necessary, so the rumor would have it, because in Koubha there were thousands of the most sexually sophisticated prostitutes in the world, and they were waiting anxiously for the blond men of the north.

When this rumor reached Lessis, she gave a wild groan and called for a meeting of all the witches on the expedition. Afterward the witches did their best to convince the men that the quinine was unconnected to their sexual urges, that the risk of disease was very real, and that there were no women in Koubha waiting anxiously to make love to an army of blond men from the east. The women of Koubha all belonged to the king and were only allowed to make love to their own husbands with his strict permission. To make love with anyone else was to risk losing their heads to the king's axman. The reason to take quinine was to avoid the terrible fever sickness that was endemic in this land and carried by mosquitoes.

But nothing could shake the image now imprinted indelibly in ten thousand male minds. Many men refused to take the quinine draft. Lessis feared malaria would soon be rife.

"It is the great secret of the kings of the river," she would tell everyone with great passion in her voice. "Without this medicine the river cannot support civilization. Without it we cannot hope to march to the Ramparts of the Sun."

Every stop, as the men ate huge meals of noodles, corn bread, and local vegetables, all drenched in pungent sauce, they cheerfully discussed the latest nuances of the rumor. The witches were in despair.

Baxander told Lessis that at the least, it had overtaken gripes about the allied forces, the Czardhans, the Kassimi, and the little armies from the Bakan nation states. Some of this griping had become too venemous for comfort.

The Kassimi, in particular, had aroused the ire of the marching legionaries. The Kassimi force consisted of just one thousand horsemen and three thousand foot. In command of this force were several hundred princelings, each with a retinue of servants and women, who regarded the expedition as a grand and dashing adventure. Each of them wore out several horses every day, galloping about the countryside hunting wild game.

Their worst attribute, as far as the legions were concerned, though, was their habit of riding up and down the columns in excited groups, their horses kicking up the dust. The marching columns had to swallow enough without this.

General Baxander was highly sensitive to the difficulties inherent in wielding an army of such disparate allies. The core of the force, of course, were the legions, but the army was weak in cavalry and the Kassimi were great horse soldiers. Even the princelings, for all their faults, had one great virtue: they were incredibly brave and driven to outperform each other at feats of arms. And so the general was slow to try and rein in the boisterous Kassimi.

The order came down for a halt.

With a roaring clatter and commotion, they broke ranks and went to work. The wood wagons were rolled up, and fires were quickly stacked. Water details struggled off, under cavalry guard, while their stored water was used to boil noodles and make broth. Woodcutting details went out into the forest. Every boil-up took several cords of wood. While they burned the wood to boil their water and cook their food, they also used the heat of the fires to dry out more wood, so that every regiment carried ten cords of wood and enough water for two boil-ups.

Relkin and Bazil drew the woodcutting detail. They groaned, but Relkin was secretly glad. The dragons loved the water detail because they got to put their huge bodies into water somewhere and get wet and just a little cooler. In the meantime dragonboys fought off clouds of hungry mosquitoes. In the woods there were far fewer mosquitoes.

They found Vlok and the Purple Green already lined up for the detail.

"Oh-ho, the usual suspects," said the Purple Green.

"What does that mean?" said Bazil.

"I don't know, but the boys have been saying it lately."

Bazil snorted. "So, what are we suspected of?"

"Nothing. Forget it."

"Baz," said Relkin, "it's just what we call a figure of speech."

This concept aroused old Vlok, however, and Relkin found himself trying to explain just exactly what a figure of speech was. This took time.

Dragon Leader Wiliger paused to inspect them briefly. The dragons carried enormous axes, dragonboys carried small axes and wore their dirks. Wiliger was obsessed with fine details these days and spent a little while fussing over the trim on Swane's trousers. They were of blue cotton twill with red braid that was supposed to stop short two inches below the waist and one inch above the ankle. Wiliger had made himself a measuring rod to assist him in inspections. Swane was just a little short on the waist side of his right trouser leg. It was hardly enough to waste any time on, but Wiliger hemmed and hawed for half a minute while they stood there, glaring impatiently at him.

At last he gave them the order to proceed.

The nearest usable wood lay in a thicket of dead and dying scrub trees, on the edge of sorghum fields.

A column of wagons and men entered the thickets. Dragons arrived, and soon there came the sound of trees being felled with enormous blows of the ax. Mule teams came forward, dragonboys darted in and out to attach trees to the mule-team traces, and then the trees were hauled back to the rear, where sawyers cut them in lengths and work details split them up for firewood and loaded them onto the wagons.

Away on the hillside they could see the water details on their way back from the nearest water hole. Huge fires were roaring in the camp, and dinner would soon be ready.

The woodcutters worked with a will, eager to be done and back in camp in time for the midday meal.

The scrubby little woods were fast thinning out, and Relkin could see more fields of grain just ahead, when there came two notes on the cornet to recall them.

Bazil put down the huge ax with a groan of pleasure.

"That thing is getting heavy."

Relkin had been impressed with the dragon's axwork that

day. Bazil was sometimes unenthusiastic for this kind of drudgery, but today he had really put his heart into it. A lot of trees he'd struck had fallen on the first blow.

"You cut more than your share today," Relkin said.

"Thank you. Boy always remind dragon of things like that."

They skirted clumps of thorn on their way back to the meeting point.

"How are the feet?"

"Feet are good. Not need dragonboy at all."

"Ho-ho, and then you'd have to go and get your own dinner."

"Not impossible to do. Even dragonboy can do that."

Relkin chuckled to himself; his dragon was ready for dinner, that was certain.

They were interrupted by a sudden thunder of hooves.

Approaching were three Czardhan knights, in full armor, with lances and pennons flying, riding right through the sorghum, flattening the crops. When they saw the dragon at the edge of the trees, they pulled up short with a chorus of raucous cries.

They'd been drinking, there was a clear edge of berserk madness in their voices. Relkin felt a sense of foreboding.

Suddenly, one of them spurred his mount closer.

"Ho, you there, the boy," said this fellow in heavily accented Verio. "I am Hervaze of Gensch. All men know that I am a true and faithful knight of my lord and liege Gaspard of Mayoux. I have never shirked a fight. Tell your beast to ready himself. I challenge him to fight me in the traditional way."

Relkin's unease deepened.

"Good knight, the dragon is due to have his dinner. The bell is ringing over there. He is tired from woodcutting. Let us joust another day. And besides, the dragon has only an ax. The ax is good for cutting wood. It is not dragonsword."

Hervaze snorted disdainfully.

"I do not care for your concerns or excuses. I will take the monster's head for my trophy whether he fights to defend himself or not. Prepare yourself for the charge."

Relkin heard Bazil hiss beside him. The dragon could understand even this barbaric Verio.

"This man wants to fight a dragon?"

The knight had avoided looking directly at the dragon; now he glanced up, but he did not freeze. Relkin marveled at the strength of fury in the man. He stared back at those huge eyes for a few seconds, and then he tore his gaze away with an effort of will and rode back to the others, uttering shrill screams as he forced his horse into a gallop.

Relkin swore. "This fellow's drunk and crazy. You can't kill him, Baz. If we kill him, there's sure to be hell to pay."

Bazil nodded gloomily. "I remember too well the matter of Trader Dook. I understand perfectly. The fool in the metal suit will charge us, and try and kill this dragon, but we must not harm the fool."

"It ain't right, it ain't logical, but you know that's the way it is."

Privately Relkin was wondering if the knight's horse would press an attack on a dragon. Czardhan warhorses were said to be uncommonly ferocious, and certainly they were huge. They had to be to carry these big men and all that armor and steel weaponry. But even so the horse was not half Bazil's size and was not likely to mistake the sight of the horse race's worst enemy, the hungry dragon.

The Czardhan knights were toasting one another from little silver flasks. Each toast ended with a series of whoops and cries as they whipped up the frenzy for combat. Then the challenger spurred his mount around, dropped his vizor, and lowered his lance. His horse moved into a canter and then to a purposeful gallop and drove straight toward them.

Relkin moved aside, looking around for something to throw. He didn't have his bow with him, and suddenly he felt terribly useless.

Bazil froze. He had only the troll ax, a clumsy, stupid weapon. The perfect thing for a troll to wield. Something shifted uneasily inside him, and Bazil felt more tired all of a sudden than he'd been in years.

All the drills he'd learned for fighting cavalry involved the use of sword and shield against any determined horseman armed with a long, pointed weapon. The defender should take the point on the shield and deflect it inward toward the horseman's line of motion. This moved the point completely clear of the defender and would also turn the rider's shoulder and open him to the counterblow. All he had was this stupid ax.

Dragons were not that good at improvisation.

The Czardhan was bearing down, his mouth open in a long, exulting scream. His horse seemed perfectly happy to charge a dragon. Relkin threw a heavy stone and missed. His next banged off the knight's shield but failed to dislodge him. His third bounced impotently off the back of the knight's armor plate.

Bazil was just standing there, not knowing what to do. He hefted the ax clumsily in both hands, and Relkin felt his throat go dry with terror. His dragon could be spitted here. He could die from this terrible stupidity.

And then Bazil convulsively swung up his hands, and by a freak of luck, the lance point caromed off the head of the ax and the knight thundered by, his blow turned.

He rode on a hundred paces and turned his mount. His friends were whooping with excitement. Relkin had already gotten Baz in motion, running away through the scrub trees. Relkin was shouting out for help at the top of his lungs. The others were only a short distance away; they should hear him soon.

Then the knight was in pursuit, Relkin could feel the thundering hooves at his back. He leapt over a stump and turned. The knight was twenty yards away. Relkin spun and tripped over a vine and fell in a tangle of branches.

When he looked up again, the dragon had stopped and was fishing something out of a tangle of fallen tree limbs.

The knight's war cry rang loud as he came in, his lance down, arrowing for the dragon's chest.

Bazil tore something free from the pile of brush and came up with a long branch, a mass of leaves.

The knight came on, his wild war scream wailing. Then Bazil swung the long branch, knocked aside his lance point, and the next moment swiped him off his horse.

The knight fell with a loud crash of steel and rolled into the base of one of the ant mounds that they had been seeing all day. By chance this was the nest of the red tropical ant of Eigo, a fierce and rather feared species.

The Czardhan was obviously stunned. He lay there against the anthill for a few moments while they watched, both equally surprised by this turn of events.

Then with a wild shriek the knight's body jerked. More shrieks erupted until his comrades rode down and dragged him away from the anthill.

Relkin was at his dragon's side by then. Relkin gave a scream of his own at the sight of the long cut on Bazil's shoulder and the red blood running down the dragon's arm, dripping into the dust.

CHAPTER TWENTY-SIX

That night Dragon Leader Wiliger brought a Kadein surgeon in to take a look at the dragon's wound. Wiliger had been much concerned earlier that "dragonboy stitch work" would not be good enough.

The surgeon was a well-seasoned sort who had been inwardly certain that this was an unnecessary inspection. He'd seen a lot of dragonboy work over the years. Dragons were always getting cut up and having to be sewn back together.

The surgeon had, however, taken the opportunity to meet the famous broketail dragon and his dragonboy. It would be something to tell his family about, if and when he returned from this expedition.

He took one look at Relkin's neat lines of stitches and patted the dragon's hide and gave Wiliger a broad smile.

"There you are, Dragon Leader, as fine a set of stitches as I've ever seen. You know something, you really don't want to worry about your dragonboys when it comes to this kind of minor surgery. They've been sewing up dragons their whole lives."

Wiliger stared stony-faced at Relkin and slowly turned crimson.

The surgeon then proceeded to chat with the dragon and Relkin and to ignore Wiliger. They discussed the Czardhans and the arrest of the knight that had attacked them. Wiliger endured this humiliation in silence and then stalked away, his face thunderous. He did not reappear that night.

The following day Bazil rode in a wagon towed by a special team of eight oxen. Relkin began the day on the wagon, too, but Wiliger spotted him there and ordered him out to march beside the wagon. There was nothing wrong with him, and therefore there was no reason to burden the oxen any further than necessary.

So it was that they slogged over a hill in the forenoon

hour and obtained their first view of Koubha. The word had come down earlier that the enemy had withdrawn, scared off by the approach of the allied army. The men were tired after days of marching, and there was a general sense of relief that there would be no immediate battle.

Koubha was a large city, built of ocher brick, and it filled a wide valley on both sides of a stream. As they drew closer they passed the wreckage of war, burned-out buildings and the bodies of men and women strung up from trees. Broken spears, arrows, and other items, like sandals and shields, were scattered here and there. Finally they marched in through a large, battered gate, hung between towers built of the same brick.

They had passed a few groups of native men and women. They were solidly built people with dark skins who now shared a hollow-eyed look that spoke of hunger and deprivation.

Inside the gate they were welcomed by a much larger crowd, clad in bright reds, yellows, and purples, with many a gaunt face among them. There was an orchestra that featured a large section of drummers and another of horn blowers; and a continual din was set up that went on and on without cease as men, women, and a horde of ragged children danced alongside the marching columns.

The dragons received a tremendous reception. The people had been told to expect them, and there was none of the terrified flight of the country folk. Swarms of children followed along behind the marching wyverns, wrapt in awe at the sight of these multiton monsters, carrying weapons and armor, wearing helmets and the leather rigging of their joboquins.

At the large open space in the center of the town, men were directed to a barracks, and dragons were sent to an empty stable. There, the scent of fresh hay mingled with the smoke of cook fires while dragonboys set about fetching water for the great beasts.

Relkin checked Bazil's wound while they waited for the evening boil. He cleaned around it with Old Sugustus and then applied a fresh poultice of herbs under a clean bandage. It was beginning to heal, an encouraging sight, although Relkin had expected little else since Bazil was in tip-top condition and the cut was only an inch or so deep. Sealed quickly and kept free of infection, it was responding well. Bazil reported a little soreness in the area, but no deep pain.

The dinner bells clanged, and dragonboys ran down to the cookshacks. There they found a large mob of hungry Koubhans drawn irresistibly to the smell of fresh bread baking. The cooks were ladling out cauldrons of noodles and broth while bakers broke up racks of bread and stuffed the loaves into the baskets for each regiment.

Relkin uneasily pushed his barrow back across the dusty ground past the starving throngs. A strong force of guards kept an open space between the hungry people of Koubha and the legions.

The dragon needed the food, and the dragon was a necessary implement of war. And so, in his way, was the dragonboy. They had to eat. The hungry people around them would have to wait until food could be brought in by their own governors.

He wheeled the barrow to the dragon, who had been joined by the Purple Green and Alsebra. They accepted the cauldrons with no comment, being ravenous, and they ate with typical dragonish fury.

Relkin turned away, appalled at the tug of conflicting emotions. Those people were starving, but it was necessary to gorge the dragons to keep them in the peak of condition.

Quietly he ate his own ration, about half of it, until his immediate hunger was somewhat assuaged, then he went back and gave his last loaf away, breaking it into three pieces and giving them to different elderly women in the line of faces that met him.

Other legionaries were already doing the same, and from the lines of men going to and from the cookshacks there flew a haphazard fusillade of loaves of bread, tossed into the crowds of Koubhans.

Relkin turned away, there was only so much a hungry army could do for the starving. Perhaps when the supply trains came up the next day, they could provide better for the Koubhans. The Argonathi legions had a job to do and a battle to fight. They were all certain there'd be a fight soon. They needed their strength.

Back in the stables Relkin found the dragons already asleep, while a mountain of empty cauldrons and sundry pots was stacked up in the central space.

"Come on, Relkin," said young Endi. "I've drawn scrub

up, too. Wiliger's really got a burr under his saddle today. He put Roos on a report charge for losing a toggle from Oxard's rig."

Relkin sighed. He'd forgotten the two weeks scrub-up detail he'd drawn from Wiliger for being on the wagon that morning. He'd only been off scrub up for ten days, too. Wiliger's malice was as heavy as Digal Turrent's had been back in the invasion days. The difference was that Turrent had been a dragonboy, and knew his business. Wiliger's mad attempt to buy himself a dragon squadron command had already turned sour. Wiliger was in a perpetual rage these days, burning from insults both real and imagined.

He and Endi loaded the cauldrons and plates and all the rest on a cart and trucked it down to the cook fires. There, with boiling water and hot sand, they scrubbed everything clean and stacked it on the cookshack cart.

It was tedious work, but during it they overheard the gossip flying about the cookshack, which was a magnet for the free and idle to loaf around in. Everything came to the cooks during the day, all the news from every corner of the army.

Thus they heard that there was a rumor that they were going to the Lands of Terror, over the mountains far away.

Nobody knew much about this place; it was at the edge of the world and few who went there ever returned.

They also heard that there was some disorder in the Czardhan camp. Bands of knights from the Trucial States had been involved in a fracas with knights from Hentilden. Other states had lined up on either side, mostly on the side of Hentilden.

Count Trego had been working for hours to bring about a reconciliation and prevent a pitched battle in the morning. The knights of the Trucial States were very prickly, aware of how disliked they were by the other Czardhans.

Meanwhile there was a mysterious problem among some of the Kassimi princelings. They had been involved in the abduction and rape of three young countrywomen shortly before their arrival in Koubha.

An old man had appeared soon after their arrival and pronounced a curse upon them while shaking a Gu-Ku head, a shrunken human skull in which burned a magical fire.

The Kassimi princelings had been struck soon after by nausea and then by a disease that seemed to rot them from the inside out. Their flesh grew soft, and blood leaked from their mouths, noses, and eyes. They cried out in agony, and no palliatives known to the Kassimi doctors would ease the pain. They were expected to die before dawn.

Relkin nodded and gave Endi a warning look. Local girls could mean trouble, and consorting with the local women of a foreign land was often an invitation to an unpleasant punishment. Endi seemed to have taken the news to heart. He fell quiet, and they resumed work in silence.

Once they'd finished the scrub up, they headed back to the stables, exhausted from the long day.

CHAPTER TWENTY-SEVEN

General Baxander had unexpected visitors to his tent. The king himself, great Choulaput, had come with a small group of advisers. Baxander had dealt with the king several times before, and knew him to be a man of sharp intelligence. However, all previous meetings had been in the royal palace.

Choulaput was a powerfully built man who carried himself like a king. He wore a suit of the light Bogoni armor, made of lacquered hide, with purple silk pantaloons and a small round helmet, also of hide. He wore a necklace of enormous, daggerlike teeth and a short, ceremonial sword with a golden hilt and pommel. On his feet were sandals bound with golden thread. His advisers were similarly clad, though with somewhat less opulence.

Choulaput explained in archaic Verio that he had come because time was short and he wanted to see the Argonathi army at first hand, without having to go through the bother of a formal review. He expected there would be fighting very shortly. The enemy had not pulled back very far.

"I fear that they have trapped you, General. Perhaps you should not have come to Koubha."

"Wherever the enemy is, there shall we go. It is our business to get to grips with them."

Choulaput smiled at the general's bravado.

"My friend from Argonath land, the Kraheen are in numbers like the leaves of grass that show after the spring rains. When I took my army up to meet them, we found we could not hold back the host of the Kraheen. They attack like men possessed of no fear. They overlapped our line on both ends, and we would have been destroyed if we had fought on. And so we were made to withdraw, although our hearts were heavy at having to allow this invasion of our land. They came here and surrounded the city. I thought that Koubha must fall when they had completed their siege engines. I prayed for the intercession of the gods, and we made sacrifices every evening. Twice the Kraheen attempted to storm our walls, and twice we drove them back. Then at last, you came and they dispersed at once. They even abandoned the engines they had been building. We have already destroyed most of them. Thanks be to the gods, for they heard our prayers."

"They feared being caught between our forces, perhaps," said Baxander.

"I do not think so. I think they wish us to believe that they fear us. They wish us to go forth up against them filled with confidence."

Baxander smiled grimly. "Good. I expect them to become emboldened now that they have seen how few are our numbers. That will be their first great mistake."

The king's dark eyes bored into Baxander's.

"They will outnumber our combined force by two to one. How can you go up against them? They are not cowards; they fight like fiends possessed."

"Your Majesty, this campaign will be fought by a professional, highly trained military force. That is what I represent. You have never seen the legions make war. No enemy will surprise a well-equipped legion. No enemy can stand before a legion's charge."

Choulaput seemed undecided.

"I expect that we shall discover for ourselves how true these claims are. The Kraheen have not gone that far away, and they will be back. We will fight again within the week."

Baxander nodded, "I absolutely agree. We will be ready."

Choulaput's expression changed. There was a hint of concern, even worry in his voice now. "In the meantime my people are suffering. We have had little food in the city for a week or more."

"Your Majesty, we will do our best for your people as soon as my supply trains arrive. They are out in the eastern hills now, guarded by our cavalry and a regiment of foot. I expect their arrival soon after dawn."

"I pray that it will arrive safely. The enemy has cavalry of his own, riders out of the deserts beyond the Nub, in the Lands of Terror. They are devils!"

Baxander felt a tremor go through him. The "Lands of Terror," that was what the witch had spoken of. Would they really have to go that far? Baxander had hoped all along that by disposing of this enemy army, they would obviate the need for the rest of the expedition.

The interior regions of the continent were largely unknown. But the legends of the Lands of Terror were known to the few who were interested in such things. Baxander had learned much of these things on his voyage from the Argonath. The legends had left him uneasy.

Baxander took a deep breath. He was exhausted. It had been a long week of marching. The mountain of planning he and his staff had constructed beforehand had paid off handsomely, and still there had been innumerable crises. The king had no idea; that was why he was so oblivious to what the legions could achieve.

"My scouts tell me that the enemy's main host has withdrawn eight miles to the west. We have contact with his outriders. I will be kept informed of his movements. If he wishes battle, then he will find it."

The king was not finished. His face became graver still.

"There is another difficulty. The armored knights have been troubling our granaries with demands for feed and grain. We have none to spare, but they are most insistent and have even drawn their weapons on my soldiers."

Baxander sighed. Those Czardhans would be the death of him!

Not for the first time Baxander wondered if it was worth having the Czardhans with them. Heavy cavalry might provide them with a grand weapon against the Kraheen, but so far the knights had been nothing but trouble.

"I will speak to the count at once."

Choulaput smiled broadly and stepped forward to clasp hands with Baxander. His smile became bitter.

"Thank you, General. Even if we die together on the battlefield, I am assured that we will give them a fight that they will sing of for a hundred years."

Baxander ignored the pessimism in the king's voice.

"My men should be rested and ready for battle by noon. How will it be with your army, Lord?"

"My men are ready, but they are weak from hunger. If we can feed them tomorrow, then they will grow stronger. They thirst for revenge upon the Kraheen, who have laid waste our land and taken many of our people as slaves and sent them into the interior. Even if we defeat the Kraheen, by the will of the great gods, we shall never see our people again. They will be lost into the Lands of Terror."

"By the Hand of the Great Mother," vowed Baxander. "We shall chasten them for these foul deeds. And if they do not disturb us for another half a day, then I can assure you we will be perfectly ready for them."

Just let the men and dragons rest; get in that supply train at dawn and feed everyone in the forenoon. Then let the enemy show his face!

"We will speak again at dawn!" Choulaput clasped hands again with Baxander. "You have filled my heart with your fire, General. We shall make war together, and they shall sing of us!"

The king left, and immediately Baxander signaled his aides and wrote a message to the Count Felk-Habren.

CHAPTER TWENTY-EIGHT

Back at the stables Relkin and Endi found, to their dismay, that they'd missed the evening water cart and therefore had nothing to set out for their dragons, who might wake thirsty in the night. As both boys knew, dragons were often dehydrated by prolonged marching.

With weary groans, they took up a barrow and pushed it down to the watering station, set up behind the regimental cookshack. There was a mountainous woodpile to one side, and a wagon park to the other. The sound and smell of great numbers of oxen filled the air. Drovers were moving their huge animals around to water them, and their whips and cries cut the night as the wagons creaked past.

At the watering station, they waited in line behind a handful of legionaries on unit water details. Freshwater was kept in hundred-gallon barrels stacked on specially designed long wagons. From these barrels smaller containers were filled as needed. When their turn came, Relkin and Endi filled a pair of drinking barrels and stacked them on the barrow. Then they started the return trip, taking turns to push the barrow.

Rounding the turn by the woodpile, they saw a party of Bogoni men, nobles from the expensive look of their armor and accoutrements. In the center was a tall, commanding figure.

Suddenly they burst into hearty laughter at a joke, the laughter was so open and honest that Relkin was moved to smile, despite the deadening sense of exhaustion he felt. The barrow was very heavy and hard to keep balanced. Endi wasn't doing much of a job on the balancing side, either.

And then with astonishing abruptness, there came a sudden rush from out of the depths of the woodpile. At least ten men, perhaps more, clad in black and with steel in their hands, sprang from concealment and hurled themselves at the Bogoni nobles.

With cries of alarm and rage, the nobles turned to defend themselves, but they were taken by surprise and they were heavily outnumbered. In a flash of steel, one of them was cut down. A second was run through and dropped to the ground.

The tall one in the center had drawn a short sword and engaged three attackers. Swords flashed and flickered, but still he held them at bay. The survivors of his party steadied around him.

Relkin came alive at the same moment.

"Push!" he yelled to Endi, and together they heaved their barrow along, the heavy barrels jouncing ominously together. With newfound strength, he got the barrow fairly flying and in ten strides they burst into the rear of the fight. The barrow took down two of the assassins, running over the back of their legs, then it went out of control and tipped over and shot out a barrel that bowled over several more like ninepins. The other barrel burst on the ground, and the barrow caromed into the center of the fight, momentarily driving back the attackers.

At this point Relkin found he wasn't carrying any weapons. He'd left his dirk back in their stall. Endi had only his knife. Then he was too busy trying to stay alive to worry about the lack. A sword parted the air where his head had been a moment before as he ducked. Fortunately, he kept his balance and now moved fluidly to kick the sword wielder hard in the belly. The man was taken by surprise and staggered back. Before his sword could move again, Relkin kicked him once more, this time in the crotch. With an explosive "oof," the man doubled up and fell to his knees. Still, Relkin could not pry the man's sword out of his hand. The man even tried to bite him.

Another came at him, and he spun away. To his right he glimpsed the tall Bogoni noble striking down a black-clad figure, and then despite a desperate duck, something hit Relkin hard on the side of the head and he fell to his knees. Some self-preserving instinct made him fall into a forward roll.

That saved him from losing his head. He bounced up against some logs and dropped back. Everything hurt, his head was ringing, but there was no time to sit there and think about it. He hauled himself back to his feet, with doubled vision and a ringing in his ears.

Still operating on instinct alone, he grabbed a piece of firewood as long as his arm and swung it around just in time to intercept a sword coming down. The sword stuck fast in the wood, and Relkin let go. The sword was pulled down, the man put a foot on the wood to pull free, and Relkin hammered him over the head with another piece of wood.

Now Relkin pulled the sword free and flung himself back into the fight. His vision had steadied, though his ears were still ringing. He put a hand up to the side of his head and felt some blood, but it was not a river of it, and he concluded he'd been struck by something blunt.

When would someone finally hear what was going on here behind the woodpile, Relkin wondered as he engaged an assassin, sword to sword.

The uproar of drovers and ox teams masked even the sounds of steel on steel, the oaths and cries of men at battle.

The assassin wielded his sword with furious energy but not the greatest skill. Relkin turned the slashes aside and sought to get in a thrust. The sword in his hand was heavy, and it seemed a little clumsy to one who had always wielded the steel weapons forged in Cunfshon.

Still it was an edged weapon with a point, and Relkin had trained and fought with such things since he was six years old. His opponent tried a kick, but gave away his intentions far too soon, and Relkin avoided it, then turned the fellow's blade and drove his point home into the man's thigh.

The assassin made no sound but pulled back for a second before attacking again.

Endi came out of the dark; he, too, had acquired a sword, but its tip was gone. He deflected blows rained down on him by a burly man with a black mask and silver workings on his robe.

Relkin noted that all but the tall Bogoni noble had been cut down, and he was standing with his back to the woodpile with two swords in hand holding off a pack of assailants. This couldn't last more than a few seconds more. Despair welled up in Relkin's heart.

Then a familiar voice boomed out behind him.

"Boys lie down!"

Relkin didn't hesitate, and as he ducked down, he saw Bazil loom out of the dark swinging a ten-foot tent pole in both hands. There came a blurring sound as the tent pole passed overhead and then a series of dull thuds, as men were driven into the woodpile like so many racquet balls.

Relkin looked up. All the assassins save one had been cleared from the field. The survivor gave a mournful croak and broke and ran away through the wagon park, disappearing into a sea of moving oxen.

Relkin got wearily to his feet.

"By the breath," he said. "It was lucky you happened to pass by."

"This dragon was thirsty, and boy had failed to provide a barrel so I was going to the watering station. Then I heard fight, and I picked up tent pole; good thing I did or boy would now be considerably shorter."

"For once this dragonboy agrees entirely with his dragon."

"This is remarkable event, to be recorded in stone for posterity."

They were interrupted by a great cry of grief. The tall Bogoni noble had survived, too, and now he knelt beside the body of one of his companions. Endi knelt beside the man.

"He's dying; his belly is cut."

Relkin saw the blood, a great pool of it beneath the victim.

The tall Bogoni cried out, and at the same time the wounded one gave up the ghost.

"I am sorry for your friend," murmured Relkin, forgetting for a moment that the man was a Bogoni and would not understand him.

"I thank you for your concern," said the tall man, rising to his feet and startling Relkin with his antique-sounding Verio.

Before Relkin could say anything, the man went on.

"I would also ask your name, and that of your dragon." He turned and stared up into the big reptilian face. Relkin feared dragon-freeze, but the man seemed immune. He looked down, and Relkin looked into a large, open face, generous features, and dark, lustrous eyes quite untroubled by signs of the innate fear of dragons.

"I am Choulaput, King of Og Bogon," said the tall man.

Relkin and Endi looked at each other, aghast. There seemed plenty in this situation to ensure trouble with Wiliger.

"And I must thank you two for saving my life. I would surely have been slain like poor Putapoz if you had not so bravely thrown yourselves into harm's way. Most of all, I must thank your great beast. It saved all of us."

"It's the king, then?" whispered Endi.

"Yes!" snapped Relkin, and they both stood to attention and did their best to come up with crisp salutes.

Relkin felt his arm tremble a little and wondered that he was even standing up. The side of his head pounded wickedly.

"Dragoneer Relkin, of the 109th Marneri, sir!" he managed to grate.

"Dragoneer Endi, 109th Marneri!"

"I see, and your dragon's name?"

Bazil leaned forward. "This dragon is Bazil of Quosh."

Choulaput jumped a little at being addressed by a gigantic animal. Beasts of this nature were known only from the legends and the tales of the Nub al Wad.

Bazil picked up the unbroken water cask and broke the seal with a huge green-brown thumb. He drank noisily.

"Long day, makes me thirsty," he said by way of explanation.

CHAPTER TWENTY-NINE

The next morning an extraordinary invitation was presented to Dragon Leader Wiliger of the 109th Marneri. Dragoneers Relkin and Endi, Dragon Bazil, and he himself as their commanding officer were invited to a banquet with the king, who intended to honor the dragoneers and the dragon.

Wiliger had only just heard the word concerning the nighttime fracas. He'd slept through it and the aftermath. His immediate reaction was unfavorable. That damned little Relkin had somehow or other gotten himself noticed by the king. Wiliger had had enough of Relkin of Quosh and his continual searching out of glory.

Then he caught hold of himself. It would be an opportunity, too, of course, and introductions among the Bogoni elite would be welcomed, by among others, his father back in Marneri, Wiliger accepted gracefully and immediately ordered Relkin and Endi to prepare for a merciless inspection of all kits.

At the appointed hour late in the afternoon, they formed up—Relkin and Endi, Bazil behind them, and Wiliger at the head—and marched off, as if on a parade ground. Every fleck of metal gleamed, Relkin and Endi's tropical dress kit was perfect in every detail. Dragon Leader Wiliger still wore some odd items, but in the main he had shifted to wearing the issued tropical kit.

The entire legion camp knew the story by this point, and hundreds turned out to applaud as they passed onto the avenue that led to the palace.

Wiliger felt a peculiar flush of pride at this accolade. They were his dragonboys, his dragon, and he bathed in the reflected glory. At the same time it occurred to him that they might just as easily have been slain, freeing him of Relkin of Quosh. Something small and mean deep inside him would have welcomed this.

King Choulaput's palace was a sprawling complex of pavilions with flagstone floors and gold-leaf ceilings. Purple silk hangings divided the space. A crowd of Bogoni nobles had gathered, and drummers thundered out a welcome.

They marched up the steps and into the main hall where the king was waiting for them seated on the Ostrich throne.

At the entry of the dragon, there was a great gasp from the crowd. Even in this great hallway, a two-ton beast standing ten feet high tended to bulk hugely, and though their imaginations had been primed, they found the reality as strange as the advance reputation.

Choulaput accepted Wiliger's salute and then rose to embrace Relkin and Endi, which brought roars from his nobles. Then he reached up to clasp hands with the dragon, the king's hand disappearing into the huge dragon paw. This brought a hush that turned into a roar when the king's hand reappeared unharmed.

Bazil, coached beforehand by Relkin, lifted his arm and waved to the Bogoni, turning from side to side to nod his big head to include them all.

By this point his keen nose had informed him that some interesting food was on its way. The boy had been right. Relkin had claimed that there would be a great feast, and it would be worth enduring the fuss.

Gold disks minted with the likeness of the king and the national symbols of Og Bogon were hung on scarlet ribbons around the necks of Bazil, Endi, and Relkin to further applause.

The king delivered a brief speech in Bogoni. Then a religious figure, clad in red and green silks, gave a long speech. Bazil grew impatient. His belly rumbled.

At last tables were pushed in, and the banquet began. Bazil lowered himself onto his massive haunches in front of a trestle on which sat an enormous platter of rice mixed with nuts, raisins, fruits, and curried goat. To eat it, he was given a shovel.

A trolley was rolled out bearing a great urn filled with frothing beer. Bazil's eyes lit up, and he raised it and toasted the king. There was a tremendous shout from the nobles, who shot to their feet en masse and raised cups to the king.

The king toasted the dragon back.

The platter of rice and goat was soon cleaned. In came a wild boar, stuffed with peppers. More beer accompanied it.

Bazil tore the cooked flesh apart and devoured it happily. The boy had been right for once. This was turning out to be a really good feast.

Many Bogoni nobles stared aghast at the sight. Here was a giant predatory reptile devouring an entire animal in front of their eyes. It popped out leg bones from its mouth like a man might who was eating a kipper. Someone compared it with a tame tiger kept by his uncle. Someone else laughed and said the tiger would be a mere snack for this monster. It was like something out of the Lands of Terror, beyond the Wad Nub.

The king, plainly in fine spirits, conversed with Relkin and Endi, encouraging them to be open and informal. They responded cautiously, all too aware of Wiliger's jealous eyes upon them. The dragon leader had received the respect due him and no more. No golden disks, no toasts, little more than a greeting from the king. He could not complain, but his resentment burned hard within him.

Choulaput's faith in the legions and in General Baxander had been confirmed most wonderfully by the events of the previous night. First Bazil and the boys had saved his life. Secondly, the supply train had come in on time and a most generous portion distributed among the hungry people of Koubha. Even the royal pantries had been replenished.

The king now plied the dragonboys with a great many questions concerning dragons and dragon keeping. They answered with that mixture of textbook certainty and dragonboy cunning that marked the professional. Thus the king learned that it was the nubs of absent wings that were the place one checked first to see if a dragon was running a temperature and the best places to scratch if a dragon's back needed scratching. Wiliger interrupted at one point to offer the king a copy of Chesler Renkandimo's awful book. The king saw the frowns on Endi and Relkin's youthful countenances and politely told the dragon leader to send the book to the palace, then he turned back to the dragonboys.

Choulaput had noticed the two strips of medal ribbon on Relkin's uniform. The king understood the technique employed in the armies of the Argonath. He understood that very few men would ever earn enough decorations to even begin a second stripe, let alone complete one. He had heard already something of the legends concerning this particular boy and his dragon, or was it the other way around? The

ing honestly didn't know. The entire experience of talking
with a dragon was astonishing to him. All this and yet the
boy seemed hardly any different from the other one, just a
little older. Then again, Choulaput detected something in the
older one, a tension in the jaw perhaps, a way of settling the
eyes on a distant horizon when he answered questions about
his past that spoke of experiences beyond his years.

"I have heard that you have fought in many great battles,
Dragoneer Relkin. I see that you bear the ribbons of many
decorations on your chest. Yet I find that you are but a
youth, barely old enough to carry a spear in my army. How
can this be possible?"

Relkin glanced toward Wiliger. The dragon leader was engaged by the noble on his left.

"Well, Your Majesty, the dragon and I, we joined the legion when we were very young. Since then, we've had more
than our share of scrapes."

Choulaput smiled. The siege of Ourdh described as a
"scrape"!

"You have fought trolls, I believe?"

"Many's the time we've fought trolls. Nasty work it is."
The beer had loosed Relkin's tongue now.

Choulaput nodded. "Now the trolls I am familiar with are
used in the Bakan. They are eight or nine feet tall and wield
clubs or hammers, and are said to be very difficult to kill.
No man can stand against them. Fortunately we were able to
ban the use of such creatures within our realm."

"They sure are hard to kill. Do we have a time with them
sometimes. But they can't take dragonsword." Relkin finished the tankard of beer. "Nor can anything else."

The king looked over to where Bazil was clearing his
plate once again. The dragon did not eat the bones, was it
because they were cooked? Choulaput made a note to ask.

"Yes, dragonsword," he murmured, "I have yet to see the
dragonsword wielded in battle. But I have seen a tent pole
used to flatten a dozen men at a time. If the sword is wielded
in the same way, then our enemies have much to fear."

Relkin nodded doggedly.

"The sword is wielded just as a man wields a heavy
sword, Your Majesty, only the dragonsword has twenty
times the weight."

Choulaput whistled in appreciation. Such a piece of steel
would cleave anything but stone.

"We must be sure to remain good friends with such grea[t] beasts as our savior, the Bazil Broketail."

Relkin noticed that Bazil was tearing into an entire side o[f] antelope, roasted in a honey sauce. Bones were piling up be[-] side him.

"I have been informed that you and your dragon were i[n] Ourdh during the great siege."

Relkin was surprised that the king had heard of tha[t] Choulaput laughed at such condescension from a youth.

"You think we are out of touch with the world here in O[.] Bogon, boy?"

Relkin flushed. It was past time he learned to keep hi[s] tongue under control.

Choulaput was smiling, however.

"Ourdh trades with the whole world, just as your city o[f] Marneri does. In Sogosh we see Ourdhi traders, just as w[e] see white ships from Cunfshon and Marneri."

The king paused a moment. The dragon tucked into an[-] other barrel of beer. The beast seemed to down about a gal[-] lon each time it raised the barrel. Choulaput wondere[d] absently, what its limits were.

"So, we heard much of the horrifying siege of the grea[t] city of the ancient land, and we heard of the great courag[e] of the men of Argonath. And we heard that the dragons o[f] Argonath threw down the evil things made by the dark on[e] that ruled in that ancient land."

"That they did, sir, and saved the rest of us."

"You were there, then?"

"Yes, Your Majesty, we were there."

"We heard many strange and terrible tales of that siege[.] Perhaps you can enlighten us about some of the things tha[t] we were told. But first, tell me this, is there anything you[r] dragon would like when the feast is finished?"

Relkin didn't have to think for a second.

"Oh, yes, Your Majesty. He would like to swim. Even jus[t] a splash in a pool would be balm for his soul. Wyvern drag[-] ons love the water."

Choulaput gave a jolly laugh. "He shall swim in our orna[-] mental lake if he likes. It lies directly behind the palace."

Relkin caught Wiliger's chilly eye upon him. He tightene[d] his jaw. There didn't seem to be any way to avoid troubl[e] with the dragon leader.

Relkin caught himself wondering how Wiliger would tak[e]

o combat, when they got into a real scrap. When the arrows
started to fly and the trolls were coming at them, nine feet
high and roaring, then they would see what Wiliger was
made of.

"Ourdh, Your Majesty? It is indeed a huge city. I've never
seen anything like it, not even Kadein comes close. The ancient land is truly a crowded land."

The banquet continued with sweet courses. Relkin tried
half a dozen things and recommended Bazil try three of
them. A honeyed nutloaf was very much to the dragon's liking, and he ate several.

Relkin could imagine a certain wyvern groaning the night
away as it struggled to digest this vast meal of heroic foods.
Relkin was beginning to feel stuffed himself, even though
he'd done his best to be moderate. He willed himself to say
no to any more beer. A good thing, since he had the feeling
that Wiliger would have interfered if he tried to have another, which would have been mortally humiliating with the
king here and everything.

A course of an incredibly rich custard followed the sweet
cakes. Relkin struggled manfully with it. Endi was looking
a little green in the face, too.

Then came a course of jellied fruits. Relkin felt he was
drowning in food. The things had no flavor, they had a rub-
bery feel, it was torture getting them down.

And then, at last, the banquet was done with. Some formal
music was played by a group of musicians with horns and
viols. The Bogoni nobles stood to applaud the dragon as a
girl ran out and placed a wreath of jungle flowers around his
big neck. The girl managed to place the wreath, then stepped
back to bow and give her little speech. This was spoiled,
however, when she looked up into Bazil's smiling face. She
froze, and the breath caught in her throat until Relkin ran
out, feeling his stomach bouncing inside him, and pinched
her and whistled in her ear to snap her out of it.

She awoke, mind blank, and ran from the hall sobbing.
Oblivious to this small disaster, Bazil waved fondly at the
king and the gathered nobles.

Led by the king, with his courtiers bobbing around them,
they left the banqueting hall and strode through the palace
gardens, redolent of moonflowers and purple urtyx. Ahead
lay a sheet of water, in fact, a small lake, with willows

weeping along its edge and a dock and a pair of boats tied up at it.

With a huge belch of contentment, Bazil made his way down to the dock and then stepped off and sank into five feet of water. He gave a great sigh of pleasure. In two strides he kicked free and pushed out into the lake with a sweep of his tail.

The king smiled at this sight.

"Some people have goldfish in their ponds, eh, Stupagaz?" He said to his cousin, the Borko of Uba Bogon. "But I, Choulaput, have a dragon in mine."

Stupagaz laughed heartily.

"Sire, you will have to spend the treasury of the kingdom to keep your lake stocked with goldfish if you let this beast live there. I have never seen such eating!"

"Nor I, Stupa, nor I. An amazing thing. No wonder the lands of the west are barren of life if this is what roams there. And they fight like men, with swords! If you had seen this one wield that tent pole like a man might swing a billiards cue, you would have felt your heart jump. The Kraheen have miscalculated, I think."

They watched as the dragon turned over lazily in the center of the lake, a huge splash followed as it slapped the water with its tail.

"The gods must have heard our plea," said Stupagaz.

"If they did, then they must have spoken to the goddess of these heathens from the eastern isles. They worship a goddess and place women on an equal plane with men."

"Horrifying thought, sire."

"And yet their armies are the most feared in the world and the most capable."

"'Tis true, and yet they are men like any others."

"They are better trained than any others, that is their secret. And they have these battledragons, that is their great weapon."

"Come, Stupa, we must go over the list of names for the ministry. I have them on a scroll in my office."

The king left them there, standing by the pool watching Bazil float lazily into the deeper water.

At the same time, far to the west of them, Kreegsbrok was brought the dreadful news. No one knew how it had happened, but a disaster of sorts had occurred.

The guard Lerodo had nodded off. The Prophet had awoken of its own, taken Lerodo's sword, and escaped.

It had gone directly into the chapel of "He Who Must," where a service was being held to initiate a dozen daughters of the new hierarchy of the Kraheen state. With Lerodo's spear and sword, the Prophet set about killing. He even slew several of the mothers, wives of the most important men of his own armies.

Kreegsbrok received the word and ran for the chapel. He arrived to find Udul and Shukk holding down the Prophet while Birond barred the door.

The young women had been slain by the door, speared and cut down from behind. The mothers had been cut open for their hearts. The priestess lay splayed across the altar. Kreegsbrok sighed inwardly at the sight. The place was a charnel house. He glared down at the Prophet.

From "He Who Must" there was no response, however, just the glazed look in the eyes and the harsh, rasping gasps of pleasure.

Now Kreegsbrok faced the task of calming parents and husbands. How could he explain that the Prophet had needed their blood for his flame? How to explain the savage lust for killing that moved in the heart of "He Who Must"?

CHAPTER THIRTY

They stood there a moment, still basking in the good feelings of a monumental dinner, watching the king and his advisers walk away.

Endi burped. "I would say that that was a very fine dinner."

"I'm stuffed," said Relkin with a slight groan.

"I'm surprised your dragon can still float."

"He enjoyed himself, he really did."

"What were you talking about with the king?"

"The king is a wise man, Endi. He has a great strength i
him. I wonder if that's the way it is with all kings."

Wiliger sniffed loudly.

"Dragoneer Relkin, make sure you're back in quarters b
the next horn. There will be a full inspection before the eve
ning meal. However, I do not think either your dragon, o
yourself, will need anything further from the legion cook
today!"

"Yes, sir." The only thing to do was to try and humor th
man.

"And Dragoneer Relkin, just because we were talking t
the king today does not mean that we should get above ou
station. You are a dragonboy; you have a job to do. I ar
your dragon leader, is that understood?"

"Yes, sir."

Wiliger stalked away.

Relkin set his eyes on the far side of the lake. There wer
some early evening lanterns lit, and slender figures movin
among the bushes of a garden. Faintly he heard music an
the voices of a women's choral group singing a sad song.

"What is that man's problem?" said Endi quietly.

"I think he's split inside. He wants to be a good leade
but at the same time he's a bit of a fool; does things impul
sively without thinking them through. Remember that horri
ble cap badge he was flourishing around?"

"Who could forget? It made me cringe every time I saw it."

"Well he would have known about that if he'd taken the trouble to check. He assumed it was just the same as it had been in the legion where they wear all kinds of cap badges. He'd never really looked at the dragon units or he'd have noticed that all dragoneers wear exactly the same size cap badges."

"By the Hand, what will he be like when we're in a real fight?"

Relkin shrugged. "In a real fight his problem is going to be staying out of the way. He doesn't have the training for being around active dragons."

"He'll get flattened sooner or later. That'll solve our problem."

Relkin laughed, trying not to sound too bitter.

Endi tossed a pebble out into the lake.

"What do you think we're going to get into here, Relkin? I mean everyone else talks a lot about it, but you don't say much."

"Why do you ask?"

"The Bogoni on my right was telling me how the Kraheen are unbeatable. They're whipped up into a frenzy by their Prophet and then they don't care about death."

Relkin shook his head at grim memories.

"Fanatics who don't fear death make poor adversaries for the dragons. If they don't have discipline, then they can't beat the legions. I've seen that myself."

"You were at Salpalangum, right?"

Relkin nodded.

"We heard about that in our village, about the time Roq grew into his final skin."

"It was a horrible slaughter, that's all I remember. Fanatics make poor soldiers."

"And after we fight them, then what?"

Relkin smiled. "I don't know, Endi, I think we're going to go inland. If the Grey Lady is involved, then we're probably going to go to the ends of the world. That happened to us once, too."

"So." Endi shook his head. "The Lands of Terror, just like everyone's been saying."

Relkin laughed again. "You know, I'd be worried sick if it wasn't for one thing."

"What's that?"

"If I'm going to this terrible place, I'm going with the best dragon squadron there is. I've yet to meet the enemy that can beat 'em."

They sat there listening to the women singing on the far side of the lake among the lanterns as the dusk settled. Eventually Bazil emerged from the lake, dripping and blissful.

"I think we should stay in this place for a while," he said even as Relkin urged him to hurry back to their quarters.

"And Wiliger will have me up on charges if we do."

"Might do you good."

"Certainly won't leave me much time to look after a dragon."

"Mmm, you have a point there."

Still feeling full and very benevolent, they reached the stables. Relkin took down all the equipment, piece by piece and checked it for the slightest harm, the tiniest blemish in the shine. Everything was in perfect condition, even the dragon's joboquin was fully repaired, and Relkin's precious store of ramgut thong had proven itself there.

Wiliger appeared, inspection was called, and the dragon leader cast his eye over everything seeking some fault, some imperfection for which he could take the boys to task. After several minutes of prodding and picking at Relkin and Bazil's equipment, however, he could find nothing to complain about and at length went on, displeased and hissing softly between his teeth.

The horn called for the evening meal, but the scent of fresh bread, hot akh, and noodles did not arouse the broketail dragon, who had already composed himself for sleep.

Relkin heard the familiar commotion all around him as boys pushed barrows and trolleys, laden with titanic portions of food for wyvern consumption. Farther away came the general uproar surrounding the cookshacks. Shouts and laughter, a distant clang as a cauldron was dropped, all the normal sounds of dinnertime in the legions.

Fully contented, Relkin laid himself back in his cot and composed himself for sleep, which came over him in moments.

He dreamed of Eilsa, with her blond hair streaming behind her, wearing a green cloak and riding a little white horse, one of the Wattel mountain ponies. Then he dreamed of himself and Eilsa, together, walking in the high vales, with the Malgun Mountains as backdrop under a clear blue sky. It was a perfectly wonderful dream.

He awoke to a blaring alarm, the rattle of drums, and hoarse voices shouting in every direction. The cornets shrilled the call to arms.

Dragon Leader Wiliger came racing through the section, calling them out by name. On all sides he heard other voices bawling orders. The horns kept calling them to battle, over and over.

He moved sluggishly at first. The aftereffects of all that food and beer, indeed he felt oddly subdued, perhaps due to the effort required to simply digest that enormous feast. He hauled on his clothes nonetheless and buckled his sword belt. The dragon was on his feet, too.

Jak stuck his head in.

"Hurry up, Relkin, come on, Bazil! There's a war on. The enemy are coming."

"But—" Words failed Relkin. It was completely unfair.

"Boy, where is tail sword?"

Relkin shook himself violently.

"I set it by the door, to take down for a better edge in the morning."

"I see it. I have it. Helmet?"

Relkin thrust himself into action.

In minutes they were parading outside the stables, then forming up and marching down to the main gate of the city.

There was a tremendous volume of noise coming from beyond the gate. It sounded like waves pounding on the shore in a winter storm, regular and powerful.

As they passed cavalry pickets, they asked for information. And now they heard for the first time that the enemy had turned about and thrust toward Koubha just a few hours before. The great horde had marched at double-quick time behind a cloud of ebon-skinned cavalry that had outfought the legion cavalry and forced it back to the edge of the city.

What at first had seemed a cavalry skirmish at dusk became something else over the next two hours, as Baxander realized, a little tardily, that the entire Kraheen army was pouring back down the roads to Koubha. By then the hordes were coming at a trot, singing their bloodthirsty hymns and building up an ecstasy of war hysteria. Long lines of torch-lights could be seen in the west and north. Meanwhile the enemy cavalry pressed hard against the battered legion troopers.

Baxander set the cornets shrieking and sent urgent messages to Count Felk-Habren and the Prince of Kassim. The city of Koubha came astir.

Alas, the riders of the Prophet were swirling into the outskirts of the city by then, having driven the legion cavalry from the field by force of numbers and the fury of their attack.

Baxander was stunned. The Talion cavalry were the best in the world. What was happening here?

The king was awake, and the drummers were thundering the call to arms to all Koubhans. Baxander urged the utmost haste upon everyone. Meanwhile the terrible thin black men from the desert scapes of the west were trying to seize the main gate. The guards were quickly reinforced with twenty bowmen, and then fifty more, but it was nip and tuck for a few minutes at the beginning when the riders, seemingly unconcerned for their own lives, set out storming ladders and swarmed up them onto the gate itself. The guards struck down dozens, but were almost overwhelmed by the hundreds coming up the ladders. Then the extra bowmen arrived, along with a hundred men roused from sleep in the nearest billets. The riders were stopped, and after a stern little battle finally thrust back over the parapet. The survivors withdrew into the gathering darkness. Behind them swarmed the torchlights as the main army gathered. The chanting hordes of the Prophet now came forth, and went up against the city of Koubha once more.

From the walls they could see them come, a great moving mass of men, with siege engines drifting along in the dark, outlined against the sea of torchlights. Their rhythmic chant rang in the hills, and then as they came in sight of the city walls so their drums began to thunder.

Baxander went to take a look. He was impressed, and appalled. They had covered the distance at a tremendous pace. They had a great number of siege engines that they were pushing forward. Clearly they had anticipated his arrival and fled as a ruse to lure him into the city. He understood their calculations, and his estimation of their leadership rose a notch.

They knew that the Czardhan knights were of most use as shock troops on a battlefield. They also knew that the walls of Koubha were insufficiently massive to allow dragons to fight atop them as they had at Ourdh, for instance. Thus both the heaviest offensive weapons available to Baxander were virtually negated by this sudden, all-out, nighttime assault. It had all the hallmarks of a carefully thought-out scheme.

Baxander surveyed the scene and pondered his options. In his mind ran an old Teetol saying, "Fight the bigger enemy by hugging him close, then stab inside." He made his decision and then ordered that the eight squadrons of dragons be formed up in a single mass, a virtual phalanx of seventy-nine dragons, the cream of the dragon force, which he would wield like a stabbing sword, a sudden blow to the vitals of the enemy army.

To go with them he massed the Kadein Alpha Regiment and the Pennar Third Regiment. To protect them from the enemy horsemen, he sent the freshest cavalry sections to hold the flank.

Outside the walls the enemy engines were looming, vast fields of torches surrounded the city. The thrub of drums and the rhythmic roar of the chanting filled the air.

Baxander waited for the right moment. He received word that the Koubhan forces were in place, manning the walls. His own units were in their places, ready to reinforce any trouble area. Even the Czardhan knights had agreed to his plan and were waiting to be used as a reserve, either on foot to reinforce the walls or mounted to follow up on the dragons' thrust.

The enemy rushed the walls under a storm of missiles. The Argonathi bowmen took a great toll, as did the bowmen of Koubha, when the enemy came in range of their smaller bows. But the horde was so great that they ignored these losses.

Siege engines were thrust up against the gate towers. A host of ladders was set to the walls. The Kraheen swarmed up to engage the defenders.

CHAPTER THIRTY-ONE

The clanging roar of warfare now rang out on the walls of Koubha. The Kraheen were attempting to break in on three sectors, previously weakened during the siege. They had brought a dozen great siege towers. The fighting on the walls quickly became desperate and the Koubhans took terrible casualties. Baxander feared they could not hold very long.

The cornets shrilled for the dragons standing in stark rows, lit by torchlight.

"Good," sniffed Alsebra. "I hate standing around."

"I agree. Waiting is much worse than fighting," said Bazil.

The Purple Green expressed his considerable feelings with a heavy growl followed by a long hiss. The wild dragon hated the tension before battle. His huge eyes glared around him, seeking a target for his rage. The younger dragons had all learned a certain wariness in their dealings with the wild, winged giant. They exchanged looks but kept quiet.

"Forward march!" shouted Wiliger at last.

They moved down the avenue toward the main gate. Atop the gate, backlit by the fires outside the walls, they could see a great mass of men, spears projecting above, arrows and rocks flying overhead.

Arrows began falling among them. A rock clanged off the Purple Green's helmet. Wiliger dodged another and took shelter under an overhang at the gate. More arrows were falling among the dragons, feathering their joboquins, glancing off their armor. The dragonboys looked in vain to Wiliger for the command. Relkin lost patience.

"Dragons, raise shields above your heads!" he called.

He was instantly aware of Wiliger's furious eyes upon him, but at least the dragons had raised their shields and were protected from the arrows.

Wiliger was about to say something when a loud groan of

metal on wood announced that the main gates were swinging open. Wiliger stared at them for a moment, Relkin forgotten. Beyond the gates loomed a sea of white cloth, torches, and dark angry faces.

A rock bounced off Bazil's breastplate with a clang. Relkin and the rest looked to Wiliger, but the dragon leader was lost in some rapture, staring out at the white-garbed mass.

Then the regimental cornets began shrieking for the charge, and Wiliger's moment was gone. Dragons dropped their shields in front of them and strode forward out of the gate.

The cornets continued to scream, and the dragons picked up their pace to a ponderous trot. The ground shook beneath them. Dragonboys ran alongside, like small active moons, their wicked little Cunfshon bows at the ready. Arrows flicked in toward them, along with stones and an occasional spear. Relkin dodged aside as one spear bounced on the ground and shot past him at knee height.

Wiliger had finally woken up to the moment. He drew his sword and ran down the line of trotting wyverns, waving his sword and screaming "Charge!" in a shrill voice. In his haste, he somewhat outdistanced the leading dragons, Alsebra and Vlok, and found himself at the front of the unit.

The dragons were not amused by the sight of the dragon leader running in front of them where he was most vulnerable to dragonsword. Alsebra stretched her neck and hissed at him, but did not gain his attention. So she accelerated her pace. As she did, so did the rest and the trot became a kind of lope as the multiton monsters reached their top speed. They overtook Wiliger, who suddenly found himself running between Alsebra on his right and Vlok on his left. Enormous haunches sprang, contorted, thigh muscles the size of a heavy man bunched and released, the ground shook and the monstrous animals thrust ahead. Their dragonswords gleamed evilly, great sweeps of shining steel. Wiliger's heart swelled in his breast. This was extremely perilous, but it was an intoxicating moment. Never had he experienced such a thrilling sense of power.

Alsebra's tail snapped suddenly just above his head like an enormous whip, and Wiliger ducked wildly and stumbled and would have fallen if Swane hadn't reached out a hand in time and steadied him. Spun half around to slam face first into the burly dragonboy, Wiliger gave an oath. His face purpled with anger. He yelled something inarticulate at Swane, but the dragonboy was already gone, hastening after Vlok.

The Purple Green and Bazil went past, then came the two young brasshides, Oxard and Finwey. He saw their tails jerking from side to side as they bounded, and he remembered the sorcerer's isle. He dropped to the ground and lay prone on his belly while the rest passed him. He looked up to see dragonboys leaping by, bows ready, dodging the dragon tails with accustomed skill, and he felt a deep sense of inferiority and outright shame. The dragonboys did their utmost not to look at their dragon leader and just prayed that he got up before the squadron behind them came rumbling through in their wake.

The leaders were through the city gates and out into the open where they could see more of the battle in progress. To either side great masses of Kraheen were bunched about the siege towers. Hundreds of ladders were thrust up against the walls.

Straight ahead was a thinner crowd of men, since no direct assault was being made on the gate towers themselves. These men held their ground as the dragons emerged, each a tower of steel-clad muscle and sinew threatening death.

The dragons hefted their swords and dressed out their formation to a line that kept expanding as each dragon squadron deployed. They did it as smoothly as if they were on the parade ground, and watching from the tower above, Baxander's heart swelled with pride at the sight.

The closest Kraheen drew back, abandoning siege ladders, pressing into the positions of their fellows on either side of the gate.

Wiliger had raised himself after the 109th and taken up his proper position, with as much aplomb as he could muster. He did his utmost to concentrate his energies on the task at hand. He stood ten paces behind the dragonboys, who stood behind the dragons, who were spaced out twenty feet apart from each other.

A cornet shrilled from above, and the dragons rumbled forward, monstrous, towering bringers of death. The waiting Kraheen stood still until the dragons were about fifty feet distant, and then they broke and ran, having suddenly realized that they could not possibly give battle to such giant beasts with only their tulwars and round shields.

The dragons kept coming in the long-legged predatory ope of their kind, sea striders, rock wranglers, hunters of the hore. Their swords glittered on high, and the Kraheen fled n disorder.

The fugitives began to impact on other divisions of the Kraheen army, and as these resisted, so there grew a thick-ning crowd that slowed as it thickened, stiffening like egg vhites under the whisk. There were still thousands of Kraheen marching down to join the battle, and these now ran up against the crowd and slowed its flight even farther.

The dragons gained, and then suddenly the dragons actu-lly reached the struggling mob. There was a sudden mur-nur, a loud basso groan of complaint that was separate from he general din. Dragonswords rose and fell, and a mad con-vulsion shook the enemy host. Somehow the men closest to he dragons compelled those behind them to give way. An explosive effect, men tumbled, scattered, rolled in every di-ection. Those who lingered were dismembered, literally cut o pieces in a matter of moments by those huge, arcing dragon blades.

Behind the dragons, dodging tails, feet and backward sweeps of dragonsword, bounced the dragonboys, eyes peeled for any infiltrators. The dragon leaders roamed be-hind them, ready to assist if needed, or to order a change in alignment. Wiliger now understood the depth of his mistake. Dragon leaders did not actually lead dragons into battle, it was simply too dangerous.

Meanwhile, capitalizing on the panic caused by the ap-pearance of the dragons, the men from the Kadein and Pennar regiments had been moving along the base of the wall cutting into the flank of the enemy's assault forces. Ladders toppled wholesale. Siege towers were captured from the rear. The legionaries took the ground floors in the towers and then sent for the engineers. The engineers brought oil and flame, and the towers went up like gigantic torches, il-luminating the wall and the turbulent battle in a harsh, flick-ering glare.

The dragons were cutting their way through the maddened Kraheen as if they were harvesting a field of corn. It was a horrible, bloody work of butchery carried on in the terrible red light of the fires.

Relkin felt his mind freeze. He reached down with his sword tip to kill a man too badly wounded to move again, but not yet dead. Something shuddered in his own heart, perhaps just a bedrock disgust. They were trampling forward now over a field of parts of men. Bodies lay everywhere, men suddenly sundered from life, cut in two and hurled to oblivion.

The only mercy was that the death was so swift and so certain. Hardly a one survived to scream his death agonies in the wake of the dragons. But the ground was sticky with blood. The stench of the opened viscera was appalling.

During this slaughter a bare half dozen Kraheen penetrated the dragons' front, and these were all slain by dragonboy arrows before they could do any harm. The dragonboys were busier putting the few mangled survivors on the ground out of their misery than they were in fighting.

And then, at last, there was open space in front of them, and the dragons had cut their way clean through the enemy army. Space was opening up on either side as the Kraheen took to their heels rather than face those great blades.

Relkin slowed up. The dragons had halted. Wiliger went forward to assess the situation. Relkin checked over his dragon. A dozen arrows stuck out of the leather outer covering on the shield. A few had lodged in the leather of the joboquin, but none had penetrated dragonhide. Relkin gave thanks to old Caymo, and then after a moment, to the Mother, too. You never knew these days just who might be watching over you.

Lower down there was a slight problem. A spear had left a long shallow slash along Bazil's thigh. Relkin swabbed quickly with Old Sugustus. Bazil hissed sharply for a few seconds. It would need some stitches later, but no large blood vessel had been cut.

Relkin did his best to examine the wound from the Czardhan lance, but it was largely out of sight under the joboquin. From what he could see, the wound had not opened. The dressing seemed dry and unsoiled, cause for further thanks to the heavens.

While the boy worked, Bazil hissed quietly, exchanging looks with the other dragons, but keeping his breath for self-renewal. Huge lungs labored in each mighty wyvern chest.

Relkin climbed to the dragon's shoulder to extract an arrow from the leather side strap of the helmet.

"We have killed many men," Bazil said after a moment. "They did not fight very well."

Relkin grunted while he snapped the arrow shaft and began to dig into the leather for the arrowhead.

"You did what you had to do."

The dragon turned his head. For a moment they stared into each other's eyes.

"Still I do not care to kill men like that."

There came a blare of trumpets on their front. The ground trembled, and with a high yipping cry a great mass of white-clad cavalry came out onto the plain before the city. The riders came on quickly, and arrows from their compound bows were soon flicking in, whining and spacking from dragon helm and shield.

Roquil was struck in the left cheek by a shaft that got through a gap in his helmet vizor. Endi darted up the leather-back's side and cut the shaft free. The dragon was able to continue. The others roared encouragement.

The horsemen came on, pressing their mounts forward despite the presence of the dragons. They could only come so near, however, and then their ponies shied away, unable to stand the proximity of dragons. From this range they plied the dragons with arrows, and the dragonboys' return fire was overmatched. Wiliger and the other dragon leaders ordered the dragons to fall back. This development was not unexpected; Baxander knew the enemy had plenty of excellent cavalry and there was no need to risk injury to the dragons since there was no reason to hold the ground. They'd done the first job, which was to split the enemy army.

The dragons retreated with shields up, but still there were arrows thudding into their shields, ringing off their helmets, slipping through gaps in their armor to lodge in joboquin and flesh.

Then with a scream of silvery cornets the legion cavalry came thundering out of the gate and passed through the dragon formation. Their legion-trained horses were quite used to wyverns, and the troopers were burning to avenge their earlier defeat. With lowered lances, they drove into the Kraheen and tumbled dozens from their saddles in the first shock. The Kraheen recoiled and fell back in disorder, passing out of bow shot.

Now the dragons regrouped in a square and marched back toward the gate, eventually taking up a position just outside it. The first phase of the battle was over.

General Baxander moved swiftly to take advantage of the

situation. The enemy host had virtually split itself in two, bisected by the space cleared by the dragon charge. The Kraheen cavalry was the only force left to dispute this zone, and that force had been disrupted as well by the troopers' charge.

The legion cavalry was regrouping quickly, as they were trained to do. The Kraheen horsemen were still in disorder.

Baxander sent two more regiments of foot out of the gate to press into the open space and hold it. Meanwhile he sent a note to the Count of Felk-Habren pointing out the opportunity for a great charge.

Within two minutes the knights were mounted and in motion. They thundered out of the gates and aimed their horses down an avenue opened up by the dragons. The light from the burning siege towers glittered off helm and lance. The Czardhan horses were bred for war, and though the presence of dragons made them nervous, it did not halt them, not in the least. The Czardhans went on in a torrent of huge horses, tall men behind long shields, with the long pennons flowing back from their lances.

They paused a moment to fix themselves on the correct axis for their attack, and when Felk-Habren had seen Baxander's signal, he ordered the horn blown. With a great shout the charge was launched and away it went. A thousand great hulking knights of steel, in a mass one hundred wide and ten deep, went through the enemy cavalry like a hot knife through steam and drove on into the left-hand enemy mass.

The effect was almost as dramatic as the dragon charge. The enemy horde, which had almost stabilized itself from the aftereffects of the dragon attack, was struck a hammer blow on the left side of the main gate. Organization broke down as the Czardhans cut their way into the crowds of men that had already run from the dragons. These men ran again, and disorder spread rapidly.

In the wake of the Czardhans came the legion cavalry, who worked to increase the rout and to fend off any reorganized cavalry response from the Kraheen.

The huge enemy mass began to break up, a section flew off and ran for the hills, terrorized by dragons and giant men on huge horses. Another segment broke down and was cut up by the legion regiments advancing along the walls. The siege engines were burned, the enemy horsemen dispersed.

Still, the enemy mass on the right side of the gate retained cohesion, and even continued the assault on the city walls. But the Koubhans had been enormously heartened by the sight of the legion way of war. Their resistance had grown stouter than ever, and now they fought furiously to deny the Kraheen the slightest foothold on the walls.

Baxander asked the princes of Kassim and the Bakan armies to press attacks against the right hand concentration of the enemy.

The dragons were readied for another stroke.

The small but immaculate armies of the Bakan city states went marching by. Men in silver and green uniforms armed with longbows and spears, other men in bright orange and purple costume, carrying crossbows. The hues were radiant and the various groups seemed filled with fervor. They deployed and advanced. Then the Kassimi horsemen went hurtling by and crashed into the Kraheen formations.

For a few minutes there was a fierce fight, but then it ebbed as the right-side mass of Kraheen withdrew, retreating in some degree of order from the walls. They abandoned their siege engines and rams, but kept formations intact.

The Kassimi charged again and again while the Bakan militias provided archer support and infantry cover.

The split between the two halves of the enemy army grew to a mile and then to two. Baxander kept the legion cavalry at work, harrying the retreating left-side mass while the Czardhans were reorganized and more foot regiments were brought through and set forward in pursuit.

Baxander allowed himself a whoop of triumph. The first real brush with the enemy had given him a victory. The legions had proved their worth and the allied forces had all contributed in good measure. The Czardhans might be so happy with their performance that they would drop their own debilitating internal conflicts for a few days.

Then he steadied. The enemy had tried a bold stroke, attempting to negate his two most powerful weapons. He had used them anyway and broken the enemy army in half. There was still the formidable job ahead of catching the left-side half and completely destroying it. There had been much slaughter already, there would have to be more before he could really claim victory.

The dragons, however, had done their part for now. With the enemy in headlong retreat, this was a task for cavalry, working with infantry and the archers. If the enemy steadied anywhere, then the Czardhans would be used to shatter them.

The surprise assault on the city had been met and broken. The swathe of dismembered men was left to mark the point of impact.

After an hour of standing around, slowly cooling down, cutting arrows out of dragonhides and joboquins, the dragons were ordered back to their quarters.

Back through the gate they marched, Dragon Leader Wiliger at their head. Relkin felt oddly depressed. Such slaughters did not improve his mood. On some obscure level, he believed that men should never be put at risk of such an attack. It was damned poor generalship.

Dragon Leader Wiliger, on the other hand, was bursting with pride. His face was flushed, and his stride was bouncy. The battle had been won in a matter of minutes by the murderous efficiency of his dragon squadron, along with a few others. Even more important, he had made it right through the battle and had witnessed the whole thing. He had been "blooded" by battle. True, he had hardly raised his sword in anger, or even given an order, but Wiliger was not concerned; it was enough that he could now say that he had fought with the dragons in a major battle, indeed, in a great victory.

Back in the stables Relkin carefully cleaned the remaining scrapes and scratches on his dragon's hide and pulled five arrows out of the back of the joboquin. Then he went down to fetch some freshly baked biscuits, slathered in butter and salt, for the dragon and himself. He met Jak, Swane, and Endi, who were on their way back. The fresh-baked biscuits smelled delicious. He was astonished at his own hunger. They ate, the dragon ate prodigiously, and then they fell soundly asleep.

They missed the arrival of the batrukh, which flew in at dawn, causing a sensation in the town.

CHAPTER THIRTY-TWO

It was another tropical afternoon, warm, muggy, with the
sun obscured by a vault of white cloud. The dragons of the
109th Marneri were bivouacked at the side of a muddy track
near a large village.

The village had been burned by the retreating Kraheen,
and the well had been filled with the bodies of the villagers.

Dragonboys were busy fetching water from a nearby
stream. Other dragonboys were stoking a fire with which to
boil such water. On the advice of the witch Endysia, all water was to be boiled whenever possible, before drinking.

Relkin, by a fluke, had avoided extra water details for the
past few days. After fetching a load of wood he had free
time.

Dragon Leader Wiliger was away at General Baxander's
headquarters for the daily staff meeting. While he was gone,
a dragonboy with free time on his hands could, in theory, relax.

Relkin knew better than to even try. There were a dozen
small, nagging jobs that needed to be attended to, and so he
dug out his sewing bag and threaded a needle with his best
Cunfshon twist. First up was the attachment of the left side
strap on his own pack. He'd been holding it together with
pins for two days, ever since it had given way while he was
putting his shoulder to the wheel of the cook wagon where
it had been bogged in thick mud. The strap itself was pretty
worn, it was more than a year old and had seen continuous
hard use since they'd landed at Sogosh. He whistled
tunelessly as he threaded his needle in and out of the leather
and the canvas of his pack.

He was sitting under a poong tree, using its outsprung
roots as a chair. The dragon lay with the other dragons, in
the shade of a grove of gums and poongs. They had marched
six miles that morning, struggling along the muddy tracks

that were all they had as roads. They were glad of a rest, but they were all in peak condition. Since leaving Koubha three days before, they'd seen no action, no sign of the enemy except for occasional parties of prisoners and burned villages, decorated with the corpses of their inhabitants. The regimen of marching ten to twelve miles a day fully laden, eating three large, simple meals, and drinking nothing but boiled water was perfect for honing dragon condition to a sharp edge. In fact, the dragons were contented, although they grumbled a lot about the lack of beer and the heat. However, during this phase of the campaign the marching schedule was light, and thus they rested during the worst part of the day and marched on into the evening before stopping for dinner and sleep.

The recent battle was already receding from their discussions. They were vastly more interested in the lands of the interior toward which they marched. The burning question now in the legion rumor mills was that of their ultimate destination. Were they just pursuing this Kraheen army until it finally disintegrated? Or were they going all the way to the Nub al Wad, beyond the Ramparts of the Sun, in the Lands of Terror? There was constant debate.

Relkin bit off the thread and tested the strap hold. It was tight and strong. He checked the rest of the pack, and finding a tear on the left side pocket, he took up more thread and set to work.

While the needle flashed through the fabric, his thoughts flew away to Eilsa. He'd sent a last letter from Koubha. They'd been told that from there on the likelihood of mail getting back to the Argonath was low. In his letter he'd told her of his love and of his hopes for the future. He never mentioned the possible destinations of the expedition; he knew such things would be censored after he handed it in. Nor did he mention the subtle fears that played on his mind. His worst, as always, was mutilation. In battle behind dragons, the sudden loss of a hand or a head was always possible. Instead, he concentrated on the future, when they would be together, he retired from legion service, she wed to him, and they would work together with Bazil to build a prosperous life as farmers in Kenor. Now he thought about that rosy future and prayed that it might come about. If old Caymo and the other old gods heard his prayers, then perhaps they'd reward him at the last. If the Great Mother was listening, then he prayed that she wouldn't be too angry with him for praying to the old gods. He was just a dragonboy trying to cover the odds.

Ever since the battle of Sprian's Ridge, Relkin had been vaguely worried over what might lie ahead of him. At that battle, he had fulfilled the destiny foretold for him. What could be left? Now that he was no longer needed by the Great Ones, was anyone looking out for him? Did the gods or the Great Mother hear his prayers? He was so engrossed in these thoughts that he never saw his visitor until she knelt down beside him.

He looked up to a familiar face.

"Lagdalen!"

"Relkin." They embraced. He held her in his arms for a moment and studied her face. There was a gauntness there, with lines beneath the eyes and around the mouth that he had never seen before.

"You have traveled far," he said in a suddenly somber voice.

"I have, and I have seen things that I would rather not have seen, but I am alive and I am here."

"Yes!" He hugged her again. "But how did you know where we were?"

"It wasn't that difficult to find the fighting 109th! We arrived last night and the Lady has been in one meeting after another, and she doesn't need me for those. All high strategy and generals and kings, you know."

Relkin nodded, eyes shining at the thought of the councils of the most high.

"So I asked where the Marneri dragons would be and borrowed a horse and found my way over here. It wasn't far, in fact, no more than an hour along the road."

Over her shoulder Relkin saw a fine white horse.

"And how goes the battle? We hear only rumors."

"Very well, everyone at headquarters was confident of completing the victory. The enemy is in flight, and we are harrying him as hard as possible. The Bogoni have been very active. Everyone had praise for King Choulaput."

Relkin was glad to hear this news. He knew the king had been much crestfallen by his defeat by the Kraheen before the arrival of the legions. He and his army would be out to exact the fullest measure of revenge.

"And Captain Kesepton?"

Her face fell. "Ah, yes, my husband. Well, I missed him. He has gone off with a diplomatic mission to the King of Pugaz. He will probably not return in time to rejoin us. So I will not see him for I don't know how long. It can be vexing at times, this life of ours."

"But he is well? I have not seen him in many weeks."

"As far as anyone can tell me, my husband is well. Someday I hope to be able to confirm this with my own eyes. Someday I would like to return to my home and my baby and stay there with her and never leave my home again."

Relkin smiled, somehow it seemed unlikely that Lagdalen of the Tarcho would ever be granted this wish. She saw his smile and allowed a sly smile to creep across her face.

"Well, perhaps not for ever." They laughed.

"Oh, Lagdalen, you must tell me about the things you've seen."

"That would take a long time, Relkin, for I have seen so much since we last spoke aboard the *Barley,* and I don't think we will have very long this time."

Relkin made a wry face. "I suppose it's all highly secret anyway, and you can't tell such things to a dragonboy."

"Well, of course, some things are. Believe me, there are things you wouldn't want to know."

From the eagerness on his face, Lagdalen was sure that she was wrong about this, so she fell silent.

"Well, one thing that isn't a secret is that you and the Grey Lady flew into camp on the back of a batrukh! Everyone was amazed. The dragons talked about it for hours. Until the Purple Green started wondering how the thing would taste."

Lagdalen laughed, and for a moment the gauntness was gone and her eyes shone with the happy light of youth he remembered so well.

"The Lady tamed him. Found him on a mountain. He had hurt his wing and was starving. His name is Ridge-eyes, and he's actually quite sweet once you get to know him and accept that he is what he is. The Lady tickles him behind his ears, and he purrs. I swear he acts like a great big house cat."

Relkin was most amused by this thought.

"What does he eat?"

"Oh, whatever he can catch, swans in flight, storks, geese.

He really likes the larger birds. Sometimes he takes a wild goat right off the mountainside."

"So how did you take to flying on the back of a batrukh like an old-time witch?"

"Well, you flew with a dragon, didn't you?"

"I did," and Relkin recalled that magical day when the green dragoness had borne him in her talons from Mt. Ulmo to Dalhousie. "It was amazing, I think of it often. You must have seen so many things!"

"Everlasting jungle, a forest that extends for a thousand miles. Mountains so high they have glaciers and snowfields even though we're in the tropics. I have even glimpsed the Inland Sea."

"Is it as big as they say?"

"It must be, it shone right across the horizon."

"It is so good to see you, Lagdalen of the Tarcho. And Bazil will want to see you, too."

"He is nearby?"

"They're in the grove behind us, sleeping I think. We came a ways this morning."

He laughed. "Flying on a batrukh. Now I've heard of everything."

Lagdalen sighed. There were more terrifying ways to fly, she knew only too well. Through the dark animantic magic, she had been made to live in the mind of an eagle for many days once. She had almost not come back.

"It's funny how different my life is from what I imagined it would be when I was a young novice in the Temple."

"Do you remember when we met, Lagdalen? You were always in trouble. I don't think you would have made it to become a priestess."

"Probably not." She sighed again. "But if I hadn't met a certain dragon and a certain dragonboy, I would have been spared an awful lot."

"It was fate, Lagdalen. The Great Ones wanted us to meet."

"After all that we've been through because of that meeting I have to admit that you may be right." She was smiling again. "Such strange and terrible things have I seen. But tell me, how did you fare in the battle?"

"Nothing more than a few scratches. Bazil got his worst wound before the fight."

Lagdalen heard Relkin's tale of the attack by the Czardhan knight and gasped in horror.

"What a fool!"

"Certainly a lucky fool. If the dragon had had the sword with him, there'd be one knight less."

"What will happen to the knight?"

"He has not been sentenced yet. But Bazil requested another joust as punishment."

Lagdalen laughed. "You mean the dragon will have shield and sword? That would be a death sentence."

Relkin nodded grimly. "It would be, but we would blunt the sword and the dragon would try not to kill."

"But why risk it? Why not let them give him fifty lashes?"

"To demonstrate why they should never try such a thing again. These knights are a hot-blooded lot. There have been several incidents besides this, though this was the worst."

"Ah, I see." Her eyes darted about him. His clothes were worn and his boots showed the signs of a long march, but the rest of him seemed in perfect health.

"But you, Relkin, you are well enough."

The lump on the head he'd received in Koubha had only just declined to insignificance, but at heart he knew she was right. The campaign had been good for him after the months at sea.

"I'll live," he said with a grin. "So, what can you tell me about where we're going?"

She put a finger to her lips. "You shouldn't talk like that. Somebody might hear you."

"Who's going to hear me out here?"

"You never know."

"This is literally the middle of nowhere. Go on, tell me something, anything. All we get is endless rumor."

"Well, I can tell you about the mountains in the west. I think we'll be going there, all of us."

"Those would be the Ramparts of the Sun."

"Yes, that is their name."

"Then, it's true isn't it? We're going to go all the way to the Inland Sea."

Lagdalen shook her head. "I don't know, Relkin. The Lady does not tell me such things. What if I were taken by the enemy? It is better if I know as little as possible of the grand strategy."

Relkin sighed, not sure whether he could fully believe this.

"But the mountains are wonderful; they are the greatest mountains I have ever seen."

"Greater than the Malguns?"

"Oh, yes, they are so high they have ice and snow on their tops, even here in this tropical land."

"How are we going to cross them then?"

"There are passes, and roads. The Impalo peoples have long tended the roads. They guard the passes against the Kraheen."

"Hmm, but the Kraheen were here already. What does that say about this guard?"

"It is known that this Kraheen army came from the south. They crossed the mountains far to the south and marched for months to reach the lands of the Bogoni unobserved."

"So." Relkin stared off into the west. "How far is it to these mountains?"

"A month's march, I would say."

"What is the land like along the way?"

"From what I saw from the batrukh's back, it is like this except that it gets drier the farther west you go."

"And when we cross the mountains?"

"I do not know, Relkin, honestly. The Lady knows, but only she."

Relkin knew he would have to be satisfied with this. In truth, he was not displeased. It was something to have confirmed his suspicion that they were heading westward, much farther than they had already come.

"And how fares the Lady Lessis? She was so good as to write me a letter, did I ever tell you, Lagdalen?"

"No, Relkin, but she did. She told me that you were the only dragonboy she has ever written to."

"She is well, then."

"Relkin, you know the Lady, she never changes much. Even when we carried her in the catacombs of Tummuz Orgmeen, she remained much the same. She is as she was, and I think, as she will ever be."

"I've heard it said she's five hundred years old."

"She is older than that by a century, Relkin." Her smile grew brittle. "I am barely grown myself, but it sometimes seems I've served for centuries myself."

Relkin sensed Lagdalen's sorrow at being parted from her baby.

There was a sudden interruption when a heavy tread behind them announced the arrival of a leatherback dragon of considerable girth.

Bazil came around the tree, scooped up Lagdalen, and put her on his shoulder.

"Greetings to Lagdalen Dragonfriend. This dragon heard boy talking with someone and then thought he recognized your voice."

"You were right. How are you, my friend?"

"Wounds are healing, none serious. The fight was not serious, either. If we had some beer, then all the dragons would be quite content, except for the heat. Dragons come from the frozen north."

"Which is why you need some beer."

"A serious lack."

The dragon set her down on her feet.

"I do not know when you will get any. There's a long march ahead of you. Perhaps when you pass through the lands of the Impalo kings there will be beer."

"That would be something."

"Relkin told me that you have challenged the Czardhan knight."

"Boy is right."

"What will you do to him?"

The dragon shrugged eloquently.

"I will not kill him."

CHAPTER THIRTY-THREE

The morning was cool and bright, as they so often were on the inland plateaus of equatorial Eigo. Only later in the day would the heat and humidity rise to the level of discomfort.

It was an important day, for it had been chosen for the punishment of the Czardhan knight, Hervaze of Gensch.

The day before had seen the trial of the Knight of Gensch, charged with assault and malicious wounding of the battledragon Bazil of the 109th Marneri. It had taken long negotiations with the Czardhan leadership to agree on the conditions for the trial.

The fighting with the defeated Kraheen army had petered out some days before. The remnants of the Kraheen were in flight south and west, into the swamps south of Pugaz. The allied army had concentrated around the market town of Douxmi, close to the western edge of Og Bogon. A couple of days of rest were in order for the expeditionary force.

The trial of Hervaze had been public and well attended, with the King of Og Bogon sitting as judge. Hervaze was defended by a skillful knight from Lenkessen, Irs Parmy. Parmy spoke Verio almost as well as he spoke his native Demmener and brought a trained advocate's skills to the task. The prosecution was led by a Major Herta of General Steenhur's staff, who favored a blunt approach that often intimidated witnesses.

Testimony was heard from Dragoneer Relkin, who had witnessed the assault, and from the dragon himself. This latter development had been highly controversial among the Czardhans. Many of the knights had still refused to accept the essential "personhood" of the wyvern dragons. Some of the most conservative knights could hardly believe that the wyverns could think and speak.

Bazil's spoken testimony, therefore, had been a shock to many. To hear a vast battle beast stand before the court and speak Verio like a man was profoundly disturbing to some. What Bazil had said, however, changed the minds of some Czardhans and threw many others into confusion.

Then Major Herta had called the companions of the Knight Hervaze to testify. At first their answers were evasive, but Herta struck home by appealing to their sense of honor. They testified truthfully, that Hervaze had been drinking a fiery distilled spirit and had challenged the wyvern dragon and then charged the beast when it refused the challenge.

Finally Hervaze himself was put to the questions. At first, aided by Irs Parmy, he had avoided incriminating himself, but at length Major Herta was able to set the knight upon his honor. He acknowledged, at last, that he had charged the dragon and speared him.

The king found Hervaze to be guilty and handed him over to General Baxander for proper military justice. Baxander announced that Hervaze had a choice of punishments. He could accept fifty lashes, given in front of the entire army, or he could put on armor and take up his lance and fight the dragon again, this time in fair fight.

There was a great gasp of wonder among the knights. Whose idea had this been? Then it was announced that this challenge had been demanded by the dragon himself. Who had ever imagined that a dragon would make such an honorable request?

Hervaze of Gensch recalled being swatted off his horse by that dragon. It had been a hell of a blow. Hervaze also thought of what he had seen on the battlefield at Koubha, that perfect carpet of dead men, cut to ribbons by dragonsword.

Yet, the men of Czardha were brave to a fault, and Hervaze was nothing if not a typical specimen of his kind. He would happily accept such a death rather than submit to the ignominy of fifty lashes in front of the entire army.

His acceptance of the challenge set off a round of cheers from the massed knights, many of whom believed that any good knight, properly armed and mounted, would dispose of a dragon. In the legions, meantime, there had been a knowing chuckle or two as they'd dispersed from the open-air court.

And so on this pleasant, sunny morning the army was drawn up on either side of a long, open space, with the ground packed hard and dry in the center. A long white line had been chalked down the middle.

General Baxander, flanked by Count Felk-Habren and King Choulaput, rode up and sat their horses at the midpoint of the white line about one hundred paces clear.

At one end of the white line was a knot of men and a great warhorse, at the other a knot of dragonboys and single, brooding wyvern. Both Hervaze and Bazil wore full armor. Hervaze's lance was tipped with a flat, and Bazil carried a dulled, legion issue blade rather than Ecator. Bazil disdained the clumsy legion sword, but both he and Relkin knew that Ecator would kill the knight. The blade was a witch blade with a mind of its own and a passion for killing.

A horn blew. An equerry from Czardha read out a proclamation, first in Demmener, then in Gelf, finally in Verio. The combat would take the form of jousts, the knight to remain on his side of the white line and the dragon on his. Each joust would begin on the sound of the horn and end when the parties had passed each other. Jousting would continue until one or other of the parties retired or was unable to go on.

A drum began to thump, and now preparations intensified. The knight was assisted into his saddle and his mount led out to the beginning of the white line. He made an imposing sight, a towering form, encased in steel plate and helm, with the oval shield and the long lance set in his stirrup cup. On the plains of Czardha, across Hentilden to the borders of Kassim, these were the rulers of the battlefield. Not even the troll hordes of the enemy had withstood the charge of the massed knights of Czardha.

The horn sounded a warning note. There came a confused cheer from the ranks of Czardhans lining one side of the ground. Hervaze's massive mount positively frisked forward to the starting point. Hervaze seemed to radiate the confidence of the ever victorious knights of Czardha.

Then everyone looked to the other end of the line. They saw a huge, crouching bulk, hidden behind a great rectangular shield with a long steel blade that rose up to rest against a mail-clad shoulder. Incalculable menace rose like a cloud of doom from this figure. There were some among the Czardhans who felt their hearts suddenly falter for the first time.

The horn blew again. King Choulaput raised a white kerchief. Silence fell across the field. He dropped the kerchief and the joust began.

With a great ringing war cry, Hervaze dug in his spurs and set his mount trotting forward. The trot quickly gave way to the canter and then to the gallop.

The dragon took a few steps forward and then halted, shield up, sword swinging loosely in the right hand. The tail was held high, bearing tail mace instead of tail sword.

The hooves of the warhorse thundered closer, the lance came down and locked into position. Hervaze dropped his vizor and bent his head over his lance. As the dragon loomed closer, Hervaze selected his target, aiming for the uncovered shoulder. If he hit that spot hard enough he might tip the great monster over onto its back. Legend had it that these brutes became helpless when they were thrown onto their backs.

The dragon was much closer then. By god, but it was huge!

They came together. Bazil shifted his feet, ducked his shoulder, and brought his shield up and over to deflect the lance away with a sharp rapping sound. Then Hervaze was past, and the horse bore him down to the far end of the white line.

A sigh went up around the field at this slight result.

Bazil turned to watch and casually leaned the sword against his shoulder while his tail drooped to the ground.

Among the watching Czardhans, there was a degree of chagrin at the failure by one of their own to achieve immediate victory. Conversation broke out among them as grooms and aides assisted Hervaze.

At length there came the signal. Hervaze was ready to charge once more. The horn blew. Bazil stood forward in a practiced crouch.

Again the great horse thundered down the line and Hervaze leaned forward, aiming this time for the dragon's helmet. The dragon loomed before him, an implacable tower of steel and sinew. A wild scream came from his lips as he bore down. Then the lance shattered as the sword swung in a mighty arc, and Hervaze rode on, bearing nothing but a stump.

From the legions there came a ragged cheer. Among the Czardhans a groan of shocked dismay rippled back.

Once more Hervaze was equipped and readied. Once

again the horn blew and he charged the dragon. This time he kept his aim flexible; he would take whatever target was available. The dragon moved too quickly for any other tactic to work. Hervaze had been unpleasantly surprised by the speed of the dragon's movements.

Again the thunder of hooves as they closed together, and Hervaze reached and lunged, aiming the lance for the dragon's throat.

And again the massive shield snapped up in time to deflect away the lance. This time the dragonsword swung around in a glittering slice. Hervaze ducked in time and only caught a fraction of the blow on the top of his own shield. Still he was almost hurled from the saddle and clung on desperately with both hands, leaving his lance to fall in the dust.

Another cheer, more lusty this time, came from the legions. Many among the Bogoni joined in. The Czardhans watched in stony silence during the minute or so that ensued as Hervaze readied himself and acquired a new lance.

The horn blew. Once again the warhorse sprang down the white line, and Hervaze leveled his lance. This time he would feint for the open shoulder and then raise the point for the upper part of the dragon helmet. A blow there might stun the wyvern.

He dodged the shield and, indeed, his lance point did carom off the very top of the dragon's helmet; but it was too late, for this time the dragonsword swept around too low to duck and Hervaze was airborne in a moment, conscious, even before he hit the ground, that his shield arm was broken. Then came the terrible impact with the ground, and Hervaze knew no more.

As the knight landed with a clanging thud in the dust, a soft moan went up from the massed knights of Czardha. They had witnessed the mastering of the flower of chivalry; it was a sobering sight.

The warhorse ran on, riderless, to the end of the line. The dragon stood back, laying his sword against his shoulder, lowering the heavy shield to the ground and leaning on it.

Hervaze of Gensch was taken up and borne from the field on a stretcher. A trumpet blew, and the equerry announced that the joust was finished.

The cheering became general as Bazil tramped away, surrounded by a mob of dragonboys. Under the trees, out of sight of the Czardhans, waited the other dragons who offered brief congratulations.

Watching the scene were General Baxander and the witch Lessis, sitting their horses off to one side.

"Well, I do hope our allies take that little lesson to heart. We've had too much of this sort of trouble with them. I think perhaps they understand now just how formidable a battledragon can be."

"Especially that particular leatherback dragon."

"Ah, yes, Lady Lessis, the broketail dragon. He has a trail of legends they say. And wonderful luck. The luckiest dragon in the legions they call him."

Lessis was moved to respond.

"I don't know about luck, but he is a great fighter. I have been privileged enough to have known this dragon, and those legends are true."

"Really?" Baxander was taken aback. For some reason he had never connected the Grey Lady to the legends of the broketail dragon. "Well may I say that I feel proud to have him in my command. I hope his presence will bring us luck. Certainly things have gone well so far."

"General, you have performed prodigies. The emperor will be overjoyed at what you have accomplished. I, myself, am amazed. Moving this army so far, so fast, and destroying the enemy host so convincingly, you have begun our campaign in great style."

Baxander felt slightly uncomfortable under such praise, but, in truth, he was most pleased by the success of his planning and the work of the Engineering Corps.

"I am glad to serve the empire, Lady."

An aide rode up and passed Baxander a note from the Count of Felk-Habren.

Baxander read the note, scribbled a brief reply that he handed to an aide for inscription in Demmener, then turned back to Lessis.

"The knight Hervaze will live. In fact, he has escaped quite lightly, a broken arm and some cracked ribs, no more. He will leave wyvern dragons alone from now on."

"Thanks to the Mother for that. We do not need any source of rancor between the legions and the knights. We will need all our forces in the upcoming struggle."

"Yes, of course." Baxander looked away; the field was emptying swiftly. From the legion tents came the sound of the "Kenor Song." They would be celebrating for the rest of the day over there.

"Our upcoming campaign, I find that I have little idea of what to expect from here on. It has been unsettling, not having any idea."

"I understand, General, and I apologize. I have spent too much time scouting and not enough time reporting to you. But after our good fortune in befriending the batrukh, I thought to take the maximum advantage."

"You have information for me, then?"

"I do. The situation is critical, and I regret even this day, lost to us as it must be."

"Surely the men deserve a day's rest. We have driven them hard ever since we landed. They have won a great victory on top of it."

"You are correct, General, and nobody would begrudge them this rest if the timing of our expedition were not so crucial. Our enemy is rapidly developing his weapon, and it will take us at least three months to reach him."

"Three months! That sounds like the worst case situation that you envisaged."

"I don't think I ever suggested that there could be any other option. Perhaps Admiral Cranx thought the expedition might not have to go all the way, but I did not agree with him. No, General, we have to go all the way, even to the shores of the Inland Sea, the very Wad Nub of legend."

Baxander sucked in a deep breath. There were legends surrounding this witch, terrible legends involving death rides by doomed units dragged into the unutterable wastes where their bones remained to whiten in the sun. Was that to be his fate?

Not a religious man, Baxander found himself offering up a prayer to the Mother just then. If She watched over them as it was claimed, then might She not give them a little aid in this situation?

"The maps are vague concerning the location of the Wad Nub. I only know that it is far to the west of here. How do you expect us to cross such a distance in only a few months?"

Lessis gave him her determined smile.

"You reached Koubha within a week. I believe it will take two months to cross the Ramparts of the Sun."

Baxander whistled. "I understand that those are mighty mountains."

"They are, and on their far side there lies the land of the Kraheen. There also lies a navigable river that flows through forest country. We shall build rafts for the army and float downstream for most of the journey. If we are in time, we shall catch the tail end of the monsoon flood, and that will speed us toward the Wad Nub."

Baxander raised an eyebrow. Two months to the Ramparts of the Sun, with this unwieldy army and all its supplies. The logistics were going to be nightmarish.

"What about the Kraheen army we just defeated?"

"They will be hunted down by the army of Pugaz, with assistance from King Choulaput's forces."

"I see."

"I won't lie to you, General. We face a great challenge, but we must hurry. We have to reach the lands of the Kraheen before they master the weapons they are building. Our enemy knows that we are coming to destroy him. He will redouble his efforts."

"We have our work cut out for us. I suppose we'd better get to it, then."

"With the Mother's blessing, we will succeed."

Baxander wished he could be as convinced as the Grey Lady, but then he was only a soldier and therefore all too aware of all the obstacles ahead. He sighed and signaled to his staff.

CHAPTER THIRTY-FOUR

It was a journey out of legend, a thing of mythological proportion. Across the savannah uplands of Eigo they marched, legions, Czardhan knights, Kassimi warriors, and soldiers of the Bakan city states. A strange polyglot army, accompanied by a screening force of Bogoni tribal warriors. Each man knew that he was involved in making history, and the weight of such knowledge lent an extra depth to every tone, every moment.

They crossed the friendly kingdom of the Impalo peoples and the unfriendly kingdom of Belatz. The King of Belatz made threats, but never followed up on them. The sight of this great host of strangers, with their multitude of wagons hauled by oxen, was so astounding that the Belatz fell back astonished and did not lift up their heads again until they were past.

To assuage the warriors, the Belatz tribal magicians assured their folk that none of the strangers would ever return from the west. They would die of disease, they would die of starvation, and if they crossed the Ramparts of the Sun, they would die over Kraheen cook fires or in the bellies of the terror lizards.

The army was blissfully unaware of these dire predictions. They trekked on, shouldering packs and weapons, faces set resolutely to the west.

They trekked through brush country that gradually grew drier as they approached the mighty Ramparts, whose snow-caps glittered in the dawn and serrated the sunset. The high savannah was a landscape lush with brown vegetation. In the day the dry grasses seethed in the hot winds; at night they whispered in cooler breezes from the interior. In the day they often saw herds of antelope and small groups of gazelle. At night they heard the roar of lions and the shrill shrieking of hyenas. The cavalry reported sighting elephants and other larger herbivores. Some were truly colossal, but these avoided the marching columns.

Each dawn found the witches in motion, casting spells against flies up and down the line, small but potent magic that kept the endemic biting flies away from man and beast all day. This was vital since the biting flies brought with them the terrible sleeping sickness that slew man, horse, and ox alike. The witches' work was so good that only a handful of men were lost to the sickness, along with a dozen horses and twenty oxen. These were such tiny numbers that General Baxander's planning staff were astounded. New respect for the witches became widespread.

The mosquitoes alone were immune to any magic, and that in part was due to their numbers. But to counter the deadly ills they carried, the legion medics issued a preparation of quinine and the march was laid out carefully to avoid mosquito-plagued places. The end result was the miraculous sight of a huge ox train moving across a land that had seen no oxen, hardly any horses, both of which were peculiarly vulnerable to the sleeping sickness, in all its history.

The legion cavalry, working in concert with the Kassimi and the small detachments from the Bakan states, roamed ahead of the marching columns, seeking out the best trails and camping places, and arranging with tribal leaders for supplies of food to be purchased and made ready.

And thus the marching host from the east did not die of starvation, and the cooks found ways to make the legion staple, noodles, out of local grains and tubers. There were even occasional supplies of native-brewed beer, strong and dark. On those nights the hyenas and lions were shocked into silence by the roar of the "Kenor Song" and "La Lillee La Loo," echoing out across the wild, empty savannah of the dark continent.

They rose early in the mornings, well before dawn, and marched until the sun had reached the eleventh house and the heat was begun. They camped and dozed through the mid part of the day and renewed the march in the evenings, carrying on until the last rays of the sun were gone. Sometimes they marched by moonlight as General Baxander pressed to squeeze every mile possible out of every day. Often they made fifteen miles in a day, occasionally more. The Czardhan knights, the Kassimi princelings, and the pocket generals from Storch and Monjon were astonished at such steady, constant progress. Their men were just as astonished by their resistance to the plagues of the tropics, and they were assiduous in taking their daily dose of quinine draft. It had been observed that those who failed to do so were invariably the ones who sickened with the tropical ague and had to be left behind in Impalo villages.

In great part this steady progress through wild country was the result of tremendous efforts by General Baxander and his staff, allied with the engineers and supply teams that had been working for Baxander since he first arrived in Sogosh. These young men saw to it that the scouting reports were evaluated and checked so that bridges could be built and ponds dug in order to collect spring water in advance of the arrival of the thirsty columns. It was these men who ensured that food supplies were received promptly. The planning staff slept barely an hour a day during this incredible march. More than anyone else, they understood what a feat their army was attempting.

Far ahead, ranging from tribal capital to tribal capital went the Grey Lady and her companion Lagdalen of the Tarcho, soaring on the back of a great batrukh. Here Lessis was in her element, casting subtle attraction spells, overawing the simple, stouthearted Impalo men with the power of her witchcraft, not to mention the appearance of the monstrous batrukh, dropping out of the skies upon their villages. Batrukhs were known only from nightmarish legends. They came from the Lands of Terror in the uttermost west and swooped down to devour whatever caught their eyes. To find one as peaceable as a horse, under the guidance of the Great Witch Lessis was a stunning experience for these men.

And so they were as pliable as rope in the hands of Lessis and gave every assistance they could to the marching army.

All day the mountains hung there ahead of them, growing larger imperceptibly as they crept westward. Wrinkles on their distant outlines turned into vast buttresses of grey stone, overhanging green shoulders and rippling foothills. Clouds often clung to the higher elevations, cloaking the snow from their view, providing spectacular banners of crimson glory at sunset.

The army marched, making history as it went.

This advance did not go unnoticed by the enemy that was its target. Most nights their campfires were overflown by other batrukhs, fell servants of the power in the West. That power watched the army's remorseless progress with mounting anxiety. In furious reaction it drove its slaves to fashion the great sword for its right hand.

Alas, there were difficulties. Such enormous quantities of metal were hard to smelt and harder to cast successfully. One accident slew sixty men who were standing too close.

Thus the enemy read each day's report of the army's march with growing anxiety. The days ahead were measured with passionate concern.

CHAPTER THIRTY-FIVE

"I thought that if they were the Ramparts of the Sun, that we'd at least see some sun. Not just this accursed cloud."

The speaker was Swane of Revenant, wrapped, like everyone else, in every stitch of clothing from his pack, and still shivering as they tramped along a trail over harsh-edged shale, drenched in cold mist.

"The sun, the sun, what I would give to see the sun," groaned Endi.

"Dragons are better off, not so hot for them," said Relkin, groping for a positive point.

"Speak for yourself, boy," grumbled Bazil, directly behind him. "This dragon would welcome a little sunlight. Anything to lift our spirits."

"This air is too thin, too cold," moaned Mono.

"Look at the bright side," said Manuel, "the way is level now, we're over the climb."

"By the breath, Manuel's right."

"That is one boy with wits about him," said Alsebra.

"We've reached the top," shouted someone else.

A cheer went up that quickly died away beneath the cold, muffling fog. Shivering, they pulled their kit around themselves and went on.

The cold was the worst thing for the dragonboys, who had only tropical kit. That morning they had had to melt drinking water again, and they would have to do it in the evening, too. This came on top of the general irritability, the constant fatigue and headache caused by the thin air.

The dragons didn't mind the cold, but they disliked the thin air, all except for the Purple Green, who was positively cheered by the experience. High gloomy places such as this pass winding through the mountains had once been a favorite haunt. But that had been in his previous life when he still had the power of flight. However, the lack of sunshine made the wyverns snappish.

For days it seemed they had been on this road to nowhere, tramping ever upward into white banks of cold mist that only seemed to grow thicker the higher one went.

At night they could see no stars, no glimmer of the moon. In the chill night air, they shivered on the ground or gathered together around the few fires that could be allowed from their dwindling supply of firewood and tried to warm themselves. It wasn't easy with so many gathered around them. They slept poorly and grew more irritable as a result.

Most irritable of all was Dragon Leader Wiliger. Now Wiliger came striding past, en route from somewhere behind them in the column to somewhere ahead. He rarely spoke to them or passed on any information. Now he passed with barely a nod, then he stopped and turned to bark.

"I want to see that joboquin fully repaired by lights out, Dragoneer Endi."

"Yes, sir."

"And, Dragoneer Relkin, I haven't forgotten those wood-splitting details. As soon as we reach a woodlot, you'll be busy again."

"Yes, sir."

Then Wiliger was gone, hastening away along the line of march.

"Where's he off to in such a flaming hurry?" groused Swane.

"Who cares as long as he stays there," said Relkin.

"I wish he'd fall off a cliff and break his neck," said Endi. "He's been riding me about the joboquin for two days now, all because a single strap was broken."

"The higher we go, the worse he gets."

"He's been strange ever since Koubha."

"He ought to be, he pulled a stupid prank. Could have been killed."

Swane shook his head in disgust. "I never thought I'd say this, but I really wish we had ol' Turrent back."

"To think that we've come to that," said Manuel from the back.

They continued to march, one foot after the other across the wet shale. It was slippery in places, and after negotiating some of these, they noticed that they were trending down.

They had gone over the top of the pass and were on the downward path.

It was an hour later that they finally broke out of the dense mists. Slowly these thinned and then all at once the sun broke through and they were out of the fog and under the bright warm sun once again.

They turned around a bend in the course of the road and emerged onto a view that took their breaths away. A green world of endless forest that stretched away into the dim distance. They cheered, but looking at that forest Relkin felt a premonition. Once they were over the mountains, they would be in a new world, completely cut off from their own. How many of them would ever return?

CHAPTER THIRTY-SIX

The raft was a beauty. Confronted with untouched virgin forest, the legion engineers had selected only mature keem and menelo trees. These provided straight trunks sixty to one hundred feet long that were highly water resistant. They had been lashed together in threes, then these triples were combined into larger and larger platforms to carry men, dragons, horses, and oxen.

Baxander blessed the planning that had gone into every facet of the expedition. The witches had suggested the route and located the prime stands of keem and menelo that they had converted into rafts. The engineers and their teams of workers had been ready to build the selfsame rafts and had brought special equipment and joiners for the task. The men and the dragons had thrown their effort into the task with a will.

In just a matter of a few days they had cut the forest, trimmed the timber, and built rafts to ferry twenty thousand men, horses, dragons, and oxen down the great river Chugnuth, which was marked on their maps as flowing toward the vaguely delineated "Lands of Terror."

The Czardhan knights had been perhaps the most astonished of all. At breathtaking speed they had seen trees cut, trimmed, assembled, and then built into rafts. They had stripped to the waists themselves to aid in this effort, under the orders of humble born Cunfshon engineers and witches. The whole thing had been an amazing overthrow of aristocratic precedent, but they had done it willingly. They and their horses were now afloat, drifting downstream at a steady pace, and they were still marveling at it.

If it had been simply left to them to do, they would still have been arguing about whose job it was to cut the trees and whose to trim them. Most likely there would have been fighting over the matter. Count Felk-Habren would have had to adjudicate half a dozen duels.

The knights had been deeply impressed by the ingrained efficiency of the legions. The Czardhans had taken part in dozens of military campaigns, all of them fought at a lethargic level, and they were thus well aware of the contrast.

It brought up unwelcome thoughts about the very nature of their quarrelsome societies. Each state in Czardha, large or small, was a seething nest of intrigues, quarrels, and constant small-scale wars.

The raft for dragons had a layer of keem trunks on the bottom and a layer of roughly trimmed menelo planks on top to provide decking. Around the sides was a stout rail and at the front end there was an outrigger fender, constructed of keem branches bound together into a huge, fat roll that was then propped up on menelo beams fastened to the raft. At the rear of the raft stood piles of firewood. The rest of the surface, forty feet across and sixty long, was given over to dragons and men.

The river they floated on was enormous, considerably wider than the Argo, and it ran smoothly enough that they had little to do other than pole off occasional snags and waterlogged trees and avoid the other rafts—a veritable armada of rafts, that was bearing the allied army down the river toward its goal at a pace somewhat faster than that of a walking man. They went steadily, with hardly any interruption, bearing the sword to their great enemy.

The river trended south and west, and bore them toward the Inland Sea and the heartland of the Kraheen empire.

The fleet of rafts was lashed together at night, anchored in the middle of the river, since Baxander could not risk losing rafts in nighttime travel. In the mornings, after a brisk boil-up on the shore, a vast breakfast was consumed and then the fleet broke up and drifted downstream all day. In the early evening, they gathered together once more and parties were sent out to find food in the forest. So far they had been able to supplement their stocks of grain with considerable amounts of game and edible foods from the forest.

In just a few weeks they would reach their target. They had made the journey from Koubha in astonishing time. With luck they would reach the enemy before he could truly concentrate his strength. General Baxander felt a surge of pride at the thought. The Empire of the Rose had thrown this expeditionary army right across the world like some enormous dagger, aimed at the throat of the enemy's enterprise here on the dark continent. They would earn a glorious place in the history of the empire, and indeed of the entire world.

The men and the dragons were, frankly, enjoying this part of the expedition. They had marched more than four hundred miles in not much more than a month. After that they were ready for the rest and here it was, floating lazily downstream day after day, beneath the equatorial sun. Being soldiers they took the opportunity to sleep as much as possible. The evening foraging was something that many looked forward to eagerly. They brought in everything, from bushpigs to edible gourds.

Relkin's raft held four dragons: Bazil, Vlok, the Purple Green, and Alsebra. In addition to dragonboys, there were a dozen legionaries, tucked in wherever they could find a crack. Traveling on another raft, Wiliger had put Manuel in charge of the unit. The legionaries were under Corporal Klake, a bluff, no-nonsense veteran of seven years. Everyone was a little crowded, since dragon equipment took up a lot of space on its own, but they had found ways to cooperate.

One dragon at a time was equipped with the big pole. Several men were assigned smaller poles and designated to assist the dragon in pushing away snags and other rafts.

Having more than one dragon moving around much on the raft tended to make it pitch, so the dragons were forced to sit in their respective places for most of the time.

When the fleet came to a halt and cooking fires were lit, the dragons would all go over the side for a swim about the river. They hunted for fish and proved adept at catching the slower ones. There were crocodiles and river sharks, too, but neither proved much of a problem since they were much smaller than the dragons and generally avoided them.

Meals were enormous, and the dragons usually contributed a few of the larger river fish to the daily pot of stew. There were some kinds of river fish that grew to ten feet in length and several hundred pounds in weight. A few of these fed a whole regiment.

During these mealtime gatherings, the witches and medics were active, making sure that everyone took their quinine-laced drink that day.

Thus they made progress, moving quite swiftly down the

river, heading west and south, leaving the Ramparts of the Sun behind them and with them all connection to the rest of the world. And throughout this period they saw almost nothing of native peoples. Once they saw distant columns of smoke, and another time they glimpsed some small canoes hurrying away from them, but that was all. They were left with the immense river, the jungles on either side, and the raucous creatures that inhabited them.

CHAPTER THIRTY-SEVEN

Relkin, Jak, and Swane had formed a hunting party that afternoon. Once the cookshacks had been set up and water put to boil, they took their bows and stalked the forest downstream.

Once under the trees, they moved through a twilight world in an atmosphere of hushed peace redolent with the stink of mud and decay. The trunks of trees were like grey pillars supporting the distant canopy. Poisonous frogs of glorious red and yellow clung to the bark. Insects murmured in the warm air. Every now and then they came upon a clearing where some forest giant had fallen. In these clearings a riot of small trees and vines competed for the light. Such places were good for finding game. Forest antelope or bushpigs might be spotted at this time of day. Bushpig was especially popular among the dragons.

On this particular late afternoon, their hunt was fruitless. The forest was unusually quiet. Even the green lizards and smaller birds were absent.

Then, in a tangle of roots around the base of a great strangler fig, Swane spotted an enormous coiled serpent sleeping off a significant meal.

Drawn by curiosity, the boys gathered around to admire it.

"It's a beauty," murmured Jak.

"Damn, but it's huge," said Swane.

Indeed, the constrictor was two feet thick except where its dinner, a bushpig, still bulged out its stomach. The serpent's skin was glossy brown, lined with black, striped with red and spotted with yellow. From a massive, spade-shaped head, two big black eyes stared at them apprehensively while a long tongue tasted the air for danger.

"What's it weigh, d'you think?" said Swane.

"Big as a dragon," said Jak.

"Big as a big dragon," said Relkin.

"Skin looks like leatherback," said Jak.

The snake looked at them with considerable anxiety. Oblivious to this, Swane reached out to touch one of the coils.

"Feels so smooth, not like a leatherback at all. More like a freemartin green."

"Some leatherbacks are smoother than others, Swane. Now, Vlok ain't smooth at all, but some are."

Swane ignored Jak.

"Feels cool to the touch. He's gorged."

Relkin was studying the snake's eyes. The pupils were as wide as they could go.

"That may be, but he's also pretty unhappy. I'd say he doesn't care for company right now. In fact, if I were you, Swane I'd . . ." Relkin's warning came a little too late.

The snake's head rose suddenly, and it made a halfhearted strike at Swane, huge fangs white and visible in the big mouth. Swane leapt backward just in time.

"Damn thing could swallow you whole, Jak."

The boys shifted several yards away while the huge constrictor slid off into the undergrowth with a fervent hiss of dislike.

"Friendly fellow," said Relkin.

"All I did was admire his pretty skin."

"Thought Swane was gonna get chomped just then."

"A lot less trouble we'd have," said Jak with an impudent grin. He looked to Relkin. "I think we really would miss old Swane."

"You'll be missing if I catch up with you, little Jak."

Jak made a face at the bigger boy, but stayed out of cuffing range.

Relkin was a few yards ahead, scouting the edge of another clearing. He gave a low whistle, and they moved to catch up with him. They soon saw that this was no ordinary clearing. The trees dwindled as the forest floor was replaced by a pavement of great blocks of stone. Ruins thrust up among vines. Occasional trees had broken through the paving, heaving up the foot-thick blocks.

Stone steps rose up into man-made hills where ancient pyramids rotted beneath a covering of small trees. Farther on there were the remains of a high wall, sections of which still rose above the short forest.

"This is an ancient place," said Swane as they trod the ruins.

"Who built it?" said Jak.

Relkin shrugged. The world was old and had seen many tides of people come and go.

"Men live but for moments," Relkin quoted the prayer to the Great Mother. "Their cities but for a day. We all come to dust in the end."

"Uh-oh," groaned Swane, "the Sage of Quosh is at it again." Relkin tossed a pebble at him, and Swane climbed up onto a pedestal of stone. A wall loomed nearby.

"Hey," said Swane, jumping down. "Look at this."

They gathered beneath the wall.

Along the top of the ruin was a fragment of bas-relief depicting the bottom half of a man wearing armored boots and carrying a sword. Rich filigree had been carved below it, forming a frame for the image.

"There's more over there," said Jak, pointing.

Two high walls rose above the scattered trees. Between were the ruins of an entranceway to a huge place, a former arena perhaps with a curved interior wall that was still ten feet high in places. On this inside wall were more carvings. They gasped in unison when they saw the dragons cut into the stone.

"Wyverns," said Swane. "Here in the dark continent."

"But I thought they came from the north."

"So much for what they taught Manuel," said Relkin.

There were, however, details that made him uneasy. The beasts in the carving walked upright and were clearly reptilian, of the same general type as the wyvern dragons, but their bodies were huge, as evidenced by the human figures carved in the background. The upper limbs were small in relation to the rest, unlike those of wyverns and the winged dragons, who could all go down on four legs quite easily. The stone dragon heads were too large as well.

"I don't know, look at these things. Are these really wyverns?"

There was a whistle to his right.

"If those are wyverns, then what are those?" Jak pointed to another set of well-preserved carvings on a fragment of wall farther around the curve.

Clearly represented were four-legged beasts of huge dimensions, with long necks, small heads, and long, long tails. In the background were men with carts drawn by small horselike animals, all dwarfed by these colossal reptilian beasts.

Swane rubbed his eyes.

"They had some pretty overweight dragons back when they made this."

"They're not dragons." Jak snorted. "Look at those heads, too small for dragons. Relkin, what do you think they are?"

"I have no idea, but they're big. Bigger than anything I've ever seen."

"They have to be dragons, what else could they be?" grumbled Swane.

"What about that?" shouted Jak, pointing to another carving.

This monster was like nothing they had ever seen. A large, bulky animal with a squared-off body, a long tail, and a large head dominated by three long horns.

They stood there scratching their heads in amazement.

"Sort of like an ox, but with horns that stick straight up," hazarded Jak.

"Never saw an ox that had a horn on its nose."

"An ox crossed with a unicorn, then."

"Unicorn? You and your unicorn, Jak."

"Whatever it is, it's pretty damned ugly."

There was a sudden eruption of noise nearby. A loud squealing began in the thickets beyond the immediate circle of ruins.

"Bushpig?" said Swane, reaching for his bow.

Relkin shook his head. "Never heard a bushpig sound like that."

"Could be a baby," said Jak.

"If there's a baby, then stands to reason there'll be a mother. Dragons would like that."

Suddenly the squealing took on another tone, one of terror. It ran sharply up the scale to agony and then cut off. Other similar animals were squealing now, and coming closer.

The boys exchanged looks. Something had just made a kill.

There came a loud, booming cry, a harsh sound filled with triumph. It was repeated three times and echoed around the stone ruins. The boys fingered their bows nervously. The squealing was much closer now.

Out of the brush burst a pack of small grey animals, striped with black, that resembled miniature elephants, with big ears and long, supple trunks.

These astonishing little elephants were no larger than dogs, and they ran like horses. The glimpse was brief, however, in a few moments they were gone.

"Damn, never got off a shot," said Swane.

"Good thing, too, we don't know what they are," said Jak.

"No bigger than dogs."

"There's another one."

"Oof!" Swane was suddenly bowled over.

Another small striped elephant had erupted out of the woods and cannoned into the back of Swane's legs. The impact knocked Swane onto his hands and knees, and left the stunned elephant sitting on its hindquarters.

While they stared at it, struck dumb with amazement, it staggered up onto its feet, eyes filled with terror.

"What the hell happened?" roared Swane, getting back to his feet and reaching for his bow.

"You got a friend, Swane." Relkin pointed to the terrified elephant.

"I really ought to shoot it. Take it back for the dragons."

Relkin had appraised the little elephant. There was something about the eyes that spoke to him.

"I wouldn't shoot it, Swane, and I don't think the dragons would want to eat it."

"How do you know? They like to eat anything."

"What I want to know," said Jak, "is what is chasing them?"

"Uh, they are," said Relkin, pointing over a low section of the ruined wall.

Three menacing shapes moved through the short forest.

"Uh-oh," said Swane as all three of them fitted string to arrows.

The little squealer was still getting its breath back. It tried to run, but could barely do more than hobble. Impulsively Jak picked it up and carried it up the slope of the crumbled arena. It wriggled like a greased pig, but he held on and lugged it up through the bushes that cloaked the lower part of the former gallery.

"What the hell are you doing, Jak?" groused Swane.

"Couldn't just leave him to get eaten."

"Here they come," said Relkin.

Into the arena came three enormous creatures like nothing they had ever dreamed of. Each stood ten feet tall, striding forward on long, massive legs, like those of an ordinary fowl magnified a hundred times. All resemblance to fowls ended with the legs. The bodies were remarkably bulky and covered in pale grey feathers. The heads were massive, ending in huge, cruelly hooked beaks.

It was the wings that were the final, chillingly ludicrous touch, for they were tiny, and held close by the body—useless appendages, no more.

The huge birds stalked forward with a cautious mien, pausing now and then to peer upward at the boys and the little striped elephant. There was food, but there was something unusual about it. The birds were cautious.

"I don't like the look of these," muttered Swane.

"Right. And if you don't like those, then what about these?" Relkin indicated two more of the terrible birds, which were stalking along outside the sunken arena wall.

"They're all around us," said Swane.

"By the breath, they're as big as trolls," said Jak.

"You know, now I've seen everything," grumbled Swane. "This elephant fellow is the size of a fox terrier, and that bird is as big as a troll."

The birds had completed their survey of the scene. With chilling nods to one another, they separated and began to edge up the rows of eroded seats.

"They're coming after us."

"Looks like they know what they're doing."

With shocking suddenness the central bird sprang toward them, its beak agape.

Three arrows studded its chest in a moment, but hardly seemed to slow it.

They scrambled upward, firing the while. The little elephant led the way, accelerating ahead of them.

On either side the other birds mounted the steps.

They hit the bird in front of them again and again to little effect until at close range Relkin finally sank a shaft into the monstrous avian skull, right through the eye. The bird halted, just a few feet from them, and with a mournful croak toppled backward and landed with a thud.

"Quick, onto the wall," said Relkin, seeing the other two birds begin their charge.

They scrambled. Fortunately there was a fragment of the exterior wall, eroded at the top but still ten feet higher than the top of the former seating area. Onto this ruin, a mere three feet wide and twelve feet long, they scrambled. During the scramble, Swane twisted his ankle and was barely able to get up to safety before one of the giant birds snatched him up. Jak had tossed the little striped animal up ahead of him. When Swane threw out a desperate hand and missed a handhold, the elephant caught his hand in its trunk and held him for a crucial moment as he regained his grip.

Then they sat there, they only had two dozen arrows between them. There were a lot of these birds, and they could not afford to waste a single shaft.

Soon the birds slipped into hiding, and they wondered for a long while if they had gone on, leaving them behind in favor of other prey.

Some antelope passed through the ruins.

With a shocking suddenness, one of the great birds burst out of concealment in some short bushes and kicked one of the antelopes right off its feet. In a moment its huge head had ducked down and seized the antelope, which was as big as a man. It lifted the struggling antelope and threw it down against the stone. Shaking its huge head from side to side, it battered the antelope to death. Then it picked it up head first in its bill and swallowed the entire animal.

The pygmy elephant gave a mournful hoot at this sight, and then sank down on its haunches and tucked its head into its shoulders.

Swane sat beside it and ventured to stroke its head.

"Changed your mind about him, then?" said Jak.

"Yeah. Saved my life. By the breath, I owe this little beast my life."

"I told you there was something about these fellows. You shouldn't shoot them."

The light of day was fading.

"One of us has to go for help," said Relkin. "I think it had better be me."

"What about the birds?"

"I'll go when it's dark enough."

"What if those things can see in the dark?"

"Then I won't make it. So you'll have to hope a search party comes out this way. But you know how they keep going on about making time. We've been in a hurry since we landed at Sogosh. I don't know if there'll be too many search parties."

"You better make it, Quoshite, or else ol' Swane is gonna be food for these damn big chickens."

CHAPTER THIRTY-EIGHT

After a last handclasp with the others, Relkin slid from the safety of the wall and slipped quietly into the undergrowth. He moved slowly, cautiously away from the walls. There was no sign of the huge birds. Yet the memory of that sudden charge from concealment kept returning to haunt him. So he moved on tiptoe with many pauses to examine the way ahead. The light was almost gone from the day, and in the dimness it was easy to imagine things lurking in every patch of bushes.

And so he took his time, forcing himself to move slowly, and not to give in to the urge to just run as fast as possible for the forest. A panicky run could easily end in disaster. It was all too easy to imagine being hammered by those massive feet, and swallowed whole, head first.

Monkeys began screaming at each other in the treetops nearby. He paused a moment beside a standing stone. He had covered half the distance to the real forest, where there were trees tall enough to provide a safe haven from ten-foot-tall birds.

Just ahead was a patch of small trees with white trunks. He stared at them, willing himself to see through the dim light and the grey vegetation. Carefully he examined the clump of trees. Were those pale bars the trunks of trees or massive legs? It was very hard to be sure, but after a minute or so he concluded that the small trees were safe; no bird lurked within.

He peered around himself in the gloom. Could the birds have gone? Was he simply wasting time being this cautious? It would be wise to get back to camp before Wiliger started searching for them. He didn't need any more trouble with the dragon leader. He'd only just gotten out from under the last load of punishment details and hardly needed any more.

Perhaps the birds had withdrawn to sleep. Relkin hoped

with all his heart that they were predators of the day and not
the night as well.

The forest loomed greyly in the near distance. He should
be on his way. And yet, something kept him back. He hesitated to leave the protective shadow by the stone. He put his
hand out to the stone. It was cool to the touch and reassur-
ing.

Then it trembled under his hand, and he looked up just in
time as a massive head was swung over the top of stone and
driven down at him. He ducked and darted away to his right.
A huge beak snapped shut just inches from his head.

The damned thing had crept up on him while he was scanning the clump of trees! By implication, that meant the birds
could see well in the dim light.

Relkin ran, forcing himself on as fast as he could go. He
broke through a tangle of vines, almost tripped and fell, but
managed to stagger on into a cleared space. Here he stretched
out in a sprint, the breath hot in his throat, his heart hammering
wildly.

The bird was close behind him, slowed slightly by the
vines. Ahead was a tumbled pile of great square stones. He
sprang among them, twisting left, then right, then right
again, while the huge bird bounded along behind him, twisting in pursuit. Again, he gained a little ground. The bird was
too massive to match him in such maneuvers.

Away in the trees the monkeys screamed at the approach
of night while he ran for his life through the ancient stones,
pursued by swift avian death. He could feel the heavy body
behind him. He could hear the thud of its feet on the ground.
On the straight it gained on him. He kept weaving, looking
for a tree he could climb very quickly. That seemed his only
chance.

And then he saw it, a temporary asylum, a fallen tree, the
trunk hollowed out. The space was just wide enough for him
to wriggle inside the trunk, but the giant bird could never
manage it.

He fairly flew over the last few yards, the bird gaining
with each drive of its huge legs. It was right behind him
when he launched himself in a dive that took him sliding
straight into the darkness of the hollow log.

The wood was slimy within, and he went in a lot farther
than he'd expected and ended with a thud against something

solid. He struggled for his dirk, and then his hand fell on the obstruction and found it to be wood.

It was too dark to see much, except for a circle of grey light at the other end. Something ran over his hand, and he jerked it back and got to his knees, holding the knife out ahead of him.

Then the whole tree shuddered as the giant bird tore at the opening behind him. Questions ran through his brain. How long was the tree? Could he get out at the other end? What else might be in there with him?

He listened intently, aided by the fact that the bird had given up attacking the open end of the tree and was stalking along the length of the hollow trunk. He listened especially for the hiss of a snake. It would be just his luck to put his hand on some poisonous serpent that he couldn't even see.

Several seconds went by and he heard no hiss, hardly a skitter. Cautiously he edged forward, testing ahead with the point of the dirk. Every so often he stopped and listened carefully. The forest beyond the log still echoed with the screams of monkeys.

Then, a little later, he noticed that silence had fallen on the forest. Nor could he detect the vibrations of the bird's feet. The bird had stopped moving. Had it gone away? Ahead was the dim grey circle of the other end. He went forward, eyes straining, hands encountering slime, mold, and insects. At some spots he had to crawl through tight places, enlarging them with the dirk where necessary. The inner wood was rotten and crumbly. As he worked insects moved about him, but thus far nothing had bitten him. He breathed a little prayer to the old gods. The divine dice were rolling for him.

At length he approached the far end of the hollow trunk. He stared at it cautiously. Was the bird waiting out there? If so, how long might it stay?

To get out meant going out on hands and knees; the opening was too small for anything else. If the bird was waiting there, it would have a good chance of catching him. This was a dismal thought, but the only alternative was to stay in the log and lose the chance of reaching the camp and getting help.

Carefully he stuck his head out for a look around. He saw the huge head coming down and scrambled back for safety. With a splintering crash, the bird's bill slammed into the end of the tree and broke off a V-shaped chunk of wood. This gave the bird pause, and it examined the place it had damaged intently.

Relkin retreated into the interior. The bird attacked the tree again. With that heavy beak, it was capable of breaking up the weaker sections of the rotted-out tree. Relkin kept moving.

Abruptly the tree jumped, and the section above his head gave way. Rotten wood showered down. He glimpsed the dark mass of the bird's head and flung himself backward with desperate energy. The head came down and the beak sank into the wood directly over him, spearing through like an enormous ax head.

He should have died then, but the bird had miscalculated. The wood at this point was weakened but not yet rotten. It was wet and yielding, but still possessed strength. It admitted the great beak and then gripped it fast.

There was a moment of stillness as this appalling news reached the bird's brain, and then the whole tree trunk shifted an inch or two as the bird heaved madly on its bill.

Relkin stared at the great hooked beak, jutting into the wood right in front of his face. The tree shook and realization dawned on him. Then he came to life and scuttled for the nearest opening.

A few moments later he burst free. A quick glance around showed no other predators. He ran for the forest. When he was among the tall trees, he looked back. It was hard to see in the dark but he detected the bird still bent over the fallen log, flapping its tiny wings uselessly as it struggled.

He ran on, keeping to the most open spaces he could find. By great good fortune he came out onto a sandy beach with the river flowing beyond it. He quickly oriented himself and headed upstream toward the campsite.

He knew he was close when he smelled the hot kalut. Dinner was already over. When he reached the cookshacks, he saw piles of dirty pans being lugged down to the riverside where the men and dragonboys on punishment detail would scrub them until they shone.

Dragon Leader Wiliger greeted him with a scowl, and Relkin sighed inwardly.

A rescue party was swiftly assembled. A dozen archers accompanied five dragons, armed with sword and shield. Relkin led the way, and after half an hour of blundering around in the dark, they found Swane and Jak still alive, holding out on the top of the wall. The little striped elephant was still with them.

At the arrival of the men and dragons, the terrible birds had faded back into the undergrowth, where they remained. The fallen log that had preserved Reklin had been broken in half and the trapped bird had fled as well.

The dragons gathered around the corpse of the bird downed by Relkin's arrow.

"That is a big chicken," said Vlok.

"Vlok is not good at telling different birds apart," grunted the Purple Green.

"That's no chicken. No chicken has a beak like that. It looks more like an eagle," said Bazil.

"I ate an eagle once," said the Purple Green. "It didn't taste very good."

"A disgusting thought," said Alsebra.

The wyverns silently all agreed. Wild winged dragons were capable of eating the strangest things. And yet they turned up their noses at fish?

Bazil poked the dead bird with his sword.

"It might be good, roasted," said Bazil.

"We certainly shouldn't waste it," said the Purple Green.

"How are you going to get the feathers off it?" said Vlok.

"Dragonboys are good for some things."

And so they butchered the fallen bird and carried its carcass away to the cookshacks. There it was swiftly plucked, cut up and set over the fires. Everyone agreed that it did, indeed, taste like chicken, only it was a hell of a lot tougher. Some parts were more the consistency of leather than meat. Dragons devoured it all anyway, and slept soundly thereafter.

CHAPTER THIRTY-NINE

At first Dragon Leader Wiliger did not know that "Stripey," the terrier-sized elephant, was traveling with them. Jak was clever in his selection of hiding places, and Wiliger spent much of the time in his tent.

The little elephant was immediately popular with the dragons, who found his antics amusing. He particularly made them laugh when he ran up the Purple Green's back and perched on his massive head. In just a day or so Stripey had become the sqadron's mascot.

Wiliger did not approve when he finally caught on. The dragonboys protested.

"There are no regulations specifically against having a squadron mascot. Some Kadein squadrons have mascots."

"That may be, Dragoneer Relkin, but I am in charge here and I forbid the presence of pet animals. Mother only knows what sort of diseases it's carrying."

Wiliger would not listen to their pleas. Stripey was dragged out on the end of a piece of rope tied around his neck. Before their horrified eyes, Wiliger picked up the little elephant and threw him off the raft.

There was a rush to the edge. Crocodiles were sliding into the stream on the near side of the river.

"Any boy who goes into the water will be flogged."

They paused. Jak looked back with anguished eyes. Mutiny boiled just beneath the surface. Feelings close to murder rose in Relkin's heart.

The raft tilted suddenly. Dragons were there, too.

"Mascot is in the river," announced Vlok matter-of-factly.

"Well, don't just stand there," said Alsebra. "Either go in and get him or let me through so I can."

Her remarks were cut off as a huge body launched itself into the water with a tremendous splash. The whole raft shuddered and shook.

A leatherback surfaced and with two powerful strokes of its tail propelled itself to the struggling form of Stripey. The pygmy elephant was rescued the next moment, and the dragon pushed itself back to the raft. Stripey was tossed up onto the raft.

It was a more laborious process to haul two tons of leatherback out of the river onto the raft, which though stoutly built, was still just a raft and tended to bend and dip under the surface when he pressed his weight on the edge. Other dragons made it worse by crowding the side in their efforts to help. At one point the whole raft threatened to tip over, and there were frantic calls to the dragons to move back from the edge.

Nor did the freshly rescued Stripey help as he danced around them, hooting and squealing with excitement. Twice he was nearly stepped on, until Vlok picked him up and deposited him on top of a pile of wood.

The crocodiles, drawn by the commotion, were getting close when at last they hauled Bazil back onto the raft, which again almost tipped over with so much weight on one side.

Wiliger had watched all this with growing chagrin. His authority had been flouted. Still something held him back from a complete explosion. The fact that the dragons wanted the animal as their mascot made it much more difficult to simply get rid of it. A dragon leader was there to guide his dragons, not to get into conflicts with them. This was so basic to the Dragon Corps that not even Wiliger could ignore it. Wiliger had a gut feeling that if this was protested to higher authority his decision would be overturned. Higher authority, in the persons of Generals Steenhur and Baxander, had shown itself to be cool, almost unfriendly to the new dragon leader of the 109th Marneri. Wiliger did not want to test his support among his superiors. There was still the embarrassment of his mistake at the Battle of Koubha. General Steenhur had said very unkind things about that.

For now, anyway, he publicly accepted the presence of the little elephant. There was really no alternative. It had become clear to him that his policy of staying aloof from the unit, following his embarrassment at Koubha, could not succeed in restoring his authority. To be their real leader, he had to win a place among them. They were all against him, and he could not win in such a situation. The squadron as a so-

cial organism had a natural strength. He had to do something
about that.

A day or so later, Relkin sat at the front of the raft, under
bright sunshine, resetting some buckles on the girth strap
from Bazil's joboquin. He felt a presence behind him and
turned to find Dragon Leader Wiliger approaching in shirt
and trousers. He murmured a hello and gave a soft salute.
Relkin breathed an inward sigh of relief.

The relief soon evaporated. Wiliger took up station on the
front of the raft just a few feet away and studied Relkin.
Relkin grew nervous. He had just cleared himself of a mountain of cookshack work details. Nervous hands were all
thumbs, and he pricked himself with the needle and cursed
under his breath.

Wiliger sat down close by.

"A beautiful day, eh, Dragoneer Relkin?"

Relkin blinked. It had been months since Dragon Leader
Wiliger had tried to be pleasant with anyone in the squad.
Relkin was vaguely shocked by this abrupt change.

"Yes, sir," he said quietly, as he always did. It was best
not to excite Wiliger in any direction.

"Dragoneer Relkin, I feel I must speak frankly with you."

"Uh, yes, sir?"

"I expect you don't much like me. You resent me coming
over from an infantry unit. You all think I don't know a
thing about dragons. Think this fellow Wiliger must be a
real showboater, big mouth, fancy uniform. I know, I know,
I have made mistakes."

"Yes, sir." Relkin found it easy enough to agree with that.

"Yes, well, it's always difficult, don't you know, when
you have a new officer and a new unit. It takes time for everyone to adjust."

"Yes, sir."

"Well, Dragoneer Relkin, it's like this. I wanted the
chance to work with the dragons. I had a career in the infantry. I've told you a few of the things that we got up to over
there, but I thought I would be happier in the dragon force.
Do you see? And since my father had the resources to make
such a switch possible, I thought I had to try it. I thought,
the fellows over there in the dragon force will probably resent me at first, but they're good fellows and they'll give me
a chance, and if I can show them that I'm as good as they
are, they'll accept me and it will all work out well."

Relkin was stunned. Of all things this was the least likely. Not after these last few months. His thoughts flew back to that terrible moment in the restaurant in Marneri.

"Unfortunately things went wrong somewhere along the way. It was a long voyage; we were all cooped up on the ship. Tempers fray, you know what I mean?"

"Yes, sir."

"So now, Dragoneer, we're going into battle soon and I want to start again with you. I want a new beginning. I think we should clear the decks and start again. What do you say?"

Relkin felt a dozen sharp retorts bubbling to the surface and gritted his teeth and did his best to smile.

"Whatever you want, sir."

If Wiliger wanted to be nice to them, rather than carrying on like some imp master, then Relkin would do his best to help it along.

This response encouraged Wiliger enormously; Relkin saw the man swell happily. His face went a light pink. Relkin shuddered; some new enormity was coming.

"I'm so glad you said that, Dragoneer. Good. You know, I've been thinking. We need a motto for the squadron. Now we have a mascot. Well, another thing we could have is a motto."

"A motto?"

"Yes, sort of thing we have in the infantry regiments. You know, the First Regiment, First Legion, they're called the "Do-or-Dies" because that's their motto."

Relkin nodded; the concept was familiar, but no one had ever suggested such a thing for the Fighting 109th.

"Well, yes, sir, I suppose."

"And, in fact, I've come up with what I think will be a perfect motto."

"Oh, yes, sir." It wasn't that he'd expected to be consulted, but Relkin still felt oppressed. Wiliger was still Wiliger.

"Yes, how do you like this: 'We'll do it. What is it?' "

Relkin stared at Wiliger for a long moment.

"Yes, sir," he said.

"Good isn't it? Because the Fighting 109th has a reputation to uphold. We'll fight anyone, it doesn't matter who they are, or even what they are, right?"

Wiliger chuckled at his own wit. Relkin made the gritted teeth smile again.

"And if we run into any of the things you saw carved on the stone, then it'll fit just perfectly, don't you know."

Relkin nodded weakly, astounded by this turn of events. Still, the important thing was to get an amelioration of Wiliger's reign of terror. If he was going to be friendly, then Relkin would let him. What the others would say, he knew, would be harsh. Swane and Jak had really suffered the last two days. Snap inspections, endless pot scrubbing. Jak had even had to polish the studs on the dragon's shield until they shone like glass. And yet, when all was said and done, Wiliger was their commanding officer, they had to get on with him. Swane and Jak would have to swallow their pride, just like everyone else.

And there was some fighting in the not too distant future. Bound to be, that's what they'd come all this way for. The Lady virtually had said as much. They just couldn't say quite what it would be they'd be up against. Relkin wondered if it could be worse than the ogres they'd faced at the battle of Arneis.

Wiliger stopped chuckling at last, and after a nod and a smile went back to his own tent.

CHAPTER FORTY

The weeks slid by effortlessly as warm, indolent days succeeded one another. The vast fleet of rafts floated down the enormous river, rigged square sails whenever a favorable wind blew, and made steady progress. Food supplies were good, if simple, and were daily supplemented by hunting and gathering in the forests. General Baxander and his staff were pleasantly amazed at their success. They had brought an expedition of unwieldly components, more than twenty thousand strong, halfway across a continent barely known to exploration. Sometimes, when he contemplated the maps and saw how far they had come, Baxander felt a flush of pride. Then, inevitably, would come a cold douche of fear when he recalled that his whole army was now effectively beyond the world, lost in the heart of the dark continent. There would be no support, no help whatsoever from here on. Everything would be up to them, alone. And if he made mistakes, it was likely that not a man, not even a dragon, would ever get back over the Ramparts of the Sun, let alone see the coast again. The white fleet would go home empty, and the expedition would go down in history as the greatest disaster of all time. The responsibility made for sleepless nights no matter how tranquil their voyage on the upper river was.

On the rafts carrying the 109th Marneri, Dragon Leader Wiliger continued to be unusually amiable. There were inspections, but instead of handing out days of pot scrubbing for the slightest, tiniest thing, he merely remonstrated with the offender for having a hair out of place, or a speck of dust on some metal that otherwise gleamed like glass.

Wiliger had taken to appearing suddenly to involve one or more dragonboys in little heart-to-heart conversations. During these he radiated goodwill like a lamp. He particularly seemed fond of Swane and Endi. This behavior left the boys puzzled, but still pleased at the relative relaxation of the former reign of terror. The dragons noticed the new mood, of course, and became quite kindly toward the dragon leader, who previously they had regarded as a witless pest.

But while the dragon leader had changed from stormy to sunny, the character of the jungle, past which they floated day after day, had slowly turned in the opposite direction. Slowly things changed until at last they noticed that they had entered another world.

They had left the hills far behind now, and the trees had grown steadily taller. They were of different types from before, and there was a progressive absence of fruit trees among them. Monkeys could no longer be heard in the forest, and the cast of birds had changed, too. They were much fewer in number and far less visible. During the day, a brooding silence seemed to settle over the landscape. At night, they occasionally heard strange raucous cries like none they had ever heard before.

Late one day, close to the fall of night, several men in the advance guard reported seeing an enormous creature swimming in the river, or possibly walking along the bottom. For when it climbed out and disappeared among the trees, it was revealed to have legs like the pillars of a temple. These men were in a scout boat well ahead of the main fleet that evening, and they claimed that the beast was many times the size of a battledragon. As big as a whale, they said.

Their report electrified a fleet that had already been aroused by the stories told by the dragonboys from Marneri concerning the carvings in the ruined arena and the giant terror birds. However, there had been no further sightings of such birds or any other large animals. Indeed, in recent days there had been very little game brought in at all. Fortunately the daytime fishing had improved markedly in the last week, but the forests had become strangely quiet.

The scouts' description of what they had seen fit no known animal, and it triggered intense speculation, and some apprehension. That same evening, a flight of very odd-looking birds had been seen passing high over the river. They were like little triangles of pink and brown, caught by the sun's last rays. Those who knew their birds remarked that they had never seen birds with such a shape.

The men of the legions shrugged and spat. That night they hunched a little closer around the cook fires. Only a few of the most determined hunters bothered to go out in the forest. They brought back very little, too, only a huge tortoise and some oversize possums. The possums made good eating, roasted over the fire, and the cooks turned the enormous tortoise into a wonderful soup, which caused much comment around the fires.

Some Kassimi hunters reported finding the tracks of an enormous animal, and a pile of dung taller than a man. This, too, became the focus for much speculation and a lot of jokes.

Several days went past with nothing more seen but crocodiles, ever-present crocodiles, and fish. The land seemed devoid of life, although at night things shrieked and gibbered in the ancient woods. And yet these night calls were fewer and much farther between than had been the case in the upland forests.

Then one day a beast, something like a small dragon in shape, sprang from concealment and attacked two Kassimi foot soldiers who were out hunting. The surprise was so complete that it was on them before they could react. It threw one man down and disemboweled him with a slicing blow from one of the giant claws it bore on its hind legs. The other man fled after wounding the animal slightly with his sword. He returned to the campfires, and a body of men with cavalry support went out immediately.

They found the creature eating the fallen Kassimi and drove it to flight with their lances. It sprang away at a good pace, and the horsemen had to gallop to keep up with it while they dispatched it with spear and lance. It proved hard to kill. Even after it had been brought down and some men had dismounted to finish it off with the sword, it managed to thrash around on the ground and bite a man on the leg.

When they dragged in the thing's corpse, it caused a sensation in the camp.

The dragons came ashore, squad after squad, to look. They were particularly disturbed, for this killer beast was definitely of their kind. It had the scaled skin, the dragon eyes, talons, and long tail. It also had a wickedly flattened head and a tiny brain.

Each dragon in turn prodded the remains. Only the Purple Green suggested eating it. Most were silent afterward, troubled on some interior level. They shrugged off questions from dragonboys and ate sparingly. That night they scanned the sky for the dragon stars, but they were late to rise and low in the sky.

Men who saw the dead brute took away an indelible image of the large jaws filled with flesh-ripping teeth, the enormous leg muscles in the thigh, and ultimately of the eight-inch killing claw that tipped the second toe on each hind foot.

The witches examined the corpse carefully during a dissection carried out by the surgeons, and conferred with General Baxander. Afterword, word came down to all ranks. From here on they would all have to exercise great caution. Going ashore would become too dangerous. Large and aggressive animals might be encountered. The legends told of the striding killer beasts, monsters larger than dragons that ate men in a single bite.

They had, at last, entered the legendary Lands of Terror. They all felt the difference. As to what it all meant and what the future held for them, that was a question they deferred to their favorite deity. For the Argonathi and the Cunfshoni, it was the Great Mother; for the Czardhans and Kassimi, it was the Lord Protector, God of the Ancient Fire; for the Bakanites, it was any one of a thousand gods, all part of their complex pantheon. But to all of these deities, the men offered up the short prayers typical of soldiers and with them the hope that they might be protected from whatever ill might come their way.

Maps of this area were vague. It had hardly been explored. All that was really certain was that the river they rode would eventually deposit them in the southern part of the great Inland Sea.

To those with the maps to look at, the strategy seemed brilliant. By going through these strange jungles, they were making a hook around the lands of the Kraheen. When they reached the coast, they would turn north and within a few weeks they would be in the heartlands of the enemy. This route to the Inland Sea was empty of human beings. The Kraheen, like all the peoples of Eigo, shunned this ancient forest. Nothing would induce them to enter. Thus, the only danger was from the terrible animals that dwelled in the deep thickets. With eighty dragons on hand, they could be sure of driving off such animals.

And so they would arrive on the field against the Kraheen

ready to give battle. Baxander's army was like a huge dagger hurled at their Great Enemy by the Empire of the Rose.

Of course that enemy knew they were coming. Every night they heard the distant screams of the batrukhs flying high above, monitoring their progress. The enemy knew what they had planned to do. He would be compelled to face an army built around Argonathi legions, with dragons and cavalry and all the formidable skills of engineers and provisioners that the Empire of the Rose was famous for. And he would have only the armies of the Kraheen with which to do it. These armies fought with fanatic determination, but they were disorganized and only lightly armed, good enough to defeat the tribal hosts of Eigo, but not to stand on the battlefield against such as the legions, or even the heavy cavalry of the Czardhan knights. In the enemy's favor was the fact that he would have time to prepare the ground, to build defense lines, and to set his tactics. Yet, in the end, he would still have to face them in line of battle and in such a clash the legions could not be beaten.

"Hektor's Formation" was the watchword on the rafts and there was much loose talk about the Battle of Salpalangum. There, a bare ten thousand legionaries had defeated an army ten times their number. In a mobile square, the legions, supported by the cavalry and mixed arms of the allies, could survive envelopment and cut through the heart of any enemy host.

Those who looked at the maps were left with a feeling that they were on the edge of a tremendous victory, a heady feeling indeed.

To those without maps there were just the legends and the rumors. They accepted these with equal aplomb. They were soldiers first and foremost. Somewhere ahead lay a large body of water. They would land on the shore there and march. Then they would fight. The one certainty was that there would be battle. They had little reason to fear the Kraheen overmuch.

And so the fears in dragonboy hearts were not for the certain battle ahead, but for the rumors of sickness that swept through the rafts. There were unusual fruits brought in from the forest. The witches tested them and pronounced them safe. However, some men became sick on one raft, and a rumor flashed through the whole fleet that the fruits were poisonous. No one would eat the strange fruits after that. Not until General Baxander set an example and ate several and survived. Then came the one about a ghost that had taken to haunting some Czardhans. Several Czardhans were said to have lost their minds as a result. Soldiers were sensitive to such things as ghosts, and it was felt to be an unlucky omen.

They saw strange beasts now every day. Often they were of the huge, placid type with long necks supported by immense, bulky bodies that seemed to come in dozens of sizes, though all with the same general body shape. In color these beasts varied from a dusky green to a sober brown, rather like wyvern dragons. This spectrum of colorations was much commented on by everyone, including the dragons themselves. The Purple Green noted the lack of any purple beasts like himself. Alsebra wondered whether they were seeing many different types of similar-shaped creatures or seeing juveniles and young adults of a single type.

There was a feeling of something akin to awe among the dragons when they spotted any of these vast, mysterious animals. They were either the ancestors of dragons or creatures very much like them, except for one very noticeable thing. These great monsters were plant eaters with tiny heads. In those heads were tiny brains, and the great ones were indisputably stupid. Most of them simply ran to the shore when confronted with the rafts and disappeared into the trees with no more than a few mournful hoots.

There were other beasts, however, that were less pleasant to meet. A water beast with a head six feet in length suddenly appeared one day beside a cavalry raft, seized a horse, and dragged it screaming into the river. Only by tremendous efforts did the men stop the remaining horses from stampeding clear off the raft.

After that guards had to be posted, and several times they were engaged in fierce battles with similar beasts that would erupt from the depths and reach in to snap up a horse or a man standing near the edge of the raft. Horses grew decidedly nervous.

So did everyone else after Legionary Gidips disappeared in the night. He was on guard in the late watch, and no one saw him taken. His body was never found. Watches were doubled after that.

The river had widened and slowed. On some days they never saw either bank, just the wide open water, as if they sailed on an ocean of calms. Then, quite suddenly, things changed when they entered a plain of reeds. Progress slowed. Conditions quickly became nightmarish. The river broke into a thousand channels that crawled through a plain of mud covered in reeds. At times men and dragons had to get out and haul the rafts through the shallowest places.

It was exhausting labor, and biting insects were a constant problem. Even though the witches used fly spells over and over all day, the numbers were just so enormous that they seeped in past any amount of magical influence. The mud was thick, goopy stuff that clung to legionary, horse, and dragon alike and made the going very hard.

Leeches in vast numbers were also attendant on them at the time, and the witches became acutely anxious about diseases. The quinine ration was doubled for every man and a noxious drink called "blue draft" was prepared for everyone, man, horse, ox, and dragon. It had a disgusting taste, but it was consumed nonetheless, with little complaint, even from the Purple Green. The Purple Green had a horror of leeches, and there were some in these sloughs of mud that could even penetrate dragonhide. The draft was supposed to discourage leeches, and it did, to an extent.

At last they worked their way through the reeds and entered cleaner, more open waters. They noticed that the water was now brackish. They had entered the estuarial length of the river. The islands lay behind them quite shortly, and the water opened out again until they could barely see the northern shore.

They floated on for another day and then, after many careful sightings of the sun and much consultation of the maps, Baxander decided they should land. They were close enough to the sea now that it was time to march north. The rafts would not be seaworthy, and once they left the great river they would be on a truly immense body of water.

A landing was made on a sandy strip within a side channel of the main river. The rafts were pulled up and lashed down. The engineers removed many of the best timbers for their siege train. Since there was no way of knowing if the rafts would be needed again, they were treated as if they would be. They could not easily be replicated.

The legions pitched camp. Around it a ditch was embedded with sharpened stakes and a wall thrown up with a palisade of wooden timbers on top. Torches were lit beyond the ditch to cast light into the surrounding area, and a strong watch was posted and relieved every hour.

After the fall of night, the surrounding forest was torn apart by a rising cacophony. The relative silence of the forest above the reeds had been replaced with uproar.

Several times that night, huge shapes showed themselves briefly in the glare of the guttering torches. Eyes set two feet apart glowed momentarily and then disappeared, their owners drawn to the fort and then dissuaded by the alien smells, the bright lights, the smoke of the fires. The watches changed on the hour, and everyone breathed a little more easily each time.

The next morning Relkin awoke to find his dragon feeling poorly. A quick inspection of the wing nubs on the dragon's back showed that he was running a fever.

By breakfast the fever had grown worse. The dragon drank water but vomited it up immediately. Solid food was out of the question. Relkin could do nothing but press cold wet towels to Bazil's forehead and pray to the old gods, and even to the Great Mother, for divine intervention.

The other boys came in to offer moral support and help, but there was very little that could be done in such a situation. Wiliger appeared after breakfast, face creased with concern, and for once Relkin withheld his customary contempt. The dragon leader seemed genuinely worried about the famous broketail dragon. After a careful examination, Wiliger left and returned with a heavy book under his arm. This was Chesler Renkandimo's *Care of the Wyvern Dragon*. Wiliger looked up "fevers" and announced that a dose of murranor was required. Murranor was frequently given to men afflicted with kneeknock and cramps. Relkin didn't think it would do much for a dragon, despite Chesler Renkandimo's claims for it. Wiliger left at once for the chief surgeon's tent.

The witch Endysia came soon after that and questioned Relkin extensively. What had the dragon eaten in the previous day? What had he drunk? Had he drunk any water that had not been boiled? Had he eaten anything uncooked? To Relkin's certain knowledge, Bazil had neither eaten nor drunk anything unsafe.

The fever raged, the dragon lay there in delirium, mouth open and tongue lolling out. He seemed so piteously helpless that Relkin felt his vision blur and he was forced to look away. How such a wondrous hulk of muscle and sinew could be reduced to this desperate state was incredible to him. Relkin was consumed by a tormenting fear that he was about to lose his dragon.

Memories kept coming up to haunt him from happier times, insistent memories that he could not shut away, such as the great day when Bazil was given the sword Piocar, his first true dragon blade. It had been paid for by a collection in the village and forged at the famous Blue Stone Angleiron works. Bazil had taken up the sword then and swung it about him with a positively gleeful abandon. The crowd had cheered lustily as the young leatherback showed off the moves he had practiced for years with a dummy sword made of cast iron. Relkin had almost expired from a surfeit of pride. He'd known then that there was nothing in the world he would rather be than dragonboy to this dragon.

Then more somber memories rose to the surface. He recalled the arena at Tummuz Orgmeen. When they'd cut Bazil down and laid him out, he'd seemed completely dead. Scorched black, stuck with arrows like a pincushion, it looked perfectly hopeless. But Bazil had come back from that, and was walking again within the month. If he could survive that, then he could defeat this fever. There never was a tougher dragon. This thought gave him a slight boost of confidence, but it was small comfort nonetheless.

Wiliger returned with a pitcher filled with a blue extract of murranor. The difficulty now lay in getting it into the dragon. Bazil no longer reacted to any stimulus. Wiliger slopped some of the blue solution into his mouth, but it only made the dragon splutter, choke, and turn his head sideways.

There was no obvious way of getting him to drink Chesler Renkandimo's prize solution. Wiliger squeezed shut his eyes and put a hand to his head.

Relkin looked away. The dragon would cure himself. He was either strong enough to overcome this fever or he was not, and if not then Relkin would have to face the consequences. He blinked away tears. He would save them for grieving, but the dragon still lived, that great heart still beat. As long as it did, there was no time for tears.

Hours dragged by. The fever continued to rage.

Then a dreadful wailing broke out in the quarters. Endi went running by, shouting at the top of his lungs. Wiliger jumped out to see what was happening. The news was like a knife to the heart. Roquil had begun to feel poorly and now had a fever. It seemed exactly the pattern that had felled the broketail.

The dragonboys gathered in Roquil's tent. A gathering sense of doom was spreading among them. They could barely look one another in the eye.

Chektor was next. Relkin came to sit beside Mono. The big orange brasshide's symptoms were pretty much the same as those of the others. Upset stomach, furious fever, eventual lapse into delirium.

"We served together a long time, Relkin," said Mono, looking up after a while.

"That's right, my friend."

"We was at Ossur Galan together. That was a hell of a fight. Old Chektor, he was in the thick of that one."

"I remember," said Relkin.

"It's going to be hard losing the old dragons."

Relkin shook his head. "We haven't lost them yet, Mono. They'll pull through, you'll see." Relkin's words sounded hollow, even to himself. All they raised from Mono was a wan smile. Both of them knew that with dragons fevers were rare, but when they did occur they were usually fatal.

The next alarm came from Calvene. His dragon, Aulay, a hard green from Seant, was sick. Then it was the young brasshide, Finwey. Then Vlok and the young leatherback Stengo. In time the entire unit, including the Purple Green, were laid low. The wild winged dragon was the last to succumb.

By that time the disaster had become general. Dragons in all eight squadrons had come down with the fever.

Orders to quarantine the 109th were abandoned. Baxander met with the surgeons, the witches, and the dragon leaders from his eight squadrons.

Dragoneer Duart of the Bea 34th was something of a herbalist. He felt that the fever was probably a waterborne thing that they had picked up during the struggle through the reed plain. Certain herbs, especially dragonfoil, were very effective with digestive complaints.

A search was made, but no dragonfoil was to be found here in the ancient forest of the Lands of Terror.

The witches had still not produced any answer. Dragons were notoriously difficult to enmesh in magic, and fever such as this was beyond most magic anyway.

Alarm flashed through the ranks of the legions, and then

leaked out to infect every man in the camp. A great sense of security had suddenly vanished. Not least for General Baxander. He had counted on the dragons being there. They were the top card for the legion front in battle. Without them the legion could fight, but it couldn't perform miracles and it could not fight against an enemy equipped with trolls.

Darkness fell over a somber scene. Dinner was a muted affair with not a dragon's bowl needing filling. The watch were nervous. With the fall of night came more visits from huge, predaceous animals. In fact, there were more intrusions on this second night than on the first. The newness of the camp was wearing off. Curiosity was overwhelming caution in the hearts of these aggressive animals.

Not long after the crescent moon rose, there came heavy footfalls from the forest, and an immense beast striding on long hind legs came out from the dark and thrust forward to the ditch.

From nose to tail tip, the monster was thirty feet of reddish brown terror. Its head was a foul mockery of a dragon's. It was huge, long, and narrow, with immense jaws. Eyes the size of a man's fist thrust up from the flattened skull and rows of saberlike teeth gleamed in the torchlight. When it snapped at the air, the sound was audible right across the camp.

It prowled along the ditch, casting red-eyed looks of hunger at the men on the parapet. This was an unsettling business, and everyone was acutely aware that they had no dragons to back them up.

The beast stopped suddenly, arched its neck, and emitted a loud, terrifying scream. All at once the Lands of Terror seemed to live up to their name. The horses and even the oxen were disturbed. A chorus of nervous neighs and moans arose from the herds. This seemed to spark the monster's curiosity, and it stepped down into the ditch. The stakes prevented it from crossing.

Arrows by the dozen thunked into its hide. It screamed again in pain mingled with rage, and bent down and seized a stake with its jaws. To their horrified amazement, it then ripped the six-foot stake right out of the ground.

More arrows struck home, along with spears now. The brute snapped at the parapet, but it was out of reach, and it still could not force its bulk through the gap between the stakes.

Suddenly it tired of the constant sting of arrows and re-treated from the ditch. Still the arrows came, and it moved farther away. It was not intelligent, but it was not that stupid, either. At the edge of darkness, it paused to scream again in rage and frustration before withdrawing into the night.

The men on the parapet breathed a sigh of relief. A fresh stake was driven into the spot at once, and the watches were doubled again. What pikes they had were broken out of the stores, and the Czardhan knights brought their long lances to the palisade.

There was not long to wait before they were needed.

The next beast was slightly smaller, perhaps only twenty-five feet in length and a pale green-brown in color. It skulked along the opposite side of the camp, sniffing the scent of the oxen and the horses, then withdrew and let out a long, wailing cry. A few minutes passed, and then another similar cry announced the arrival of a second beast of the same type. They let out more wailing cries and jumped up at each other in threat displays that shook the ground. Their cries attracted a third and then a fourth beast, of the same type. They gathered and displayed to each other with tremendous bounds in the air, threw their heads back and emitted the long, wailing, sobbing cries that sent shivers down the spines of everyone in the camp.

Quite suddenly, all four together made a concerted attack on the ditch and the parapet. This fight was much longer and more fiercely pressed than the first. The beasts darted down into the ditch and attempted to jump over the stakes. Two struck the stakes and fell back with loud shrieks of complaint. One impaled its thigh and was left screaming in pain and rage stuck in the ditch. The fourth got through the stakes with a lucky carom. It mounted the earthen wall, kicked a hole through the flimsy parapet, and broke in.

By then it sported a dozen arrows in its hide. Eight men opposed it, shields and spears at the ready. More men were coming. Bowmen kept up a constant fire, trying to hit it in the eyes.

Still it attacked. The men stood their ground, thrust upward with their spears. The beast was stymied a moment, then it kicked with one of its hind legs and tossed two men onto their backs. In a moment it had bent over and ripped one man's head off his shoulders.

A brave soldier name Licius ran in and rammed his spear deep into the brute's side. It emitted a scream of pain, lashed out with its forearm, and ripped Licius open from neck to crotch.

More men came up led by old Corporal Praxus. Their spears sank home in the monster's belly, and it suddenly tumbled backward, crushing more of the palisade before falling into the ditch. There it thrashed and wailed, lashing the ground with its tail and limbs.

The archers now concentrated their fire on the beast that had impaled its thigh. A lucky shot struck home through the eye and slew the thing. It slumped over, still on the stake.

After some mournful screams, the remaining two beasts withdrew into the forest.

Within minutes a horde of smaller things had appeared out of the darkness to dispute possession of the remains of the two dead beasts.

The sound of the quarreling and feeding was nightmarish enough. But soon it drew much larger beasts, and these not only fought each other but also sought to invade the camp and had to be fought off. So it went for the rest of the night.

The smell of meat kept the monsters coming all day as well. The camp was permanently invested by great carnivores, only some of whom contented themselves with the carrion. More carrion resulted, and it was simply impossible to do much more than clear the beasts away from the wall long enough to drag the bodies a short distance. Then the men would beat a hasty retreat as things like hyenas, but four times as large, would mass and make a charge at the meat.

All that next night the process was repeated, except that the numbers of predators involved had increased. Everything from miles around was gathering, drawn by the increasing smell of meat.

CHAPTER FORTY-ONE

Lessis returned to her tent from a long, exhausting attempt to rouse some of the dragons through magic. They were impervious as always. Lessis was hot, very tired, and somewhat afraid. Better than anyone alive, except Ribela of Defwode, she knew what was at stake. They absolutely had to have the dragons for that edge in the upcoming battles. The enemy would be sure to have a few trolls. The reports had spoken of trolls months before.

General Baxander was waiting in her quarters, a small tent erected behind the headquarters tent.

"You are tired, Lady."

"I am ready to sleep for a week. Yourself?"

"The same. I take it that we still cannot rouse a single dragon?"

"We cannot. But we can also add that we have not lost one, either. They are prostrate, but they live. The broketail dragon, the first to show the fever, still has it, but we think it has ameliorated slightly."

"Praise to the Mother for that much. Yet our difficulty remains."

There was a sudden uproar from the southern end of the camp. Another pack of predators was climbing into the ditch in pursuit of carrion. Cornets blew, and men tumbled out of their tents and ran to their stations.

"Have there been any further casualties?"

"Not today. The Czardhan bitten last night will live, we think."

Lessis nodded vaguely and mumbled her thanks and shifted to the side of the tent and sat on a chest. The uproar continued on the rampart.

"Forgive me, General, I'm too tired to stand any further."

Baxander squatted down on his heels.

"From my understanding of the maps, it seems we have

two weeks' march ahead of us to get clear of this accursed forest."

"That is probably a slight underestimate. The country ahead is not difficult, but the forest is uncut and completely wild."

"It is galling to have come so far and to be so near our target and yet to fail."

Lessis came awake. "We have not failed, General. Do not say that!"

"Well, Lady, we cannot move without getting the wyverns on their feet. They are essential to defense against the animals."

Lessis changed the subject abruptly.

"How go our supplies of wood?"

"Getting very low. We must cut wood for burning, but at the moment it is too dangerous. The last work party lost three men. I can get volunteers, but for how long will that last?"

"How difficult would it be to carry the dragons? Could our ox train manage that?"

Baxander shook his head sadly. "Our wagon train is pared down to the essentials of equipment and grain, plus some wood-carrying capacity. To put eighty sick dragons on wagons and pull them through untamed jungle would require far more wagons than we have at our disposal."

Lessis nodded glumly. "As I thought. Then we must redouble our efforts to bring the dragons around. There must be some way to break through this fever."

"I pray there is, Lady."

But neither of them was prepared for the next shock. The witch Endysia came to Lessis's tent with a face the color of ashes.

"What is it, Endysia?" said Lessis.

"The worst news possible, Lady. I have just come from the surgeons. They have been getting cases of legionaries coming down with the fever. A trickle of cases a couple of hours ago, but now they are coming fast. While I was there, I heard of ten men down in Czardhan camp, all within the half hour."

General Baxander stared at her for a moment. Then he swallowed hard and stood up.

"We have plans for this situation; it was not unanticipated.

I must go and set things in motion. We will defend the camp to the last, that much I can assure you."

When he had gone, Lessis allowed her face to sag into the exhaustion she felt.

"I must sleep for an hour, Endysia. Then I will come to the surgeon's tent and see what I can do."

Endysia slipped back through the darkness. The shrieking battle at the rampart had died down again now that a large carcass had been torn free from the stakes in the pit and dragged back into the undergrowth by a pack of sickle-clawed monsters of yellow and scarlet hue. Among the men the news of the sickness had brought on a new set of anxieties. A gathering sense of doom was enveloping the camp.

Far away on the shores of the Nub al Wad was a scene of frantic activity. Great barges had been hauled up on the sands. Around the barges struggled an army of slaves. Over their heads cracked the whips of their drivers.

Kreegsbrok arrived in the hour before midnight.

"What kept you?" said Gulbuddin. "We've had a bloody time of it. Did you hear that we lost a barge?"

"What happened?"

"Damned metal tube went right through the timbers when a big wave struck. Must have broken loose from its restraints. Barge tipped over and went straight down."

"You lost the slaves, too?"

"We recovered some, perhaps half. A lot never got out of the barge."

"A pity to lose slaves. We will need all that we have to haul these things to the site."

"Each one of them weighs twelve tons."

"I know."

"And then there are the balls. Five hundred of them, each weighs half a ton."

"There are no worthwhile draft animals in this land. We have to rely on slaves and donkeys. There are only so many slaves available."

"Then the Kraheen must put their shoulders to the wheel."

Kreegsbrok laughed bitterly. "The Kraheen are too proud now to do such labor. They exist only to wield the sword like aristocratic lords of creation."

"Such pride will not sit well with the Master."

Kreegsbrok nodded. Gulbuddin made a fist and drove it
into his palm.

"The drum is beating. There will be war soon. We must be
prepared. The Kraheen must understand this."

"Praise to the Great Master. He will make them understand, and our enemies will be destroyed."

"Verniktun comes." Gulbuddin pointed down to the beach
and the struggling masses. "He is not alone."

Kreegsbrok nodded, stepped forward, hands clasped behind his back, and watched two men approach.

"That will be the man from the weapon shop. I was told
he would come with the tubes."

Kreegsbrok took a breath and tried to dispel the fatigue he
felt. It had been a frenetic few days. He'd known that some
crisis approached, but he had not known when it would arrive. All at once the alarm had been sounded on the Bone.
All leaders, all men, were to double and redouble their efforts. Kreegsbrok had been doing without sleep ever since,
getting by on nips from a flask of the black drink.

Keeping the Prophet under some semblance of control had
been getting harder and harder, too. Whereas once an hour
of killing had been enough to sate it, now it could go on for
hour after hour, killing any man, woman, or child placed
under its knife. The word had leaked out. It had to. There
had been too many bodies, too many trips to the volcano to
incinerate them, and too many incidents when the Prophet
went mad and began to kill his own followers.

Then had come the orders to prepare for the transportation
of a dozen enormous objects of metal. Each was a huge tube,
sixteen feet long and five feet across weighing twelve tons.
They were to be taken inland some twenty miles, to a ridge
overlying the field of Broken Stone, Tog Utbek.

As if these tubes were not enough of a burden, there were
also several hundred enormous stone balls, marvelously
smooth and perfectly round, chipped that way by slave labor
in the dungeons of the fortress on the Bone.

Finally, there was to be a special cargo, which would be
brought across only when the tubes were in position. Special
precautions were to be taken during the shipment of this
cargo.

Kreegsbrok had learned long ago not to question orders.
He existed only to obey and expedite. And he had expected
some kind of frantic activity. The Great One had as much as

warned him, months ago. The hags would attack; the Master made magic here that would end their rule forever. They would come, they would have to come.

The problem was the slight lack of slaves, caused in part by the blood-crazed Prophet and his killing orgies.

The weapons officer and Verniktun came up. Verniktun was sweating, his voice hoarse from bellowing orders all across the waters from the Bone.

"Hail to the Master!" said Kreegsbrok, extending his fist in salute.

"Hail! I am Durmer. I am close to the heart of the Great One, and he has lifted me up."

"Hail, Durmer!" said Kreegsbrok. They clasped hands.

"How quickly can my tubes be landed?" Durmer went right to the heart of the business.

Kreegsbrok turned to Verniktun.

"They won't be ashore before daybreak," said Verniktun. "Not with the slave squads we've been given."

Durmer's face clouded.

"That long? Are you absolutely certain?"

"With just these paltry slave squads, yes. Give me twice as many slaves, and I'll have them ashore in a couple of hours."

Kreegsbrok fumed. He envisioned all the slaves that had been wasted by the Prophet.

Durmer shook his head angrily. "You must do better. Remember that the batrukh flies tonight."

Even under the wan light of the moon, Kreegsbrok could see Verniktun pale at these words.

"We will get them ashore as quickly as we can. Let us not talk of such things as the batrukh."

CHAPTER FORTY-TWO

The plague progressed with a steady, remorseless stride, first decimating the legions, then the Czardhans and Kassimi and finally the men from the Bakan states. It worked with a horrible swiftness. By lunch a full third of the legionaries were too sick to stand, and a quarter of the Czardhans were affected. By the middle afternoon almost all the Argonathis and Cunfshoni were down and more than half of the Czardhans, too. Only among the Bakan soldiers was there more resistance, and though many fell ill, a good third of them did not.

This informed Lessis that the plague was native to Eigo and that the Bakani were partly immune. Whether it was the same plague that had struck the dragons was another matter. The surgeons said it was unheard of for wyverns and men to suffer from the same disease. Chesler Renkandimo's tome on the *Care of the Wyvern Dragon* said much the same. Lessis's spellsay did not address the problem, and she had no resources of ancient spellsay in written form on hand to consult. In the end it didn't seem to matter. Lessis fell ill in the hour before sunset, and there was nothing she or Lagdalen could do. Lagdalen brought cold compresses, but like everyone else the Lady soon slipped into unconsciousness.

By the day's end there were only a hundred or so Bakani left standing, along with a handful of resistant souls among the rest. The men from Cunfshon had succumbed to a man. Even General Baxander had been taken from his tent at last, virtually unconscious. General Steenhur had already fallen.

Left in command was the Count of Felk-Habren. The count called the survivors together in front of him. He spoke in Verio and Demmener. He swore them all to an oath. They would stand and die in defense of their comrades now lying in their tents.

Felk-Habren was a large man with a shock of pale silver hair and big blue eyes that took on a ferocious luster when he spoke of matters concerning honor and war. He impressed all of them with his passionate sincerity. For a moment, morale was high.

Then they drew for the watches, two hours on, two hours off, through the night. Not long after that Relkin found himself on the rampart. The line was thin. They would have to reinforce each other quickly in the event of an emergency.

Relkin and Swane were the only survivors of the 109th. They checked the unit's resources in arrows and divided them between them.

"Eye shots. These damned beasts don't care for those," said Relkin with feeling.

"I hit one yesterday. One of those yellow horrors. Killed it, too."

"Yes, I heard about that. Good work, Swane."

Swane felt that strange sense of pride he always felt when Relkin praised him.

On the rampart they were spaced a hundred feet apart. A couple of Kadein dragonboys were in the watch, but they were situated on the other side of the camp. To Swane's right was a Czardhan knight and to Relkin's left was a Bakani.

The situation was deceptively calm. The forest always fell quiet around dusk. The beasts of the daytime were repairing to their lairs while the night-loving animals awoke, scrubbed the sleep from predatory eyes, and moved out of their dens.

During the day the men had made two sallies to cut up and haul away the stinking carrion lying in front of the ditch. It was the carrion that drew the beasts. Those work details had been very lucky that day. The hyena-like things had refrained from attack, and the huge, two-legged predators were inactive. They had cleared most of the remains, even the large bones, from the ditch and thrown them into the margins of the forest.

As night renewed its grip on the world, they heard things stirring. Harsh screaming cries from the right told of a pack of the formidable, though small, yellow demons. A coughing roar from the left warned of one of the huge, brown-red beasts that had enormous heads and relatively puny upper limbs. Then came booming cries from the south and wails from several other directions. That meant there were the greenish-hued long striders on hand as well.

The carrion had called them, and they had responded.

Soon the woods were filled with snarls and roars and the sounds of terrible conflicts. Bones crunched in great jaws as tasty, rotting carcasses were consumed.

Soon, all too soon, the carrion in the woods was finished. Now the scent of hundreds of oxen and horses, penned up in the camp, became overwhelmingly interesting to the beasts. Now began a night of desperate struggles.

The worst were the packs of yellow demons, as the men called them. These were bipeds about ten feet long from nose to tail tip that stood about shoulder high to a man. They bore enormous sickle claws on the second toe of each hind foot. Their mouths were lined with serrated teeth. They were horribly active animals, and quite capable of squeezing through the stakes to mount the rampart. They were vulnerable to arrows and spears: A thrust in the belly or chest was enough to discourage them; an arrow in the throat or the eye usually killed them. However, they were fast and they were deadly if they got close. Many men had been gutted by the slashing movement of those hind legs bearing the long sickle claws.

Also to be especially feared were the long-legged green "striders" as they called them. These could step over the stakes and lean down with their long necks and snap off a man's head with their formidable jaws.

During several fights on their side of the rampart, Relkin and Swane found themselves working alongside a Bakan soldier, Bakdi of Fute.

Bakdi was a cheerful, round-faced fellow with glistening brown skin and laughing, dark eyes. He was short and full-bellied, but surprisingly agile and a good shot with his curved compound bow of horn and wood.

His arrows slew three yellow demons in succession at one point. This provided enough of a feast for the rest of the demons in that pack that a lull developed while the horrid meal was devoured on the edge of the ditch.

Relkin and Bakdi watched with somber eyes.

"I am wondering if I will ever see Fute again," said Bakdi.

"Don't wonder. Bad to think about things like that. Have to live for the moment."

Bakdi pursed his lips. "I think Argonath boy have wisdom, yes? Better not to think about it. Anyway, I came on this mission because I wanted to, so no complain, yes?"

Bakdi's Verio was slow and oddly accented, but still comprehensible.

"Better not to."

"It is good. I am a maker of carpets. I finish a good carpet, oh, but it was my best! So I think, I take a rest from carpets. Go on expedition."

"You wanted some excitement."

"Oh, yes." He sighed. "Excitement. Foolish Bakdi."

Ferocious growls broke out in the nearby thickets.

Long-legged striders appeared. They stepped to the ditch Swane released. His arrow stuck in a shoulder. Relkin fired and his arrow bounced off tough strider neck and ricocheted into the dark. Bakdi released, and his arrow sank deep into the leading beast's side.

It gave a wild shriek of rage and pain and tried to leap the stakes. Fortunately it could not leap that far and impaled itself instead. It screamed in further agony and bit at itself.

Its fellows then turned on it and tore it to pieces in the ditch.

Relkin and Swane put up their arrows.

"No need to waste a shaft," said Relkin.

"Right."

"As long as they eat each other we leave them alone,' said Bakdi.

"I wish they'd just eat each other up and get it over with. How many of these things can there be out there?"

Neither Relkin nor Bakdi had an answer to that, and they turned back to watch the dimly outlined forest. The green striders growled and crunched their way through their former companion just a few feet below.

When the watch finally ended, Relkin stumbled to his tent and checked on the dragon. Baz was still asleep, but the heat in his wing nubs had lessened. Relkin lifted a big dragon eyelid. By lamplight it was hard to be sure, but it seemed that the eyeball was less yellow and inflamed. He felt the pulse, steady and strong, but then it had never really faded The great hulk seemed less feverish. It was no longer trembling in the slightest. Just the rhythmic, easy breathing, great lungs lifting the rib cage and then deflating with a sigh.

Was it possible? Could the dragon be making a recovery? Relkin laid himself down and prayed to the old gods and then to the Great Mother for his dragon's recovery. Praying had never been one of Relkin's strong points, and he fumbled the words of most of them, but at length he satisfied himself that he'd asked all the deities he knew of for their help. He wondered if it was worth praying to the Sinni, except that he didn't think they were actually gods—at least that was the impression he'd received from the Great Witch Ribela.

He fell asleep, almost immediately, and dreamed he saw the white stone city of Marneri, as if from a ship. The white walls seemed to float above the dark water of the Long Sound.

Then he was in the city, moving among the crowds. A parade was coming down Tower Hill, people thronged the sidewalks. He watched Lagdalen go by in the parade, marching with a group of senior witches, all wearing the quiet grey robes of their order.

Abruptly there was a loud noise in his ears. Someone was shaking him roughly.

He awoke. Uproar. There was a terrible screaming of horses.

A man yelled something in his face. Relkin could smell the fear on the fellow. Then he ran out of the tent. Relkin pulled his wits together and stumbled to his feet. His hands strapped on his sword belt. He picked up spear and shield.

A small four-legged shape came hurtling through the door and almost cannoned into him. It was Stripey. The little elephant gave a violent trumpet of terror and hid behind Bazil's recumbent form. Relkin pushed through the flap.

The screaming in the horse corral was accompanied now by a ghastly reptilian shrieking.

He staggered outside the tent, still fogged by sleep. He was back in hell.

In the horse corral were two of the terrible striders. They had killed several horses already. The rest were at the far end of the corral, desperately trying to get out. The oxen in the farther pen were also panicked. Men were running to the side of the pen to hold back the oxen. Other men were pumping arrows into the green striders, so far with no effect.

Then there was a human scream of terror from behind him. Relkin whirled around and saw a huge form, one of the brownish red beasts, standing on the rampart. It tossed its head and part of a man's body flew away to land among the tents. Two more men with spears were thrusting at its legs and belly, but it took no notice of them and stepped down inside the camp and made for the oxen. As it went it gave out its distinctive coughing roar.

The oxen went mad. The fencing gave way, and the terrified beasts jammed in a gap where it had gone down. Men leapt for safety to either side.

Without seeming to move, Relkin found himself alongside several Bakani, all with spears, thrusting at the monster's back. One man thrust home, his spear sinking in near the base of the tail.

The beast swung around with terrible rapidity. Its head darted down and clamped on the man's shield. It lifted him off the ground and shook its head and sent him flying twenty feet. As it did so, Relkin ran in from the side and thrust home into the thing's thigh.

Again the head whipped down and the jaws snapped shut. Relkin had anticipated them and darted sideways, heaving his spear free with a jerk. Blood fountained from the wound.

A Czardhan knight came running forward, screaming his war cry, holding a shortened lance in front of him aimed directly at the beast's belly.

The giant beast adroitly stepped out of the man's way. The huge head bobbed down, and the jaws seized the Czardhan and lifted him off his feet. His final scream cut off as the jaws champed and severed his head and legs.

The helmeted head bounced in front of Relkin's eyes. By then Relkin had picked up the cut-down lance. It was much heavier than his spear, but longer and far more deadly. He cradled it and drove at the monster. Again it avoided him with a move practiced against generations of the huge horned beasts on which it preyed. Relkin's forward lunge carried him into fatal range. Fortunately, Bakdi darted in at that moment and put an arrow into the hulking beast's throat. It gave a scream of pain and lunged after Bakdi, who spun backward until his foot struck the severed head of the Czardhan knight. He stumbled and fell, and the thing was on him in a moment. With a roar of fury, Relkin drove the lance at its head and at the last moment it jerked aside, distracted from Bakdi.

Instead the huge jaws snapped shut on the end of the lance. Relkin felt himself heaved off his feet before he could let go. He fell back and turned to run. The lance was tossed aside. The ground shook as the red-brown beast pounced after him. On instinct, Relkin flung himself sideways. He heard the immense jaws snap in the air where he'd been. He cut around an overturned wagon, feet scrabbling for purchase, and then he slid to a stop with his mouth open.

Standing there, head nodding a little from fatigue, was a leatherback battledragon, holding dragonsword in both hands.

The monster behind him had come to a halt as well. He heard its heavy hiss of surprise. Now it took a sideways pace and snarled to itself as it took in this new development. A smaller beast, like itself in some ways, except that there was a long sliver of bright metal in its forehands.

"Boy, get out of way," rasped Bazil.

Then the red-brown giant attacked, leaping forward, head plunging down and jaws snapping.

There was no time for gauging things, no time for thought. Bazil took the beast's measure quite instinctively, as if it were simply some oversize troll and hewed into its neck with Ecator. There was a moment of equipoise, then the shock struck home. The beast pulled sideways in a fountain of its own blood and gave a death shriek. Bazil plunged after it and ran Ecator through its belly with a tremendous thrust.

The monster collapsed and shook the ground with its falling. Relkin ran to his dragon and leaped to his shoulder with a triumphant yell.

CHAPTER FORTY-THREE

Slowly the camp recovered from the plague. The dragons awoke, weak and shaking and staggered out of the tents. Relkin and the other dragonboys worked furiously in the cook pits putting out an enormous quantity of stirabout. To flavor it, they rifled the stocks of akh. Dragons ate quietly and took up swords when necessary to subdue invasions from the forest.

The recovery was patchy at first, although there was little mortality among the dragons. Only two, both brasshides from Kadein, failed to awake. There was greater loss among the men. In the legions there were sixty dead and another fifty permanently damaged by the fever. Some twenty Czardhans were buried along with a dozen Kassimi and a handful of men from the Bakan states.

The dragons were burned in the usual manner, the men were buried according to the various rites of their religions. For several days the survivors struggled around as their strength slowly returned.

During this time the wild beasts continued to investigate and at times to besiege the camp, but the sight of dragons armed with swords atop the rampart seemed to deter most attacks. On occasion, however, hunger drove the flat-headed monsters to burst the stakes and mount the rampart, whereupon dragonswords flashed and great beasts expired.

Lessis of Valmes awoke from her own bout of the fever to find the situation teetering back from disaster. There were other losses, however, most grievous to her being the loss of the batrukh, Ridge-eyes, who had flown away when she lost consciousness and her spell on him was broken.

Still the initial news was so much better than she might have expected that her heart soared. As soon as she had taken some soup, she asked Lagdalen to help her walk across to meet with General Baxander.

Baxander had only recovered half a day previous, and he was still shaky. He had, however, taken stock of the situation and was able to brief Lessis extensively when she appeared at his tent, barely able to walk, leaning on Lagdalen for support.

The news of the losses caused Lessis despair.

"I blame myself; it was some kind of plague that we had not considered. I had hoped that we would be protected by the spells and the use of quinine. It had worked well for most of the journey."

"Lady, it worked very well. Everyone on my staff was surprised that we even reached the Ramparts of the Sun. You could not expect to have knowledge of every plague that haunts these fevered forests."

Lessis accepted Baxander's reassurances gratefully. Yet there was a greater concern still troubling her.

"We have lost time, precious time. Every hour is priceless now. We are so close, and our enemy has been making haste to prepare for our arrival for weeks."

Baxander had anticipated Lessis.

"We can march in two days. We took some losses in the ox teams, but not that many. We lost seven horses to the wild beasts."

"From what I was told, it was something of a miracle that we were not devoured in our beds. Our thanks must go to the Mother and to a certain leatherback dragon!"

"Indeed. Now, as to the line of march, if you would care to look at the map, Lady? We go north, along a riverbank for part of the way. Scouts report it makes a good path, surprisingly firm."

Two days later they struck camp and marched out. Around the camp rampart they left a drift of bones from dead beasts. Many of the men had collected strings of daggerlike teeth to sell for necklaces. Others had gathered sickle claws. There would be a relative dearth of predators in that region for years to come.

And now the Mother seemed to smile upon Her children, for the rain held off for seven full days. The ground firmed up and in the last three of those days they made almost thirty miles, as much as they'd managed in the first four.

They were aided also by the relatively flat terrain, sloping upward to the north. Whenever possible they moved along the open banks of subsidiary rivers. When necessary the engineers cut trees, built bridges, and hacked out crude roads. Everyone worked incredibly hard, digging, clearing brush, pulling out trees when absolutely necessary.

Occasionally predatory monsters came out of the woods to investigate the oxen, or even the work crews. The cavalry dispatched most of these, although a few of the largest and most obstinate had to be confronted by dragons with dragonsword.

The land around them was changing, though. As they climbed northward, they found a new kind of forest around them. Flowers reappeared, and with them came the birds, many of them brightly colored, darting through the green canopy. And every day the sightings of the great beasts declined in number. The very air seemed to grow fresher, and there was a cool breeze at night blowing in from the nearby waters of the inland ocean. Finally, at night the forest was noisier than ever, far noisier than it had been down in the bottomlands, but the men did not complain about such noise anymore.

In the 109th the mood was one of relief and expectancy. They had suffered no casualties. There was one casualty they would have welcomed, but their dragon leader, too, awoke from the fever unharmed and in a foul mood. The sunny disposition of just a few days before had vanished. The dragon leader was distant and cold with everyone. He called inspections every morning, though, and demanded spotless joboquins. This was unreasonable, since they were marching through wild country and the dragons were doing all kinds of intensely physical things every day, whether cutting and shifting trees or digging or occasionally whacking some predator too hungry or stupid not to leave them alone.

Relkin sensed that something was wrong. Wiliger was back to behaving as if he was hurt and insulted by his own unit. Like it had been on board ship and during most of the march. Perhaps the constant repetition of "We'll do it. What is it?" jokes that kept the boys sniggering had reached him. His unfortunate motto had sunk to being the butt of endless jokes in these days of improving morale. Wiliger was a creature of fragile pride, easily dented.

"What are we, lads?" Endi would say in a stage whisper.

"We're the 'We'll do its'!" would come back from several others.

Then someone else would say, "Wrong! We're the 'What

is its?' " This tepid humor was enough to get the boys giggling again and again. They were in a wild mood, alternating between silly relief at escaping plague and the dark forest of antiquity, and tense excitement at the thought of battle at the end of the march and an end to this long campaign.

Relkin watched with some concern. He even tried to dampen the giggles over "We'll do it. What is it?" jokes, but did not succeed. The earlier reincarnation of Wiliger as Delwild the Nice had done something to his spell over the younger boys. Whereas before they had been in fear of him and his endless punishments and inspections, now they had nothing but contempt.

They marched, a process that included shoving wagons out of mires, cutting and hauling timber, while engineers built rickety bridges across endless winding streams of murky brown water. They marched, or more accurately they covered ground. In the process they got covered from head to toe in mud every day. Keeping equipment ready for parade ground inspections was almost impossible. Yet Wiliger kept riding them. Punishment details were being handed out again in broadsides.

At the end of the first week, the rains came. For two days they sat in camp while the brown waters rose around them and then subsided. The ground ahead was mired thickly. Their progress slowed dramatically. On the first day they barely made five miles. On the second only three. Then as the ground firmed up again to the point where it could take iron-shod wheels, they began to improve.

On the twelfth day they saw the last giant beasts. A pair of loping two-legged animals, harmless and inoffensive, about the size of wyvern dragons. These beasts, colored light green on the upper surface and a dusty ocher on the lower, were grazing on bushes at the edge of a long glade. They ignored the marching columns of men and ox wagons, although they stopped and stared for a long moment when they saw dragons march by. When the Purple Green noticed them and stopped to consider them, they grew nervous and shifted back into the forest and disappeared from view.

The Purple Green tried to inveigle Bazil into a scheme for hunting the herbivore beasts, but the Broketail was too tired at the end of every day to consider any extra effort. It was all he could do to eat several big tubs of noodles lathered in akh and then turn in and sleep every hour allowed.

Still they made progress and by the eighteenth day had crawled up the northern side of the basin and entered a different land. They saw the first human villages they'd seen since they'd crossed the Ramparts of the Sun. The villagers had long since fled. The batrukhs had not ceased to stalk them every night. They were in the land of the Kraheen, and the Kraheen knew they were coming.

CHAPTER FORTY-FOUR

At length the army came to a plain covered in shattered rock known to the Kraheen as the Tog Utbek, the place of broken stone.

The rock came in all sizes, from that of a fist to lumps as big as a man. The volcanic origin of the rock was clear enough, and its source lay out in the midst of the waters of the Inland Sea, the Island of the Bone.

This barren place was a surprise to the men, who'd grown used to greener pastures. For days now they had tramped along muddy farm roads through a region lush in grainfields and orchards of tropical fruit. They had found large villages, emptied by their approach, stripped of most provision.

Denied the stores in the villages, the army had harvested the almost ripe grain from the fields and taken green fruits from the trees. These were a welcome addition to their now-dwindling supplies of grain.

Even more importantly, they cut lush fodder for oxen and horses, and this put new impetus into the scouting operations going on far ahead of them.

The plain of stones seemed harsh, almost unreal to them for a while. Relkin thought he'd never seen uglier ground in his life. Manuel scoffed and mentioned the sorcerer's isle. Relkin had to agree that that had been bad, yet there was something about this place that he did not like.

They marched a third of the way across the plain, and Baxander ordered the halt for the day. It was still early, but camp was set up while the surrounding ditch was dug. Baxander and his staff met under canvas, with the maps spread out before them. Being unsure about what lay ahead, he waited for the final report of the day from his scouts. In truth, they were feeling their way through this land. The Imperial maps were vague about this entire region. Imperial surveyors had never been here, and everything was mapped

according to the sketches produced by explorers of many
types. From a dozen accounts of varying qualities, the maps
had been cobbled together. There was a lot they did not
know.

What they did know was that there were low hills,
scooped up from the rock-strewn plain, about five miles
ahead. To the flanks, the ground rose gently on either side in
a long flat plain. Beyond the ridgeline the land sloped down
toward the Inland Sea. Thick forests choked the lower
ground. On the right, the hills rose to higher masses extending back many miles from the plain. For the legions, engaging a larger force, the ground resembled a possible trap,
a box in which they could be shut.

Shortly, Baxander was closeted with Steenhur, Felk-
Habren, Prince Ard Elac of Kassim, and Lessis of Valmes.
Around them a camp was being hammered to life. A ditch
was dug, a rampart thrown up above it, and along the top of
the rampart was set the palisade they carried with them.

Baxander unrolled the general map of the region and
pointed to its center.

"Beyond this plain lies the heartland of the Kraheen. They
must give battle soon. They cannot risk letting us get past
those hills."

"If they sit up on those hills," said Steenhur gloomily,
"they will have good ground."

"They will attack us. They cannot stand on the defensive
with untrained troops. The fanatic is ill suited to discipline.
They will want to use their numbers as quickly as possible,
while they have the fervor hot and strong."

The Count of Felk-Habren rubbed his hands together.

"If they attack, we will be ready for them. Horses are well
fed now, eager for the charge."

Prince Ard Elac agreed with the count. The Kassimi were
eager for battle. The battle at Koubha seemed long ago and
far away.

All senior commanders reported good spirit in their units
and a general readiness for battle. Effects of the great fever
had largely worn off.

Lessis was quiet and added nothing of her own. When the
others left, Baxander asked why.

"The question I must ask myself is simple: Have we come
too late?"

"Dear Lady, we have brought a great army, capable of

smashing our foe, halfway around the world in the matter of less than half a year. He has had advance warning of our coming only for a few months, since we landed at Sogosh and defeated his invasion force at Koubha. He cannot be ready to face us."

"I understand what you have done, General, and it has been magnificent work. Your staff has wrought a new kind of magic. I trust that they will infect all our forces with it. It has a miraculous strength. No one could have asked for more than this army has given our cause."

These words evidently pleased the general.

"A good staff, the best engineers in the legions, and willing men. With such weapons we can defeat any foe."

Lessis nodded and did her best to suppress her fears. The army was doing everything that General Baxander ·could want in preparation for battle. Still, the loss of those weeks in the swampland, brought low by the fever, cut at her. Who could say what the enemy might have accomplished in that time?

She left the general and made a swift tour of the medical section. Most of the remaining fever victims were still weak; all were still being carried in ox carts now emptied of food and materials. Lessis was more interested at that moment, however, in the veterinarian report on their stock of horses. The recent renewal of good fodder had done wonders for their condition, but there were still problems, particularly for the Czardhan warhorses, which were large brutes with rather fragile dispositions. The Czardhan leaders were still sanguine about their horseflesh, but the veterinarian was worried. He thought that they had yet to regain their endurance.

"Such horses must be as strong as trolls. They must carry a man in full armor with heavy weapons. Weak horses will walk rather than charge!"

Lessis listened and did her best to boost morale. She reminded the vets that they would probably fight a defensive battle and in such a battle the knights could fight dismounted, as part of the shield wall.

As for the dragons, to the surgeons it seemed that the wyverns had completely recovered from the plague. They were well fed and hardened by the weeks of marching. Lessis could be assured that they would fight as well as ever.

At last Lessis made her way to her own tent. Lagdalen

brought her some hot soup and fresh-baked bread, and she sank down to eat it.

Hardly had she touched it when a courier came running up. The scouts were in, and the enemy army had been sighted. Lessis darted up, all fatigue forgotten and left the soup to grow cold. She went at once to the command tent, but found the generals already gone, galloping for the camp gate.

Baxander and his staff spurred their mounts forward to a little rise a mile ahead. From its top they could spy out the enemy position.

The plain dipped down in front of them and then rose up ahead to the low hills. The enemy had formed a battle line on the farther slope some three miles distant.

"They have chosen good ground," said Baxander.

"Indeed," agreed Steenhur. "They hold heights overlooking a long slope. If we attack, we will have to fight upslope and cross a broad field of fire for their archers."

"Whereas if we sit on the defensive . . ."

"They outnumber us. They will maneuver down those side slopes, seek to envelop us."

"Some have found it is a mistake to envelop a legion army."

"True, though that has usually been an army with more than two legions."

"We have worthy allies. A good force. Eighty dragons."

Baxander shook his head. "To keep the initiative, we should attack."

"Should we risk the casualties of an attack? How long will this campaign last? We need to husband our forces."

"The witches say it will be a short campaign. This may be the only real battle. The Kraheen have only recently become a warlike nation. They are fierce fighters, but their formations are crude, they fight in a disorganized way. If we strike them now, pitch into them, and knock them away from their prepared positions, we may panic them. They will not dare to take the field again."

Steenhur nodded. "I am sure you are right, sir. I only propose the alternatives for the sake of argument. We must consider all the possibilities."

"Yes, of course, you are absolutely right. They are too far away to make an attack today. We will rest tonight and leave early in the morning. By dawn I want to launch our assault, right at their center."

CHAPTER FORTY-FIVE

They awoke when it was still dark. The camp was astir despite the hour. Horsemen thundered by in small groups as they moved out to their mustering.

"So we fight today, eh boy?"

"We fight."

"Good. It is time. We have been traveling forever. Now we get it over with and then can rest."

Bazil took down his great sword and examined it carefully. The white steel was flawless, a magic blade and a terrifying weapon. At times he could almost feel the personality that inhabited the blade. It was fierce and merciless and eager to drink the blood of servants of the Great Enemy. Holding it always gave him strength. He took out the whetstone and passed it a few times across the edges. In truth, it was already as sharp as it could be.

Relkin rolled out the empty cauldrons from breakfast.

"Rest," he muttered to himself. "When does a dragonboy get a rest?" Dragon Leader Wiliger had been riding him hard lately. Sometimes it seemed he was not supposed to sleep at all.

Cornets shrilled, orders were barked. Men began to assemble now that breakfast was done. The army believed in fighting on a full stomach.

From the Czardhan camp came the distinctive note of their bugles. From the Kassimi section of camp came a light rattle of drums.

Soon Wiliger appeared, and a few minutes later the squadron formed up and marched out. Ahead marched the Kadein 92nd, led by Dragon Leader Jendenter. Behind them came the Bea 34th, led by Dragoneer Duart.

All dragons wore full battle kit, including breastplate and vambrace, and they carried their big shields over their backs.

Outside the camp the land was hushed under dew. The order was to march as quietly as possible. Conversation was hushed. Thus there was just the clank of metal and the rhythmic tread of men and dragons as they progressed through the dark. The way was lit, but barely, by a series of dark lanterns, which could only be seen from one direction.

Cloud cover obscured the stars while a soft, warm wind blew steadily across the line of march from the land to the Inland Sea.

The dragons were happy enough. The air was still cool, and they appreciated that, considering that they were marching in full armor. They swung along as steadily as any well-drilled squad of men. Among them was a general desire to close with the enemy. The nature of the wyvern dragon was naturally combative, and having made this vast journey, they were eager to get to grips.

After almost an hour of marching, the first faint light of the sun began to tinge the eastern sky. They found themselves passing between massive volcanic boulders up a gently sloping ridgeline. Before they reached the top, they halted and deployed into a short battle line. The 109th Marneri were set directly behind the Kadein 92nd. On their left were a regiment of Bakani pikemen. On their right were troops of the Kadein legion. The double ranking of dragon units meant they were going to attack. Dragonboys immediately checked their dragons' feet. But after the weeks of marching the wyverns were hardened and ready, though that could hardly satisfy a dragonboy.

Relkin nudged Swane as he went past.

"Good luck, Swane, don't get whacked by the tail."

"You watch out yourself, Quoshite."

Wiliger hissed for them to be silent.

And so they stood still, each locked within himself in contemplation of the coming fight. Relkin thought of Eilsa, far away in the land of the Wattels. He imagined her with her long hair flying, riding one of the little Wattel ponies across the high bek. How he wished he were with her, if only to spend one more day. A little guiltily he then offered prayers to the old gods and to the Great Mother, continuing his policy of seeking all the help he could find.

Bazil thought of his young, the winged dragons Grener and Braner, who dwelt even farther away than Wattel Bek and which he would never see again in this life, no matter what happened on the field of battle. Bazil did not fear the coming struggle. It was unlikely there would be trolls to ace. Yet, it was still good to know that a part of him would ive on no matter what happened.

The strengthening light revealed the Czardhan cavalry lrawn up nearby on the left in two lines. With their steel armor agleam and their bright flags and pennons aflutter, they made a brave sight. Along the front of the army, keeping below the ridgeline, messengers galloped to and from the central command. These were the only interruptions in the view of the barren ridgeline, dotted with chunks of rock.

They waited for half an hour or so and then a messenger an down the line passing instructions to the dragon leaders. Wiliger turned to them with a gleam in his eye, and then with a shout of command they went forward at the march step.

They went up the slope of the ridgeline, dodging around the larger chunks of lava. Then they reached the low crest and came into view of a wide shallow valley with a long slope ahead leading up to a low prominence.

"There they are," said someone, and they all looked up and saw a dark mass clumped along the side of the prominence. The enemy was in view at last!

They had a fair distance to march, perhaps a mile, perhaps more, and all in the open. The enemy would have perhaps twenty minutes to pull himself together and prepare to receive their attack.

One thing in their favor perhaps was the sheer size of the Kraheen horde. The dark mass straggled along the prominence for half a mile at least. There were tens of thousands of them up there.

The cornets shrilled and on they went, marching steadily through the stone-strewn landscape, keeping to their formation as rigidly as possible. Bazil had the Purple Green on his right, Alsebra on his left. Vlok was beyond Alsebra and Chektor was on the other side of the Purple Green.

Relkin looked around himself and felt a surge of pride. Here was the flower of the empire in irresistible motion with banners flying and every arm of the military service in action. Moreover Relkin knew that he belonged to the very heart of the legions, the Dragon Corps, the cutting edge of the legion sword. And he felt his heart swell further when he looked along their line. What a grand sight the dragons made, huge, grim towers of sinew and steel, with their sword hilts rising above their shoulders like a row of steel crosses as they strode on with that peculiar predatory lope unique to the wyvern kind. And around them went dragonboys in the blue of Marneri or the grey-green of Kadein and Bea. Even Dragon Leader Wiliger cut a fine fig ure, striding at the rear, his cornet tucked under his arm, his jaw jutting forth, his cap set perfectly on his head, and his regulatory cap badge gleaming in the dawn light. Dragon Leader Wiliger had come a long way, Relkin decided. They had to try and get along with him, live and let live. Relkin felt full of generous notions.

They crossed a small stream that wound across the plain. Some wild goats were running away to the left. The Czardhans, walking their horses forward, gave a cheer at the sight of the white rumps bouncing away.

They passed out of the belt of large stones and now they could make out clearly the frenzied activity in the enemy's lines. Men moving in disorganized groups, spears waving in masses above their heads. Shouts, drumming, even screams echoed from the top of the slope.

A small group of enemy horsemen approached the ad vancing line. Burly bowmen ran up between the dragons and tried a few ranging shots. One of the enemy toppled from his horse. The rest withdrew at a gallop.

On they went, dressing out to the right under Wiliger's eye as they came out of the confinement of the large boulders. Throughout they were keeping their line as straight as possible aligned with the second rank of legionaries on their right.

The Bakani pikemen on the left were also re-forming. And now they moved up the slope smoothly together. They would soon be in arrow range. The bowmen were coming up from behind to begin their covering fire.

General Baxander rode beside Lessis, with General Steenhur a short distance away. A messenger rode in from Count Felk-Habren. The knights were ready to charge, just give the order.

The enemy front was disorganized. Once they closed, Baxander was certain his army would cut through the bigger host like a hot knife through butter.

"We have them, Lady. I think we actually surprised them by closing so soon."

"You doubt that they will stand!"

"They know they cannot do that. Not against legions equipped with dragon forces. Look at them, they're trying to launch an attack of their own, they want their force to meet us with some impetus behind it. They know that ill-disciplined troops will not put up a good defense."

"So their attack will meet ours head on."

"And disintegrate. It will be poorly organized, almost chaotic. We shall let them break up on our front and then send in the Czardhans to cut them in half."

"I pray that they break and run, and that the casualties will be few in number. There is too much bloodshed in the air here." Lessis stared up at the enemy lines. There was no sign of the weapons Ribela had told her to fear. Then again, Ribela had also warned her that the weapons would not necessarily be visible. They might be hidden and at a considerable distance from the rest of the fighting. Lessis felt that great fear again. They risked so much here, and they absolutely had to win!

A few minutes later the enemy's front dissolved as an order to attack blared from their trumpets and the Kraheen streamed toward them, screaming the name of their Prophet as they came.

"Ajoth Gol Dib!" went the cry, again and again, like a susurration of death. Relkin watched as Kraheen men with white and brown shields came rushing toward them. They bounded forward at full speed, leaping over stones with their long shields in the air.

Arrows were arching over in greater and greater numbers. Bazil's helmet rang as one struck the very top. Then he swung his shield up for cover and soon it was studded with a dozen or more. Relkin ducked back behind the dragon, his own shield raised. A bowman stopped beside him and fired. The range was still too great for his own bow.

The dragons drew dragonsword and held them on their shoulders. On came the enemy spearsmen. Now! They were in range. Relkin slung his shield, pulled his bow around from his other shoulder, and took careful aim at a fellow running straight for Baz with his mouth open in a long ululating cry. Relkin fired; his arrow stuck on the man's shield. Other dragonboy arrows flicked out. Kraheen stumbled and went down here and there. Relkin knelt by a rock and steadied his bow. The onrushing warrior was still screaming the name of the Prophet. Relkin released and saw his arrow suddenly stand out of the man's shoulder.

It hardly slowed him, perhaps a step. With a renewed shriek he spun and came on, still eager for battle. Behind him came dozens more.

Relkin's mouth was dry as he fumbled a third shaft into

the bow. These were true fanatics. The dragon was getting settled. Ecator came down off Baz's shoulder.

And then, very suddenly, the two forces came together and battle was joined. It was a wildly disparate struggle. The Kraheen had enormous numbers, but they remained a force of lightly armed tribesmen. Their superb cavalry was occupied far off on the flanks, dueling with the legion troopers and the Kassimi. This left them with a single style of attack to throw at the oncoming legions.

Still, they came on with a fanatical rush and maintained this even against the dragons, where they sought to get close enough to wield their spears against dragonhides.

Unfortunately for the Kraheen warriors, the dragons were well trained to prevent such efforts. Dragonswords moved in steady, slaughterous curves, humming through the air and cutting down the brave but foolhardy men that came against them. In frustration, many Kraheen threw their spears from a distance of forty or fifty feet, but they had little success. Most were absorbed on dragon shield or deflected by armor. However, a few spears did damage and one or two dragons were forced to pull out of the line. Their places were taken immediately while dragonboys and surgeons worked on the wounded wyverns.

Against the men of the legions, the Kraheen had little more success. They piled up against the legion front, where they engaged with spear against sword and shield. As they fought, they faced a rain of arrows and javelins thrown from behind the frontline soldiers. The Kraheen compressed themselves along the line, and soon their bodies began to pile up there, and their charge lost impetus. Within half an hour they were exhausted, and the attack petered out.

The legion was itself in attack mode, and as the Kraheen began to ebb back, so the men and the dragons went forward, sweeping away stragglers and accelerating the Kraheen movement toward a rout. The vast Kraheen horde wavered dangerously.

The time had come for a decisive blow. General Baxander sent a message to Count Felk-Habren requesting that the Czardhans press home their famous charge and break the Kraheen mass apart.

Czardhan bugles began to blow. In their full magnificent panoply the knights moved out, each a tower of steel atop his warhorse. Their lances glittered above their heads. Baxander's battle plan was unfolding exactly as hoped for.

The sense of expected victory was rising high in the legions. Dragonboys whooped at the sight of the charging knights going away. The Kraheen were running.

And then there was a distant boom, and the ground shook slightly. A curious sound, very loud, but far away. Then there came a second boom, exactly like the first. Again the ground shook a little. More of these distant bursts followed, and then there came a sudden, louder, heavier noise, as if several of the things had spoken at once.

"Look," cried Endi, pointing way up the slope ahead of them. Columns of smoke were rising from the ground, dark and ominous. Relkin glimpsed something black and solid hurtling through the air high above.

"Up there!" shouted Swane.

A moment later something struck the ground in the midst of the retreating Kraheen host, about fifty yards from where Relkin stood. There was a loud crash, a thud, and a collective shriek from the Kraheen. Relkin saw men, both whole and in parts, go flying up in the air.

A moment later there was a second impact directly ahead. Relkin saw something dark and round skip toward him at terrible speed. Instinctively he ducked and felt the wind of its passage above him.

There were screams all around him, and the ground shook and heaved as several huge projectiles struck the battlefield at once. Great polished balls of stone smashed on the rock-strewn field, some shattering into a thousand knife-edged shards that slew everything around themselves. Others bounced and hurtled through the packed masses of Kraheen and the legions. One passed straight through the charging Czardhans and brought down thirty knights in a moment.

Then it was over. The crashing ceased. All that remained were the screams of the wounded and the crying of the panicked. Relkin saw horror all around him. Poor Finwey, a big brasshide from Marneri, was down. Dragonboy Aris was screaming his dragon's name and frantically undoing the buckles on the joboquin. Relkin could see the blood under the great body. Finwey would not move again.

His eye caught on the upper half of little Roos's body almost underfoot. The sight did not register for a moment since he was still looking at his own dragon, who seemed perfectly untouched, but bewildered.

"What is happening?" bellowed Baz.

Relkin couldn't respond because he was too busy staring in horror at the torn torso of little Roos. His gorge rose. He almost stumbled and fell. Roos's dragon, big Oxard, gave a harsh hiss of dismay. Relkin turned away, sought comfort in his own dragon's survival.

The legion advance wavered, the front dented, and casualties struck right through the columns behind. The Czardhans kept going, however, ignoring their losses, plunging on into the Kraheen mass, who fled in utter rout.

"What was that?" shouted Swane in Relkin's ear. Relkin shrugged in hopeless ignorance.

And then there came another distant boom, followed by another and then more in a solid ground-shaking crash. Fresh fingers of cloud loomed above the retreating Kraheen, and a moment later the ground jumped and shattered as a dozen great solid stone shot slammed home and ricocheted through the legion formations.

Little Shutz was smashed to a pulp in front of them by something that hummed through the air. Big Oxard, still holding poor little Roos, was felled by a piece of stone that slammed into his breastplate at chest height with tremendous violence. The Purple Green was almost knocked senseless by a similar piece of stone.

Dragon leader Wiliger lost the little finger on his left hand, plucked from his hand by yet another speeding fragment that he never saw.

The legion advance was stalled. Lanes had been cut through the ranks. Men knelt by the bodies of their friends, stunned by the suddenness of their deaths. It was inexplicable and therefore more frightening than any of the known hazards of the battlefield. Disbelief and horror filled the air along with the cries of the wounded.

Another round of booms sounded far ahead. Once more the clouds of smoke rose. Men looked up, eyes searching for some sign of this weapon of the enemy. Then came the carnage as the enormous stone shot smashed and splattered its way through the legion ranks. A moan went up from the Argonathi. In that cry of grief was the fear that the world had changed in some inexplicable way and the rules of warfare by which they had trained all their lives had been torn up. Disaster rode high in the sky, borne up on the dark clouds of smoke jetting from the hilltop.

CHAPTER FORTY-SIX

Fighting off panic, Lessis rode up to General Baxander. This was the weapon she had been warned of. This was the end of the world. Worse, they were too late! And they could not defeat it with their usual tactics.

She found Baxander in the act of giving orders for a renewal of the attack, only now the legions were to speed things up. It was necessary to close up with the mysterious sources of the deadly fire that was falling upon them.

Lessis tried to convince him to change his mind. General Steenhur rode up. Both generals insisted that they had to press the attack and capture the enemy weapons now that they had shown themselves. Lessis despaired. She struggled inwardly against the prohibition on the use of magic to influence the military. She and Ribela had broken the prohibition during the battle of Arneis, but they had been sworn before the emperor not to do it again. Yet she was sure that to renew the attack was a recipe for further disaster, and the only way to stop it was to resort to magic.

The ground shook to a fresh fusillade. A moment later there were screams all around them. Then General Baxander and his horse were destroyed when something struck the ground ten feet ahead and flew through their position. The horse spun over, smashed, fountaining blood. Baxander flew away, turning like a broken doll and landing in a loose heap. Lessis knew instantly that he was dead.

Steenhur was sitting his horse, blinking. His eyes were wide, and there were tears coursing down his cheeks.

"What is happening?" he cried. "What are they?"

"Explosive devices, General, that throw a heavy weight a great distance at tremendous speed. We have to destroy them."

Steenhur closed his mouth and snapped back together. "You are correct. We must attack."

"No, General, I think that would be a mistake. We must get our forces away from this field and regroup."

But Steenhur was no longer listening. He was talking to his aides. Others investigated poor Baxander's remains.

"He was a damned good man," Steenhur said bitterly.

"The best, sir!" said someone with great emotion. All of Baxander's staff had tears in their eyes. They had worked miracles together these last few months. They had expected, somehow, to continue.

"You can see the enemy weapons now, sir," said one young staffer holding out a telescope. "Appear to be long tubes, resting on heavy wheeled carriages. There are a great many men standing around them."

"Explosive catapults of some kind, I think, sir," said Major Romer.

"We have to smash them."

"Yes, sir."

"Let's do it for old Bax!"

"Yes, sir!"

Lessis was ignored. The cornets blew moments later.

"What are the Czardhans up to?"

"They are still advancing, sir, but their horses have slowed on the upper slope."

"We were right to worry about their condition. Those big horses were not ready for this. Have we contact with the rest of the cavalry?"

"We have had word within the minute. They engage the enemy's horse, things are about even. Our advance will be covered on the left flank. No attack is expected from the right."

The booms of the enemy weapons came again. Smoke rose in towers from the curve of the low hillside. Moments later the ground around them shuddered, and the ranks were thinned once more. Two dragons in the Bea 34th were killed.

Lessis pushed her horse close to Steenhur.

"General, may I say something?" He blinked. She rushed on. "If you order the men to lie down, they will present less of a target."

Steenhur looked at her blankly.

"If they lie down, Lady, they will not be able to attack. We must attack. We must destroy these weapons."

In vain did Lessis plead with him. The cornets blew once more and shortly the legions moved forward.

On up that deadly slope they continued. Far ahead they could still glimpse the Czardhan knights, pennons fluttering as they rode slowly toward the even more distant enemy weapons. At this distance, almost a mile, the knights formed a dense mass, seeming to slide slightly rightward as they went like some dark creature with a thousand legs and spikes along its back.

While they pushed their exhausted mounts onward, the enemy manning the great tubes was frantically at work, shifting them around, knocking out wedges to lower their snouts until they were aimed directly at the oncoming Czardhans. Then they were loaded with the blasting powder charges as usual, but instead of the great balls of smooth stone, the men were ordered to pack the tubes with jagged shards of iron and slag from the piles placed nearby.

To the oncoming legions there was a welcome respite from the invisible projectiles that had done such deadly work. They moved at a steady trot up the slope, their lines tight and well formed. Indeed, they were moving considerably more quickly now than the Czardhans, who were still pushing their desperately tired mounts, but who could get little more than a walk out of them.

To Relkin and many others in the legion attack this was a timeless, soundless moment. Their hearts had been numbed by the loss of so many comrades. That numbness would change to rage in time, but for now they marched in virtual silence. Apart from the rattle of the snare drums, there was just the clank of metal equipment and the creak of leather to interrupt the hush.

Abruptly the quiet was broken by a near simultaneous volley from the great tubes. A wedge-shaped cloud of smoke arose, and the Czardhan pennons fell in a clutter. The distant mass of knights was virtually gone. A mere handful remained.

General Steenhur put down the glass with a groan. "It is too bad, too terribly bad."

"They have been annihilated, sir."

Steenhur slapped the spyglass into his palm. His mouth tightened to a line.

"We go on, sound the cornet, tell the drummers to raise the tempo."

And on they went, striding toward the ridgeline while the enemy worked furiously to shift the great tubes again and reload them with powder, wadding, and tons of scrap metal and slag. Once more there was nothing but the snare drums beating out the tempo to break the hush of the morning.

Lessis found Lagdalen riding beside her on a cavalry horse. The girl held out a canteen. Lessis took a swig to clean the dust from her throat. She had a sense of impending disaster.

"What is it, Lady? What do they do that kills like this?"

The nightmare was plain to see in the fear that filled young Lagdalen's face. It seemed a great magic to her, one filled with an awesome power.

"Think of a catapult fired with an explosive powder rather than by twisting ropes. It is a terribly simple device, once you have mastered the key skills required for making it."

"They say that the Czardhans have been destroyed? Can this be true?"

"Alas, 'tis all but true. They are retreating now, too few to press home their attack."

And Steenhur was impervious to her pleas that he call off the assault. The rest of the army was marching into the same inferno.

When she looked along the marching lines of men, she had to wonder if even magic would stop them. There was a spirit there that would refuse orders to stop now. There was nothing to be done but to ride behind them, her heart in her mouth, as they marched into the gates of hell.

They met the Czardhan remnants tottering back on completely exhausted mounts, a few handfuls of men, some openly weeping, some walking, others borne limp over the backs of their mounts.

Ahead lay a bright carpet of the flower of Czardhan chivalry, a patchwork of steel armor, horseflesh, and blue and yellow silk tied together with threads of scarlet.

The legions passed over this carnage, ignoring the cries of terribly wounded men, grimly setting their sights on the line of dark-mouthed tubes two hundred yards ahead. The crowd of men around the tubes were very active.

And now flowing forward from hidden positions behind the tubes came an army of imps stiffened with fifty trolls. At the sight of more traditional enemies the legions gave voice with a defiant shout. The cornets sounded, the drums thundered, and they pushed on for the final assault, returning to a full trot, readying weapons for the moment of contact.

But before the two sides could meet, the ground trembled once more and the great dark mouths spoke again in a vast cloud of smoke and vented forth a hailstorm of iron and slag right into the oncoming legions. The army of the Empire of the Rose staggered, a moan went up, and thousands fell, cut to ribbons.

The survivors broke into a run, and with a shout of "Argonath" they crashed into the imps and trolls.

At last they were at grips with an enemy they could understand. A ferocious battle of sword and spear and arrow took place. The legions unloaded a tremendous charge of hate that had built up during the earlier slaughter at long range. The imps and the evil men who commanded them were battered, cut up, and slain in droves. Dragons pitched into the trolls, and though the trolls fought well, the dragons fought magnificently and in the matter of fifteen minutes had destroyed most of them.

The tide had turned, but the enemy was still engaged, the struggle pressed back virtually to the mouths of the tubes in dense clumps and knots of struggling figures, and now the legionaries were attacking the men who served the new weapons.

Behind the tubes a command was given, men touched slow-burning matches to small holes in the upper side of the tubes, and a moment later there was a great bellowing roar and the scene of battle was lost in a cloud of smoke as the enemy fired another deadly volley of iron right into the back of its own forces.

But the iron that cut through imps and trolls also struck the legions, and with deadly force at such close range. Relkin saw something decapitate the troll that Bazil was engaged with, and that same something flew on and killed a bowman notching an arrow some ten feet to the right. Other things flew all around him, humming like arrows. Men sank to the ground, horses fell screaming, and dragons, too, went down with groans of agony.

Some units were hit harder than others. There wasn't much left of the Kadein 92nd, and this volley completed their destruction as the last brasshide fell alongside the remaining two leatherbacks. In the 109th, Aulay was slain, and the Purple Green was wounded in the thigh.

Everywhere you looked there was slaughter and terrible, inexplicable death. With cold fury Relkin slew an imp that had survived like himself and was still showing signs of fight.

He saw Wiliger, holding up a hand that dripped blood while someone tried to bandage it up. The dragon leader's face was ashen, but at the same time lit by an inner fire Relkin recognized.

And then Relkin was moving on between the great tubes, and the men there were fleeing as Bazil Broketail cut at them with the gleaming white steel of Ecator. Alongside the broketail were the others, Alsebra, old Chektor, even Vlok, and their swords made short work of anyone that stood in their path.

The legions swept the entire area clear of the enemy and halted. A sense of common exhaustion filtered through the army. They had come a long way, through excruciating tension and horror, and finally they had routed an enemy force. Most important of all, they had captured the enemy weapons.

A thin cheer went up from the victors, most of whom were still busy killing imps and clearing out pockets of resistance.

They had won the day, or so it seemed. Except that the cost had been catastrophic. The army had been beheaded. General Steenhur had died in that final, terrible fusillade. As much as two-thirds of the dragon force was dead or incapacitated. The Czardhans had been annihilated, and the legions cut to pieces. It was a small, grim-faced force that occupied the hill and began to turn its attention to its wounded.

CHAPTER FORTY-SEVEN

It was still early in the morning. The sun was only now beginning to grow warm. The legions stood on the ridge crest
and stared at the things they had captured, the weapons that
had done such terrible damage. Blackened by smoke, the
tubes sat on their heavy carriages like so many burned offer-
ings to the gods of war.

Commander Voolward, now acting commanding officer,
was huddled around a folding table with Major Herte and
Commander Flades of the Cunfshon Legion. They had captured the objective, but their small army had taken terrible
casualties. Half of the command was dead or incapacitated.

Shortly the commanders were joined by Prince Ard Elac
of Kassim and the Count of Felk-Habren. The count had
been in some fierce fighting and bore a fresh wound on his
forehead.

The count asked the whereabouts of the witch woman and
was told that Lessis was with the engineers, seeking a
method to destroy the tubes.

Felk-Habren laughed bitterly at that. "Maybe we should
keep these things; they are more powerful than we are upon
a battlefield." Then he stared at the map spread on the table,
covered in notations in Baxander's fine hand.

"General Baxander will be much missed among the
knights of Czardha. He was a good man, we mourn him."

"As do we, Count."

"You will have to work very hard to fill his place."

Voolward pursed his lips. This was not news to him.
Baxander had been a fanatical worker, one reason why they
had come so far with so little trouble.

"The witch comes," said Commander Flades.

Lessis rode up, accompanied by Lagdalen and the chief
engineer, Absalt of Andiquant. Lessis kept to the background while Absalt explained what needed to be done. Pits

were to be dug in front of each of the tubes. Then they would be packed with blasting powder and the mouth of the tube sealed. When sealed, they would be tipped over until their mouths pointed down into the pits. Dirt would be packed over them, and finally a volunteer would light the torch hole and run for his life.

"What will happen?" said Count Felk-Habren, whose eyes kept returning to the wan face of the witch. She was hiding herself, he thought, and he wondered if she felt guilty for this butchery she'd unleashed. It was because of the witches that they had come to this hellish place. Come to die. All the fine young men of Czardha, lying out there ripped to pieces. A lump formed in the count's throat.

"The explosion will be trapped within the tube," said Absalt. "It should burst the metal. That will ruin them. They will be useless."

Felk-Habren nodded; his somber eyes sought out Lessis. She looked away.

"By the Hand, how are we to turn such things onto their ends?" said Voolward, who had been much impressed by the sheer mass of the huge tubes.

"If we dig a large enough pit in front of each one, it will be easy enough. Discharging them will be the hazardous job. It will require volunteers."

"Why so?" said the count.

"The tubes will explode most forcefully, Count. Anyone close by will be killed."

"The power in these things is so strong. I wonder if we should not keep them. Let us learn to use them and do to the enemy what he has done to us. Most piteous damage he has done."

Count Felk-Habren broke down for a moment. "Such good knights we have lost," he said in a bitter voice. "Brave men, great fighters, men who would throw themselves into this great expedition with no thought of reward except in honor! Now we shall honor their graves!"

Somehow, it did not seem at all odd to see this huge, ferocious man openly weeping.

Lessis heard him, but in truth she was distracted by her fears. These were the first, crude weapons from the path of power, and they had shown themselves to be monstrously deadly. And yet, as she had been told, these weapons were so primitive that those that would come after them, their descendants, would make these seem almost harmless. The count's expressed desire to wield the weapons was what she most feared. Now this secret was out. To keep it suppressed would become more difficult.

Voolward broke in to end the silence afforded the count's tears for his fallen comrades.

"First we need some kalut, perhaps some food. Where are the cooks?"

"They're on their way, sir," said Captain Keeven, now the eldest member of the support staff.

"Some hot kalut, some food, and we'll get digging."

"Transportation teams are coming forward. The question is where are we to take the wounded?"

Voolward contemplated the surrounding terrain. They stood on the crest of a low hill with long, flat slopes all about. Back the way they had come, through the volcanic boulder field, lay other smooth sloped ridges. Ahead were more of the same. To the west lay some smaller forested features. Small hills arranged in a line north south.

Voolward indicated the hills to the west and ordered scouts to investigate them for possible campsites.

Kalut was brewed and distributed along with hot bread and pickles and akh. About an hour after the capture of the guns, the first pits were begun.

The wounded were gathered in, then loaded onto the ox trains, and sent westward under cavalry guard.

Not long afterward the scouts out to the north brought reports of enemy activity. A large force of Kraheen had been reorganized and was moving south to engage. This force shortly crested the next ridgeline to the north of them and spread itself out in a long attacking line.

The digging was hastened. The Kraheen moved forward, their uluations rising into the warming air of the day. Within minutes they were engaged, and the space around the embattled legions was filled with a howling multitude. Arrows flicked in from the hovering mass, which hesitated to close with the legion survivors, now set in double lines, with dragons at the corners for a defensive square. Such a line bristled with death.

The digging, however, was slowed by the need to defend against the Kraheen. Still it continued, and the Kraheen could do no more than threaten and harass with archery.

Thus the situation stabilized and persisted for several

hours. The Kraheen hordes remained at the limits of bow shot, surrounding the legions and avoiding close contact. The sun rode through the high part of its arc, and the digging continued unabated. What they removed from the pits was used to build up a parapet around the position. While the pits were dug, the tubes were packed with the explosive powder and sealed with wet mud. Eventually the pits were deepened enough for Absalt to signal for the tubes to be tipped forward by a team of dragons.

They had barely begun this task when they heard that dreadful sound again, a distant booming thud. There came another and then several more. To the north, perhaps a mile, they saw a cloud of smoke shoot up. The enemy had brought up another set of his terrible weapons.

Lessis put her hand to her mouth. Too late, too late, came the cry whispering in her heart. All would fall to ruin, the work of centuries by her order would be lost. And with the work would be lost another world.

The enemy showed scant regard for their own troops. There was nothing unusual in this. Projectiles fell among the Kraheen and skipped across the barren plain like terrible bowls from some game of giants until they either exploded against rock or disappeared into the distance. Either way their effect on the Kraheen was dramatic. Amid a collective wail of fright, several dozen were slain while most of the rest withdrew at high speed. Avenues opened up in the circling masses.

Voolward saw the opportunity and set things in motion at once.

Volunteers, the first dozen who had managed to get their names in the hat, gathered by the tubes. Among them were several dragonboys, including Relkin of Quosh.

Relkin was still a little puzzled by his decision to volunteer for this. He'd been in the legions long enough to know that you never volunteered for anything because sure as hell it was going to come around to you anyway. He wasn't the sort to go volunteering for death or glory missions. He'd had quite enough death and glory shoved his way by the gods, or the Great Mother, or all of them combined.

And yet there was an anger burning inside him lit by the loss of so many comrades to this new weapon of the enemy. He wanted to destroy them.

Jak had volunteered, too, and was standing there with a

suspiciously large pack on his back. Then Relkin noticed the pack move, and the tip of something trunk-like showed through. He grinned happily at the younger boy. Trust Jak to weigh himself down with potential trouble in a situation like this!

The second volley from the enemy bellowed to the north. This time the balls landed much closer to the legions; a few skipped overhead. Everyone ducked, including the dragons, and cursed the damned things.

Voolward ordered everyone to hurry. They had to take advantage of this situation. There were openings in the Kraheen hordes on the west. Out there beyond the Kraheen foot soldiers were the legion cavalry, engaged with the Kraheen horse. If he could break out of the ring, then he would have some protection in a foot race for the western hills. Once on one of those hills, he could set up defense again.

Unless, he realized, with a deadly chill, the enemy brought up those tubes once more. That would place them in a deadly race. He would have to keep retreating, staying ahead of the enemy, and outpacing the deadly tubes.

But with so many wounded to carry, including wounded dragons, their progress would be slow. Perhaps the enemy would be able to match it, and they would never escape these terrible bombardments.

Voolward swallowed, his mind confused for a moment with dreadful portents. By the Mother's Hand, he thought to himself, panic was the most destructive force on any battlefield. He pulled himself together. It was up to him now; he had to bring the small army out of this.

They could not stay where they were.

The cornets blew. The men readied themselves, and when the command came, they formed up and headed west, dragons in the center. Behind they left the twelve volunteers, gathered around a crackling fire.

The enemy's third volley was fired, and for the most part it missed them, overshooting a little. Everyone crouched down as the air above them was filled with the urgent sounds of the great balls whipping past. A second or so later they could be glimpsed ricocheting away across the distant plain, and disappearing over the ridge to the south. A couple, however, landed short and skipped through the ranks of the legions, killing another eight men and wounding three.

The cornets blew once more, and the legions moved into a quicker step, abandoning the ridgeline and getting down below the line of sight of those manning the enemy weapons.

When the legions were some two hundred yards distant, the Kraheen began to trickle closer from eastward.

The small ring of volunteers watched nervously as the Kraheen approached.

"Light your tapers," said young Lieutenant Jeeks of the Pennar Third Regiment.

Relkin and Jak lit their tapers, then ran to their assigned tubes, fortunately placed adjacent to each other. At the command they pressed the smoldering tapers to the touch holes. Jak's took, as did everyone else's except Relkin's. Relkin's taper had blown out.

Everyone was running for their lives, except Relkin, and little Jak, who was tugging at his sleeve.

"Leave it, come on, Relkin."

The Kraheen were pressing in now on the position. They would be on them in moments.

Relkin pushed Jak away.

"Run," he said. "I will stay."

Little Jak looked at him amazed for a moment and then threw himself into a small hollow in the ground. Relkin followed a split second later.

The Kraheen were just yards away.

The tubes exploded almost as one, in a last titanic volley.

The ground heaved, the world was reduced to shattering sound, and a huge cloud of dust and smoke arose that obscured everything.

Shards of metal and superheated rock continued to fall from the sky for several seconds afterward.

Relkin and Jak were coughing fit to burst, even Stripey was snorting and snuffling inside the pack, but the hollow had sheltered them. The Kraheen who had rashly entered the position had been annihilated.

It was safe to stand up. Relkin took his taper back to where the fire had been. It had been scattered. A fragment of metal as big as himself had dug into the ground there like a giant knife.

He searched frantically for a few moments until he found a smoldering brand. This he took back to the surviving tube and pressed it to the touch hole.

"Run Relkin," screamed little Jak, taking off at a wild pace, his pack jouncing on his shoulders.

Relkin took out after him, pushing himself. He slipped on a patch of bloodstained ground and staggered.

A moment later the tube behind him blew, and the force of the explosion lifted him off his feet. Something hard struck him a glancing blow on the back of the helmet, and he never felt the landing.

CHAPTER FORTY-EIGHT

Commander Voolward struggled to keep the lid on the panic he felt rising up to overwhelm him. The situation was very difficult and could at any time become nightmarish.

At first the retreat had seemed quite a tactical success. The enemy weapon tubes were destroyed in a series of cataclysmic blasts, and all but two of the volunteers were recovered. The legions, guarding the wagon train, had reached the western hillocks. The cavalry had selected a defensible position straddling two adjacent small hills that acted as towers, with good clear fields of fire, allowing good protection of the space between them. Here they cut down the forest to build a barricade and threw up a rampart. Behind this they packed the ox train and set up tents.

While they fortified, the Kraheen infiltrated the woods around them, and a harassing rain of arrows began to make operations more difficult. The legion bowmen and dragonboys did their best to counter this fire, but they were greatly outnumbered. Dragons were used to hurl sudden barrages of rocks in the direction of particularly troublesome enemy archers. Yet the enemy clung on out there, circling, calling out to their Prophet, while their drums rumbled and thundered.

The legions did their best to ignore them while eating a necessary meal and taking some rest. The Kraheen showed no inclination to risk the casualties involved in attacking a fortified legion position, especially one as well protected as this. Thus a generous schedule of rests and watches was set up, leaving most of the men free to grab some food and then some sleep. It had been a long, exhausting day. Despite the danger of their position, they slept like the dead.

Still the drums thundered and arrows flicked in out of the dark, occasioning more casualties. The surgeons, aided by the witches, were working flat out to try and deal with the worst cases from the battle, but there was a mountain of work. And yet there was a steady dribble of freshly wounded men.

After the very worst cases had been dealt with, Lessis excused herself from the surgeons' tent and went with Lagdalen on a tour of the position. Wherever the Grey Lady went, morale soared, and the effect remained even after she had gone. It was not as if the men loved her, or any witch, that much. Indeed, they tended to regard the witches with suspicion. Nor was it the presence she projected, for that was ordinary to a fault, like her plain grey clothing. And yet when she had gone, with her small smile and honest grey eyes, the men felt better, stronger, and ready to take on the enemy no matter what they brought against them.

Lessis studied the situation, then went to see Commander Voolward.

"Well, Lady, what is the situation in the medical tent?" Voolward had the drawn, attenuated look of a man taxed to the limits.

"Not good, Commander, there are many men who should not be moved."

"Well, they needn't be for a few more hours, but I'm afraid they will have to move before dawn."

Lessis nodded, feeling relief that Voolward understood what was happening.

"The enemy is bringing up his weapons in the night."

"Yes, Lady, and he will assault us with them in the morning. We must be gone from here before then."

"What direction will you go?"

"I think south and west from here. Through country much like this, but there is a useable road that runs about eight miles westward of here. We can take it for as much as fifty miles south and west."

"You intend to remove the wounded from the scene, get to a place beyond the range of the enemy weapons."

"As a first step, yes."

"And then you will reengage?"

Voolward hesitated. "With such casualties, I am not sure that we can do that."

"There are still thousands of us, we must go on. We must stop the enemy from developing this weapon any further."

Voolward fell silent for a long moment, then he shrugged. "Well, whatever we hope to do, we must withdraw first

and recover. Our wounded must be seen to a place of
safety."

Lessis agreed with Voolward's plan and did her best to
improve his mood with only the mildest of spell effects. The
prohibition against the use of magic to influence the military
was only absolute when it came to changing the minds of officers and overruling their judgments. Morale improvements
were not considered real breaches of the rule.

The witches returned to the surgeons' tent after taking
some hot kalut at the cook fire. Once more they took up
washbasins, towels, and bandages, and returned to the grisly
tasks that are the residue of war.

Lagdalen had some saddening news. Relkin of Quosh had
been lost in the retreat. He had been one of the volunteers
for destruction of the enemy tubes, and had not returned
from the explosive blasts. The broketail dragon was heart-
broken.

Lessis gave a sigh. In the five centuries she had lived, she
had seen a great many men and women come and go. She
had regretted many an undeserved and early death. And yet
she shared the dragon's grief, for this one came very close
to her heart. In a very real way Relkin had saved her life on
one occasion, in the catacombs of Tummuz Orgmeen. He
had given much to the Argonath and would be missed by his
friends. Lessis of Valmes felt a shaft of sorrow at the
thought of this loss. That young rascal from that obscure village with the laughable name had come to personify for her
the strengths of the Argonath itself.

The parade of the wounded went on and on, though the
worst cases were finally behind them. These had been
loaded directly onto the wagons that would go out in the
second wave in the morning. This would allow them to recover slightly before they had to withstand the jolting progress of the wagons going through rough country. Meanwhile
the lesser cases, men with cuts and gouges, some broken
limbs and ribs, came in an endless tide.

Sometime around the midnight hour, however, there came
a new development that made everyone very nervous. Suddenly the Kraheen began sending in fire arrows. At first just
a few, then more and more, until there were Kraheen arrows
sunk in many trees, burning steadily.

The trees were not that dry that they could be lit in this
way, and wherever small fires did begin, the men soon put

them out. Still the fire arrows came, and Voolward realized with grim horror that they were simply helping the enemy aim the tubes.

A minute later they heard the first distant boom. It was loud, and thus they knew the enemy had brought the tubes quite close to them. It was followed by a volley of eleven more.

The aim was poor, and the first few volleys crashed mostly into the forest, quite short of their position. Some of the balls ricocheted over their heads, screaming through the air, and one or two slammed into the wagon park, overturning wagons and slaughtering oxen.

This had Voolward on the edge of panic. Any loss in the ox train would be a deathblow. They would be forced to abandon their wounded. In practice, that meant they would have to kill them because no one would leave a comrade to the torments of the Kraheen.

Inevitably they had to move even sooner than anticipated. The cornets shrilled, orders were distributed, and while the enemy continued to fire volleys at them every twenty minutes or so, the legions made shift to move from their prepared positions.

A strong party was sent out on the preferred route, to clear the Kraheen out of the way. They burst through the Kraheen screen and dispersed the enemy on that side of the camp. Bowmen flooded the woods there to pick off enemy snipers.

The ox train began rolling. The cavalry went out ahead, working through the pitch-dark woods, seeking the best trail for the wagons.

By now the enemy was finding the range, and volley after volley fell on the hilltops or within the vale between them. This hurried the retreat, and things began to grow a little ragged. Even the training of the Imperial legionaries began to fray under these conditions.

Once they were out in the woods, a new phase of the struggle began as near invisible bands of Kraheen filtered in around them and engaged in hit-and-run attacks.

It became very difficult to maintain cohesion in these conditions. The long wagon trains had to be protected, and this stretched out their forces along the rough path they were taking. Dragons were essential to cutting and clearing the route they were following, which made them vulnerable to sniper attacks. There was a constant battle at the front of the column to keep the Kraheen away from the dragons and engineers, working to build the way for the wagons.

All this slowed their progress toward that promised road, eight miles to the west. Voolward was left to pray, helplessly, that the enemy would be just as slow in bringing up his terrible weapons.

Conditions approached a crisis, but the real catastrophe began when a great stone ball struck a pine tree right over Commander Voolward's head and dropped half of it right on him and Commander Flades. Both men were crushed into the muddy stream that the engineers were bridging with a rough-hewn construction of trees cut down with dragonsword.

The legions struggled on; everyone had their job to do, and they continued to do it, but there was a fatal gap of time before Major Herta and Captain Denk rode up to take command. Count Felk-Habren was left in charge during this period and he called for volunteers to turn back and attack the enemy weapons in the dark. This dreadful retreat from an enemy they had bested on the battlefield was not the count's idea of how to wage war.

Dragon Leader Wiliger was taken with this idea and committed the survivors of the 109th to it at once. They grouped with fifty surviving Czardhans, some Bakani foot soldiers, and a dozen Kenor bowmen, and moved out, straight back on the road they had hacked out of the wilderness. The Grey Lady accompanied them, determined to destroy the enemy weapons if at all possible.

The legions continued the retreat, harried by the Kraheen for the rest of the night. Major Herta and Captain Denk drove themselves mercilessly and were finally brought a little good news from scouts riding in from a mission that had penetrated all the way to the western road.

They had the welcome news that the road was there, and that it seemed like a good one. Once they reached it, they would be able to make much better time. They would soon outdistance the enormously bulky enemy weapons.

Unfortunately, their progress was slowed by a stretch of deeply cut ravine land. Getting the wagons through in the dark was a horrendous task, and as they jolted over rocks, the wounded gave out piteous screams.

The dawn found them stretched out for miles in this difficult country, surrounded by packs of Kraheen. Chaotic fights were in progress at many points.

At the rear of the column, packs of trolls and platoons of imps had joined the Kraheen, and they began to overwhelm the resistance.

The imps reeked of the black drink, and under its spell they happily risked death as they sought to bury their blades in Argonath flesh. The fighting grew more desperate, and several times groups of trolls managed to cut their way through and get into the ox train, where they slew oxen and wounded quite indiscriminately.

But a sudden cessation of bombardment from the enemy weapons gave the escaping columns a fighting chance. By the forenoon, the front half of the wagon train was safely on the western road and moving away. The surviving fighting forces concentrated on extricating as much as possible of the rest. Dragons set several fierce little ambushes during the afternoon and soon made the pursuit turn cautious. Still the enemy took prisoners, both wounded and fit, and there was nothing the men of the Argonath could do to save their comrades. In the end the remnants of the army escaped onto the western road and fled as fast as they were able.

CHAPTER FORTY-NINE

Consciousness was slow to return, and fitful. For a long while Relkin lay in the dark and drifted in and out of dreams in slow waves that broke on unseen shores of the dark. There was a dull ache in his head, blood crusted down his cheek and neck, and a very tender area on one side.

It was very dark, cool, and damp, and he wondered how he had come to be in this place.

His memories were hazy, however. For a long time he thought of Eilsa Ranardaughter, and of the life with her that he dreamed of. He thought of her wild blond hair, the determined jut of her chin, and her keen, well-directed intelligence. She had a startling honesty that sometimes made him love her so much it felt as if his heart would burst. He and she were made for each other, a match blessed by the gods and the Great Mother.

One day they would build a cabin in the forests of Tuala. And together with the dragon they would clear land and plant their first crops. While the crops grew, they would start a family.

Even in hazy dreams this thought was startling for Relkin, whose only family had been a two-ton leatherback dragon and the 109th Marneri Dragon squadron.

Then, gradually, memories came back of the long, arduous campaign. The march, the terror birds in the ruined temple, the monsters that haunted the eerie, ancient forest, the little striped elephant, images of all these things kept popping up in his mind until the pieces fitted back together. Finally came memories of the battle on the place of Broken Stone. The defeat of the Kraheen, the savage fight with the imps and trolls, and the terrible destruction wrought on the legions by the enemy's secret weapons.

When he remembered it all, his heart sank. The legions

had been hard hit. The fantastic journey across half the world had been for nothing.

The very last links in the chain of memories eluded him, however. How had he come to be lying in the cool darkness, in a place that smelled of wet stone and mold?

A chilly thought struck him at last. What if this was death? Had old Gongo, the god of the afterlife, collected him from the battlefield and brought him to lie in the halls of stone until the end of time? If so, it was going to be a pretty boring wait lying here in damp darkness. He hoped something would happen occasionally. Then he chided himself for his irreverence. It was no wonder he was always in trouble.

And then an aching sadness came over him as he realized that if he was dead he would never achieve his dream of a life with Eilsa Ranardaughter. Nor would he ever see his great dragon again.

He lay there, cold and damp and very low in spirit, for a long time. Oddly enough for one who was dead, he felt his wits sharpening and his head clearing in a more or less steady progression during this period. He could feel his breath coming evenly, steadily, through nostrils to chest. This struck him as strange. Did the dead breathe in the Halls of Gongo?

Suddenly he heard a loud snort and a mutter. He held his breath and listened with every fiber of his being while he tested his bonds.

There was no easy way out of them. Thick leather thongs had been used. He could tell at once that it would take him a long while to gnaw through them.

How could he be dead and have his wrists bound?

The conclusion was obvious and of little comfort. He had been captured by the enemy and left here with who knew what in this dark place. Perhaps he was the next meal for some troll or other fell beast of the enemy.

Where were the gods when you needed them? It seemed that the gods had rolled the dice on him again and come up with singles. He prayed that they might roll them again, and he promised to make sacrifice as soon as he was able, if he could only get out of this place.

Then, without warning, he sneezed at the cold.

The breathing sound was interrupted; a familiar voice said, "Who's there?"

"Jak?"

"Relkin, is that you?"

"Of course it's me. How did they capture us?"

"Relkin, I'm so glad I'm not in here alone."

"Is there anyone else?"

"Not that I've heard."

"Is anyone there?"

The silence convinced them that there wasn't.

"I was trying to get you on your feet; I didn't see the one that got me; he sneaked up from behind."

"I don't remember."

"You're lucky to be alive. We lit the fuses on the enemy weapons and blew them to pieces; something must have knocked you cold. I thought you were going to die. There was a lot of blood."

"Yeah, I can feel a big cut on the top of my head. I guess old Caymo was rolling the dice for me after all. Where are we?"

"Inside some big building, that's all I know. I was put in a closed cart for three days and could hardly see anything since I was tied up. Then they pulled me out, and a great stinking troll carried me inside a wide door and down a passage and put me in this room. Someone shut the door, and I've been here ever since. I don't know when they brought you in, I was asleep for a while."

"Then we're a distance from the battlefield."

"Miles."

"They didn't kill us, that's significant."

"Of course not, they're gonna sacrifice us. That's what they do to prisoners, Relkin. You heard the stories. They rip your heart out of your body while it's still beating and offer it to their god."

"Yeah, I heard." Maybe old Caymo had rolled the dice pretty damn badly. "Except we're from the legions, Jak. They'll ask us questions before they kill us. You'll see. We might get a chance to escape."

"That's what I hoped you would say. If the madman from Quosh says we're gonna get away, then I'll believe it."

"What happened to Stripey?"

Jak's voice dropped. "I don't know. I hope he got away. He was in my pack when they took me. They tore it off. I don't even know if he was still in there at that point."

They lay there in the dark, talking bravely to keep each

other's spirits up. Relkin recalled a similar situation in the Temple of Gingo-La in the faraway land of Ourdh. This time, however, there was no lovely Miranswa to save him. This time the orphan boy from Quosh was going to face the music.

Food and water had been brought once before, according to Jak. The service had been dismal. Someone had crouched over him in the dark and shoved wet bread into his mouth. Relkin hadn't eaten for days, however, and he was so ravenous even this would have been acceptable. He was also terribly thirsty. After a while his dry throat made him stop talking. He dozed, awoke, and dozed again. His thirst had grown unbearable.

And then the door suddenly crashed open to admit a fierce red light. By it they saw a pack of squat, dark-skinned men in leather aprons and feather headdresses. Heavy gold chains hung around their necks, huge rings flashed on every finger.

Relkin's heart sank. These gentlemen looked every inch like priests. Maybe little Jak was right after all.

The priests pulled them to their feet and hustled them out the door and down a corridor of stone. The leather between their ankles slowed them, and the Kraheen goaded them with sharp blows and hisses of impatience.

At length they passed some guards and entered a larger room. A fire blazed at one end, throwing a harsh light across a scene of fantastic savagery.

On a dais stood a single figure, clad in cloth of gold like a shimmering pillar. Before him groveled a small army of men in leather aprons and feather headdresses. In a cage set to one side of the dais were a dozen poor wretches, crammed into a space big enough for half their number.

Five stout imps armed with bludgeons, whips, and swords guarded this cage.

Behind the figure on the dais was a stone altar. On the altar was the corpse of a woman, her chest torn open and her heart removed. The man in the cloth of gold held up the woman's heart and squeezed it so that drops of blood fell into his mouth.

Relkin and Jak exchanged a grim look.

"Old gods have ratted on you, Relkin," said Jak.

Relkin and Jak were pushed through the milling horde of priests while the man on the dais harangued them with a voice of electrifying power. Relkin couldn't understand a word, but he sensed the excitement in the crowd around him. They were spellbound.

Then they climbed some steps to the top of the dais and were brought before the figure in the cloth of gold.

A devil's face looked into theirs. A devil splashed crimson from nose to chest. A face cut by harsh lines with deep-set eyes that blazed with an insane fire. The devil smiled evilly at them. His hands came up and made clutching motions at them, then he barked something to his servants.

Drums were beaten, horns blared, the priests shouted for joy. Doors opened at the far end of the room, and Relkin and Jak were hustled through them and onto a huge balcony overlooking a great amphitheater. Down below was a mass of Kraheen waiting expectantly under torchlight.

At the sight of the figure in the cloth of gold, a roar went up. When the prisoners were brought out, the roar increased and a harsh chant began, a few syllables repeated over and over again while the crowd raised its hands en masse.

From the cage the imps brought in a pair of Talion troopers captured the previous day. Both men had been beaten and stripped, but they retained their native bumptiousness. When an imp struck one of them, he struck back, hammering the imp in the face with an elbow, then putting a knee to good use in the imp's midriff. For this he was struck repeatedly with whips until the tall golden one shouted at the imps and made a gesture with one hand at his throat.

The crowd roared; they hated imps. To see the Prophet kill imps would be wonderful. Lustily they called for the death of the imps. But it was the Talion troopers who were pulled forward and bound to thick poles set on the edge of the balcony. The crowd fell into an expectant hush.

Relkin didn't want to watch, but found it impossible to look away. The Prophet began his incantations and raised his hands to the heavens again and again in supplication. His voice grew harsh and then rose to a demonic shriek that cut through the listeners' thoughts like a hot knife through snow.

The air grew dense with energy, a feeling of doom pulsed in the air. The troopers gave out hoarse cries of agony that mounted quickly to shrill squeals.

The crowd murmured expectantly as the Prophet moved closer to the doomed troopers with his hands extended toward their chests and his mouth open in an obscene rictus of a smile.

The troopers began to jerk madly against their bonds, pulled by a force greater than anything in their own bodies. It was eerie to see these big men pulled off their feet, the bodies contorting as their pink chests surged out to meet the brown hands that grasped at them.

The power rose, the air crackled as if lightning was about to break loose, an unbearable tension lay over everything, and then with a sound like small trees being split with an ax, the rib cages of the two doomed men broke asunder in a fountain of blood.

A moment later the bloodstained Prophet, drenched with gore, had the men's hearts in his hands as he raised them over his head.

The crowd let out an ecstatic roar, a terrifying cry of monstrous lust, a satisfaction with dreadful evil.

For a full minute they roared while the tall man in the bloodstained cloth of gold capered back and forth before them, squeezing and shaking the hearts in his hands so that drops of blood rained down on the fortunates in the audience who were positioned right below him.

Eventually he slowed and let his hands drop. The hearts were exhausted. The pleasure had faded. Gradually the crowd's excitement dimmed, and the noise died down. The Prophet turned and signaled to the imps standing behind Relkin and Jak.

In moments the boys were lifted up and borne to the poles, and Relkin felt a sense of utter hopelessness overcome him. This seemed such an unclean way to die. But there was nothing to be done and he was bound to the stake, positioned so that he stared across ten feet of space to little Jak, who was plainly terrified.

"Commend your soul to the Mother, Jak!" he called. "She will protect you from now on."

Jak heard but made no response. He was frozen with terror. Relkin tried again and drew an angry slash from an imp's whip. This time, though, his words had gotten through to Jak, whose face softened a moment and then firmed with new strength as he overcame the terror of death.

"If you live in the Mother's Hand," he shouted back, "you need not fear death."

An imp stepped up to snarl in little Jak's face. Jak spat in his eye. The imp staggered back and snarled and plied his whip on little Jak.

Once again the Prophet checked the imp with a snarl. The crowd murmured in appreciation. The Prophet spread his arms wide and began to summon up his power once again. Relkin felt his heart flutter oddly in his chest, and he was struck by a sudden nausea. From nowhere came a blow; it was as if he'd been kicked in the chest by a mule. He heard himself bellow involuntarily.

The crowd roared. The Prophet came close, and Relkin stared up into those mad eyes above the thick gore. So this was death, thought Relkin. Old Gongo could not be any more horrible. He felt his ribs starting up, bending under the invisible pressure of the mad Prophet's magic. It felt as if a hand with cold fingers was actually prising his chest up and up until it must burst and send his heart flying to the Prophet's hand.

And then, with shocking abruptness, a huge man clad in black leather appeared in his field of vision and shoved the Prophet aside. The spell collapsed.

With a strange crawling sensation, Relkin felt the pressure on his heart ebb away. His skin itched unbearably. Tears ran down his cheeks, and there was a ringing in his ears.

More men in black leather, with the conical helmets of Padmasa, appeared around them. Relkin and Jak were cut free and hustled away while the crowd groaned its disappointment.

Down a labyrinth of stone corridors they went, before exiting from a narrow side door that opened onto a dark alley. It was night, and a soft moonlight pervaded the upper air. A torch flared, and by its flicker, Relkin saw a dozen men with swords and helmets of Padmasa style in the alley. Several had their swords drawn, and now they danced ahead on the lookout for trouble.

They went on through another alley, then down some stairs and through streets lined with rough-hewn houses built of stone and thatch. They emerged onto a harbor; Relkin could just see the outlines of the headland to his right. Beyond that was the openness of the sea, the great Wad Nub, the Inland Sea.

Now they were taken out onto a generously proportioned two-masted ship, something that was at least as large as the river-going boats of Kenor.

Aboard this ship they were driven down belowdecks and confined to a narrow dark compartment. The door was bolted on the outside. Soon afterward they felt the boat leave the dock and begin to make its way out onto the waters of the Inland Sea.

Behind on the wharf a small creature scurried out of the tunnel mouth and into the protective shadows of a pile of barrels being unloaded from the next ship up the wharf. It gave a soft, mournful hoot at the sight of the first ship leaving the harbor. Men in black loaded the barrels into carts and drove them off the dock. Other men went aboard the ship and disappeared below.

Before the unloading was complete, the creature had managed to reach the side of the dock. For a moment all was still. The small animal scurried up the gangplank and hid itself beneath a heavy coil of rope.

Not long afterward more men came to the dockside, boarded the ship, and cast off the ropes tethering it to the dock. The sails were unfurled and quickly filled with wind, and the ship headed out of the harbor and into the Inland Sea.

CHAPTER FIFTY

The man called Kreegsbrok came to them once again.

"You will be questioned by the Great One himself, quite soon. I have come to warn you not to attempt to dissemble or deceive the Master. He will detect any untruths, and you will regret them at once, believe me."

Kreegsbrok's Verio was good, albeit with a strange accent. He had questioned them himself, thoroughly. At first Relkin had given him only his name and rank and unit, as he was trained to. Jak had been taken away to be questioned separately. Kreegsbrok learned enough from them separately to converse intelligently about the expeditionary force. The more Kreegsbrok knew, the harder it became for Relkin to keep silent.

"Why does a Great Master want to question me?" said Relkin. "I'm just a dragonboy."

"I have served the Master for many years, dragonboy, I have learned never to question anything he does. He will have a good reason. Perhaps he will share it with you. Just be sure not to anger him with some silly attempt at deceit. He can sniff out the slightest untruth, and then he will be cruel."

"I have answered your questions, Kreegsbrok, will you answer one for me?"

Kreegsbrok looked at him. It was odd, but he liked these youths. Servants of the enemy they might be, but they showed a grit that he had to admire. Even in such dire circumstances, they kept their heads. Kreegsbrok had seen many a man confronted with an imminent interrogation by one of the Great Masters of Padmasa shake, tremble, and even foul themselves from fear.

"All right, speak, Dragonboy."

"That man, the Prophet of the Kraheen, why does he kill like that? Is it to entertain the people?"

Kreegsbrok pressed his lips together. His dislike for that part of his life was so great that it was hard for him to talk about it.

"He is not properly alive. He lives only to kill. It is his greatest pleasure."

"Why do the people love it so?"

"We have made them great and given them power and slaves. They think the deaths increase their power, though in truth, they are a cruel people eager to have revenge on the world."

"What do you think of the killings, Kreegsbrok?"

"I do not think of such things. It is not my job."

"You are a man of honor, Kreegsbrok. I see that from your weapons, from your dress, from the way you carry yourself."

"I command the Master's forces in this region."

"Then you must be a great general. You must have a sense of honor. How can you obey such orders, doesn't the killing sicken you?"

"Shut your mouth, Dragonboy. You people of the East are weak. You let women rule like men, and so you are weak like women. You know nothing of the world."

Relkin laughed to himself at that, but thought better about letting Kreegsbrok hear him.

"You know something, you're wrong about that, but never mind. You're a brave man, a soldier, and you must have once had honor. I think you must have shut your heart away somewhere and lost it in the darkness. Now you serve a thing that kills for the pure pleasure of it. Now you have no honor, do you?"

Kreegsbrok stared at the boy for a moment and raised a fist.

"I would make you pay for that, Dragonboy, but you are wanted by the Master." Abruptly he turned and stalked away.

Not long afterward men came and blindfolded Relkin and led him away. There was a long tramp through an echoing place, perhaps a cave. Then he was forced to ascend a great many steps, and as he climbed them, the air grew thick with sulfurous fumes. It became hard to breathe after a while, but his captors would not let him stop. If he slackened the step, they jabbed him with knife points to keep him moving. At last they reached their destination, and he was pushed against a wall and shackled there with heavy chains. The sulfur smell was very strong, and the air was hot and heavy. From somewhere below there was a constant harsh roaring sound broken occasionally by louder crashes. His captors took their leave, and he was left, blindfolded, alone, in a high place over great peril.

He was there for perhaps an hour when he felt the first touch of the presence. It came directly into his mind, a little thought, a sort of warmth, even friendliness. A kitten of a thought, just out to be playful.

Another mind was surfacing within his own thoughts. It spoke to him, and it did a whole lot more.

Of all dragonboys serving in the legions of Argonath, Relkin was perhaps the most practiced in the arts of magic, all on the receiving end, of course. He had spoken with the Great Witches, Lessis and Ribela, on the mental plane, so he was not struck dumb with terror.

On the other hand, the witches had never "arrived" in his mind like this. They came like still, small voices "speaking" in his head. This was different. This was as if a part of him spoke to himself. It was as if he no longer completely controlled his own mind. He disliked it intensely.

The arriving presence was amused by his dislike.

"I know you," it said. His lack of fear had confirmed everything it had learned.

"Kreegsbrok has done very well to bring me this dainty," said the voice in his mind. It turned to him; he felt the power grow enormously. His mind was gripped as if by huge, unseen hands. He felt his memories invaded; flashes of thought rushed past, looted from his private places.

Relkin hissed and spat, enraged.

"You have involved yourself in the affairs of the great too many times, dragonboy Relkin, to escape me now. When you left your village, you hoped for great things. And you have achieved them."

Relkin struggled not to feel the false pride that the thing in his mind pressed upon him.

"You have fought in many campaigns. You have seen battle again and again, and you have survived and emerged covered in glory. Why, they even gave you the Legion Star after your exploits in Tummuz Orgmeen."

"We threw down the Doom." Relkin spat back, taking control of his own mind for a moment.

"Yes, you did," said a huge voice in his brain, as the invisible grip came down again, but much, much tighter.

"Do not think to resist me, child. You cannot, and I do not wish to hurt you. No, not in any way, despite all the injury you have done to me and my cause."

Relkin struggled to spit out his reply, but could only manage an incoherent snarl.

"Listen to yourself, now you are snarling, like an animal. That's what those witches have done to you. Don't you see? You've been raised under witches' sorcery. From the earliest times they indoctrinated you with their bizarre theories. People are not equal, boy, this you must understand. You are not equal to me. No living man is equal to me. Comprehend this truth. Then listen to the message I bring you, for it will liberate you and set you on the true path to enlightenment."

Relkin's struggles had lessened. His thoughts had grown confused. It was true that he'd seen plenty of sorcery performed by the witches, but it had always been for the good of all and the peace of the Mother, or so he thought. And yet there was another thought, which spoke of the sacrifice that dragonboys made, losing limbs, dying, all for the comfort of a society that valued them little and rewarded them meagerly. For ten years of extremely dangerous service, you received a mere forty acres of virgin land in Kenor.

Well, the dragon received eighty more, so between you, you had one hundred and twenty acres. It was also possible to buy more, and if you saved, then you would have enough to add to this total. This way a sizable farm could be built up quite quickly. Relkin's optimistic views of the future were strong; he'd spent many hours daydreaming them into fantasy life.

But the other voice would not be quiet. "The life of a small peasant farmer!" it bellowed, "for risking your life for them over and over again." At the siege of Ourdh, at the great battles of Salpalangum and Sprian's Ridge, or in the catacombs of Tummuz Orgmeen, Relkin and his leatherback dragon had served them well. And for all that suffering and sweat, terror and toil, they would give him land enough to be a peasant.

Another view swelled up. After service with the new power, the power brought by the Masters, someone like Relkin would retire to a country estate with a pension of considerable value and high honors. He would have hundreds of acres, and hundreds of servants. His life would take place on an altogether more exalted plane.

Relkin rejected it. This was all falsity; he knew how the servants of Padmasa lived. He had seen Tummuz Orgmeen.

"But come, I have no need to contend with you. You are simply dwelling in ignorance. I shall show you the way. Listen to the words and learn, child."

The voice in his thoughts grew to become the universe, absorbing everything into itself.

"In the center of all there is nothingness," it said. "The nothingness is what we come from and what we return to. While we live, we are given the world to enjoy. It is ours to use while we have it. There is nothing that is forbidden.

"Of course, the pursuit of the better things is to be preferred. The higher elements are much worthier of our efforts than the animal urges of our flesh. We have developed the way to pursue the higher elements and to overcome the limitations of the flesh."

The voice plucked at something in his mind.

"Yes, you were marked by the Sinni. And you saw them, I think, during another of your depredations. Think how the Sinni live! At higher energies, where power is vast and pleasure limitless. You, too, could have this, if you master the subtleties of our method.

"All this can be open to you, child, if you will but open your heart to us."

"I have no master," said Relkin aloud, with a great effort. "Leave my mind alone."

There was a long moment of suspense. As if a great avalanche were falling on him from a height.

"Oh, but you do have a Master!" roared the voice, taking over the universe once more.

"I will empty you and re-form you. You will become my golem, and you will live forever."

"Never!" Relkin screamed back with everything he had.

CHAPTER FIFTY-ONE

The small group of men and dragons were now fugitives from the enemy. They had successfully destroyed the enemy's weapons, but since then they had been driven westward and had lost hope of rejoining the main army.

They halted for the day when they finally struck the main stream of the river. They had spent much of that day hacking through undergrowth surrounding small tributaries, getting closer and closer to the river itself. It was getting dark. They were exhausted. Dragonboys were on their last legs, but they struggled up and set about checking their dragons for cuts and abrasions. The older men, many of them wounded, simply fell asleep wherever they lay down.

Dragon Leader Wiliger made his rounds, limping, with a large bandage on his wounded hand and another bandage on his lower jaw. Wiliger's bark had long since ceased to frighten the boys, and he had abandoned his martinet pose. Something had happened to Wiliger. He had become a good dragon leader, eternally solicitous of the boys and their wyverns. Somewhere in the white heat of days of fighting, seeing boys and dragons die under the enemy bombardment, he'd lost his arrogance and gained a genuine humility.

With the dragons who'd lost dragonboys, the Broketail and Alsebra, Wiliger tried to tend to them. He took scraper and points and attempted to fill in. The dragons ignored him as they usually did. Bazil was sunk into his own interior gloom. Alsebra simply felt numb at the loss of her second dragonboy. She had already lost her dragonboy since her young days, Bryon. She knew what the Broketail was going through. And at the same time she genuinely missed young Jak with his cheery ways and his skill with cuts and bruises.

Wiliger tried to change the bandage on Alsebra's slashed left forearm, but she withdrew it after she realized how clumsy he was.

"Mono will do it, later," she said with a hiss.

Bazil merely glared at him when he sought to check the leatherback's cuts.

Once, Wiliger would have been offended and would have gone off in a rage. Now he accepted the situation and left quietly, going over to comfort Manuel, who they had picked up from the battlefield unconscious and who later despaired at the loss of the Purple Green, who had been slowed by his wounded leg and had become separated from the rest of them in the dark. Manuel had come into the Dragon Corps to care for the wild dragon. Despite the Purple Green's temper and ingratitude, there had grown a bond that was very strong. The young man's heart was breaking as he contemplated the strong likelihood that he would never see his wild dragon again.

The bond between dragon and boy was that powerful kind that can come between species, such as a dog for a human. But between the battledragon and the dragonboy, the bond was stronger by far. Dragons were not only intelligent and incredibly fierce, they were capable of great emotional involvement. They tried not to show this, but it was always there.

Bazil, of course, was utterly desolate. His boy was gone. He had lived with boy Relkin for most of his life. They had grown up together. Bazil had often warned that boy that this would happen, and it had. Now the dragon was alone. Memories crowded in his thoughts, all tinged now by sadness.

He felt a presence and raised his head. Alsebra leaned closer so that he could see her eyes clearly.

"Jak was my second boy," she said. "I mourn his loss. Your pain is deeper, though. I know. When I lost Bryon, I felt as if I had lost a part of my self. We grow close to our boys over the years."

Bazil could hardly speak. He slumped beside the water, sitting back on a fallen tree, Ecator in its scabbard before him.

"It was not like boy to volunteer for anything. Why this time? It seem damned foolish."

"Someone had to do it. Boys have to prove themselves not completely worthless. Relkin was angry. We all angry."

"Yessss."

Bazil hissed with a deep boiling kind of rage. His hands

clenched on the pommel of Ecator. Someone would pay, by the ancient gods of Dragon Home, he swore it.

The word was passed around that there would be a share-out of the available food.

They could not risk a fire. The woods behind them were alive with Kraheen scouts. Sergeant Worrel had organized the collection of every scrap of food they had. Now he split it up and shared it out equally. It was meager. A scrap of dried biscuit with a thin slice of sausage and a fragment of cheese. Even without a fire, the food distribution point became the center of the little camp. A ring of hungry, exhausted men formed around it. The dragons were settled farther away, where they could stick their big feet in the river. The dragons did not expect any of the food; there wasn't enough to even give one dragon a snack.

"Anybody know where we are?" said Spearman Rikart.

Nobody answered for a while.

"Ask the witch, she'll know. She knows everything," said someone else in a bitter voice.

"It's not her fault. We had to stop them firing those things at the column."

"It's not her fault?" said someone else, incredulous. "That's a joke, right?"

"Pass over, friend. That's wrong. It's no one's fault. We had a job to do. We done it, but we paid a price."

"Damned witches brought us here."

"You join the legions, you join to fight."

The witch they argued over was too busy right then to answer the question, even if she had heard it. Not that she could have said precisely where they were. Lessis knew they were close to the Inland Sea, and that this river must run into that sea, but how close that sea was she did not know. And besides, there were too many badly wounded to treat right away for her to spend much time thinking about it. She was helped by Lagdalen, who was completely covered in mud, blood, and general filth, from head to toe, but continued patching and bandaging men with stolid indifference. Lessis noted that Lagdalen had developed an endurance almost equal to that of a Great Witch. Her years with Lessis had hardened her.

They left the worst till last, when Swane joined them.

"I need you to hold him down, Dragoneer Swane."

Swane understood. He was big for his age, already a well-developed man.

The gangrene had begun in the patient's arm. The imp blade had cut to the bone, and the wound had turned bad. Lessis had never performed an amputation before, although she had witnessed hundreds over her lifetime. Cutting through a screaming man's flesh while others held him down was not the same as watching and assisting the surgeon. Trying to tie off arteries with shaking fingers and vision blurring from fatigue was even worse in some ways. With Lagdalen's deft fingers moving around hers, she struggled through it. Somehow they kept the young man alive. He went into shock before it was over, and that made the latter parts of the operation simpler. Swane helped with the sewing; like all dragonboys he was deft with needle and thread.

They wrapped the amputee in a blanket and prayed over him for a moment. The Hand of the Mother hold him close. Swane returned to his dragon, who was already asleep and snoring thunderously. Lessis went on to her last call, Legionary Petto, who was obviously going to die that night. Peritonitis had taken hold from the spear thrust in his belly. Lessis had nothing to dull the pain except a flask of black drink she'd taken from a dead imp major. She gave some of this to the worst cases. The ones who were dying anyway. It dulled their pain even as it excited them. It was hard to lie to Petto, who didn't want to die and was afraid of going to the Mother's Hand. He knew what was happening. It was difficult to ease his fear. Lessis spoke with him for a while and worked subtle magic on him. Despite the intoxication of the black drink, he calmed, his breath came more easily, he struggled less. He made ready to go to the Hand.

At length Legionary Petto slipped into unconsciousness, and Lessis left him and went to sit beside Lagdalen under a tree. There was a piece of hard biscuit in her pack. They shared this, the last food they had. Neither spoke. Both were close to exhaustion.

Then Lagdalen's head dropped suddenly against Lessis's shoulder. In a moment she began to snore softly. Lessis laid her head back against a tree. The sight of Lagdalen sleeping brought on a tremendous urge to sleep herself. She felt tired to the bone, just so, awfully tired.

She awoke to a gentle shake of her shoulder. She sucked in a breath with a gasp as her hand went to her dagger.

"It is I, Count Felk-Habren, Lady."

"Ah, yes, pardon me, Count." Lessis remembered where she was. Lagdalen still slept, curled up like a kitten beside her.

The count continued to have difficulty with the concept of dealing with what looked like beggar women as if they were his equals, but he had seen the work of these same beggarly looking witches when they blew up the enemy's tube weapons, and he had seen them fight during the long, crazy retreat from the battlefield. He had seen this fragile-looking drab parry a sword thrust, go inside, and kill an unwary imp with the long dagger she carried at her hip. Thus, his discomfort was now matched by a healthy respect for their power and their courage.

"We must talk."

"Good idea, Count."

Felk-Habren grasped at the air with his hands.

"I do not know what to do. I knew we had to smash those weapons, and we did that, but now I am lost."

Lessis pulled herself to her feet.

"Lost? No, my friend, we are not lost. We know several things about our location. We can't be far from the Inland Sea. We've traveled westward since the battle. This river will take us to the sea. That seems the way to go. So we have an idea of where we are and where we're going. More than that, we seem to have given the enemy the slip, too. No signs of them for hours now."

Felk-Habren squinted at her.

"I wish I could believe that. There are thousands of Kraheen out there searching for our trail."

"Then I suggest we use the river to escape. Let us build a raft of some kind and float downstream."

Felk-Habren stared at her. Where did she get such an idea? Why did she think he would know how to build a raft? Just because Imperial engineers were always building things? He was a Czardhan knight, a pinnacle of chivalry. He knew how to ride and how to fight and that was it.

"Don't worry, Count," she said, reading his thoughts. "The men have built many rafts in their legion careers. They can do it, if anyone can."

The Czardhan nodded slowly. The witch was right. Count Felk-Habren had seen these soldiers produce one amazing feat after another during their journey across this accursed continent.

"What will we do when we reach the Inland Sea?"

Lessis pursed her lips. That was a good question. She was not altogether sure. Obviously the original plan was finished. The legions were in full retreat. She would never turn them around now. She just prayed that the legions succeeded in escaping the enemy. Perhaps, she thought to herself, the main column of fugitives would decoy the enemy's attention away from a small force bent on infiltrating the very heart of the enemy's power.

"Well, Count, I think we shall seek the opportunity to get as close to our enemy as we can. I think the dragons would like that. How about you?"

CHAPTER FIFTY-TWO

Heruta Skash Gzug, Great Master of the Dark Arts of Padmasa, wielder of the power of the vanus void, adept of the black fire, lord of ice, overcomer of death, ruler of millions, summoned his inner strength. As an "enthraan" or wizard of the Tathagada Dok, he was able to draw strength from the stuff of the world, to amplify that which he generated within himself.

Feeding off the energies of the fire pit beneath them, Heruta built a field of titanic properties. With it he sought to crush Relkin inside his own skull.

Relkin, unable to see and feeling utterly lost, fought back with a dumb, relentless persistence. Despite the agony it caused, he struggled free of each engulfment. Ignoring the fire that seared his mind, he refused to succumb.

Heruta the Great, who could literally hammer dozens of men unconscious with a single blast of mental power, was stunned. There was a streak of stubborn willfulness in this bastard child of some seaside slum that would not give up. Each effort to bind it down ended with a corner popping up again. The bonds would snap, and the defiant curses would spit from the boy's lips.

Heruta felt a rage such as he had rarely suffered building within him. It became so intense that it actually affected his power of concentration, and for a moment the pressure on the boy ceased.

Relkin pulled his head away from the stone. He could see nothing through the blindfold, but he sensed his enemy was nearby, standing over him. He turned his head to face him. "Never," he croaked.

Heruta's rage suddenly cooled, imploding like a black balloon. He became icily determined. Immediately he summoned up a mental probe, something that sliced through the boy's crude defenses, and searched deep within the mind.

Relkin writhed as this mind rape went on, and spittle foamed at his lips and his limbs twitched unnaturally.

Heruta looked and then withdrew. It was there all right the subtle marks of great magic wrought on this boy. In fact Heruta could discern several layers of such marks. The boy had been involved in the affairs of witches, that was known The child had been involved in the catastrophe at Tummuz Orgmeen. He had also been present in the overthrow of the Demon Lord in Dzu. Something had toughened him. The boy was clearly more than he seemed to be on the surface

Could this be the work of the Sinni? Did the Sinni dare to interfere so obviously in a world like Ryetelth? This armoring of a child seemed unlike the witches, who kept their miserable secrets to the inner circles of their mad cults. But for the Sinni to involve themselves like this would break a dozen great treaties on higher planes. Huge powers would be brought to the brink of conflict by such a thing. An incredible thought to Heruta the Great, but the workings of every little worm were important in the struggle across the sphereboard of destiny.

And then again there was that odd echo of another kind of magic, a power that Heruta had not felt in an aeon. The boy had had some kind of run-in with creatures that, in his simple way, he thought of as "golden elves." Could the ancien Danae still walk the fields of Ryetelth? Heruta had thought the ancient race long gone, withdrawn to the purer land of Illius.

Heruta wondered if the child might even be a weapon against him, deliberately molded in combat and finally offered up to him like this. The Great One gave a soft hiss and checked the chains that bound the boy. No, there was nothing to fear, no human boy could break those chains.

Suddenly there came an interruption. Verniktun approached and genuflected, proferring a message scroll. With a sniff of irritation Heruta scanned the message, then he hissed and rasped in rage. The fools had cracked the barrel of the first of the quick-firing cannon. It would have to be redone. Recast completely. Heruta went at once to the forge He would oversee the casting of the next barrel himself. The steel master that had cracked the barrel would be fed to the fires.

Relkin was just as suddenly left alone. His head lolled back on the stone from immense exhaustion. The heat from

he lava below and the sulfurous fumes made his head
swim, but it was better than having his mind raped by the
Master. Nausea wracked him and left him gasping for air,
fouled, and weak. His situation had never seemed quite so
desperate.

After a while the exhaustion finally overcame him, and he
slept, sagging to his left in his chains. His dreams were not
pleasant, and he whimpered occasionally and twitched
against the stone.

He awoke from evil dreams to find the blindfold had been
removed. Bright daylight, white clouds above, and Relkin
observed that he was set on the rim of the volcano's cone.
Then a face swung down in front of him, a face contorted
into a hellish mockery of a man's. Whorls of green-black
horn spiraled outward from eyes that glowed like windows
onto hellfire, a flickering orange-red. The mouth and jaws
had fused into a beak.

The vast mental presence of the Master surrounded his
mind once more. He struggled, and was rewarded with the
image of a stupid worm struggling on hot rocks beneath a
relentless sun.

"Surrender," spoke the voice.

Relkin swallowed; his mouth had gone dry. How long
could he stand against this power?

"I am tired of your resistance," the voice said within his
head.

There was a movement. Behind the gold-carapaced figure
of the Great Master, a pair of imps pushed forward, holding
little Jak between them. The boy had been ill used. Blood
and bruises marred his fair face. There was a long, diagonal
cut across his chest. Jak managed to smile. His front teeth
were gone.

"Don't give up, Relkin," he spluttered through split lips.

"That's how you treat prisoners of war?" Relkin threw at
the thing covered in horn.

The voice of power within his mind "spoke" in a voice
ringing with steel and might.

"You will cooperate or I will hurt him."

"I should have expected that. Seems pretty cowardly to
me."

The great presence grew cold. Jak screamed, and his face
contorted into a rictus of agony.

Relkin looked away.

"I do not like to do this, but you give me so little choice," said the voice, now in a less strident manner.

Relkin fought off despair.

"You'll die one day, and then old Gongo will come for you, that's all I know. Everything that lives will eventually die."

"Oh-ho, old Gongo, is it?" rasped the Master suddenly breaking into speech. "What have I here? A true man among the female-worshiping Argonathi? You remain faithful to the old gods, eh? None of this worship of their so-called Great Mother."

Relkin felt a sudden nervousness. He had been so ambivalent about all the gods, even the Great Mother, his beliefs were in a state of confusion.

"Gongo will take you for a judgment. Think on that, thing of horn and fire. One day you will stand in front of a much greater power and be judged. How will you fare on that day? With all the blood and horror you have chalked to your name?"

"May the old gods watch over you, child. I am glad to learn that they still have their followers among the benighted folk of Argonath."

"Leave Jak alone, it's me you want."

"Such conceit! Especially from a little orphan bastard."

Relkin felt a flush of shame. This thing knew how to hurt him with a phrase.

"What do you want?" he said at last.

"To be your friend, child," spoke the voice inside his head.

CHAPTER FIFTY-THREE

The waters of the Inland Sea broke in surf upon a silver strand about half a mile from their position. Sea grass dotted the sand dunes. From where they stood, on a slight eminence, covered in scraggly gum trees and deep purple greasebush, they could see well out across the water. On the horizon lay the dark mass of the Island of the Bone. Jutting up at one end was the cone of the fire mountain, which rumbled and emitted a thin stream of dark smoke.

A mile to their south lay the ruins of a former Kraheen village, burned to the ground a few months earlier. Overgrown fields were rapidly being claimed by the sea grass and the gum trees. All the people were gone, except for a handful of men controlling a small force of imps. Every so often a small swift-moving sailing craft approached from the direction of the Bone and docked at the abandoned village. The men there were apparently unaware of the enemy presence nearby.

The dragons were asleep, tucked away beneath the gum trees. The legionaries were spread out across the gentle landward slope of the little hill. They, too, were catching up on their sleep except for a party of three that was netting some fish for dinner.

There had been no sign of their pursuers for days. It seemed that their use of a raft to float down the river had baffled the Kraheen.

Count Felk-Habren was left monitoring the seashore with the spyglass. It was a beautiful instrument, not much larger than his sturdy middle finger, which unfolded to three times its length and produced a tremendous magnification of the viewed image. Felk-Habren was impressed with the deftness of this piece of Cunfshon technology. The witch Lessis had given him the instrument, shortly after they had climbed up

here from the river. She had suggested that he keep a look
out.

The seashore was largely disappointing. There were a few
seabirds visible, but that was all. The place was empty. As
Lessis had predicted.

"Our enemy must use this dock for communications,"
she'd said. "That is why the land around us is devoid of peo
ple."

The witch was right. As she always was. Slowly, Coun
Felk-Habren had become amazed at the talents of tha
woman. To think that such a drab could be such an effectiv
leader went against the grain for any Czardhan knight. Th
women of Czardha cared for the hearth, for the children an
the cooking fires. They did not roam the world. They did no
produce fabulously expensive miniature telescopes from
their sleeves. They did not indulge in magic.

Felk-Habren shivered. He had been seeing things tha
weren't right. There was the mark of devils all over it. H
prayed to the Father Protector to look after him.

Now the witch was up to some new weirdness.

It had started soon after they'd climbed up here after
ditching the raft. Lessis had given him the spyglass and gon
a short distance downslope, toward the sea, and vanishe
into a clump of trees. She was alone except for her assistant
Within a few minutes all kinds of birds had started to fly to
her side. Count Trego had been stunned at the motley floc
of pigeons, gulls, hawks, and even eagles that swung out o
the sky to visit with the witch briefly and then loft awa
again. He lost count sometime around the sixth eagle. B
then dozens of doves and seagulls had been released. Felk
Habren had seen many of them head out to sea in the direc
tion of the Bone.

Later that day the birds had begun to return to Lessis, wh
remained in the same place, meditating, according to the lis
some young woman who was always at the witch's side ex
cept for brief visits to the top of the hill for water.

For several hours birds continued to come and go. The
the disparate birds were replaced by a flock of crows tha
grew in size and gathered in the trees all around the spo
where Lessis sat.

While the witch crafted her spell, reciting a thousand line
from the Birrak from memory and building several sma

volumes with magical declension, the crows gathered and formed a great croaking mass within the trees.

Felk-Habren had gone down to ask the witch what it all meant, but was intercepted by the girl and turned back. The witch had cast a great spell and could not be interrupted. The girl had been extremely determined. The count believed she would have even drawn steel on him if he'd tried to press the issue.

Felk-Habren had given way. In truth, there was something spine-tingling about the way the witch was sitting, her back unnaturally straight, her head lifted up, her arms at her sides, her legs crossed in a strange position.

She had taken no notice of the count's near interruption. He had retreated up the hill again beneath trees groaning with blackbirds that cawed at him as he passed.

Then the birds had grown silent, and a strange tension began to build in the air. Something made the hairs on the back of men's necks rise. They'd suffered from nervous fits. This tension had continued for an hour or more. Then it died away, leaving the men exhausted.

Felk-Habren raised the spyglass to the distant volcano again. The enemy was out there apparently. Lessis thought they should go and try to take him unawares. She hadn't explained how they were going to do it, but the count was sure she had some plan up her sleeve.

There was a distant flash of red light on the Bone, down below the volcano. Felk-Habren caught just a flicker of it and shifted the glass slightly to focus on the spot.

At this extreme distance he could make out only a headland of a somewhat lighter shade of gray and beyond it a dark mass that sloped up to the cone of the volcano.

The light came again, a distinct flash. The enemy was up to some fresh devilry. Felk-Habren shivered. At night, when he sought sleep, tears would often well from his eyes as he mourned the good men of Czardha, lost to those hellish weapons. Long would the lands of Czardha weep over the deaths of the fair and the brave on the field of Broken Stone. Rage and despair would fill their hearts when they looked to the east at the dread enemy of Padmasa.

There was the light again. The enemy had made more of the tube weapons. The count moaned. How would they prevail over such weapons when they were so few? Any charge at the weapons would see them all swiftly killed. Count

Felk-Habren had grown up wedded to the charge, as did all Czardhan knights. He could conceive of no other form of attack.

Watching the red flashes, which kept coming, the count grew depressed. It seemed that their mission was doomed to failure, despite all they had done. After such a journey, with victory over the savage tribes at Koubha, and after surviving the plague and then the monstrous animals of the ancient jungles of the Land of Terror, that they should finally succumb seemed terribly wrong.

And then, cutting through this gloom came a new sensation: a strange rush of joy welled up with him. A burst of light was spinning in his breast, and he raised his eyes to the blue vault of the sky. The trees came alive with thousands of raucous crows, and the birds lifted up en masse with a tremendous beating of wings and flew up and up and then broke apart and dispersed.

Openmouthed, Felk-Habren watched them go. He looked down into the grove of gum trees where the distant figures of Lessis and Lagdalen sat unmoving beneath a tree. Something was happening, but he had no idea what.

The strange, but wonderful, mood of elation passed and faded, yet left a mark. The count's mood remained improved. He ceased to ponder the difficulties ahead, but thought of the chances for revenge.

The day passed. The sun set in a lovely riot of orange and red. For a while the Isle of the Bone was silhouetted on the horizon. The flashes of the enemy weapons were still coming, in bursts every hour or so. In the gathering darkness, the flashes were more noticeable, and might even be detected by the naked eye.

The moon rode high in the western sky when Lessis arose and, leaning slightly on Lagdalen, made her way up the slope. Lessis was very tired, but seized with a fervent hope. Victory might yet be snatched from disaster.

Felk-Habren was asleep. They left him and moved down into the gum trees that sheltered the surviving dragons of the 109th. There they searched for the Broketail and Alsebra.

Lagdalen woke the dragons the dragonboy way, by lifting an eyelid and blowing on it. In moments there were two somewhat irritated wyverns sitting up.

Lessis had their attention. Not for the first time she marveled at how uncomfortable that could be.

"It is an old story, my friends," she began.

"What is?" said Alsebra waspishly.

"Well, I have some good news and I have some terrible news."

"Boys live?" said Bazil Broketail, scarcely able to believe it possible.

"They do."

Both dragons sat up straighter, with audible hisses.

"I knew it," rumbled Bazil. "It take awful lot to kill worthless boy. In many ways this is boy's best attribute."

"By the fire of the ancients, I am much relieved to hear this," said Alsebra. "Where are they?"

"Ah, that is the bad news. They are over there on that island, up on the cone of the volcano. They are held captive by our Great Enemy, and he torments them most grievously."

The dragons became dangerous again, instantaneously.

"We will swim to the island," said Bazil.

"We cannot swim," said the green freemartin. "This is the ocean."

"Actually," said Lessis, "that is a matter of debate. This is a completely landlocked body of salt water. It has no connection with the greater oceans. I think the prohibition can be ignored in this case."

"Then we swim," said Alsebra. "I take sword only. I find Jak."

Bazil's eyes locked on Lessis suddenly.

"Do you come with us, Lady?"

"If you will allow me to, yes. However, I doubt that I could swim so far unaided."

"You ride on my back. Lagdalen Dragonfriend knows how to do it."

Lagdalen smiled. "I will never forget that night we crossed the River Oon."

Lessis nodded. "We go, then, and bring a surprise to our Great Enemy."

CHAPTER FIFTY-FOUR

The water of the Inland Sea was warm and salty, and thus not really to the taste of the wyverns, who would have preferred colder water. Still, they swam it happily enough, Bazil, Alsebra, and Vlok, who had volunteered at once and would not let anyone talk him out of it. The remainder of the survivors of the unit were left hidden on the wooded prominence. They were to wait there for three days, and then if no word had come to them, they were to slip away southward and seek to join up with the rest of the expeditionary force.

The dragons carried two persons apiece on their backs. Bazil carried Lagdalen and Lessis. Alsebra had Dragon Leader Wiliger and Spearman Rikart, and Vlok bore Swane and the Count Felk-Habren.

Lessis had tried to persuade either the count or the dragon leader to stay with the main party, but neither would be budged. To the count, honor and the need for revenge made it imperative that he be included. Wiliger had pointed to the Bone. "Those are my men out there. I'm going to get them free."

The wyverns experienced the shocking effect of ocean water, and the call to the wild thrilled through their beings. Each overcame it in turn, in very different ways. For Bazil it was expected and familiar, and he turned it aside as he had done before. His boy was on that island, and he was going to rescue him and bring down the enemy that had done them so much harm. Alsebra rationalized it skillfully. She had also expected it, and she placed her legion career and a future prosperous life on the frontier of Kenor above the appeal of living wild. Vlok was the most vulnerable, except that he was so puzzled by the new emotions that he became afraid of it, and grew determined to ignore it and concentrate on swimming to the island and the job ahead. This time, Vlok was adamant: Vlok was going to be in at the kill.

Since wyverns are great swimmers and the water was calm as a millpond, the passage was uneventful. However, there were occasional reminders of the perils of these ancient waters. At one point the waters parted about two hundred feet ahead of them, and a long neck rose up topped by a head brimming with teeth. Eyes like saucers regarded them intently. The dragons were too big to be prey. After solemn contemplation, the sea monster decided against troubling them. The head subsided beneath the waves, and they were alone once more.

Later, they saw a triangular sail, somewhat to the north of them. Soon they made out a small fleet, one large ship and three smaller ones, all with triangular sails. The fleet passed to their north, heading toward the island, and gave no sign of having noticed the dragons or their passengers, who dropped down into the water and clung to the dragons' shoulders and scabbards.

In time the island, fringed with beaches of dark grey sand, grew large in their sight. Beyond the beaches rose tumbled cliffs of friable lava. Here and there grew patches of scrub forest. The place had a stark, spare beauty to it. It was a work in progress, and the author was the volcano, which rumbled and gave off a short stream of dark smoke.

They came ashore on a beach littered with volcanic debris. The sand was harsh and gritty. At the top of the beach it turned into volcanic shingle, a mound of thumb-size pieces of pumice. They found a way up the cliffs through a place where the lava had crumbled under wave action, and a series of giant steps had been left behind.

Up above they found a scrub forest, small palms clumped in the watercourses. In places, the scrub was thick with thorn bushes. This slowed their progress considerably, and they were still but halfway to the cone when night fell. Now when the volcano rumbled, which it did once or twice an hour, they felt the ground shake every so slightly. They could also hear the sound of hot gas seething from lava on occasion.

They rested while Lessis conferred with Wiliger and Felk-Habren. She knew where the boys had been during her inspection of the island on the hidden plane. They were perched on high, over the crater, where they were in danger of smothering in the hot gas. The steps to reach them ran up behind the foundry complex built on the volcano's southern side. Here, behind stern walls and towers of guard, Lessis had sensed the great presence of Heruta Skash Gzug himself. Caution had impeded her search. Heruta was sensitive to witch magic, but no living witch had a lighter touch than Lessis of Valmes. She might dare this visit where few other magi would dare to tread. At any moment Heruta might sense her presence and ensnare her, so powerful was he on the higher planes. A true enthraan of the Tathagada system, he had overcome the resistance of the matter of the Mother's Hand and fed off it with parasitic vigor. Thus inhibited, she had made no effort to penetrate the fortress on the volcano's side. From a distance, it was hard to see clearly on the astral plane, especially when you trod as lightly as she did, and thus she had no more than a vague idea concerning the inner parts of this complex of buildings.

Wiliger was caught up in a strange, personal epiphany, and was subdued and attentive. He felt as if he moved in the midst of a fevered dream, and that somewhere behind the scene, great music was being played for an unseen audience that represented eternity. The count was also in a strange state of mind. It was as if he saw the scene ahead with crystal clarity. He now understood the reputation of these witches. If anyone had ever suggested before now that a woman with grey hair would ride across the sea on the back of a great swimming dragon, Felk-Habren would have laughed at them. If they had told him that the same woman would be visited by seagulls, and by hordes of other birds, he would have taken them for crazed. Now he had seen such things, and many others, enough to turn anyone's hair to grey.

Ahead, the count saw the enemy, pent up in that large fortress attached to the lower slope of the volcano. The tasks ahead would require a flexible strategy. He himself had none other than to crash in and destroy whomever he was pointed at. If the witch had a plan, he would go along with it happily.

The ground was too treacherous, too cut up with gulleys and pits to risk the dragons on it at night. They slept, changing the watch through the night, and moved on at dawn. There was nothing to eat, and only a little freshwater. The dragons were very hungry.

They headed for the mountain. After an hour they stumbled on a road, cut down into a shelf of ash. Lessis and

Wiliger examined it. Wiliger wondered what it might be used for, since it was uncommonly well made. Huge flagstones had been laid along a trench forty feet wide cut in the brittle ash. Lessis hesitated to use the road. It might easily lead to their discovery by the enemy, even though it was certainly the quickest way to reach their destination. She had no doubt that it connected the fortress with the ocean side.

Their caution was rewarded quickly enough. There came a series of sharp cries from the direction of the volcano, and then a blaring horn.

The dragons slid back into the scrub with the natural skill of predatory beasts. In a few moments the party was entirely hidden.

Down the road came a heavy wagon pulled by an army of slaves being driven by brutal-looking imps in the black of Padmasa. Loaded on the wagon were dozens of immense stone balls, more ammunition for the weapons that would change the world.

The wagon ground on, heavy wheels creaking and groaning. Rough-skinned imps with the faces of gargoyles rode the wagon and wielded long whips over the sweating backs of the slaves. The slaves were of all races, from dark-skinned men of the Impalo kingdoms, to olive-skinned types from the Bakan and even a scattering of pale skins, their hair now bleached by the tropical sun. In the eyes of all of them there was little except a mortal exhaustion. They were beasts of burden, no more. They had been reduced by cruelty, starvation, and the liberal use of the whip. They worked like beasts all day and were fed from troughs like animals. They slept on bare floors and were hosed down in the mornings by the imps.

This terrible procession rumbled past followed by a second wagon and a squad of marching imps, heavyset creatures with sword and shield, just in case of trouble from the slaves.

The dragons itched to slay these imps. Big hands clutched on the air, and blazing eyes exchanged looks of fury. But discipline held and no dragonsword was unsheathed.

Then at last the imps were gone, and the road was empty once more. The party of dragons and men crossed the road, climbed up into the ash hills on the far side, and went on.

CHAPTER FIFTY-FIVE

The treatment of the captive dragonboys had changed. They had been taken down from the volcano's lip and placed in an apartment of three spacious rooms, furnished in the Kraheen manner with carved wood and silken wall hangings. Jak's attendant imps were taken away. Kreegsbrok came to check on Jak's condition, and summoned a nurse to clean the boy's cuts and bandage them where necessary.

They were given water, and a little food. Ravenous, they spoke little while they ate, and afterward they slept.

Kreegsbrok came back for another check on Jak. Before he left, he raised a finger in admonition.

"Don't try to lie to him, he'll know it at once. Remember that, both of you."

Relkin understood then that he had seen more of the Master's power displayed than Kreegsbrok ever had. That strange request, "I want to be your friend" echoed and re-echoed in his mind. It was laughable, but Relkin could find no energy for laughter. His situation was too precarious. Death or slavery loomed on either side, and he walked a knife edge over darkness. Kreegsbrok left. Soon afterward the door opened, and the Master entered, floating in, holding himself off the ground with his own power. Relkin felt his jaw drop. The Masters could fly!

In the center of the room, Heruta let his feet touch ground again. Such feats were exhausting in the extreme. It astounded him that he debased himself so much! Deigning to try and impress this young thug from the witches, except that this was such a valuable little thug. Once converted, he would be a marvelous fount of information. Reining in his temper, the mighty Heruta spoke as sweetly as he might with a mouth of horn and bone.

"Come, walk with me awhile, young man. I have much to discuss with you."

Heruta indicated a doorway that lead to a gallery built above a central courtyard. Relkin could hear water flowing somewhere nearby. The courtyard had flowers and shrubs growing in thick profusion. A fountain was playing in the middle. It seemed churlish not to accept the invitation to talk. Perhaps he could save at least Jak.

"You are a special young man, Relkin of Quosh. You have been marked by the Sinni. Things like that cannot be hidden from my eyes, believe me. You have been a formidable foe. You and your great dragon have dealt my cause some terrible blows. They say that you're the best-known pair of the legions, don't they?"

Heruta knew this from plundering young Jak's mind for all references to Relkin. He knew a lot more, as well.

Relkin kept his voice as level as possible.

"I don't understand this. You wanted to crush me, to make me into a slave. Now you flatter me. Why?"

Such charming insouciance for a little street thug from a filthy little Argonathi city!

"Because, child, I think you are too special to waste. Of course, I could have you destroyed. Or even given to the slave gangs and worked to death. But I do not. I seek to show you what it is I am fighting for. It is for the greater good for all."

Relkin's head jerked up.

"What?"

"Open your mind to me, let me show you the world we shall make."

"You can't," Relkin began in disbelief, "mean . . ."

"Come, oblige me in at least this one thing. Let me show you what I am talking about. All your short life you have been the manipulated tool of a massive conspiracy. You must see the other side of the story."

Relkin said nothing, still shaken from the surprise of this. Heruta purred next to him.

"Come. Let me show you a world without rancor, without hate, a world where war will have been abolished. Where people in all walks of life will serve a single cause, with joy in their hearts."

"I saw Tummuz Orgmeen. That is how your world works."

"Of course you would have that opinion if all you knew was a frontier city full of soldiers. You know that soldiers are rough company. A society of soldiers seethes with aggression. These things have to be worked off somehow."

"And always your rule is that of master and slaves. We are free men in the Argonath."

"Free men?" The Master made a buzzing sound within the horned beak. "You are enslaved by an ancient cabal of undying hags, child. Do you know how long some of those witches have lived?"

Relkin knew that Lessis had served the cause of the Empire of the Rose for centuries. It was one of those things that made everyone uneasy.

"I do."

"Long before you were born, child, they had erected their fantastic system. It cannot last. It only holds together with enormous effort on their part, it is quite unnatural. They will be unable to maintain it much longer. Our way is the better way. There is some necessary brutality at first, but later such things will be obsolete and out of the question."

He saw the disbelief in Relkin's eyes.

"You have been ruled by these women all your life, child. You do not understand the rule of men."

That brought life to Relkin's tongue.

"I understand the rule of just men, for that is what we strive for in the Argonath. Just men believe in equality before the law for all men and women, I know that much. Just men allow for no slavery within their realm."

"And, in truth, for a lad with little education, you are a wise one, Dragoneer Relkin. You have held to the old gods. I like that. That's always a good sign. The old gods were gods of men! When men ruled and women obeyed."

"We don't have slavery. We are free men."

"Free men are the rulers in their own homes. Free men rule women in all things."

"There is no need for either to rule the other; each is as important for the race. Every man has a woman as a mother, so they say in the temple. Can you deny that?"

The boy recited that babble from the so-called "Great Weal of Cunfshon," which guided them as constitution and book of social rules. It was soft-brained stuff for men afraid to harden themselves so as to triumph over the world and dominate it.

"That does not mean that women are fit for equal status with men."

Seeing Relkin's frown, the Master shifted gears. The indoctrination ran deep, it was clear to see.

"But come, I want to show you what you might achieve. I want to show you the possibilities that are open to you."

Relkin stared at him.

"I will give unto you a kingdom."

And Heruta moved a hand before his eyes, and Relkin beheld a fair city, of white stone like Marneri, with long pennons streaming from the towers. A fair folk walked before him, in celebration of his rule. Golden trumpets played, white horses ran across the green field. It was all his.

"You will be king of the eastern shorelands. You will be known as Relkin the Just, and your rule will last for centuries."

A king! A golden glow attached to the thought. Wouldn't that be something? For an orphan boy from the Blue Stone country, it would be quite remarkable. The glow burned on.

"And as a ruler of a great kingdom, you would have the opportunity to do good. You would be able to erect a realm of true justice, where just men would do as they are bid by enlightened rulers."

The white city seemed to float there, quite tangible, with bright colors, in the air. Relkin wanted to stretch out a hand and touch it for some reason. To be a king!

Relkin the Good, a name that would go down through the aeons of recorded time. He was irresistibly drawn. Rising toward the lure like a nail being pulled up from the wood.

Then another voice spoke in his heart, a voice that echoed all the lessons of his early life in his village. It named the Master as the hissing serpent, and seducer of hearts.

There were no kings in the realm of Padmasa. The Masters ruled through their agents, the Dooms, the things they gave intelligence to in the Deeps of Padmasa. Their rule was uniformly cruel and harsh.

"You would become a master of jurisprudence. From you would come the body of laws that would forever after govern the affairs of men. You see how I need you, Relkin of Quosh? I, we, cannot do everything. We have so much to do to remake the world so as to achieve peace and harmony for all."

Fury broke to the surface on Relkin's face.

"Like when you build your weapons that kill from a great distance? Always you build to kill and destroy!"

"Come, child, we have to defend ourselves. The witches have never accepted our overtures for peace. Many is the time we have begged them to desist and agree to negotiate. Never have they answered us with fair words, not even with politeness. Where is the justice in that?"

"I know nothing of matters of the state. You know that. But I know what I have seen. I have seen the way your cities would be run. They spill blood there for amusement. They traffic in human slaves. I have seen too much blood, too much war."

Heruta knew how true that was. The great one had been appalled by the memories dredged from the mind of the other boy. These children had lived their lives from battle to battle. It was another example of how the hags toyed with human lives.

"We employ imps for our defense forces because their lives are of little consequence. The same for our trolls. The only men we risk in war are volunteers, who flock to our banner from all over the world, I might add."

"I have seen how you make imps. In Tummuz Orgmeen we saw the breeding pens."

Ah.

"Yes, a tragic thing, but necessary for us to stave off the constant assaults of the witch armies. Without our imps, we would long ago have been destroyed. And yet we judge it better that imps, which are like animals, after all, be slaughtered rather than men."

"I have slain imps. I did not think of them as animals. They can think and speak. They have lives, too."

Heruta gaped inwardly. The indoctrination of the hags was strong stuff. Here he had a dragonboy expressing concern about imps!

"Well, I see that you have a natural respect for all living things. That is as well as good, but we must remember that in extreme conditions, such as those of war, we must make difficult choices. So we prefer to lose imps on the battlefield rather than men."

Relkin had lost a great many friends in war, friends both human and wyvern. Anything that would save casualties would be good. Could it be right to use imps as soldiers? After all, the legions used dragons, and dragons took heavy casualties. There was none but Baz and old Chek left from the original 109th Marneri Dragons.

"Young man, you have great potential. Will you at least do one thing, keep an open mind for a few days. Let me show you the powers that can be yours."

"I am a dragonboy."

"You were a dragonboy. You are about to become something far more important. You must ascend to higher matters. We need you to help craft our great peace. Perhaps with your aid we can produce a peace initiative that the witches will accept. Think of that, child. You can become a prince of peace."

Relkin knew that the Master could not understand. To be a dragonboy meant you were half of an organism. The other half was two tons of wyvern. Where was his dragon? How could he have a future life that did not include the dragon?

"And you would be the King of Marneri, or perhaps of Kadein, if you would prefer the big city?"

Heruta dangled the juiciest bait he could think of. This boy was an amazing mixture of openhearted fanatic and sly little sophisticate. Relkin had spent time in old Ourdh after all, a notorious cesspit of the flesh. Heruta shuddered. The lure of women, how odious it was! Men were so weak toward it. Complete sexual abstinence was the only way for the achievement of the great power.

Relkin's mind was turning over the options available. Backing up the Master's attempt to seduce him this way was the unspoken threat to little Jak. Surely if Relkin refused, then little Jak would suffer some horror. It seemed Relkin had to dissemble. Yet, as Kreegsbrok had said quite correctly, it would be hellishly difficult lying to the Master.

"How could I be sure of such a thing?" he said slowly.

Heruta buzzed quietly for a moment. Ahah, the price had been found. The kingdom of Kadein, complete with the great fat city of Kadein itself.

Finally, Heruta would have someone who had spent considerable time with such creatures as the hag Lessis. The prospects were most encouraging.

CHAPTER FIFTY-SIX

The volcano loomed above them. When it rumbled, the ground shook. Occasionally gas seethed so loudly in the vent that the small group of men and dragons could not hear themselves speak.

In front of them stretched an open plain of lava and ash cut by gullies and ravines. Across the plain stood the walls of the Master's fortress, twenty feet high and studded with towers twice that, all built from stone quarried at the farthest end of the island. A road, constantly repaired by gangs of slaves, ran to the great gate that bisected the wall.

Behind the first wall bulked the buildings of the foundry, which sprawled up the side of the volcano. Roofed in copper, grown deep green with corrosion, these buildings presented windowless walls up to a hundred feet high and two chimneys that stood even higher. The whole vast thing trembled with each motion of the fire mountain.

Heruta Skash Gzug cared little for the risk. His slaves would rebuild if the volcano destroyed everything. And with his pet batrukh tethered in a high tower, he was assured of escape at any time.

The day was waning rapidly, as it always did in the tropics. Count Trego of Felk-Habren was eager to be off. He and the spearman Rikart were to make a reconnaisance. Their object was to find a way inside the enemy's stronghold.

Lessis had wanted to go alone. None of them could move as quietly as she, none of them could see in the dark as well, either. The men, especially the count, would not accept this. Despite the changes in his opinion of the witch he could not allow a woman to undertake a dangerous mission when he was there to do it himself. The witch pondered the use of magic to change their minds, but abandoned the thought with a sigh. That was how the enemy fought, with programmed slaves. The men of the Empire of the Rose were free.

As soon as the darkness grew thick enough, the two men slid out from their place of concealment behind rough-hewn boulders of lava and shifted down toward the nearest gulley.

Lessis watched with her spyglass, until the darkness made it impossible to see anything.

"I hope they'll be able to find their way back," said Lagdalen.

"I hope so, too, my dear. I wish they would have listened to me."

"I have never seen him so agitated as when you suggested that he stay while you went alone."

Lessis nodded. That male pride again; it made heroes out of ordinary men, but it also made for foolish mistakes. Then she reassured herself. With the constant noise of the volcano, it probably didn't matter how much noise the men made since no one would hear them.

There was a heavy movement behind them, and they felt a big presence slide into place alongside.

"Are the boys in there?" said the broketail dragon.

"I don't know," said Lessis. "They had them up at the crater before, but I'm sure that was only to terrify them."

"They kill them?"

"No, I don't think so. They could be very valuable, especially Relkin. He has seen a great deal for one so young. They will want to pry deeply into his mind."

The dragon grunted. Lessis could have sworn the great monster was laughing.

"That not take too long then," Bazil said.

Lessis smiled to herself. It was always this way between dragon and boy. No matter how grave the adversity, dragons had to show their superiority.

"Why does the enemy build this place here? The mountain will destroy it."

"He does not care. Slaves will rebuild it. He needs the heat generated by the mountain. With that heat, one can make fine steel."

Bazil digested this for a moment. Alsebra had suggested much the same thing a little earlier.

"We stop him."

Lessis approved of the finality with which the dragon said this. The dragon spoke again.

"First find boy, though."

"Yes, of course. We all owe Master Relkin that much."

They lapsed into silence, their eyes scanning the dark plain. There was nothing to see except a distant gang of slaves, working under torchlight to repair the great road. There were many bridges built across the wider gulleys, and these were under constant assault from the vibrations of the mountain and the sudden widening of gulleys and ravines. Thus gangs of workers were constantly employed at repairs.

On the walls stood imps, visible occasionally by the torches they carried as they went about their business. Once or twice Lessis had seen a troll with her spyglass. The walls were well defended. She prayed the count would be cautious.

An hour passed.

Suddenly they heard horns blare on the gate tower. The gates were swinging open. Lessis prayed, but her prayers were not answered. With the spyglass she could see a horde of imps come forth with torches waving above them.

Other imps came behind them, and with them were other things, taller and deadlier than imps. With horror she saw they were yellow beasts brought from the jungles of terror. They stepped forward with a peculiar, dainty stride under the command of fell imps, who held them by long chains to their necks.

Imps ran in from the plain, gesticulating wildly. The chains were released, and the sickle-clawed beasts bounded forward on their long hind legs, the small front legs tucked up beneath their chests. Lessis felt the breath freeze in her throat.

"They've been seen," said Lagdalen.

"How can we help them?" said Wiliger.

Lessis shrugged. "If they're caught they're done for, but if they can get back here, we can ready a hot reception for their pursuers."

It was agreed in moments. Wiliger ran back to the other dragons; Bazil moved off to join them. Lessis remained on the rock with her spyglass trained on the dark terrain in front.

The monsters came on quickly; she could see them bound along the plain, leaping the gulleys when they came to them. Lessis shivered as she recalled scenes from their earlier struggles in the jungle.

Then at last she caught a glimpse of the men. They had a lead on the pursuit, but when they were forced out of a covering ravine and across a stretch of the plain, they were seen. Now it became a virtual foot race, and that they could not win against the bounding yellow demons that came behind.

Swane dropped down beside her. He had seen the gathering crisis and had an arrow notched in his Cunfshon bow.

The men came on, desperately urging their tired bodies on, legs extending mightily before and behind. The beasts were gaining.

Now they struck the slight incline that led up to the line of rocks behind that sheltered the dragons.

The count was losing the pace, winded. It had been years since he had run this hard, this long. Spearman Rikart stopped, looked back, and saw the first of the yellow beasts as it lunged in at the count.

Rikart sprang back and intercepted the beast with his spear point. It gave a shriek of rage and pain, and tried to reach him with the massive claws on its hind feet, but the spearman did not give way and pressed home the point, until the thing was pinned to the ground.

More were coming, though; it was time to run. Rikart jerked his spear free and bounded on, catching up to the staggering figure of the count just before they reached the rocks.

Big hands reached out of the shadows, seized both men by the arms, and pulled them out of sight.

"Well done, Rikart man," said a dragon voice.

The beasts leapt up the slope and then to the top of the rocks. Three dragons rose up from the darkness beyond, and great dragonswords swept around in full roundhouse cuts. The first three beasts went down instantly, cut in two at the waist.

The next three yellow beasts came on with no thought of caution or concern for their fellows. They ignored whistles from their imp handlers. Two leapt over the rocks. Vlok spitted one cleanly, running "Katsbalger" right through it as if he were putting a lamb on a kebab stick. Alsebra chopped the other one down with a neat backhand slice. Unfortunately, Vlok's spitted beast did not behave as if it was ready to be turned over the coals. It attacked Vlok with teeth and claws, ignoring the fact that a huge wedge of steel had been passed clean through its vitals. Claws skittered off Vlok's tough hide, and fortunately for the leatherback, the beast's gutting claw got hooked into Vlok's joboquin and could not be freed. With a snarl the beast clamped its jaws on Vlok's arm. Vlok bellowed in pain and punched it between the eyes, knocking it cold. At last it consented to fall away.

The third beast avoided leaping into the unknown, and instead pressed into a gap between the stones. Swane put an arrow into it, but it spotted his movements and leapt for him unfazed by the arrow in its chest. Swane dodged back and bumped into Count Felk-Habren, who had drawn steel and was waiting for the onrushing beast.

The count pushed Swane aside. He anticipated the beast's move, which was to leap with its feet foremost, the long sickle claws extended to slash him to ribbons. Count Trego met it with his sword, which cut deep into the thing's feet.

The impact bowled him over, and the beast bore down with its jaws, seeking his throat. Swane was about to hurl himself on it when a big hand caught hold of him from behind and pulled him up and back. Then Bazil struck with Ecator and hewed the beast down.

The count struggled free from the still-kicking lower half of the creature. He was covered from head to toe in gore.

The beasts were slain. Their imp masters were alerted to the fact. The imps were closing in, moving cautiously now. Something had stilled their charges, which they found difficult to believe. Normally those things ran down men and tore them up like cats taking down small rats.

"We must move," hissed Lessis. "Before they see us."

This was such obvious good sense that the count did not argue. The group, with Swane in the lead, bow at the ready, moved off to its right, circling back through an area of rough lava to get past the flat plain before the walls. The wall continued up the side of the volcanic cone, but they were not so formidable up there, and Lessis thought they might be garrisoned with fewer imps.

They moved as quickly as they could, Vlok complaining of the bite on his arm from the beast.

The imps let up a wail behind them. The corpses of the beasts had been discovered. Such damage could only be done by one force, wyvern dragons with dragonsword Gazaki! Filthy great Gazaki were loose on the Island of the Bone! There was a sudden burst of activity on the walls of the fortress.

Lessis called a halt while she studied the situation. Squads of imps were trotting out the gate; a half dozen trolls armed with heavy axes came out after them.

There came a screech from high up the mountainside, and with a sinking heart Lessis saw the shape of a great batrukh take to the air.

They could not remain in the open; batrukhs could see well in the dark. Unfortunately, the only cover here was provided by overhangs of roughly cooled lava. Everything else was bare to the sky.

Despair gripped Lessis's heart. If they were seen, the enemy would direct his forces to surround them. There was nothing to be done except to slink into the shadows and lurk there while the batrukh prowled the sky above. Every so often they heard its shrill scream as it wheeled by. Yet, they could not remain where they were. The imps would find them sooner or later.

Lessis scouted forward, slipping invisibly through the pools of deepest shadow. She found a way that even the dragons could take, down through a tumbled section of huge blocks of stone to a deep gulley. Lava had welled up here and made a dome, which had then broken open to allow the gulley to spew forth.

She returned and successfully guided them down to the gulley. There they crouched as close as possible to the steep sides. The batrukh flew past but not directly over them, and so they were safe for a moment.

Safe, but trapped. Lessis wracked her brain for a way out, but could think of nothing. Lagdalen was looking at her intently, hoping that she could think of something. So were the count and Dragon Leader Wiliger.

Lessis had never felt less inspired. It seemed she had led her small force into a trap, and she could not think of a way out. From the beginning this had been a quixotic adventure, a last throw of the dice, and it seemed to have failed.

The batrukh flew past again, but again it missed them. How long this could go on before they were detected, she did not know. Where to go? To go downslope and leave the gulley invited immediate detection on the flatter surface beyond. To go up the gulley offered little improvement. Their target lay inside those walls, guarded by who knew how many aroused imps and trolls. It seemed very far away.

Just when despair was closing over her in waves, she

heard a strange, soft hoot from somewhere above her head. Lessis looked up.

Above them on a cliff overlooking the gulley was a small, triangular head outlined against the dark sky. It was hard to see except when it moved. It seemed to have large ears.

Then there came another soft hoot, this time with overtones of wonderment and joy.

Swane let out a barely suppressed cry. The dragons extended long necks to examine the creature.

"What is it?" said Lessis.

"It is mascot," said Bazil.

Lessis looked to Lagdalen for enlightenment, but she knew no more than the ancient witch. Meanwhile the head had disappeared. A few moments later a small, rotund form barreled out of the shadows at the base of the gulley and began romping around Swane.

Wiliger stared at it in amazement.

"It's that damned pest that Jak was keeping. What's it doing here?"

"He must have brought it to the battle with him," said Spearman Rikart.

At the sound of its master's name, the little elephant pricked up its big ears and tentatively trotted over to Swane.

"Perhaps it knows where Jak is?" said Lagdalen.

At the sound of its master's name, the little elephant lifted its trunk and gave a soft squeal.

"It does, it knows where the boy is," rumbled Alsebra.

Stripey turned and scurried a few paces up the gulley, where he paused and looked back over his shoulder at them and cocked his big ears quizzically.

"It wants us to follow it," said Lagdalen.

"Well, at least it has an idea of what to do," said Lessis. "I suggest we follow it."

They scrambled up the steep little gulley, dodging from each patch of the darkest shadow. At length they came to a huge hole, perhaps ten feet across, that had opened up in the floor of the gulley. Here the elephant paused and circled around the hole until it found a spot where a slope of rubble led down into the dark. With a squeal, it disappeared down into the hole.

It was a large hole, but it was pitch-black in there.

The dragons exchanged grunts. They did not relish climbing down into that place.

Swane was edging down, trying to feel a way down the steep slope of the collapsed floor of the gulley.

"What can this be, Lady?" said Lagdalen.

Lessis was radiating hope. A blaze had been rekindled in her heart. The men soon felt it, as did Lagdalen, who was familiar with this sort of thing from Lessis. Lagdalen knew the Lady was inspired once more.

"A lava tube, I'd say. That little elephant may have given us the keys to our enemy's kingdom."

Lessis followed Swane and found that her hopes were realized. The hole lead to an inky dark space, still warm from its fiery creation. The walls were still radiating heat. The floor was hot.

Lessis put up a hand and murmured the words of power, and a stone on her ring gave off a soft blue light that lit up the place. Walls of lava, still rough from their creation loomed away in both directions. The little elephant had moved a few feet farther in and gave another soft hoot.

Lessis pointed as the dragons descended into the darkness. Alsebra looked at the ring very closely as she passed.

"This is the ring Capsenna, it is an ancient piece, something of an heirloom in my coven."

Alsebra was impressed. Her opinions of the magic of the witches had improved markedly in her years in the 109th Marneri Dragons.

"We follow our little guide." Lessis pointed up the dark lava tube.

"What lies that way?" said Vlok.

"The lava flowed the other way, so that must be the source, the hot heart of the volcano. That is where the enemy will have his forge."

"To the forge, then."

CHAPTER FIFTY-SEVEN

Relkin awoke and for a moment stared blankly at the unfamiliar surroundings. It was a sumptuously furnished room. He lay on a wide bed, covered in soft brown suede. On a heavy chair lay his new uniform and weapons. On the walls were luxuriant tapestries, mandalas of red, black, and white. The floor boasted a spectacular Kassimi rug.

He rose and dressed. There was a mirror at the far end of the room; Relkin caught sight of his reflection. He wore the black leather uniform of Padmasa, with heavy boots and a short sword, a weapon very much like his own dirk. He looked the very image of a swordsman for Padmasa, one of the grim mercenaries that directed the armies of imps and trolls that gave power to the word of the Masters.

He was torn between revulsion and a strange attraction. The surroundings were so comfortable, he thought again of the Master's offer. To be a king! That thought just wouldn't die. Who wouldn't want to be the king of a fair city? To rule wisely and justly in true majesty?

Eilsa would be his queen. If he were King of Marneri, then of course Eilsa would consent to wed him. Even her clan would go along. The older generation would stop opposing her engagement to him. All the social obstacles would be swept away.

Then he would rule through a peaceful era of plenty, bringing in a golden age that would be sung of for all eternity. From his seed would come a mighty dynasty.

And the route to that dream began here, putting on this black uniform of leather and steel. The dream vanished with a sudden, bitter laugh. The vanity of it was preposterous. He was just a dragonboy trying to survive. And what kind of kingship would it be that would be given so freely by Padmasa? He knew better than that.

Outside the room he found himself in a corridor that led-to the suite of rooms he and Jak had been in earlier. They were empty now. Where might they have taken Jak?

The younger boy had not followed Relkin's hints and had maintained his defiance of the Great One. Jak had been aghast when Relkin had accepted the enemy's poisoned offer. Relkin didn't want to remember the things Jak had said to him. Nor the cold triumph he had felt from the Master. Relkin had had to leave them, and he feared for young Jak under the lash of the power of the Master.

There was a rap at the door, which opened without any word from him. An imp with a head like that of a giant weasel, stuffed tightly into a satiny black uniform, called on him to attend to Kreegsbrok at once. The weasel head would show him the way.

Relkin followed the weasel head along corridors, down stairs, and into a large chamber, paneled in dark wood. There was an air of urgency in the room. Kreegsbrok stood on a dais with a small desk beside him where another weasel-head imp sat writing at a furious pace. One at a time a line of black-clad men approached Kreegsbrok with message scrolls. He read each one, then spoke to the imp scribe, who wrote down his answers. The men came and went constantly.

Kreegsbrok looked up at Relkin's entrance.

"Ah, the young captain. Welcome aboard! We have some rather trying work ahead of us today." His smile was oddly forced. Kreegsbrok was a hard man to read, his true thought deeply hidden from any but the Master.

Relkin made no reply. Kreegsbrok completed another dozen messages in rapid-fire fashion and then called a halt.

"Come," he said.

Relkin was ushered out to a large room filled with Kraheen notables, many wearing feathered headdresses. Kreegsbrok led Relkin to the dais on the far side of the room, where a group of heavyset men in black leather and armor acted as guards. Relkin had a sudden sinking feeling in his chest. A moment later it sank completely when the eerie sight of the Prophet hove into view.

The Prophet's oddly animated face danced on the end of a long neck. The eyes glittered for a moment as they settled on Relkin.

The Master would be watching, of course. From somewhere high up probably. This was to be a test.

The Prophet recited prayers for the crowd and then addressed them with words of ancient prophecy. They were to be the Great Ones whom all other peoples would worship. For them there would be a carpet of human hearts thrown up to celebrate their assumption of glory. They would tread across a prairie covered in the skulls of their enemies. For them there would be cities of gold and splendor. For the rest of the world there would be ashes in the mouth and the lash across the shoulders.

The Kraheen greeted this with cries of ecstasy.

The chanting and the prophesying went on for a long time and then at last ended with a clash of cymbals and a rattle of drums. Now imps pulled out men on the end of leather leashes. With harsh cries they lashed the men forward, driving them to kneel in a row before the Prophet.

Relkin saw, with horror and disgust, that they were legionaries, most of them with wounds. One man could barely walk, and tottered to his place and virtually fell down in a heap. Relkin ground his jaw. If he made a wrong move now, then both he and Jak would pay, possibly with their lives. The Master would cease toying with him and destroy him. Still he wanted to draw steel very badly.

Kreegsbrok was watching him.

"It is not easy, believe me," said the man. Relkin swallowed his first, hot retort. He couldn't trust himself to speak.

"Sometimes, my young friend, we must show we have the strength of will that is necessary to serve the Great Ones."

Kreegsbrok knew. He had slain many men, many friends, on the orders of the Master. He had put his knife through their throats at the command. Could this young man from the hag cities stand the test?

Now two of the prisoners were hauled to their feet and bound to the stakes set beside the Prophet. Drums thundered as the Prophet summoned his grisly power.

The men's chests bowed and quavered. Thin screams of horror came from their throats, and then with the sound of ripping bones their chests burst and their hearts flew out to the waiting hands of the Prophet.

Relkin wanted to vomit. The room echoed with the ecstasies of the Kraheen. For a long moment Relkin asked himself if it might not be better to die than to live defiled by this evil. He could die so easily here, too.

There were trumpets blowing now and drums thundering. He looked up.

"The first of our surprises today," said Kreegsbrok.

Through open double doors came a platoon of slaves, men with blank staring eyes, as naked as beasts. Cracking whips over them were squat, powerfully built imps. The slaves hauled an immense cart into the room. On the cart was the Purple Green, strapped down with thick cables.

Wide-eyed with barely controlled horror, Relkin watched them position the Purple Green's body just below the center of the dais. The crowd of Kraheen notables was abuzz with wonder and anticipation.

Then Kreegsbrok stood up, reached over, and grabbed Relkin by the black leather uniform. Relkin was taken by surprise. Gently but firmly Kreegsbrok tugged him, toward the edge of the dais.

The Purple Green's hide was marked by hundreds of cuts. They had beaten him long and hard. Still, in those eyes blazed elemental fury. Relkin imagined what might happen if the wild one could get free of those cables. Their eyes met. The Purple Green blinked, then recognition flowered. Then rage exploded, and the wild dragon screamed the dragon speech equivalent of "traitor" at him.

Kreegsbrok was positioning him by a butcher's block. Sunk into the block was a long sword, handle toward him.

"This honor is for you, young Captain. To show the Master that your heart is truly his!"

Relkin saw the Prophet, who seemed to be quivering with the urge to kill.

"Kill the dragon," said Kreegsbrok.

Relkin looked out at the brightly dressed crowd of nobles. In their eyes was an unholy lust. It strengthened him for what he had to do.

Relkin edged around the block, not thinking, his mind a blank. When he spoke his voice was loud and firm.

"No, I will not do this thing. It is evil."

A gasp of astonishment went up. The Prophet hissed curses under his breath. Kreegsbrok shook his head.

The weight of the Master fell upon his mind in an instant.

"Worm! Think to trifle with me?" roared the Great One from within the center of his thoughts.

Relkin detected enormous anger. He allowed a smug thought of his own.

"That got to you, didn't it?" he whispered.

"Silence, impious little fool!"

Relkin's tongue clove to the roof of his mouth and could not be moved. His teeth ground together, and his elbows seemed to want to push together through his ribs. He sank to his knees, barely able to breathe.

"If you will not do this, then my other dragonboy will do it."

Jak approached with a long knife and expressionless face. Jak stepped up to stand over Relkin. He lifted the knife. Once more the crowd of nobles grew excited.

"You see how easily I could have you kill one another? You cannot trifle with my power."

Jak went past Relkin to the block and took up the sword. Relkin felt the grip slip off him just a fraction. He got his breath back.

Jak raised the sword over the Purple Green. The wild dragon struggled to break his bonds, heaving from side to side, rocking the cart off its wheels, hissing like a boiler about to explode.

The Master's grip had slackened further. Relkin sprang from where he knelt and collided with the back of Jak's legs, knocking the smaller boy aside. The sword fell to the dais.

Relkin had it the next moment and swung it in a wide backhand that forced Kreegsbrok to duck and roll away. The Master screeched and flung a disabling blow at Relkin, but it was too late; in that instant he had brought the sword back and thrust it home, right into the chest of the Prophet.

There was an explosion of blood and a horrified shriek from the Kraheen.

"Thank you, boy," said "He Who Must" with a strange grin.

Relkin was smashed to the ground the next moment by Kreegsbrok. The breath was gone out of him, but a cry of triumph echoed in his mind. Then his mind was crushed into blackness by the Master's rage.

Kreegsbrok hauled him to his feet, still gasping.

"I take it back," roared the Purple Green, still trying to heave the cart over.

Relkin's foot brushed against the corpse of the Prophet. The Kraheen were wailing and tearing at their headdress.

"Examine him!" bellowed Kreegsbrok to Gulbuddin, and the others clustered beside the Prophet's body.

Relkin spun out of Kreegsbrok's hands, his thoughts no

longer his own, his body no longer his to control. The Master gripped his mind so hard he could barely think.

"First you will kill the boy, then you will kill the dragon. You see, you cannot resist me."

Jak staggered over and kneeling bared his throat. With hands that seemed to think by themselves, Relkin grabbed a handful of Jak's hair and unsheathed the knife.

"Cut his throat!" came the command. Without knowing why, Relkin put the blade to the neck of his friend.

And then the doors burst open at the far end of the room with a tremendous slam. Screams of terror rose from the Kraheen as they stampeded, and right behind them came battledragons, led by Bazil Broketail, with Ecator gleaming in his hands.

CHAPTER FIFTY-EIGHT

So stunned was Heruta Skash Gzug at this sudden eruption of enemy power in the very heart of his realm that his spirit quailed as Relkin's knife clattered to the floor. Heruta never noticed the presence of Lessis, nor did he sense the subtle spell of affliction she cast his way. The spell took hold and a great fear mounted until he upped and fled in panic, skittering into the corridor on horn-covered feet, his thoughts fixed on the batrukh and immediate flight.

With the Master gone, the men under his command took the prudent course of escape, scrambling for safety, jamming in the doors behind the dais.

The dragons tore the doors off their hinges, but could not get their bulky bodies through them. Dragonboys looked through; the enemy had gone.

The Kraheen crowd in the meantime had flattened themselves back against the wall. Terror showed on every face.

Suddenly released from Heruta's crushing pressure on his mind, Jak had blacked out. Still dazed, Relkin caught him on his way to the ground and propped him up on his feet.

"Boys are tired," said a familiar voice from behind him. "Can barely stand up."

Relkin was lifted up by huge hands.

"Put me down," he said in a dazed voice. "We've got to get out of here."

"We go, but boy ride on dragon back. He tired."

The Count Felk-Habren was pulling at the dragons to get them to hurry. The surprise had been complete, but the enemy would soon regroup. They had to move. The dragons abandoned the doors at the back of the room. With the boys recovered, they turned and stepped past the stunned Kraheen notables and out through the larger, double doors into the main passage.

The fortress contained a veritable warren of passages.

some of them large enough for dragons to use freely, others
barely wide enough to admit Alsebra, let alone the Purple
Green, who, now freed, was limping along with them. He
was extremely hungry. He was even angrier than that, a
somewhat awesome thing to contemplate.

"Why is boy dressed like enemy?" said Bazil, expressing
a deep uneasiness.

"Jak cannot speak, so I don't know," said Alsebra.

"They tried to make him kill this dragon," said the Purple
Green.

"Yet you are alive," said Alsebra.

"Boy refuse to do it. They were going to have Jak kill him
as punishment. I saw all this with my own eyes."

"What else could you do since you were tied down?"

"Boy did well, then. Still I hate that uniform."

Lagdalen came running up with the spearman.

"Found it," she announced, and passed a small sack of
powder to Lessis. For once Lessis's feelings showed clearly
on her face.

"Good girl, where is it?"

"Not far. Big place. Stinks of horse piss."

They ran after her and shortly burst into a room filled with
barrels, raised tubs, and other heavy equipment. Piles of
grey powder mounded up in the nearest corner. Stacks of
small barrels and sacks lined one wall beyond, which was a
loading bay. A sour stench filled the air.

Lagdalen pointed to the barrels.

"That's the final product, I think."

Lessis broke open the seal on a barrel and poured out a
handful of black powder. This was exactly as it had been described to her by Ribela.

"This is it. We need as many of these sacks as can be carried."

"Where to, Lady?" said the count.

"To the foundry."

Outside the manufactory they found a line of wagons, but
the slaves manning them had fled. They filled three of these
with the barrels and sacks, and then pushed them down the
long, flagstoned halls of the widest passage to the foundry.

The foundry was a large space, hewn out of the volcanic
rock and tapering toward the inner core of the volcano.
From that end came the hissing of hot gas and the glow of
lava in the pool below.

In the foundry great trolls had worked until quite recently, maneuvering the larger instruments, the tongs and cranes, while gangs of slaves had hauled ropes to power the lifts and swing the buckets of hot metal. All this activity had ended with the invasion by the dragons, erupting out of the lava tube with Stripey at their head.

Now the trolls lay dead, scattered by dragonsword here and there, and the gangs of slaves had fled. Two of the latest versions of the tube weapons lay cooling on beds of sand. These were slimmed-down versions of the weapons they had met on the field of Broken Stones. Lessis noted with horrified fascination that the enemy foundry had been making rapid progress in its development of this field of weaponry. These new tubes were markedly superior. She tested the barrels with a finger. One of them was already cool enough for her plan.

She called for the men to stuff the barrel with sack after sack of powder. Meanwhile Lagdalen scouted out a long iron bar and had Vlok use it to tamp home the sacks of powder and then to plug the barrel with a heavy wooden block torn from a block and tackle. The block fitted snugly into the barrel and was rammed home by Vlok and Bazil together until it was solidly jammed.

Lessis primed the firing hole on the tube and began to compose a spell for delayed combustion. In preparation for this mission, she had spent time studying such spellsay in the Imperial Library in the city of Andiquant. Now she thanked that time of study, for the lines sprang from her memory and the spell soon came together with a little quiver in the air. Everyone felt a sudden race in their pulse and a cool breath on their brows as the ancient magic was knit from thin air once more.

Meanwhile, with the aid of the dragons, the powder kegs were taken down and stacked around the packed tube. When it was done, they completely hid it from view.

It was done.

"We must leave. This place will soon be a shambles."

Lessis allowed herself a small thrill of achievement. This had been a success beyond her dreams. Now all they had to do was escape, somehow.

A moment later she felt a sudden drag on the higher planes. She shivered inside. A great power was coming, and she had no doubt who it was. It had been foolish to hope that her spell could completely spook him. A moment later she felt him, the massive power, the brutal intellect of the Master, the Great One, Heruta Skash Gzug himself. He came.

He had overcome the maddening fear. He knew of her presence from her nasty little spell. He was enraged.

The main doors were suddenly gripped by a tremendous power and torn open, ripping free their bolts. The Master strode in; this was no time for wasting energy on levitation. He was encased in gold-chased steel armor, but wore no helmet. The eyes blazed like fires in that face of glittering black and green horn.

"You thought to bewitch me, hag!" he snarled. His voice buzzed with rage.

Lessis made no reply. This was a contest she had dreaded all her life. In truth, she had none of his terrifying strength. He was a true enthraan of the death force. No witch, not even Ribela, could stand openly against such a one.

"You shall pay for this assault upon my realm! And when you are taken, then shall you give up to me all that you know. I will drain you, Witch, until you are nought but a cipher, a dead leaf rustling in the wind."

Dragons stepped forward, their long swords in their hands. Lessis felt sudden encouragement.

"If you come alone to do all this, you may find yourself in peril, Master Heruta," she said. "Perhaps it would be better to, ah, negotiate."

"Negotiate? With you? You are surrounded by my power. The presence of a few of these great beasts of yours will not save you. Madness, that is all you have to offer. All of you hags have long since lost all semblance of sanity. Why should we talk to you?"

"We work for the good of the world."

"You hold back the march of history. Men must have dominion over the world. We guide them, that is all."

"It is not the dominion of men that you seek, Master Heruta. It is dominion for yourself. Why do you need such crushing rule? Why must the men be guided the way you choose to do it?"

"You dare to question me?" Unbridled fury engulfed the Master, and his grip slackened for a moment. Lessis struck with her affliction spell again, but he recovered before she could penetrate.

"You dare to assault me, again! You will beg me for the release of death before I am done with you."

He brought down all his power to squeeze her to the ground. To the rest of them, it seemed as if an enormous shadow had filled the upper air of the chamber and pressed down on the Lady Lessis.

Around Lessis the air sparkled with a fragile white light. It resisted the shadow even as it pressed. The resistance grew, and the space where they met began to glow strangely. Polychromatic flashes of light struck their eyes and threw rainbow shadows on the walls.

Even in the midst of the struggle, the great Heruta found a moment to marvel at the strength he detected within the witch. Great strength, greater than any he had ever encountered, except among his own guild in Padmasa.

"You have misused the power that you discovered," Lessis hissed. "Why assault the world? Why do you not join with us in the use of the natural powers? The world can be made a benign place, with just rule and a place for all."

"You will achieve nothing like that. There must be strength of will and fanatical devotion to rulership!"

"Why? What is the need for such things?"

"Only thus can real power be concentrated, you fool. We are not interested in this world alone. There are boundless opportunities for those capable of wielding the greatest power."

"But why do you want such power?"

"You cannot understand, because you lack the true masculine will to rule. It will be done because we want it done."

"Why is this masculine? Anyone with power can misuse it for selfish ends. Surely this is nothing but egoism. Is this not unworthy of your vast talents? You and your peers, why do you sit in a tomb of stone and impose your harsh will upon the world? Why do you not come out into the light?"

"Silence, hag!"

A squad of trolls came in on either side of the Master. They lifted heavy axes off their shoulders. With them came fell men in black armor, swords at the ready, plus a squad of heavyset imps.

The foundry was a large place, but even so, to pit five trolls against four dragons was to fill it to the bursting with huge bodies and terrible weapons slicing through the air. As huge swords flashed and mighty axes whirled, every-

one else scrambled back to the walls for safety. The Great
One dodged back hurriedly to the entranceway, safely behind his line of trolls.

The dragons were eager for the fight. Bazil exchanged a
round of blows with the first troll, then he dug his shield inside the troll's shield and pulled it clear. Ecator thrust home,
and the troll died in the instant. Bazil felt Ecator hum in his
hand, gorged on life force for a moment. When he raised the
blade, it had a familiar glow about it.

A troll's head flew past him, and he looked up to see
Alsebra standing over the remains of the first, engaging the
next with overhand and shield thrust.

Then came a gasp from the right as Vlok missed his stroke
and was rammed in the belly by a troll shield. Vlok barely
fended off the following blow with the ax. The troll pressed
hard. Swane's arrow caromed off its steel-pot helmet.

But, before the troll could gut the leatherback, it was
stopped in its tracks by the impact of the long iron bar
wielded by the Purple Green. It staggered back, off balance,
and fell within Alsebra's range. In a moment she had hewn
it down.

"I hate all these wizardly men," roared the Purple Green
as he hurled the iron bar in the direction of the Master, lurking in the doorway.

The bar shot through the door and ricocheted off the wall
and felled a line of imps. The Master threw himself flat as
the massive piece of metal bounced off the wall just above
him and skipped on down the passage, killing three of his
men. For a moment Heruta crouched there, quivering, appalled at such violence. He discovered that he had fouled
himself in his sudden terror.

Suddenly there were but two trolls in the chamber, and
these nervously edging backward. Alsebra drove in with
Undaunt whirling, and the trolls scuttled back, almost crushing Heruta Skash Gzug beneath their huge, homely feet. The
Great One was backed against the wall, confronted by
battledragons.

Heruta suddenly faced the unimaginable—death. He dug
deep for hidden strength of will. A calm coldness settled
over his mind. His anger mastered his fear. He reached for
his ultimate weapon.

With a long, ululating cry he wove harsh syllables of
power in the air. Lessis felt her hair stand on end; the room

was filled with peculiar energies. Then with the sound of an ocean wave crashing down on molten lava, a black mirror opened in the air above them. Purple light bathed the chamber.

Lessis was awed. To open a mirror on one's own like that, it was incredible to her. To open a mirror by the witch method took three people and long, precise incantation.

The bizarre glare of chaos flickered across the foundry, throwing stark shadows against the walls while a fat, seething hiss pervaded the air.

With a thrill of horror, Lessis understood the peril and began a counterspell.

The dragons, every one, stood still, struck rigid by the weird light that flowed from the six-foot-wide circle of chaotic nothingness that had just snapped into existence between themselves and the Master.

Heruta retreated through the doors with an evil smirk. He knew there was a Thingweight close by in the chaotic ether. It often lurked around him. Even across the membrane between its awful realm and the real world it could sense the power of Heruta Skash Gzug. Such power was like nectar to it. It would lurk there, hoping that the power might come closer so that it could be taken and devoured. It made use of the black mirror for journeying virtually impossible.

Heruta mounted his seat. Eight strong slaves hurried him away from the scene, lashed on by his will. Their feet thundered on the stone. Heruta drove them hard because he knew that behind him came wild, terrible death.

Lessis called a warning, but it was useless, how could mortal men even comprehend what threatened them? She concentrated on her counterspell, which began to take shape as she hurriedly drew down the lines from memory; still it would take some seconds to set.

A moment later she saw the first wispy line of green fire flicker across the mirror. A Thingweight was there already! A shudder ran through her soul. Nothing now stood between them and the horror.

The line of green fire was joined by a second, and a moment later there were ten of them and then the monster was there, at the mirror's edge where light suddenly wrinkled in green and purple lines of fire, whorls and whiskers rippled. The green fire leapt high and tentacles lashed out into the world of Ryetelth to seize prey, any prey they might encounter.

The tentacles sought warm bodies; any living thing was taken. A huge troll was whipped off its feet and pulled to the mirror, where it was sucked into the chaos beyond.

Lessis hurled her counterspell against the mirror. One side crackled and went dark, but the other side still offered a portal to the Thingweight. The dragons, spooked by the bizarre mirror, had already moved back sharply. Now they fled under Lessis's command.

A tentacle of fire slapped around Lessis the next moment. She tried a disconnecting spell to break it. She almost succeeded, but the tentacle re-formed and kept its grip.

She was lifted up, her feet left the floor, and she was on her way to the most hideous death, consumed in the dark by the Thingweight, sucked slowly down into agonizing nothingness.

Then a flash of silver caught her eye as Ecator hurtled past and struck the tentacle. It rebounded with a wild flash of white fire. Brazil gave a grunt and hewed again, on the backhand. This time he got every ounce into it, and with a tremendous blast of green fire it gave way.

The air cracked with the sound of a gigantic whip, and the green fire around Lessis evaporated with a strange chemical stench. Suddenly released five feet in the air, Lessis fell to the floor, lost her footing, and pitched onto hands and knees. Lagdalen caught her by the shoulders and helped her to her feet.

"Lady, are you all right?" They retreated quickly.

"My dear, I think I really am getting too old for this."

An imp was pulled through the mirror with a final hoarse scream.

"Come, Lady, the door." Lagdalen was in motion.

But Lessis climbed the wall of powder kegs and stood above the tube they had primed to explode, a mad idea blossoming in her mind. She conjured, and a brilliant flower of bright energy lit up above her hand.

The tentacles from the bright side lashed down for this glowing tidbit, but Lessis cast it into the hulking metal tube and it sank into the steel, leaving a small glowing patch. The tentacles wrapped around the barrel in a flash and lifted it away.

"Run," she shouted to the rest of them, leaping for the ground once more.

The sight of the tube rising into the air wrapped with green fire set everyone in motion again.

Relkin, Bazil, and Wiliger caromed off the wall inside the main doors and tumbled down the flagstone floor.

The cannon entered the mirror, and as it went, Lessis let go of the ignition spell and a moment later it exploded, just as it crossed into the realm of the Thingweight. Lagdalen and Lessis were tossed through the doors and bounced off Bazil's back before landing on the floor.

The blast was deafening in the foundry, but in the maw of the Thingweight it was so intense that it cracked the monster's carapace. A moment later a searing flash of green fire exploded through the mirror, struck the wall, and melted the stone like wax. Hot molten rock spattered outward, and then the mirror began to spin wildly. The green fire cut across the wall, bringing down hundreds of tons of rock in a spreading avalanche, and then it lanced directly into the heart of the volcano, where it pierced the magma chamber itself.

The ground rumbled menacingly beneath the fortress. Lessis, covered in dust, staggered up to Relkin. The air was already thick with fumes. The floor shook.

"Must catch the Master. Take him now, our best chance," she said. "No time to waste."

Relkin agreed. He was eager to settle his debts with the Great One.

"Where?"

"Climb. He will be going for his batrukh."

The ground leapt under their feet as the volcano bellowed. The foundry filled with superheated smoke and gas.

"Can't stay here anyway," said Bazil as they ran for their lives, "much too hot for dragons."

CHAPTER FIFTY-NINE

Heruta Skash Gzug preferred his buildings to be on a heroic scale. Accordingly the staircase that lead to the batrukh aerie was massive, with steps hewn from the lava some twenty feet wide beneath an arched ceiling decorated with polished slabs of black crystal.

This made the ascent easy for a wyvern dragon, who went down on all fours, with his sword over his shoulder, and climbed enthusiastically, as if he were back on the obstacle course at Dashwood. The men had to step smartly to keep up with him.

After they had climbed seven turns of the stair, the volcano gave a sudden sharp jolt, stronger than before. Dust flew from joints in the ceiling. Something fell with a crash. More dust flew up.

Everyone redoubled their efforts. Lessis, however, was reaching the limits of her strength. She found it hard to keep up this pace and began to lag behind. Lagdalen fell back to be by her side.

Dragon Leader Wiliger was in front with a strange light in his eyes, as though something mystical had seized him. As they climbed and Relkin's legs began to tire, he noticed that Wiliger was moving ahead, apparently untouched by fatigue.

The dragon climbed on without a break, Relkin marveled. Bazil was really mad this time. He'd turned this into a personal fight. Now he'd never give up until he'd made the enemy pay. Ecator swung rhythmically back and forth over the dragon's shoulder as he climbed, seeming to promise retribution.

Wiliger was out of sight now, around the curve. Relkin dug for reserves, though his thighs ached and the breath came hot and harsh in his throat. The air was getting thick with fumes.

Ahead of them Wiliger suddenly emerged onto the batrukh aerie, a paved gallery cut in the side of the volcano. Here dwelled the batrukh, and here came the great Heruta to meditate. The view was wide, the whole island was spread out beneath with the sea beyond it and far in the distance the smudge of the land. The volcano shuddered again, and stones slid off the upper slopes to bounce off the flagstones.

A loud hiss greeted Wiliger's entrance. On a perch, projecting from the wall a few feet off the floor, crouched an enormous deadly form. Huge red eyes fastened on Wiliger, and a mouth filled with fangs snarled a greeting.

Wiliger blanched, but stood his ground, drawing his sword. A sudden hush fell on the huge space; even the volcano seemed quietened. A narrow door had opened in the wall right behind the batrukh's perch. Out of it stepped the Master, his face submerged beneath green horn, his eyes glowing like coals.

"A brave but foolish effort!" He gestured toward the dragon leader.

Instantly a black tide crashed down on Wiliger's mind. He fell to his knees with a gasp, clutching his head. A stream of spittle ran from his lips. Then he screamed.

Relkin stepped out behind him. The screams cut off.

"Ah!" snapped the Master, "my prodigy! So, child, you have come to me after all."

Wiliger let out a long groan as his mind was released from the dreadful grip. His eyes had rolled up in his head, his mouth was open, slack, dribbling. Relkin kept his eyes on the Master.

"I have come, and I will slay you if it is within my power," said Relkin with utter conviction.

"Such honesty in the young, I commend it, I truly do."

Heruta raised his fist, and the power came down on Relkin like a mallet on a mouse. Everything went black for a moment, and Relkin staggered and almost fell, but finally found the strength to resist. Again came the power, and now Relkin resisted with every fiber in his being and, incredibly, threw back the wizard's assault. Heruta the Great had been rejected.

The Great One's wrath boiled over, and thus he was fatally blinded to his peril. Instead of mounting his batrukh and making his escape, he concentrated his strength, bellowed the harsh syllables of power, and directed his fury at Relkin. This impudent pup would be crushed, here and now!

Relkin lurched to the wall and clung there, slowly sliding down it.

"See, child, you shall have no will but mine!" Heruta raised his fist again. Relkin felt a terrible hammering in his head; he could no longer breathe. His hands went to his throat.

"Leave boy alone!" said a loud, inhuman voice suddenly. The next moment two tons of angry battledragon stepped out onto the floor of the aerie.

The batrukh uttered a thunderous snarl and unfolded its wings, which billowed like black canopies to the sky. The Master was knocked off the perch and fell heavily to the floor below. His concentration was gone, and he lost his grip on Relkin.

Heruta cursed himself. He should have expected this development. One of those damnable reptiles had stuck its snout into his business again. The situation was becoming somewhat difficult. He dragged himself to his feet. He had to get out of this place. The volcano seemed on the verge of an eruption.

Then another complication arose. With a gasp, a young woman reached the top step and entered the aerie. What were they doing sending this girl against him?

A moment later another figure entered, and instantly he felt her power.

"You!" he breathed. The damned hag herself had dared to climb here to challenge him.

With a great cry, he unleashed such a spell on them that its very strength took Lessis by surprise. She found she could not move a muscle. Poor Lagdalen was driven to her knees. Indeed, everyone within a mile felt the lash of the Master's power. They clutched their heads, groaned, and groveled on the ground.

The leatherback dragon, however, was barely affected. It moved forward cautiously, drawing that terrible sword from its scabbard, filling the room with the sound of huge lungs laboring for air. In truth, Baz was exhausted from the climb.

"You have hurt the world," it said suddenly.

Heruta stared. What must one do to destroy these thrice-damned battledragons?

In the presence of Heruta, Ecator began to glow with anticipation.

"See, Wizard, my blade hungers for your soul."

With a trace of desperation, Heruta jerked Relkin and Wiliger to their feet. Their bodies were no longer their own to control. They drew their weapons and lurched toward the dragon's unprotected back.

Lessis felt her tongue sliding backward into her throat as Heruta sought to strangle her with it. She struggled to complete a defensive spell, but unable to make a sound, her strength was greatly limited.

"There, hag, feel the power of an enthraan!" said the Great One with a ghastly chuckle. "For many years I have dreamt of such an occasion. At last I have a hag beneath my fist! You filthy creatures with your muddy little religion, what do you know of power? You dare to throw yourself across my path. You dare to oppose me! I will crush you like a worm!"

And he forced Lessis to her knees. A dark, crushing cloud was coming down over the Grey Lady's mind.

But now even the Great Heruta was spread thin. Lagdalen managed to scream a warning to Bazil. His head snapped around, and he saw the men at his back. Dodging in time, he knocked Wiliger away with a slap of the tail.

Relkin swung in, eyes glazed, face contorted in torment. Bazil stopped the boy with a big hand and lifted him off the ground. Relkin struggled weakly in his grasp.

"What have you done to my boy?"

"Silence, foul monster!" The Master stretched out his arms and reached into the roots of the mountain for strength. With a deep breath, he summoned all his power and hurled it at the dragon.

Bazil gave a gasp and shook his head. It was hard to move all of a sudden. He dropped Relkin.

Heruta gave a sigh of inward relief as the dragon froze in place. At last he had found a way to control these brutes. But at what a cost! He was stretched to his limit, indeed, he could no longer hold them all down. The hag was beginning to stir despite the enormous exertions he made to hold her down. The boy was slipping from control as well. He struggled to regain his grip on them.

He neglected to consider Delwild Wiliger, who had been knocked silly by the dragon's tail. The blow had cleared his mind dramatically. Now he pulled himself to his feet. One of his legs felt all wrong, and his mouth was full of blood. Still he was able to take up the sword.

The Master was focused on the dragon and that huge blade in its hands. The sword glowed oddly, Heruta felt a spirit presence there, something so strong in its way that it was frankly terrifying. Most odd, and quite frightening in the hands of that leathery monster.

And then all at once the man had crept up on him, a sword flashed, and Heruta staggered as he was struck. The sword did not penetrate his armor but the blow nearly knocked him off his feet.

Wiliger and the Great Master exchanged a glance. Wiliger snarled defiance and raised his sword again. Heruta disabled his mind in the next instant, and the dragon leader stiffened in place while his sword dropped from his fingers.

The damage was done, though; the dragon was slipping free, damn, but the brute was hard to hold down. Heruta looked up and saw the dragonboy stumbling toward him with a long knife in his hand. This was ludicrous. He snatched at the child's mind. In doing so he lost the dragon.

Bazil lunged for the wizard, Ecator a blinding blur. Heruta hurled himself backward. This was becoming damned awkward.

Then the stupid batrukh struck down from its perch at the dragon with a shriek of hate. Its jaws snapped shut an inch from Bazil's neck, the dragon backhanded the fell creature, and Ecator hewed off its head. It collapsed in a heap. Ecator gave off a tiny cat scream of joy.

Heruta shrieked in horror. How was he to escape without a suitable mount?

The dragon came on. The Great One could no longer get a grip on the beast. There was only one place to go. Heruta fled, scrambling up the steps that lead to the high place, overlooking the volcano's crater.

The mountain jerked again, and a great cloud of dark smoke towered into the sky overhead. An angry roar burst from the volcano's throat.

When the ground stabilized once more, Relkin climbed unsteadily to his feet. Lagdalen was crouched over the Lady Lessis. Wiliger was sprawled on the floor. Relkin swallowed. The dragon leader had come through in the end. Poor Wiliger had shown his courage. Relkin turned his eyes upward; stepping around the dead batrukh, he started up those steps to the high place.

It was a long climb, but in the end he came to the place

where he and Jak had been chained. There he saw the Master stand at bay.

The lava down below was boiling, and the heat and the gas made it hard to breathe. Far below, the searing blast of the Thingweight's death had awoken the volcano's heart. A long rumble in deep basso shook the ground. The Master wobbled. Relkin fell against the wall. A gout of flame shot up from the lava pool. On the outside of the volcanic cone the foundry buildings collapsed in clouds of dust and slid down in ruin.

In desperation, Heruta conjured and stretched out his power to crush the dragon. A great weight fell on Bazil's mind. His thoughts seemed to coagulate. To move forward was almost impossible, as if an invisible but unbreakable membrane was stretched in front of him.

Dragon teeth ground together in his long jaw as he struggled to break the wizard's grip. He could barely feel his arm; all sensation was fading as time seemed to slow to a crawl.

Out of the corner of his eye Bazil saw the boy slip past, knife in hand. The Master was tiring and did not react quite quickly enough, and Relkin struck. Forced to defend himself against renewed physical assault, the Master had to switch his attention to the boy. This freed the dragon for a moment. Bazil lifted an arm that felt heavier than lead and brought Ecator around in a gleaming arc of death.

The Master stepped back. Bazil gave a grunt of satisfaction. His muscles were responding once more. Bazil stepped over Relkin—who was sprawled on the ground—shifted his weight, and swung again. Ecator flashed and took off the Master's arm at the elbow. The blade sang in a high wild tonic, but Heruta screamed in incomprehension. Shaking his head, blood fountaining, he stepped backward, missed his footing, and plunged over the edge and fell with a long, wailing cry into the heart of the volcano.

For a long moment there was nothing but the rumble of the volcano and the seething of the lava. Then the mountain leapt under them. A tremendous blast convulsed the world.

Bazil fell on the flagstone and scrabbled for fingerholds as the mountain shook and shuddered and threatened to toss him into the fiery crater, too.

Relkin crawled to the dragon's side, holding on for dear life as the ground jumped beneath him.

"We did it, Baz. Put an end to him."

A section of the crater wall slid down, taking the stairs with it. Below them they saw the batrukh aerie break up and fall away. They were trapped now.

"Boy celebrate too soon."

Relkin never got to answer because at that moment the ground heaved again and their entire section of the mountain broke away from the cone and slid down the side. Behind it billowed a pillar of smoke, reaching high into the sky.

For a moment Relkin was in free fall, then he returned to the floor with a thud. Bazil had a fingerhold in a metal ring sunk in the stone. They were on a ride like no other, sliding, gathering speed, as their giant fragment of the mountain roared down the slope like a huge stone sleigh.

Then they left the mountain and arched out from the mountain's side; the sea was beneath them, rushing up, flecked with foam. Boulders were flying all around them. Relkin glimpsed an incredible jet of lava that was blasting forth from the volcano's ruined side beneath a cloud of incandescent smoke.

Then all was lost in black smoke and dust for a moment before they struck the water, and Relkin was thrown high into the air, turned a somersault, and landed feet first in a wave of extremely hot water.

He screamed, choked, and almost drowned, but somehow struggled to the surface and broke through successive shock waves as huge objects crashed into the sea around him. Each time he felt himself hurled up, out of the water for a moment. The last one was the greatest of all, however, and it tossed him out of the hot stream of water into a cool one, and just in time, for he was already half scalded. He tried to swim, but the waves flung him from side to side until at length he felt himself picked up by one larger than the rest and hurled down deep into the cooler water.

For a while he waited, lungs bursting, to simply drown, but the current that had taken him down now moved him upward again. He surfaced, sputtering, beneath a vast cloud that filled the sky. More waves were coming, lifting him high for a moment before dropping him back in the deep troughs between them. The sky beyond the waves was a mad riot of scarlet and orange fire, toiling with huge coils of black smoke. The volcano had blown itself to pieces, along with much of the Isle of the Bone.

Relkin did his best just to keep his head above water as the waves carried him farther from the island, which was split in two now by a wall of fire.

Sizzling lava bombs fell into the sea; some burst quite close to him, but he took no notice, his thoughts dulled, his heart numbed by the loss of his dragon.

And then there was a different sort of explosion in the water beside him. A huge shape surfaced, and his dragon swept him onto a broad leathery back.

"I thought I saw boy. Hard to fool this dragon's eyes."

Relkin gave a prayer of thanks to all the gods and clung there to Ecator's scabbard as the wyvern swam, his great tail boosting them out into calmer waters while volcanic bombs continued to rain down around them every so often.

The waves continued, but the wyvern powered on, leaving the boiling cauldron of the drowning volcano behind.

He swam for a long time, during which the world behind them continued to vent steam and smoke with unmitigated fury, but they were spared the lava and blast effects, and eventually Bazil grounded on a wide beach covered in warm grey ash.

Relkin slipped down to splash ashore. It was a steaming desolation. Seaweed was strewn across the wreckage of palm trees. A fishing boat perched high on a dune. The half of the sky behind them was covered by the death throes of the volcano. The half ahead was hidden in white haze.

A thin wind blew in from the sea with a whiff of sulfur. They stood still for a moment and gazed about them. They were utterly alone, but they were alive.

CHAPTER SIXTY

The volcano blasted westward, blowing out one-third of its crater and hurling it into the sea. Superheated lava struck the water and generated a vast cloud of steam, which soon hid even the smoke of the eruption.

To the east, however, very little material fell, and thus the band of survivors was spared. They staggered out of the hot, stinking mist onto the beach under a strange, bloodred light. Alsebra led them, carrying the Lady Lessis over her shoulder. The Purple Green was still on his feet, and carrying Dragon Leader Wiliger, who drifted in and out of consciousness. Vlok, Swane, and the Count Felk-Habren came behind, followed by Lagdalen, of course. Nothing could kill Lagdalen of the Tarcho, it seemed.

With grateful groans, the dragons waded into the water and let the waves crash over them. The sea was a turmoil of waves moving in different directions, but it was blissfully cool on their overheated skins. All the bruises and singed spots felt better at once.

"We been through far too much, we need rest," said Vlok in tired complaint.

"Listen to Vlok," said Alsebra, "for once he's absolutely right."

"We lost the Broketail," said the Purple Green.

"And boy Relkin."

"I grieve for them."

"I, too."

"We fought side by side, the broketail dragon and me," said the Purple Green. "I don't know how many fights we were in, but he was always at my side in every battle. He saved this dragon's life, not once, but many times."

"And this dragon's life," said Vlok.

"And this," said Alsebra.

"Since they came to me where I was starving to death in

a dismal cave and showed me how I could live a better life, with honor and the chance to smite our enemy, I have been with them. We even ran off and starved in the forests once to try and save boy Relkin."

"Oh, yes, we remember that," said Alsebra.

"I cannot believe he is gone."

Alsebra glanced up to the skies, hidden beneath the volcano cloud.

"He will lie under the red star now. Across the long leagues that span the stars he will be running, and to the red star he will go. That is the fate of all dragons in the end."

A pall fell across them, and they spoke no more.

They stood in the surf while the world around them hissed and shook. Every so often a fresh gout of lava would hit the western side of the island and unleash a great blast of sound. The rest of the time there was the rumble and the distant roar of the seething crater. It was a dark, inchoate world, filled with terror, but they were not afraid. They had seen too much death now to ever fear it. They waited there until the Lady Lessis awoke from the coma brought on by Heruta's magic. Count Felk-Habren sat at the edge of the surf and stared out at the water. Lagdalen sat by the Lady. Wiliger awoke, stared about himself with a completely lost expression on his face. Then he saw her and seemed to relax. He did not speak, but sat there looking out over the waves and the three towering dragons standing in the surf. Swane had gone out to scout the coastline to the south of their position. They were still too close to the volcano.

And then the Lady's eyes opened, and she gave a sigh that Lagdalen heard at once. *She tires of this life.*

Lessis was slow to get to her feet, but steady once she was on them.

"Heruta is gone," she said in a calm voice. "The greatest wizard in the world, our tormentor, he is dead."

She looked back to the volcano, as a rift in the clouds exposed the eastern side for a moment. The cone was still intact on the east, but beyond it was a halo of fire as the western side of the island was reforged with fresh lava.

"And they will sing the songs of Bazil Broketail long after men have forgotten everything of Heruta Skash Gzug, the mighty maggot and dark Lord of Padmasa—wound to the world, corrupter of men's hearts, and a mortal bane to their women. He is gone, but they will sing of an orphanboy from

Quosh and the broketail dragon for as long as men can sing."

The big dragon eyes were all fixed on her. Lessis felt a momentary flash of fright, dragon-freeze she supposed. After all this time spent working with dragons, it surprised her. And she had never suffered it before. But there was a penetrating intensity in their gaze that she could not recall feeling before.

Lava crashed into the sea on the far side, and the noise overwhelmed them for a moment.

Lessis bowed her head. She hoped she had not trespassed on their feelings.

"They will sing," said Vlok after a long silence. "We will sing first, though."

The others agreed with urgent hisses.

Lessis took a breath, and then urged everyone to move into the water. "We are in the Mother's Hand, that is clear, but we should move away from here as quickly as we might."

They waded in and found the water still cool; despite the fury unleashed on the far side of the island, the eastern water remained its normal temperature.

They swam, or more accurately, the dragons swam, while the people clung to them or rode on their shoulders. The waters were rough, but the dragons swam slowly and steadily through the chop, finding some great renewal of strength in the contact with their most natural element.

For a long time they swam thus, resting at intervals, allowing themselves to drift, and then powering on with smooth strokes of their tails, away from the thunder of the fire mountain.

When they were many miles distant, they noticed that the mists and smoke were thinning around them. A breeze from the south was coming up. Their hearts rose a little at this sign of peace, and they went on.

In time they were spotted by three lateen-rigged single-masted ships from the south, fishing craft of the Xiphura people of the southern coast. To their joy they found legionaries on these boats, each of which had a crew of six.

The ships weren't big enough to take the dragons, but the wyverns could take a tow line and thus get assistance. Lines were paid out over the end, and the wyverns took hold. The strange little fleet was slow but it kept an eastward heading, and in time they reached the shore, not far from the party of fugitives from the battle of the field of broken stones.

The great news went out. The wizard was dead, and so was the prophet "He Who Must."

More fishing ships came up from the south and bore them all away to safety in the land of the Xiphura. There they regrouped and tended to their wounded. The expedition had ended in a disastrous battle, but their enemy had been destroyed along with his secret weapon. Overall it had been a great victory, despite the terrible casualties. The passage of history had been interrupted with a grand stroke.

Peace was slow to reestablish itself, however. The Kraheen peoples underwent a period of anarchy. The oppressive, bloodthirsty culture of the Prophet collapsed. For a few days, raw red chaos ruled and many wrongs were righted with the sword and many oppressors were laid in the dust while gracious homes were torched.

When the fury had begun to burn itself out, leaving the Kraheen people completely desperate and disorganized, the legions moved north again and occupied the capital. Lessis and the other witches began a program to rehabilitate the Kraheen tribes. Their society needed to reknit itself, and that could best be done in the old culture, with the simpler life of farming and fishing on the Inland Sea. They would put aside the swords and shields and take up the plough and the tiller.

At the same time the witches organized an immense effort to destroy all traces of the enemy's secret weapon. The pieces of the metal tubes were collected on carts and thrown into the deepest parts of the Inland Sea.

The stone balls were more of a problem, and in the end they were left, a puzzling array of perfectly spherical, smooth boulders scattered across the plain of Broken Stones. In time the legends about them would grow and magnify to include a cast of saints, who fought monsters from out of the southern forest and turned them into big stone balls.

An investigation of the Isle of the Bone, once the volcano had quietened again, showed that no one else had survived. All the wizard's craftsmen had perished, along with the trolls and slaves in the foundry.

Word of the weapons, however, would be taken back to the lands of Czardha, Kassim, and the Bakan coast. The men of the Argonath legions would also carry away the news. All this posed a continued threat, for clever men were spread across the world, and spurred by such stories they might begin to re-create the fire tubes of Heruta.

The witches worked to confabulate the recent battle. With artful rumor and some wit, they turned the fire weapons into living monsters in the minds of most of the men. There were so many wild stories about the things that the reality was almost tedious and unbelievably flat. Serpents that spat balls of stone into the sky was the most common belief by then, although there was another story about owls, giant birds that seized the stone balls in the sky and dropped them on the legions. All anyone could be certain of was that whatever the weapons had been they were deadly because the expeditionary force from the Empire of the Rose was coming home with appalling losses. Less than half the initial force would ever return to their homelands, and in the case of the Czardhans, there were but eleven surviving knights for the Count Felk-Habren to command for the return trip home.

In time a relief force from Og Bogon reached the legion forces, having marched over the mountains on the old roads. The Argonathi engineers, with a large force of former Kraheen warriors at their disposal, were busily improving the roads to the frontiers.

The legions gathered themselves up and then began the trek to the east, returning over the mountains and across the waist of the continent to Sogosh. It was a long march and took several months.

Along the way they stopped at Koubha to report to the great King Choulaput. The king was greatly distressed by the news of the loss of the broketail dragon and dragoneer Relkin. He proclaimed a national day of mourning in their names and ordered statues to be carved of them and set up in the palace.

But at last, two years since they'd first set out on the march to the interior, the legions embarked at Sogosh and started the long voyage home. By then, of course, Lessis, accompanied by Lagdalen, had long since reached Marneri. Lagdalen rejoined her family, finding Hollein Kesepton already there after the success of his diplomatic mission on the southern coast of Eigo. Lessis had gone on at once aboard the frigate *Lyre,* bound for Andiquant and a grim interview with the emperor. Their losses had been terribly heavy, but they had destroyed the enemy's weapon and halted, for a while, the spread of such things. They would have to remain vigilant, however, for as they had seen, the use of such weapons would quickly change the nature of war.

All the way across the Bright Sea, Lessis kept to herself, either in her cabin, or walking on the quarterdeck alone. She did not dine with the captain or anyone else. The packet with all the names of the casualties was heavy. The emperor would be shaken by these losses. Some regiments were but a tenth of what they'd been when they set out. In some ways, Lessis thought, it was a pity she'd survived the destruction of Heruta.

And still Lessis's heart felt the heaviest when she thought of a particular pair of casualties, a certain battledragon and a young dragoneer with whom her life, and the fate of the entire empire, had been much entangled. Never in all the five centuries of her life had she felt more inclined to beg for the release of death. At the very least she wanted to retire after this mission.

She would go to Valmes. It had been years since she had lived in her own home. She would go to Valmes and pick apples and spend her time in peaceful meditation. Perhaps she would retire into the mystic. Perhaps she would be able to persuade young Lagdalen to come to the Isles and undergo the training for a witch. Whatever she did, she wanted to have plenty of time for her garden. It would be in ruins by now, she imagined, unless her neighbors had been kind and intervened. She could barely remember when she'd last spent more than a week in Valmes. A cell in Andiquant when she was lucky, and a rock for a pillow when she was not, had been her lot for years. She wondered how the old pear tree in the garden had done this year. And the delphiniums, did they still thrive on the walk by the front door? She prayed they did, she would need to see them after she'd endured this meeting with the emperor. The delphiniums and then the roses, and then to eat a pear, that's what she would do.